THE SANDLER INQUIRY

Also by Noel Hynd:
Revenge

THE SANDLER INQUIRY

BY NOEL HYND

THE DIAL PRESS 🦁 NEW YORK

Published by
The Dial Press
1 Dag Hammarskjold Plaza
New York, New York 10017

Manufactured in the United States of America

First printing

Book design by Holly McNeely

Library of Congress Cataloging in Publication Data

Hynd, Noel.
  The Sandler inquiry.

  I. Title.
PZ4.H9984San   [PS3558.Y54]   813'.5'4   77–10184
ISBN 0–8037–7545–8

for
m.a.k., d.h., and e.d.h.
with love

PART ONE

Chapter 1

Who'd want to burn him out? Destroy his records? His office? His livelihood?

Thomas Daniels considered the hundreds of enemies his father must have made. He wondered whom he knew who liked to play with fire.

"This was a good professional torching," said Corrigan, a lieutenant from the New York City Fire Department. "High-intensity, quick-spreading fire. Would have taken the whole building if the custodian here hadn't found it." Corrigan pointed to the filing room. The air was gray with the vestiges of smoke, and the law offices were permeated with the sweet smell of ashes and water. Thomas Daniels's eyes smarted. He was looking at the charred remnants of the old wooden files.

"No one was here when it started," Corrigan continued. "That's the usual. A good arsonist uses a fuse."

"An electricity fuse?" asked Jacobus, the janitor, in slightly accented English.

Corrigan shook his head no. "A timing fuse. A candle, a wire, a clock, even a cigarette sometimes. Anything that will burn down slowly and not ignite whatever chemical, papers, or rags are being used until the torch man is gone." He glanced around. It was a few minutes past four A.M. "If the fire had done the whole building we'd never have known where the flash point was. Here we know where the blaze started. So we'll go through the debris in the filing room, inch by inch. We'll find a fuse mechanism in there. Bank on it. I'll show you something else."

Corrigan led Jacobus and Daniels through the two adjoining rooms. He pointed to places and showed them how the flames appeared to have traveled in a path from the flash point.

"See?" he said. "Tracks. Tracks made by trailers that our firebug left. If we hadn't broke in on the fire early, we wouldn't have these, neither."

The trailers, Corrigan explained, had been some highly flammable substance—chemically treated rags, paper, or plastic—which had been left by the arsonist to be triggered by the fuse. When the fuse had burned down, the trailers had been sparked. And a rapidly spreading blaze had shot in every direction. The intense flames consuming the trailers had left the tracks.

Thomas Daniels, though working up a dislike for Lieut. Corrigan, knew he was listening to an expert. But the questions which kept recurring to Thomas were ones Corrigan couldn't answer. Who? And why? A premeditated fire made no sense. "A pyromaniac?"

The lieutenant seemed amused. "No. Too neat a trick for a pyro. Pyros are sloppy. They leave so much evidence you'd think they was trying to get caught." Corrigan shook his head. "Nope. This was set by somebody who wanted all the tracks covered but wanted the whole area destroyed. Usually that points to one thing."

"What's that?" asked Thomas Daniels.

"Something else was involved. Another crime. Sometimes you dig in the rubble of a fire like this and come up with a grilled cadaver. Get it? No stiff here, though. That means something else. Burglary, maybe. Anything of value kept in the office?"

Thomas shook his head.

"No art? Jewels? TVs, typewriters? Nothin' like that?"

"Nothing."

Corrigan shrugged and used a thick forearm to wipe grime and sweat from his forehead. "Then there's something else that the detectives are going to suggest."

"What's that?"

"Insurance. A failed business somebody wanted torched to cash in on a policy."

Thomas visibly bristled.

Corrigan pursed his lips. "Not necessarily you. Maybe the guy upstairs. Or downstairs. The fire spreads and you all go up in the same puff, making it that much harder to figure who lit the fuse."

Corrigan turned to the janitor. "By the way, how'd you find the fire so fast? Doing your nighttime rounds?"

Jacobus considered it, thinking back over the events of the early morning. "I vas mopping," he finally declared, trying to sound as American as possible, "and I smelled smoke."

Shassad and Hearn stepped from the unmarked car and held their shields aloft to Officer Renfrow and a second uniformed patrolman. Renfrow recognized them anyway. The flash of red lights from the blue-and-white New York City police cars was reflected off the wet sidewalk and windows.

"Looks like he resisted," Renfrow suggested.

The homicide detectives looked down. The body was covered by a police blanket.

"That's a heavy finance charge for not coughing up a wallet." Shassad said. He looked at the trail of blood on the sidewalk, leading from the body and running along several yards of pavement to the doorway of number 246. The blood on East Seventy-third Street was already partially diluted by the rain.

"Want a look?" Renfrow asked.

"Why the hell not?"

Shassad reached down himself and pulled back the blanket. It was heavy and soggy from the rain. He gagged slightly, though he'd seen hundreds of equally repulsive scenes. "Jesus."

The dead man's face was chalk white. Below the neck, on the right side, was an obscene gaping wound, a huge bloody hole carved into the flesh just below the jawbone. A blade, perhaps of butcher-knife dimensions, had slashed upward into the victim's throat, tearing and ripping everything in its path and cutting into the mouth. The front of the man's suit, coat, and shirt was scarlet of varying shades.

Shassad mumbled, "Can't a guy even step out of the house after dark?"

"No identification," said Renfrow. "Just some change and keys."

Hearn looked up as Shassad put the blanket back in place, affording the dead some privacy. "No wallet?" he asked.

"All gone," said Renfrow.

They looked to the end of the block where an ambulance was turning the corner and approaching silently, its white headlights and red top lights glaring. The only sounds other than subdued voices were occasional raspy bursts from police radios.

Renfrow's partner waited for it to pass and then crossed the street, coming toward them.

"You from Homicide?" he asked Shassad and Hearn collectively.

"We're not from the garbagemen's softball team."

"It's your lucky night."

"Yeah?"

The young patrolman turned and pointed across the street to a small frightened woman standing in a doorway, wrapped in an old overcoat and clutching one hand in the other. "You got a witness," he said.

"Hell," muttered Shassad, "I was going to slip the Medical Examiner a few bucks and have him mark it 'natural causes.'"

The young patrolman watched Shassad as the detective walked across the street to Minnie Yankovich.

Minnie was a bent-over little woman with gray hair, a suspicious wrinkled face, and a prominent aquiline nose. She was also an occasional insomniac, given to sitting up all night watching the streets. Mrs. Yankovich had seen everything. She had been sitting in her window for an hour in the darkened bedroom. One of the cats was on her lap. She'd seen two men, apparently waiting for something or someone. They had, in fact, seemed ordinary enough as she described them for Aram Shassad.

Shassad went back up to the woman's apartment with her and, still somewhat shaky, she insisted on brewing them both a cup of tea as they spoke. Routinely and accurately, and without contradicting herself at any time, she was able to describe what she'd seen.

The two men had been standing on the block for thirty minutes before attacking their victim. One had stayed in a shadow near 246 East 73rd Street. The other twice walked to the corner of Third Avenue, where there was a telephone booth. But both men were near 246 when the door opened and a young man stepped out.

"I thought he was what they were waiting for," Minnie Yankovich said as Shassad sipped tea from an antique blue-porcelain cup. The apartment was small and faded, but comfortable and warm. "They went toward him right away. I thought they knew him." She scowled and shuddered slightly. "But they turned out to be robbers, officer. They surrounded him, one to each side. They talked. Then they shoved him and he tried to run back into the building."

"But you couldn't hear anything?" he asked.

"No."

"Or see their faces?"

She shook her head. "The next thing I saw was a knife. It was big. Like a butcher's." She nodded.

"What happened next?"

The victim struggled, said Minnie. He fought and clutched his wounds as the two slashed at him. The man went down onto the sidewalk. The last thing Minnie saw, before she moved to her telephone and called the police was one of the pair leaning over the fallen body. "That's when they took his wallet," she said. "From his inside pocket."

"I see."

"He should have just given them his money." She frowned. "Money isn't worth such . . ."

"Some people feel otherwise," he said gently. "It's unfortunate."

"And they didn't look bad, either," she said hopelessly.

"Excuse me?"

She set aside her cup. "They weren't badly dressed at all. Nice raincoats. And white." She laughed sourly. "I guess that's unusual, Mr. Shadash. White muggers."

He took his notes carefully and was still writing when she added her postscript.

"Officer, I don't mean to complain . . ."

He looked up.

"Something simply must be done. You tell your commander. It took your policemen seven minutes to drive here." She shook her head contemptuously, indicating that this would never do. "It wasn't like this when LaGuardia was mayor."

Shassad crossed Seventy-third again. The rain continued. He approached Hearn, who saw him and spoke first.

"What'd the old lady say? Any help?"

"Some," he said. He looked toward the body. A night unit from the Medical Examiner's office was there to make official what everyone already knew. The anonymous man on the sidewalk was dead. Shassad and Hearn watched the body being placed in a police van.

"Looks like a standard cash-and-carry street job," said Hearn. "No?"

Shassad surveyed the doorway of 246 and the shadows in which the killers had lurked for half an hour. Then he looked toward Second Avenue, though he was partially blinded by vehicle lights.

"I wonder, Patty. We got to think about this."

By six A.M. Corrigan was gone. Two city fire detectives had arrived. A uniformed police officer had cordoned off sections of the fifth floor. Ropes and signs reading "CRIME SCENE" separated the Zenger and Daniels offices from the rest of the building.

The managements of the offices on the floors above and below were asked to give their employees the day off, pending an assessment of any structural damage.

By seven thirty a few maintenance workers began arriving. They were perplexed and intrigued by the investigatory activity on the fifth floor.

Just before eight o'clock Thomas Daniels was allowed into a neighboring office by Jacobus. He borrowed a telephone and began calling his two associates.

Gerald Derham, a friend of many years who'd been a year behind Thomas in law school, lived in Mamaroneck with his wife and year-old daughter. He had already left for work.

The other attorney, Sam Leverman, lived in the city.

"Why didn't you call me sooner? I've been up since five." Leverman sighed. As was often his habit when faced with despairing news, he changed the subject completely. "See the *Times* yet this morning?"

"Are you kidding? All I've seen is smoke and ashes."

"Your beautiful friend Andrea has an article in section two, page one. A woman with brains. That's like a fine watch that actually tells the correct time. Good article. How did she know about—?"

"I haven't seen her all week," Thomas answered. "I'll see you when you get here."

Thomas next telephoned a secretary and two clerical employees, telling them what had happened and advising them not to come in for at least that day. They asked if they'd be paid. Thomas assured them they would, though when he hung up he wasn't quite sure how. There simply wasn't much money. And, given the suspicious nature of the fire, the insurance company could be counted on to delay payment indefinitely.

For a moment Thomas stood up from the borrowed desk and stared out the window, watching people coming to work in the steady January drizzle. He wondered what it would be like to be in another line of work. Such as? He didn't know. He was aware of someone at the door.

"Mr. Daniels?" It was Jacobus.

"Yes?"

"The detectives want you. I think they found something."

"Paraffin," said Frank Bianco, a dark, heavy-set Fire Department detective. "And celluloid. An old technique, but reliable."

The fire investigator stood at an impromptu work area that he'd established on a damaged desk in Thomas's office. On the desk he'd spread a clean drape. On the drape, beside a cardboard container of coffee, he'd spread various items which had been found in the debris of the filing room. Another detective, Jack Shoenbaum, had photographed the area extensively and was still sifting through the wet rubble.

In the ashes of the filing room, Schoenbaum had found seven separate puddles of molten paraffin, blackened by fire but easily recognizable.

"Seven paraffin candles, strategically set where they'd pick up crosscurrents of air," explained Bianco. "The perpetrator used the candles as his timers. Once he'd lit them he had about an hour before they burned down."

Thomas looked at the amorphous black substances. He felt a slight tremble of fear looking at the instruments of the knowledgeable but faceless man who had intentionally burned him out. Thomas examined one of those paraffin deposits, then wiped his fingers on a towel.

"See this?" asked Bianco, holding up a four-inch black strip with his rubber surgical gloves. The strip looked like a negative from a roll of film. Thomas held up his hand to examine it, but Bianco pulled it away. "Don't touch! I want it treated for fingerprints. Know what it is?"

Thomas shook his head.

"Any reason why it would be near your files?"

"None that I know of," said Thomas.

"One of the burning tables collapsed on this strip. That pinned it to the floor and protected it while the other side of the table burned. Several long strips like this were used as trailers. Celluloid. It ignites immediately and can spread a blaze through an entire room in seconds. Perfect trailer," said Bianco with grudging admiration. "I'll tell you one thing, Mr. Daniels. Whoever torched you sure knew what he was doing. He wasn't a virgin."

"Super," grumbled Daniels after a few seconds. He looked at Bianco carefully. "Based on what you've seen here, do you have any chance of catching him?"

"Oh, there's a chance," said Bianco slowly. "I suppose that a snowball has some chance in hell, too." Bianco shook his head. "This guy didn't exactly leave much to start with," he said. "Unless you've got some idea who might have done it."

"None," said Thomas. "None at all."

By eleven A.M. the arson detectives had completed their work. Soon afterward a thin, gaunt man named Marvin Jupiter arrived. Jupiter was an investigator for National Fire Underwriters of Hartford. Jupiter spent an hour walking around, rubbing his chin, sniffling, taking notes, and not speaking. Thomas knew already that the next suit he'd be filing would be against his own insurance company.

During the afternoon Daniels, Leverman, and Derham attempted to begin a cleanup operation. Quickly, they realized that theirs was more a salvage operation. What the fire hadn't destroyed, smoke, water, and ashes had rendered unusable. The firm was, indefinitely at least, out of business.

By seven thirty that evening, Thomas Daniels was unlocking the door to his apartment. He opened it and was immediately aware that someone was there.

Andrea.

She'd let herself in. Sitting in the living room, leafing through an afternoon newspaper, she'd been waiting for him. She stood there, radiant as ever. He tried to speak but couldn't. The day had been like a death in the family.

"I know all about it," she said. "I know how you must feel." She kissed him gently.

He shrugged, then embraced her. "I'm not letting it defeat me," he said. "Worse things could happen. I'll get by some way."

"Thought we'd have some dinner," she said. "I'm sure you can use it."

"We'll go out," he said. He motioned toward the kitchen. "I don't think there's anything here."

"I brought everything we'll need for the evening," she said. "Everything." She held her arms around him just below the shoulders and nipped playfully at his ear. "I'm not leaving till tomorrow morning," she said. "I've got a couple of days off." She gave him a mischievous smile, her brown eyes alive with intrigue.

He smiled for the first time. He released her and she disappeared into the kitchen. Thomas reclined on the living-room sofa, closing his eyes, trying to erase the images of his burned-out office. He listened to Andrea rattling something in the kitchen. She could be so considerate when she wanted to be, so gloriously feminine, kind, loving.

And then she'd go sleep with someone else. He cared not to think of that right now. For the time, at least, he was to be treated to her good side. She had read him perfectly. He hadn't wanted to be alone and now he wouldn't be.

He glanced at the coffee table. On top of the clutter was that afternoon's *New York Post.* She had left it there.

He was about to open it when an item at the bottom of the front page caught his eye. The headline of the story was suddenly shouting out at him, staring him in the face.

VICTORIA SANDLER
DEAD AT EIGHTY

Last Living Member
of Millionaire Family
Found Dead in Mansion

The story recounted the final years of Victoria Sandler, a woman who, though one of the wealthiest in America, had spent the last three decades going quietly but spectacularly insane.

She'd lived alone, since the 1954 death of her brother, Arthur Sandler, who'd been three years younger than she, and the departure of the final servant in 1955. The family mansion, originally fashioned after a French château of the 1870s, had acquired grates on the windows, an iron fence and gate in front, and a twenty-foot-high concrete fence in back to protect a rear patio. The fencing included electrified barbed wire all around. Victoria lived within. The once elegant but fading mansion, the symbol of the family, was now a fortress in a tough, changing city.

Victoria, the article continued, wore heavy galoshes without shoes in all weather. Thick, black woolen stockings and the same ragged, frayed dress was her outfit day after day. There were seven marble-and-zinc bathtubs in the mansion, but for twenty-five years Victoria Sandler had remained a stranger to all seven. Matters of personal hygiene were, to phrase it kindly, questionable. Victoria suffered from—among other things—aquaphobia, and touched water only when absolutely necessary.

"Dollars and doggies," as she termed it, were her only two passions. She liked crisp one-dollar bills and would take nothing else from local merchants. She gave them to her brother, she explained; he had use for them. Local merchants kept stacks of crisp money just for Victoria, despite the fact that Arthur Sandler, who she said was receiving the money, had been dead for years.

And then there were the dogs.

Since the 1930s, Victoria had had a succession of canines, mostly poodles, and each named Andy. The dog would be fed steak in the morning and walked for at least an hour each afternoon. The "walk" would be in the courtyard behind the mansion—with the dog in a baby perambulator.

As each Andy passed away, Victoria would commission a walnut casket to be built. Then, it was said, when the current Andy died, he would be entombed on a velvet pillow somewhere within the mansion. No outsider ever saw exactly where. And former servants were notoriously lacking in memory.

Victoria Sandler was a woman who had rejected reality as ardently as reality had rejected her. Estate management by Thomas's father, William Ward Daniels, until his death in early 1975, had kept her afloat financially and out of asylums. Since his passing, the estate had drifted aimlessly.

Thomas devoured the story, not speaking again until he'd read every word. He grimaced with suspicion. And infirm old woman had died. Seven paraffin candles had been strategically left in his office. No connection, of course.

Andrea stepped out of the kitchen. My God, Thomas noticed, even now she turned him on.

"Tom. I hate to add to your worries," she said.

"Feel free."

"Did you know there was a murder in front of your building last night?"

He put down the *Post.* "No."

"Between three thirty and four o'clock," she said, drying her hands on a dish towel. "A mugging." She cocked her head inquisitively. "Wasn't that about the time you were leaving?"

He thought for a moment. "Yes. It was." He considered it and shrugged. "Strange. I didn't see or hear anything."

She seemed to consider it for a moment, letting the subject hang heavily in the air. Then she moved over to him and sat down beside him.

She kissed him on the cheek, more affection than he'd received during several of the last weeks in their fading relationship.

"Tom?"

"What?"

"Do me a favor."

He answered with silence.

"No matter what happens between us," she said, "if this . . . this arson thing develops into anything good . . ."

He sighed. "You can have the damned story. If that's what you're worried about, you've got it."

Andrea smiled. It was the smile he liked. "Promise?"

"Promise."

She kissed him again with slightly more passion.

Chapter 2

The crimson maple leaf was barely visible through the driving white snowflakes. Leslie McAdam trudged through the deep accumulation of snow packed on the sidewalks. She paid little attention to the Canadian flag on the pole across the street. The flag's red borders and red leaf were discernible now as she was closer to them. But she chose to walk with her head down, not seeing the flag, back to the comfort of her small apartment.

The city of Montreal was being blanketed again by a heavy, freezing snow. Standard weather for January. Eight fresh inches. That on top of the half foot they'd received four days earlier, which in turn had landed on top of a foot already fallen. All the auto routes of Quebec were closed, again, as were the airports. Whiteness was everywhere. Snow coated the buildings of McGill University, the giant illuminated cross which overlooked the city from the hills of Westmount, the stone statue of Jacques Cartier which dominated the old square which bore his name, and the ancient little church of Notre Dame de Bonsecours in the old town close by the gray frozen Saint Lawrence. The snow was impartial and resolute, yet Montrealers had learned to shrug and live with it. The Métro always ran. And beneath the icy streets, there were underground cafés, shopping centers, and a type of urban camaraderie among the natives, a sense of having defeated the elements above.

Leslie turned a corner, was blasted again by a ripping snowy wind, and then walked up the steps to the wooden row house where she lived. Just a few blocks from the McGill campus. Behind her rumbled a massive, hulking snowplow, scraping out the street, flashing red, blue, and green lights and equipped with everything except a tail gunner. Leslie's second winter at McGill. One more, plus a thesis, and she'd have her doctorate.

Once inside the house she shook the snow off her head and coat. The warmth of the house was soothing. Thank God for Canadian oil, she thought. Much more dependable than the wood and coal used back in southwestern England near Exeter, where she'd been born and raised. At least Canada would never be frozen into submission by a cartel of greedy sheiks.

She pulled a wool scarf from around her throat and lower face. She shook the snow from it and pulled a wool hat from her head, letting her brown hair fall to her shoulders. She clomped up the wooden stairs to her second-floor apartment, leaving wet tracks from her heavy boots on the worn carpeting in the stairway.

Five minutes later she was alone in her warm cozy apartment. Her wet outer clothes were drying above an old bathroom tub. India tea was brewing in the small kitchen and a Mozart piano concerto was playing softly on a KLH system. She listened to the music as she made herself comfortable. On the walls of the apartment were numerous pastel-shaded prints, mostly nineteenth- and twentieth-century European impressionists.

She wasn't a bad artist herself. Had her past and childhood not been a factor, she might have been torn between pursuing either an academic career or a career as a painter. She had her father's gifted hands, she told herself. Gifted at creation, gifted in destruction.

She shuddered at the thought of him. The source of her greatest joy, the creation of art on a blank canvas, was also the root of her deepest fear. She could never exhibit her work, at least not under current conditions. She'd had several invitations to stage private showings. But why bother? Her own name would turn into a death sentence.

She walked to the bedroom. The classical music from the next room was faint but still audible. She stood for a moment before the large bedroom window. The snow outside was still falling beautifully and lay untouched on the quiet street. It was illuminated by the soft light of the streetlamp.

She sighed. Snow. And she'd have to travel, anyway.

From a closet she withdrew a single suitcase. Within twenty-four hours she'd be gone, missing the last two weeks of the semester. Her professors, she hoped, would understand. If she fared well she'd be back within a few weeks, able then to see her thesis through to its conclusion.

But meanwhile, there was unfinished family business. Victoria Sandler was dead.

Leslie began to pack.

Chapter 3

Why did a man take off his wedding ring and slip it into his pocket? If there were two reasons, neither Shassad nor Hearn could think of the second one. No matter. The presence of the ring and its location in the victim's pocket indicated that there had been at least one extra woman in his life. Within the band was engraved: *K.F.-M.R.—6-12-72*.

The report from the Medical Examiner arrived at the Nineteenth Precinct toward three that afternoon. Shassad was the first to glance through it. The report confirmed what he and Hearn had already surmised. The Seventy-third Street victim had had sexual intercourse less than an hour before he'd been transformed from a live man into a butchered corpse.

"The penis," said Shassad philosophically as he handed the report to Hearn, "is mankind's tragic flaw. If this guy had kept his prick in his pants, or at least home where it belonged, he'd probably be alive today."

"Probably," mumbled Hearn, reading the report.

"So," said Shassad aloud and ruminatively, "he's screwing around till three in the morning. Then he gets up, gets dressed, goes down to the street, and meets a reception committee." Shassad paused. "Why did he leave? Is he going to come sneaking home at an hour like that?"

"Maybe he's divorced," offered Hearn.

"If he's divorced why does he carry the ring at all?"

"Habit?" shrugged Hearn.

"Habits are for nuns. I say he was still married."

Neither man was satisfied. But it was essential that they toss ideas back and forth like tennis balls, keeping it up until something made sense. Knowing each other so well for so many years, they'd refined this Socratic method of crime detection to a fine art.

"Why is he leaving at three A.M.?" mused Hearn, leaning back in his chair. "Maybe his girl friend's husband arrived home unexpectedly."

"Or," said Shassad, a man familiar with the delights of the flesh, "maybe he didn't pay for the entire night."

They held that thought for a moment. It was three twenty, almost twelve hours exactly after the slaying. Their telephone rang.

At Bradford, Mehr & Company, an investment firm at 440 Madison Avenue, one of the junior account executives had not appeared that morning for work. At first, since the man came in from the suburbs, his office believed him snarled in the trains which, with luck, bring commuters in and out of the city each morning. But when Mark Ryder had not yet appeared by noon, a secretary called his home.

His wife answered the telephone and was immediately alarmed. No, she said, her husband had not been home last night, either. She explained that he'd called her late the previous afternoon and maintained that he'd be having a late business conference and then had stacks of paper work to catch up on. So, he'd explained to her, he'd chosen to stay overnight in Manhattan at his university club. Did she mind terribly?

One call to the club indicated that he'd never registered there. One glance around the office revealed that he'd never arrived for work on the morning of the twentieth, not even a fast in and out. So one hour later, at one o'clock, the Missing Persons section of the New York City Police Department was notified. They were given a description of the man by a very, very upset wife named Kyle.

The call went through the proper channels, through hospital lists, through precinct reports, and through the city morgue. Eventually lab assistant Gary Dedmarsh, whom on prior cases Shassad had dealt with, thought the description sounded familiar.

Dedmarsh checked the recent arrivals, then telephoned the Fourth Detective Zone headquarters to learn who was assigned to the case.

Several more minutes passed. Then at three twenty, Dedmarsh, a gangly pale twenty-two-year-old, telephoned Shassad and Hearn's desk.

"Mr. Shay-sod?" Dedmarsh asked, pronouncing it as if it were the infield turf where the New York Mets play. "Guess what I got in the freezer. A gorgeous red-haired teenage prostitute. Came in last night. Strangled. Not a mark on her."

Shassad already knew Gary. A "weird kid," as Shassad termed him. "What's the real reason you're calling, Gary?" Shassad asked with impatience. Gary sounded particularly gleeful today and would whistle faint tunes when he wasn't speaking.

"A missing person named Mark Ryder," Dedmarsh said. "He sounds like the guy you sent me last night."

Shassad considered the initials within the gold band. He listened to the Missing Persons description as Dedmarsh falteringly read it over the telephone.

"Indeed, it does," Shassad said. The Seventy-third Street corpse had reassumed its real name.

Thomas Daniels sat in the lone cleared area in the charred ruins of his offices. The entire suite stank of smoke and obviously would for weeks to come. Ashes and soot were everywhere; much of the carpeting was still wet. The arson investigation was going nowhere. What Thomas had left was a free desk, telephone service which had been restored, and a vivid memory of a day six years earlier, the day he'd joined his father's firm. Age twenty-seven, an iconoclastic young lawyer with an affinity for civil-liberties cases.

His father's son? It would hardly have seemed so at first. The father, the archconservative criminal attorney, and the son, a hard-eyed idealist, had had to come to an understanding before they'd join each other. The younger Daniels could handle as many freedom-of-speech or civil-rights cases as he'd handle of tax law or divorce. The son would defend none of the racketeers or white-collar frauds whom the father seemed not only to relish, but also acquit with astonishing frequency.

"Tom," William Ward Daniels would often postulate while his son was in the midst of a civil-liberties case, "sometimes I think there's too much freedom in this country."

"How can you say that?" the son would implore, taking the bait. "How, in light of the people *you* defend?"

"Ah," the old man would opine, throwing back his curly head of graying hair, "all *my* clients are innocent. Check the court records."

Thomas reached to the restored telephone. He dialed Andrea's number at work. It was Tuesday evening, seven thirty, but she would be at her desk in the *New York Times* building, retyping a feature article not due until Wednesday, the copy spread neatly on her desk.

"Andrea Parker," she answered.

"Want a story you can't print yet?"

"Sure," she said. "Give it to me in confidence tonight, read it in the *Times* tomorrow."

"This is serious," he said.

"Can you tell me over the telephone?"

"I know why my offices got torched," he said simply. "I think I know what they were after."

"Who are 'they'?"

"I can show you everything. It's a story."

"Now?"

"If you're interested."

"I am," she said. "Twenty minutes?"

"Twenty minutes."

She hung up, straightened the copy on her desk and locked it into the desk's bottom drawer. She left the *Times* building, walked out onto Forty-fourth Street, found a yellow cab which had just discharged theatergoers, and arrived at 457 Park Avenue South fifteen minutes later.

Thomas was waiting in the locked lobby. Jacobus, the night custodian, unlocked the plate-glass doors, admitted her without speaking, then cautiously relocked the doors. Jacobus remained in the lobby watching their elevator, making sure that the young Daniels kid and the girl went to the right floor. Jacobus was even-natured: He trusted no one at any time.

Thomas led Andrea through the front doors of his offices. It was her second look at the destruction.

"Do I still need hip boots to walk through here?" she asked.

"Just a clothespin for that reporter's nose of yours. It'll be months before the next tenants get the stench out of here."

"Next tenants?" she asked.

It was too late to retract his words. He stammered slightly.

"It's not—ah—what I called you down here for," he explained slowly, "but, yes, I'm giving thought to closing the offices. For good."

They arrived at his cleared working area. It was adjacent to the filing room, the flash point of the blaze.

"Quitting law?" she asked. "Is that what you're talking about."

"I guess it is," he said without emotion, his hands in his pockets.

"I don't understand people who quit things," she said flatly.

"I know you don't. But you show me the alternative. My two associate attorneys need work at a steady salary. They've already contacted other firms. Take a look around here." He held his hand aloft, indicating the scene of ruin. "Damned little that can be salvaged. And the insurance company isn't going to pay. I've got to drag them kicking and screaming into court. *That*'ll be my big case for the year."

"What did you bring me down here for?" she asked. "To give you a pep talk on why you should stay in law?"

He sat down on the rim of his desk and looked at her. "No," he answered. "That's just what I don't want. The proper circumstances have been presented for making an exit. It's time for me to get out."

"Ridiculous. Quit your only livelihood?"

"My only livelihood?" he scoffed. "My only livelihood has been killing me all my life." He stared at her. "Christ," he said, "if your father had been *the great* William Ward Daniels and if you'd been shoved along in his footsteps, you'd have been a lawyer, too, by now. But that doesn't mean your old man's shoes would have fit you, either."

Andrea looked at him, half with contempt, half with understanding as she thought of her own father, who had worked for United Press.

"And you'd hate it, too," he said, "just as I do. You would have been seduced along the way with the summer jobs in law firms, the clerking for important judges, the tricky legalese draft deferments, and the silver-platter offer to join the firm that bore your name. Ah, yes. My ordained future. But no one knew I wasn't going to be brilliant like the old man. And no one knew that once he was gone the clients wouldn't flock to me."

Thomas paused. In the mind's eye of the son, William Ward Daniels stood in the center of a silenced courtroom, a somber expression on his craggy face, his hands thrust into jacket pockets, his graying head lowered and gazing absently at the floor. He would seem to be contemplating the process of justice, all eyes on him—the virtuoso. Then the trained voice would rise and fall as the large, square-shouldered, fastidiously dressed attorney launched into defense arguments that could draw tears from a jury of granite blocks. Opposing attorneys wondered what had hit them.

Thomas looked up. "Do you remember the Luther Adley case?"

"The black militant?"

He nodded. "1970," he said. "Adley was up on charges of armed robbery and possession of narcotics. He'd been a militant in the civil-rights movement and—"

"—and claimed he was being framed," she recalled.

He nodded again. "My father brought the case into the firm," Thomas said. " 'Good practice for you,' he said to me. And he dumped it in my lap. 'Here,' he said. 'Here's a *big* liberties case for you.' "

"You won it, didn't you?" she said.

"Sure," he said sullenly. "On perjured testimony."

"What?" Her mouth flew open.

He remembered that she was a reporter as well as his friend. "Off the record, of course," he said quickly, raising his hand. She grimaced, conceding the point, and so he went on. "My dear father arranged a key witness for me. The witness was pure fabrication. Perjury all the way." Seeing her incredulity, he added, "I had no idea at the time. None at all."

"But afterward?"

"We were hardly back in the office when my father told me what he'd done. It was to serve a point," Thomas said, "a point my father considered a crucial principle of courtroom justice." Thomas paused and recalled with acrimony, " 'That will teach you two lessons, Tom,' he said to me. 'Nothing, but *nothing*, is black and white. And never trust another attorney. Even me.' "

Thomas let his words sink in, waiting for her to speak next.

Her face was contorted into an inquisitive frown. Her mind was racing ahead, wondering if someday she could print the story.

"Is that what you wanted to tell me?" she asked with a certain degree of sympathy.

"No," he said, "that's only background. It explains why I'm a bit of a disappointment. I wasn't honest enough to come forward to tell the court the truth after the trial. I wasn't *dis*honest enough to do the same sort of thing again. It was as if the old man had been testing me, seeing how corrupt he could make me."

"A strange sort of challenge to throw down to an only son," she said, hoping he'd keep talking. She almost felt like taking notes, but her memory would suffice.

"He was a strange man," Thomas said. "Sometimes I think I never really knew the man. He left me with that feeling. And the feeling that he must have been disappointed because I'm just plain nowhere near as good as he was. Similarly, I disappoint you."

"What?"

"Which is why you and I will never make it on a permanent basis, and why you persist with your casual liaisons with other men. Which, as you know, drive me insane."

"Thomas—" she snapped.

He held up his hand, cutting her short. "Please. My final point."

She was silent.

"There is, however, someone I have not disappointed. That person burned me out. And that is why you're here. That is the beginning of the story I'm letting you in on. But it's also all I know."

"Who burned the offices?" she asked flatly.

"I don't know," he said. "But someone had to have a certain folder from my files. Imagine. Something so valuable in those crumbling old files that someone went to these lengths to get it. The old man would have appreciated that, wouldn't he?"

"All right," she said. "You've got me. I want to know. What was it?"

"Don't know," he said with exasperated amusement. "Something long forgotten, but so valuable that it had to be taken without anyone even learning that it was missing. Want more?"

"I didn't come for the lecture," she said.

"Wonderful." He smiled. "Follow me."

He led her into the filing room and gestured her toward the burned frames and ashen contents of the wooden filing cabinets. He could see her discomfort.

He walked to one of the remaining files. A drawer was open, just as he had left it before calling her.

"I have a good memory," he said, pointing toward the cabinet. "These drawers were the S's." He patted the charred frame of the file. "The beginning of the S's. 'S' as in Sandler."

"Sandler as in Victoria Sandler?"

"The same."

"Cut the bullshit, Tom. I want to know what you're talking about."

"With pleasure," he said.

Carefully he drew her closer to the open file drawer. He fingered the drawer's contents. The drawer had not been tightly shut during the blaze, and much of the fire had crept in. Yet the folders and papers hadn't been completely destroyed. The tops and corners had been burned or blackened, but the lower half of each particular folder was intact.

"I would never have noticed this if I hadn't seen Victoria Sandler's obituary," he said. "Her death was reported the day of the fire."

"Yes." Andrea had an inquisitive frown on her forehead. "So?"

"So it made me curious. My father represented the Sandler family in several cases. Zenger and Daniels handled the Sandler fortune for years. So Victoria finally died, long after most people had forgotten about her." He smiled and his tone changed. "What do dead people leave besides bodies?"

"Wills."

"Exactly. That old woman had been out of her mind for years. Probably didn't know where her own will was. The previous will, Arthur Sandler's, was probated by Zenger and Daniels. That made me wonder if—"

"—if Victoria Sandler's will was in your file," she said. "And if you were sitting on a massive probate case."

"Brilliant deduction."

She smiled coyly. "In other words, if the probate fee were enormous enough you wouldn't mind being a lawyer again?"

"With the probate fee on a will like that I'd gladly accept it as my first and last big case. Then I'd take the money and get out of this sleazy profession. To be specific, I'd be able to buy my freedom."

Her grayish-blue eyes glanced to where his fingers ran up and down the charred center drawer of that filing cabinet. "What did you find?"

"A black hole in space," he said. "There's enough left in this drawer for me to know what was here when the fire started. The beginnings of the S's. Look." He fingered each file as he spoke. "Eugene Sabato. Margaret Saichter. Robert Samuelson." He reached a space filled only with ashes from the other folders. "Here it skips," he said excitedly. "No Sandler. It continues with Saperstein, Howard. Then Saxon, Reginald. And that's the end of the drawer." His hand moved back to the center. "Nothing but ashes and an empty space where the biggest frigging folder in the whole office should be."

He looked at her. Her expression was pensive yet skeptical.

"What do you think?" he asked.

Her eyes met his. "Flimsy," she said.

"What's flimsy?"

"Your whole theory."

"Why?" His tone was almost belligerent.

"One of your associates could have taken the file."

"They'd have no reason to," he said. "Anyway, I asked them. They didn't."

"When's the last time you definitely saw it?"

He shrugged. He had no idea.

"See?" she asked. "The Sandler file could have disappeared months ago. Maybe even years ago. Linking its disappearance to the fire is an excellent theory. But it's farfetched. Where's the motive?"

"I don't know," he said.

"Who's alive who'd even have a motive?"

He shrugged again. "Somewhere someone must be," he said. "Whoever burned me out knew what he was doing. And he didn't start in my filing room for fun."

"I'm not disputing that," she said. "But I say you're leaping to conclusions. Whoever burned you might have taken twenty folders out of your file. And who knows what they might have been taken for. He might have used them for kindling in this same room."

He thought about it. "Possible," he conceded. "But I could have some fun with the only clues left to me. I could find out what was in the Sandler file."

"How?" she asked.

A sly smile crossed his face. He led her from the blackened filing room back to the one clear working area in the office.

"I talked to the old man's former associate," he said.

"Zenger?" she asked.

"Zenger."

"I'd forgotten he was even alive."

"It's not hard. He's eighty-two. Lucid, though. His mind works even though I suspect the body is failing. He lives on Nantucket. Genteel retirement."

"What did he say?"

"About the Sandlers? Nothing."

"Big help that is," she said. He sat behind the desk. Failing to find a chair, she sat on the edge of the desk. He was aware of her gracefulness and figure as she sat and looked him in the eye.

"He said he'd talk to me personally about it," Thomas said. "I'd have to go up there to meet him."

"How's he going to remember what's in a ten-year-old file?"

"He's not," Thomas said. "But I think with old Victoria dead he's ready to tell me about the Sandler family."

"Are you going up to Massachusetts to see him?" she inquired.

He leaned back in his chair and folded his arms in front of him. "It would be intriguing," he said. "But no. I won't. It doesn't matter enough. I'm ending my involvement with this once-corrupt firm here and now."

"What's that mean?" she asked.

"Remember I told you I was thinking of closing the office?"

"Yes," she said.

"I'm not 'thinking' about it. I'm doing it. I'm closing this office on Friday and I'm getting out of law."

There was a silence as she weighed his words. "I don't believe you," she said. "You'll come back to it. It's . . . it's in your blood."

"No," he said, shaking his head in resignation. "If I don't do it now, I'll never do it. I'm broke. The office is bankrupt. All the past has been burned gloriously away."

He looked out the dark window at the empty office building across the street, a building much like the one he was in. The lights were off across the street. But the offices waited for their workers the following morning. And the morning after that and every morning thereafter.

"I'm thirty-three," he said. "I figure I have half of my life ahead of me. I'm not going to spend it in this office. I'm not going to grow old and die doing something I hate and something I'm not that good at."

"What *will* you do?" she asked.

He held his hands apart, as if in wonder. "All I know is what I *won't* do."

He moved back to his desk and sat down. He folded his hands behind his head and leaned back. "I'd love to solve a mystery," he said. "And I'd love to play amateur sleuth. But nothing here matters enough anymore. Everything was my father's, not mine."

He glanced in the direction of the charred filing cabinets. "I'm closing the doors," he said. "And you know what? I'm not unhappy about it."

Chapter 4

It was well past four o'clock on Friday afternoon. The young woman in the camel's-hair overcoat tried the front door to the Zenger and Daniels offices. The door was locked.

She looked at the dark walnut door. She knocked again at the door and tried the knob. Again, no response. The door was unyielding. Yet she knew she was in the proper place—she could smell the stale odor imparted days ago by the smoke. Besides, the newspapers had mentioned Zenger and Daniels and that was the name on the door.

She noticed a doorbell to the left of the entrance, a feature of an older New York office building. She pressed it. Several seconds passed. She was just about to turn to leave when the door abruptly opened and a man spoke.

"Yes?"

She was almost startled. The man before her wore no tie. His hands were dirty, his hair disheveled, and his sleeves rolled beyond the elbows. His clothing suggested maintenance rather than the practice of law.

"I wasn't sure anyone was in," she said. "I . . . I don't have an appointment but I wanted to see someone."

"Anyone in particular?" he asked.

She glanced at the names on the door. "William Ward Daniels," she said. "If he's available."

He smiled slightly. "You're a bit late for him," he said. "He died a year ago."

"Oh, I'm sorry," she said. She seemed taken aback, searching for the next words but not finding them immediately.

"I'm his son," said Thomas. "Maybe I can help you."

She thought for a moment. "Perhaps you can," she said. She looked him up and down, wondering what to make of his attire. It was the last Friday in January. Thomas had been packing what was salvageable in cartons and storage crates. On Monday the landlord would be bringing in construction men to rebuild the entire suite. After today, the offices would be made habitable for new tenants. Zenger and Daniels would exist only as a memory.

Thomas looked at himself and suddenly realized her apprehension. "I've, uh, been moving things. Don't mind my appearance. What did you want to see my father about?"

"Could we discuss it inside?" she asked. She hesitated again, then added, "I understand your office had something to do with the Sandler estate."

He looked at her carefully, almost in disbelief. She was well-spoken, nicely dressed, and she possessed a face that might brighten a magazine cover.

"Of course," he said. "Come in."

He held the door open and she followed.

She was apparently struck by the condition of the office. Blackened walls, packing crates, the scent of smoke even stronger now. Blackened furniture had been shoved against sooted walls.

"I should explain," he said. He did, about the fire.

"Your offices are relocating?" she asked.

"In a sense," he said. He led her to the one room in the suite that was presentable and functional. He removed two crates of papers from the top of his desk. He avoided mention of his intention to leave the practice of law. He'd listen to her and guide her on to someone else who might be able to help.

She sat down in a hard-backed wooden chair near his desk, attempting to sit comfortably on what was essentially a rigid and uncomfortable chair.

"I don't know whether you'll be able to assist me or not," she said. She glanced around and began to sense the moribund state of the office. He was now aware of her slight English accent. "You might not even believe me. And you might be too busy moving."

"It doesn't take much space to listen to a problem," he said.

"I suppose not," she said. She eyed him carefully, deciding whether or not to go on. But he did sound sincere. And this *was* the firm mentioned in the newspapers. "I read last week that a woman named Victoria Sandler had died," she said. "The article stated that this firm once handled the Sandler family's business."

"At one time," he said. Thomas mentally pictured Andrea, who'd written the *Times* article which other newspapers had picked up.

"Victoria had a brother. Arthur Sandler. Born in 1899."

"That's right," he said. He began to wonder where this might lead and whether or not it would be worthwhile to be led. He studied her. The English accent was more noticeable now. She was well-spoken. Educated. Her clothing conservative, yet flattering to her lithe figure. A navy-blue suit hemmed below the knee. A light-blue print blouse and a carefully knotted pale-blue scarf. The camel's-hair coat was now across her lap as she sat with her ankles slightly crossed.

"How much do you know about Arthur Sandler?" she asked.

"Not an awful lot. It was my father and Mr. Zenger who knew him personally. Before his death, that is. 1954, wasn't it?"

"No," she said. "It wasn't."

"Wasn't what?"

"1954. The newspapers said that he was a murder victim. Some sort of street execution."

"That's right."

"That's *not* right. He was alive past 1954. *Well* past 1954." She spoke calmly and methodically.

He leaned back in the chair. He folded his arms and looked at her in a new light. He wondered if she might not be better served at Bellevue than his office.

"How do you know?" he asked.

"It's a long story."

"I'm sure it is."

"I'm prepared to tell it if you're willing to listen." He made no comment. He only looked at her, trying to assess her grip on reality.

"He wasn't killed in 1954. I don't know who was, but it wasn't he."

"You've *seen* him since?"

"*After* his 'death' in 1954," she said. "And then again in 1964."

"Uh huh," he said. "That's very nice. Did you come here to warn me?"

She looked up from her lap into his eyes. Her blue eyes, formerly soft and warm, were now sharp and intense, wide with emotion, almost with fear.

"I'm not a crazy lady," she said. "I didn't come here to be patronized."
She paused. "Arthur Sandler was my father."

He considered the assertion for only a second. "I see. Was he married
to your mother?"

"Of course. During the war."

"War?"

"World War Two."

"Arthur Sandler was never married," he said. "And when he died in
1954 it was established legally that he had no children, legitimate or
otherwise. His estate went in its entirety to Victoria, who—"

She tossed a folded paper from her purse onto his desk.

"—was the sole inheritor," he finished. He picked up the paper.
"What's this?"

"I assume you can read." He opened it and examined it. She spoke as
he read. "It's my birth certificate. I was born at Exeter in England in
1945. See for yourself." The document had the appearance of what she
claimed. "The marriage was a secret," she added.

"A hell of a secret. His own sister didn't know about it."

"Victoria didn't know about anything. She didn't even know what year
she was in."

"Uh huh," he said.

Studiously, she drew back her head and looked at him. "Skeptical,
aren't you?"

"I'm afraid so, Miss . . . or Mrs. . . ?"

"McAdam. Leslie McAdam. And if it matters, I'm unmarried."

"What you're here to claim is that you're an heiress to the Sandler
estate. Or at least part of it. Correct?"

"All I want is what's due to me," she said.

"I can have this certificate checked," he said. "We both know that. But
by itself it won't be enough. Can you *prove* who you are? Can you *prove*
who your parents were? Can you *prove* they were married?" He paused
for a moment, trying to be tactful. "What you're embarking on will take
years in the courts. It's bound to be challenged by hundreds of other
people, some with verifiable claims, others who are merely crackpots. It
will be difficult enough to convince an attorney—including myself—to
take on a case like this. Then it will be twenty times more difficult to
convince a court that your claim is justified."

"I know."

He said nothing. She understood the skepticism evident within the
silence.

Leslie spoke. "I have spent my life being brutalized by the facts surrounding my birth. I'm not afraid of Arthur Sandler anymore. Whether he's dead or alive. I only want what I deserve."

With perfect composure she unpacked a ribboned group of letters from her purse. She laid them on the desk in front of him.

"Letters, Mr. Daniels. From my father to my mother. 1942 to 1944. You may look through them now. Eventually you may have the handwriting verified. But at no time do these letters leave my possession."

He glanced at the letters. Then, with interest, he fingered the stack, examining the browned envelopes, the return addresses and the old postmarks over British wartime stamps. If Leslie McAdam was an act, he began to concede, she was a good one. And if she was *not* an act, he wondered.

"There's more," she said. He looked up.

From her purse she pulled a small aged black book. The frayed leather cover and gold-edged pages were well worn. Thomas recognized the book for what it was even before he saw HOLY BIBLE embossed in gold on the binding.

"Open it to the inside front cover," she said. And she handed him the Bible.

Thomas took the book with his right hand. His eyes left Leslie. He examined the Bible with genuine interest, opening it as she had instructed. He could in no way stifle the deep chill he suddenly felt when he read what was before him.

Bound into the Bible's front cover was a marriage certificate. Enscrolled, embellished, and fully notarized, it was dated October 20, 1944. Arthur Sandler of New York and Elizabeth Ann Chatsworth of Tiverton, bound in holy matrimony at St. George's Chapel in the Devon township of North Fenwick. The names of two witnesses were signed to the certificate. A third signature appeared at bottom, to the far right. The signature was that of Jonathan Phillip Moore, D.D., the pastor.

Thomas examined the document for almost a full minute. Then, with increasing intrigue, he glanced through the Bible. He noted the Roman numerals on the title page.

ANNO DOMINI MCMXLII, it said. Printed in Great Britain, 1942.

He looked up at her. His skepticism was diminished, but not dismissed. "Anything else?" he asked.

"You're probably wondering why I didn't come forward in 1954," she said.

"It crossed my mind," he said.

Leslie McAdam pushed back the light-brown hair which almost

touched her shoulders. She pushed the hair behind her ears, then unbuttoned the top two buttons of her blouse. She reached to the scarf at her throat, untied it, and pulled it away with one graceful motion.

"Lean forward, Mr. Daniels. The light here is not the best."

She looked directly at him and opened the collar of her blouse. She exposed the bare white flesh of her throat, the area formerly covered by the pale-blue scarf. She craned her head slightly to allow him a clear view of her neck.

Thomas could see a long thin line of reddish-pink scar tissue which circled the midpoint of her throat. It was readily visible against her delicate skin.

"Piano wire, Mr. Daniels," she said. "It can make rather a mess of a nine-year-old girl's skin."

Thomas looked at her without speaking.

"It's something else my father gave me," she said. "My best memory of him. 1954. Alive enough in that year to attempt to garrotte me."

She let Thomas gaze at her damaged throat. He could envision the razor-sharp wire digging into her flesh, savaging the jugular vein and unleashing a red torrent of blood. He no longer wondered if she was telling the truth. He wondered why she was alive.

She let the collar fall into place again, gently retied the scarf, and modestly rebuttoned her blouse. She hadn't lost her composure in the slightest. Thomas was able to regain his.

Several seconds passed. She looked to the birth certificate, the Bible, and the time-worn letters on his desk. She did not exude patience. Nor did she appear to be a woman who'd be in any way swayed from her appointed mission. She was again conscious of the faint, stale smell of smoke as she broke the silence.

"I'm here to collect my inheritance, Mr. Daniels," she said. "And I'm afraid you're the only one who can help me."

"Why me?"

"Because of your father. And his relationship to my father."

"There are other attorneys in New York," he said. "Men much better than I."

She was already shaking her head, shaking it with a definitiveness and a finality which did not suggest—it stated. The decision was made. To look at her one saw delicacy and perhaps what might be mistaken for a feminine form of tenderness. But within there was a spirit as resistant as an anvil, as insistent as a hammer.

"You see," she began, "I'm a scholar and an artist. I have the inquisitive temperament of one, the creative instincts of the other. But I'm also the daughter of a vicious man. Arthur Sandler. I have some of his blood, too. I know how to hate."

"I hope you also know how to explain," he said. "I'm not following this. I'm sorry." And, seeking now to keep an emotional and intellectual distance between them, he tried to tell her of his decision to leave the practice of law.

She interrupted. "I'm here to ask you to fulfill two roles," she said. "Attorney and detective."

"Neither suits me."

"Don't be too certain. People's marks in life have a way of finding them."

"Do they?"

"That's what I've always observed. What is it that Camus said? 'A man gets the face he deserves'? I've always thought a man or woman also gets the métier he or she deserves."

He shook his head. "Very, very wrong," he said. "I've spent the last eight years resisting this profession. Want to know the truth? I've been burned out here. Want to know the real truth? Secretly I'm happy about it!"

"Happy?"

"It's my out. These files, these records which my father and Adolph Zenger spent a lifetime building. They're nothing now. Nothing. Wiped out." An elusive smile crossed his face. "It's like a clean slate," he said. "It's like being liberated. You see, I can do what I want with my life. It doesn't include practicing law or playing detective."

"What does it include?"

"I'll decide," he said. "Eventually. You know what? I looked in the mirror this morning and I looked younger than I have for years. As if a burden had lifted. It has been."

"Don't be too sure," she said.

"Of what?"

"That it's lifted."

"Your tone of voice," he said. "It sounds like either a threat or a warning. Which is it?"

"Neither, really. But one's fate often comes looking for him, not the other way around. That's what I've always found. You didn't *happen* upon a fire. It found you."

He gave her a look which mixed suspicion with intrigue, a look which seemed to ask a deeper explanation of who she was, what she wanted, and from where she'd materialized.

"You seem to know a lot," he said, feeling very much on the defensive now.

"I know arson when I see it," she said. "Or smell it." She smiled.

His own smile was gone. "I'm sure you have a theory," he said.

"Of course. That's why I'm here."

"I hate theories," he said. "I like facts. That's why I hate law. Law deals with permutations of truth and misrepresentations. Obscuring of facts."

"You want facts, do you?" she said. "I'll give you facts. I tell you a story which has a direct bearing on why I'm here. And why you had a fire."

"All right," he said, easing back in his chair. "I'd love to hear it."

Chapter 5

"It's all past history now," she said. "Cold war and all that."

Thomas frowned. "Cold war?" he asked.

"Yes," she said casually. "I should think so. I should think that had very much to do with it." She added matter-of-factly, "My father did intelligence work. Or didn't you even know that much?"

Thomas fumbled for a response but felt himself drawn into her story. "My father handled the bulk of the Sandler business," he said.

"You *didn't* know, did you?" she asked, surprised.

"No."

"No matter. There's probably not much that's known, anyway. Even I have never figured out for whom he was spying."

"Which government, you mean?" he asked.

"That's right," she answered. "I suppose there are only a few possibilities. He was on one side or the other. East or West, I mean."

Thomas's gaze, shrouded with curiosity, fixed upon the fair face before him. "How do you know all this?" he asked.

"From the two times in my life that I saw him," she said. "The rest of the time he was a nonperson. Officially no one would admit he existed." She laughed slightly. "Don't worry. My mother revealed enough of the rest when I was a little girl. As an adult, I've drawn my own conclusions."

"I'd like to hear them."

"My mother raised me until the time I was nine years old," Leslie said.

"She was a good mother. But embittered. She'd been abandoned by my father. An American man."

"Your mother was British?"

Leslie nodded. She clasped her hands in her lap and sat a trifle stiffly on the wooden chair.

"A wartime romance," Leslie said. "There were thousands of troops billeted near Exeter during the war. British, American, Canadian, French in exile. And there were others, military and intelligence people who didn't wear uniforms. Our whole area later became a staging area for airborne troops immediately before the invasion of Normandy. But I'm skipping ahead."

Leslie backtracked to wartime England. Her mother was working class. The daughter of an Exeter innkeeper, Elizabeth Chatsworth was twenty-one in 1942. She worked in an Exeter pub which, generally, was off limits to uniformed soldiers. But many foreigners did come by. Included among them was a cultured American man who gave his name as Arthur Sandler.

Sandler, unlike most of the pub's patrons, was a loner. He would be in Exeter for several weeks, be gone for several weeks, then return. His habit when in town was to kill his evenings in the pub, staying until closing time and sitting sullenly alone, lost in thought as he sipped warm beer.

Early in 1942, he began to chat idly with the barmaid, whom he knew only as Elizabeth. She too was lonely much of the time. Then one rainy February evening, as it approached the one-A.M. closing hour, Sandler asked if he could walk her home. She agreed. The walk was only four blocks. When they arrived at the stairs to her flat, she invited him up. He stayed the night.

They were two people of drastically different backgrounds. But the politics of the world had brought them together. And each needed the other, each initially fearing loneliness in that dark year rather than feeling any deep attraction to the other. But they soon discovered that they were compatible. They enjoyed each other's company and liked each other. When Arthur disappeared at the end of four weeks, he promised her he would return. But he couldn't promise when.

Weeks passed. Elizabeth remained at her job, watching the days pass on the calendar, listening carefully to the censored war news, and starting to lose hope daily that her American admirer would ever return. Three full months passed. It was June of 1942. On a sticky summer evening she looked to the end of the bar and saw him. He was smiling and watching her. She let out a loud gasp, dropped the tray she was carrying, and rushed to embrace him, he returning her warmth with equal enthusiasm.

He said he'd be there for three weeks. He was, seeing her each evening, staying with her each night and vanishing during the day. Eventually he left again, only to return again. And so it continued, weeks there, weeks gone, for eighteen months. Finally she summoned the courage to ask what she'd been wondering all that time.

"When you're not here," she asked, "where do you go?"

They both knew that he shouldn't answer. But he did. "Austria," he said. She was staggered, and realized that he was telling the truth. She asked nothing further, not even which side of the war he was on. She did not want to know. Nor did she ask, at that point, whether or not he had a wife somewhere else. She considered herself lucky to have a man, even part-time. Most women she knew had none at all.

1943 passed, then the early half of 1944. On a visit in October, he grew increasingly despondent over a period of two weeks. She asked what was the matter. Initially he refused to discuss it. Finally he did.

He said that his participation in the war was reaching its final—and most dangerous—stages. "There's a strong chance," he said, "that I might not see you again until the war in Europe is over." He paused and then with faltering calm added, "I'm trapped in the center of a treacherous game. I suspect that I'm going to be killed before the war ends. By one side or the other."

They embraced each other. His face was away from her but she wouldn't look at him. She didn't want to let him know that she knew he was crying. When he was able, he spoke again. For the first time, he told her that he loved her. He said he didn't wish to leave her, but he'd have no choice.

"I want to do what's best for you," he said. "If I'm lucky enough to survive the war, I'm going to come back and take you to America." He hesitated, then added, "If I don't come back, I want you to be provided for." Then for the first time he spoke of his origins. He stated without elaborating that back in New York he was a man of considerable wealth. On the next day, October 20, 1944, they drove from Exeter out into the countryside. There, among green hedgerows in a small rural churchyard in the township of North Fenwick, they were married.

Thomas Daniels glanced down at the threadbare Bible in his hand.

"Ten days later," said Leslie, "he departed during the night. He never returned, even after the war. Nine months later, I was born."

"And at the conclusion of the war . . . ?" asked Thomas.

"My mother waited. Nothing. No communication. No letters. No messages. No Arthur Sandler."

"Did she attempt to trace him?"

"Of course," said Leslie. "But she ran into two walls of resistance. One

British, one American. The British authorities maintained that no such man could ever have been on English soil. Then my mother tried to trace him through the American Embassy and the United States Army Head-quarters in London. Again, nothing."

"Did she show the marriage certificate and explain that she was search-ing for her husband?"

"Yes," she said. "But the Americans were worse than recalcitrant. They were outright secretive and untrusting. Do you know what they said? They said that no such man ever existed. And they told her that if a bargirl such as she continued to make these wild accusations about marrying an Ameri-can millionaire they would turn her over to the local police or a London mental hospital."

"And so?"

"And so that's how it stood. My mother raised me herself. And as the years passed she became more convinced that a cruel hoax had taken place, with her at the center. She was stuck in her job as a barmaid in a section of Exeter which declined after the war. She was a woman without any education. She couldn't do anything to support us except work in that bar, subjected to dirty labouring men whose drunken hands wandered nightly."

"She never married?"

"She never trusted another man in her life, Mr. Daniels," she said. "Given her situation, I'm not sure that it was a bad idea."

Thomas fidgeted uncomfortably. He glanced away from Leslie. Outside it was dark now, almost six in the evening. ?

Leslie skipped to 1954, the year of Arthur Sandler's death.

It hadn't exactly been of natural causes. Arthur Sandler had been walking on Eighty-ninth Street, where three gunmen had been waiting for him. Victoria, with him at the time, screamed hysterically when she saw him being shot. She dropped the shopping bag she'd been holding and out tumbled no less than a thousand crisp, new one-dollar bills. The assassins ignored the money and were never found.

"The murder of an American millionaire like Sandler was newsworthy throughout Europe," said Leslie. "A shooting on the street like that, a prominent man executed, would find its way into most newspapers. The British news journals carried it. All of them." She took a breath. "My mother saw a picture of him. Recognized him. And of course she recog-nized the name. She had always felt that somewhere he was still alive."

"What did she do?"

Elizabeth Chatsworth, Leslie explained, went to half a dozen solicitors, each of whom dismissed her as a fortune-hunting fake. She went to a local petitioner who said he'd look into her claim. He may or may not have, but he quickly reported back to her that she had no case at all. Then she tried the American Consulate in London. After a few days of investigation, the Americans icily informed her that she was a fraud.

She took the only course left. She sent several letters to the Sandler address in New York.

"Did she get a response?" asked Thomas.

"Yes. But it wasn't in the mail."

On an afternoon in 1954, two weeks before Christmas, Leslie returned to the small four-room row house where she and her mother lived, opened the front door, and shouted that she was home, just as she'd done countless other days. There was no response. Leslie called a second time. Odd, the girl thought. The door unlocked, yet her mother not home. She stopped in the kitchen for cookies, and a few minutes later climbed the stairs.

Her mother's bedroom door was open. And beyond, the room was a shambles. Clothing, dresser drawers, and bedding were all over the floor.

The girl's voice broke now. *"Mother?"* she called plaintively.

She stood at the doorway. The bed had been turned over. She walked past the half-open door, and saw the bedraggled, bloodied sheets. With another step she saw her mother.

Elizabeth Chatsworth Sandler. The body was lying faceup on the floor, broken and fully clothed, the face contorted. Below her mother's chin was a messy line across the throat, where the neck had been severed.

The girl bellowed, nearly felt her heart stop. The door behind her crashed shut.

Terrified, she whirled. He was a large man with a powerful build, his suit and tie black, his skin sallow and white. There were heavy black rubber gloves on his hands.

"You must be Leslie," the man said evenly. His accent was American. "Your mother wrote about you."

A second or two slipped by as the man started slowly toward the cornered girl. He pushed back his sleeves.

"Come to me, Leslie," he said. "I'm your father."

Sandler fumbled with something in his other hand, a pair of silver rings with several inches of wire strung between them. He quickly looped the wire over her neck. She kicked.

Her foot cracked directly into his kneecap. He yanked at the wire. The wire tore the flesh across her throat. But he was unsteady. She pulled away. He lost his grip on the wire and it fell as she rushed by him and down the stairs, shrieking, the deep red gashes dripping blood to her dress and coat.

Exactly how Sandler escaped Leslie never knew. When the police returned to the house Sandler was gone. He'd left behind no trace of himself. Just the body of Elizabeth Sandler. A thoroughly professional killing.

"I have an instinct for self-preservation, Mr. Daniels," she explained. She continued calmly, with only the slightest quaver in her voice. "At age nine I learned. I've never forgotten. I remember him grabbing my wrist so tightly that it hurt. I remember how his face looked. I was paralysed with fear. But I knew I had to do something to protect myself."

Leslie's left hand played with a strand of her hair. She noticed Thomas watching her hand. "I have something else to show you," she said. "This is something you can keep."

She opened her purse and pulled from it a small envelope, the size used for personal letters. She reached into the envelope and pulled out a small glossy black-and-white photograph. She held it by her thumb and forefinger, considered it for a moment, then handed it to Thomas.

"My father," she said without emotion. "Arthur Sandler."

Thomas took the photograph by the edges and looked into the face. "What year?"

"It was Mother's photograph. 1942. Maybe 1943. Probably not much use now."

Thomas shrugged noncommittally. He tucked the picture into another envelope. "So you were a nine-year-old orphan," he said. "What next?"

"Mother hadn't any relatives. Normally that would have put me in a children's home in Devon. But there was more to this case than that. Scotland Yard was involved from London the next day. And they must have turned it over to British intelligence immediately."

"Why do you say that?"

She managed a sardonic smile. "Because that's what happened," she said with sudden authority. "I was driven to London by two plainclothes policemen whom I'd never seen before. I was taken to a large Government building which had Union Jacks and official portraits of Churchill and the Queen on every wall. I may have been nine years old, Mr. Daniels, but never underestimate a child. I knew what was happening. I was to be hidden away, shielded from the man who officially was already dead. They didn't even let me attend Mother's funeral."

"Who's they?" Thomas asked.

"A man named Peter Whiteside was in charge," she said. "I liked him, actually. Tall, thin, very handsome. A sensitive, educated man, most unlike the crude working-class men I'd been exposed to all my life." She paused. "Peter Whiteside was the only man who understood what it must have been like for me."

"This Whiteside," Thomas began, "is—?"

"Long since retired from government service," she said quickly.

Thomas nodded. "You sound like you were close to him."

"For a brief part of my life," she said. "He was the only man I could trust." She allowed her eyes to stare into his for a moment, as if trying to read them. "May I continue?"

"Please."

"Peter Whiteside said he'd take care of me," she said. "Said he'd put me in a new home. A good safe home. He did. He sent me to live in Vevey, Switzerland, with an older British couple, a man and his wife. George McAdam was his name. I adopted the surname immediately, of course."

"Ordinary British subjects?" Thomas asked.

"No one in my life is *ever* ordinary," she intoned. "McAdam had recently been 'retired' from Government service due to a 'car injury.' I always suspected that the truth was being withheld. Years later I put together the correct story. It was 1955. McAdam had been a British operative in the Middle East. Suez. He'd been shot in the lower back by an Arab. He'd never walk properly again. So he'd been 'retired.'"

"And they became your surrogate parents?"

"So to speak. Actually, I was happy there. While it lasted it was the happiest part of my life. I was in a private school which overlooked the Lake of Geneva and the French Alps. I had good clothes, a nice home, and friends. Girl friends and boyfriends. I learned to speak French and German."

"Sounds idyllic," said Thomas.

"My father found me," she said. "Ten years. But he found me."

It was 1964, summer. Her school year ended; she had finished gymnase. In July she took a job working in a boat basin in Lutry, on the Swiss side of the Lake. On the job she met a young man named Roberto Gicarelli. He was dark-haired and handsome, and said he was the son of a manufacturer in the Italian Swiss canton of Ticino. He seemed to have money.

She saw him each evening. He was assertive, athletic, older than she, and, after a week, began asking her to sleep with him. At first she declined. Gradually, she changed her mind. Having known him for about a month, she spoke to him one evening when she was leaving work.

"My family is away," she said. "The flat is empty."

They returned to her home and, inevitably, after sipping wine and listening to jazz during the evening, went into her bedroom. Without speaking they began to undress. She was excited. She liked Roberto—his firm body, the wide muscular shoulders. The anticipation of a strong young man in her own bed aroused her. She'd never done it there before.

Then they lay back, enjoying each other passionately. He was good to her. Rarely in her life had she enjoyed such unrestrained physical pleasure. When it was over, she nuzzled against him, pressing her breasts to him and relaxing in the warmth of his body.

"You were gorgeous," she said. Then, looking at him, she asked eagerly, "Want to do it again?"

"No," he said. "I don't think so."

She frowned, sitting up in bed by leaning on her elbow. The only light was from the window. "Did I do something wrong?" she asked.

"No," he said. "It's me."

"What are you saying?"

"Look out the window, Leslie."

Naked, she went to one knee on the bed. Outside there was nothing as she peered out the window. An empty street. Moonlight. A man standing in the shadow of a streetlamp across the cobblestones at a trolley stop.

"You're being silly," she said. "I don't see anything."

She felt his hands on her shoulders.

"Don't you see the man?" he asked.

She looked again. The man below was gazing up at her. She couldn't clearly discern the face. But suddenly, in a hot flash, she knew. Her hand shot to her face while one arm covered her breasts. Roberto smothered her scream.

"I'm sorry, Leslie," he said. "I have my instructions."

As she turned toward him his hands went tight around her neck. The hands, moments ago affectionate, were now murderous. He was shaking her viciously and squeezing her throat at the same time.

Oh, God, she thought. *He's done it. He's succeeded! My father's having me killed!*

She struggled wildly, but was no match for him. He forced her flat on the bed. She groped for the sewing shears that she'd always kept beneath the mattress.

She was losing consciousness. Her fingertips skimmed the handle of the shears. But Roberto yanked her. Her fingertips slid away.

She groped for them a final time, clenched them in her fist; and the fist was out from under the mattress and slamming into his back.

He bellowed with pain. The twin blades dug deeply below the left shoulderblade. His grip was suddenly gone from around her throat. She coughed painfully. He bent back and tried to get off her. But she stabbed the shears even deeper into his left side.

She had hurt him. Badly. He arched back, straddling her, and looked as if he were trying to reach the open wound in his back. He looked at her with crazed eyes, not comprehending how a naked woman could harm him.

She threw her arm forward a final time. He curled forward on the bed and struggled for life. . . .

It grew quiet in Thomas Daniels's office. "There's not much more to say. Whoever he was, he died. His identity was false. My only regret was that it hadn't been my father. Arthur Sandler escaped again. It was the last time I saw him."

"What about—?"

"The police in Switzerland?"

"Yes," he said.

"It was taken care of. My foster parents flew home from Majorca immediately. They contacted London. My foster father had, shall we say, friends in the usual places. The British Consulate in Geneva straightened things with the Swiss. But I had to leave the country. My identity was worthless. And besides, the Swiss don't like people who import trouble."

"Of course," he said in a low voice.

"I had a British passport, so I used it. I relocated to Canada, where I continued my education. Before I left, my foster father gave me the Bible and the letters. Said they'd been given to him to hold for me until the proper time. I guess that was the proper time." She shrugged. "That brings us to the present, actually."

She fell silent. Thomas searched for the words. "You don't look like someone who's actually killed a man," he said.

"Don't deceive yourself, Mr. Daniels," she warned. "I'm not helpless."

"I can see that."

She paused. She shifted her position slightly and seemed to try a tack that was almost totally contradictory, almost as if a different person were speaking.

"Look," she said, "I'm coming across all wrong." Her manner was sweeter now, less abrasive, less harsh. "You can see what I've contended with all my life. I *do* value human life, just as much as any other civilised person. But I want to live without fear. And I can't do that with uncertainty."

"Uncertainty . . . ?"

"About my father. I want to *know* that he's dead. He dealt with your firm. You must have had records."

Thomas glanced toward the charred remains of the files, but said nothing. Facts. All the facts were gone, he thought. Destroyed. Where else could they be found?

"What if I find your father?" he asked. "Alive."

"I hope you don't," she said.

"But if I do?"

"I've told you," she said. "For me to live, he must be dead." There was a long awkward pause. Then the tension in her face melted and she seemed to relax again. "I'm sorry," she said. "I know how that must have sounded."

"But it's your basic position," he assessed.

"Yes," she said. "I'm afraid it is." She offered him an agreeable smile. He recognized it for what it was, one of her more subtle weapons. Meanwhile she appraised him carefully, wondering if he'd believed her story. "You *will* be able to produce a Sandler file?" she asked.

"Of course," he said, marveling at the ease with which he could lie. "It might take a few days. And I might speak with my father's former partner, Mr. Zenger."

"Good," she said pensively. "Now, your fee . . . ?"

"My normal hourly rate," he began to explain slowly, "is—"

"I have no money," she said, "other than what's due to me from the Sandler estate. I'm willing to offer you twenty-five per cent of what you eventually collect. In the meantime, I can't pay you anything."

Thomas agreed with little hesitation.

"Why don't I contact you Wednesday of next week," she said. She glanced around the burned office. "By the way. Where will you be?"

Thomas thought for a moment. "I have an office in my apartment. You can contact me there." He wrote his telephone number on a sheet of paper and handed it to her. He looked up. "There's one thing you didn't explain," he said.

"There is?"

"From what you tell me your father and mother had a nice enough romance during the war. He loved her enough to marry her. What happened that made him want to come back a decade later and kill both of you?"

"Maybe you can help me find out," she said.

She stood, straightened her skirt, and appeared thoughtful as she saw him watching her.

"I suppose I should add one other thing," she said.

"Yes?"

"You might be wondering. Men unnerve me. So I never sleep with them."

There was a long silence. "I thought I'd mention this," she said. "If you're like most men, you were probably wondering."

"It never crossed my mind," he said, lying again.

He watched her close the door. She was gone before he realized that she'd left him no way to contact her.

PART TWO

The small eleven-passenger de Havilland STOL belonging to Air New England left New York's Marine Air Terminal at nine forty-five A.M. Thomas Daniels was one of nine passengers. For most of the flight, he was deep in thought.

Strange about old Zenger, he mused. The man had once been close to a legend in New York legal circles. Bill Daniels's partner. Or "Shifty Little Adolph," as his detractors called him. Once he'd been brilliant. Once he'd been a firebrand. But then, abruptly in the mid-1950s, he'd lost his stomach for law. One day his desire was gone and courtroom machinations no longer interested him. He was, as William Ward Daniels described it at the time, "a different man," a man far more concerned with a leisurely and reclusive retirement than with the daily torment of a Manhattan legal practice.

Privately, Bill Daniels had explained it to his son. Zenger's retirement was somehow connected to the Sandler estate. But it never really made much sense. A visit or two by Zenger to the Sandler mansion and the attorney had decided it wasn't for him, after all. Now, two decades later, who cared anymore? Who even remembered? Thomas had never known his father's partner well.

The small airplane arrived in Nantucket at twelve fifteen. From the airport Thomas took a taxi to the residence of the long-retired attorney.

The taxi found Zenger's home with little difficulty. Zenger lived in a rambling, white-shingled old house on a promontory which dramatically overlooked the ocean. Thomas saw a curtain move near a downstairs window as he stepped from the long blue Chrysler taxi and paid the driver. Thomas glanced around as he passed through a gate and followed a flagstone path across a brownish-green lawn. A comfortable site to spend one's later years, he thought. Free from crime, pollution, and the real world.

Beyond the old house, and to the side of the promontory, a path led down to the ocean. The surf broke briskly against the sand beach which bordered Zenger's land. A sturdy wooden pier jutted out into the water.

Curiously, Thomas noted that two large pleasure boats—Chris-Craft they appeared to be, the type used by sportsmen for deep-water fishing —were tied up to the pier, rocking somewhat with the waves. Obviously somebody, Thomas thought, liked to venture into the deep waters beyond the Nantucket shore. Obviously Zenger, his father's former partner, since the boats were tied to Zenger's pier.

Zenger's daytime housekeeper, a dowdy dark-haired woman named Mrs. Clancy, opened the solid oak front door.

"Mr. Daniels?" she asked.

Thomas nodded. He was taken to a downstairs sitting room congested with old overstuffed furniture. There sat Adolph Zenger. The old man, considerably whitened and wrinkled since the last time Thomas had seen him, sat in a large leather armchair. An afghan covered his lap. Before him was a paneled window overlooking Nantucket Sound. Zenger's gaze did not leave the water.

"Come in," he said as Thomas stood somewhat uncomfortably after walking a few feet into the room.

"I already am," said Thomas.

Zenger turned toward the younger man. The aging face creased into a slight grin. "I know," he said. "I'm not blind."

"You look well," said Thomas.

"Damn you!" snapped Zenger with convincing bitterness.

"What?"

"You know you've got one God-damned foot in the grave when people say that to you," he said. "People stop asking you how you are and start telling you how well you look. Do I look that bad?"

"I only meant—"

"It's obvious what you meant. Most people my age are dead." He eyed his visitor with keen interest. "So. Bill Daniels's boy come up to see me. How long have you been practicing law now, Tommy?"

"Six years."

"Ever won a case?"

"Mr. Zenger," Thomas said with fading patience, "I—"

"Answer me, God damn it, or I'll have your obscenely young ass heaved out of here!"

"Of course I've won cases," said Thomas evenly.

"You'd never know it, boy," he said. "Never know you were Bill Daniels's kid. You haven't learned a thing."

Thomas was silent. Then the sharp old eyes mellowed and the smile was more friendly. "I've had you on the defensive since you came into this room," said Zenger. "Be that in a courtroom, boy, and you're dead."

Proud of his point, Zenger eased back in his chair and offered his hand to his visitor. Thomas smiled and took it.

"I appreciate the lesson," said Thomas. "But nothing's changed. I'm still not all that interested in courtrooms."

"Rubbish," snorted Zenger. "You came up here because you're working on a case. What do you think I am, senile? You're your father's son. Bloodlines don't wash out in the bath. You're even starting to look a little like Bill."

"Am I?" Thomas was genuinely surprised.

"Yes, yes," said Zenger, drawing out the words and looking the younger man up and down. "Don't forget I knew Bill way back when he was your age. A hundred years ago or whatever it was. Hungry?"

"I could eat something."

"You damned well better. I've had lunch fixed for both of us. If I don't drop going from this room to the next, we're all set. If I do drop, go ahead without me."

Zenger climbed to his feet with the help of a sturdy cherrywood cane. Thomas put out his hand to help, but Zenger motioned the hand away. The older man's physical movements were slow, to a degree where Thomas was embarrassed for him. But after a few moments of fumbling, Zenger was able to move to the adjoining dining room, a small cozy room with two dark beams across the ceiling and a bright window which looked out on a small garden area and the water beyond. A china cabinet stood before one wall and a ship's barometer dominated another.

Zenger spoke as they sat down. "Know why I live up here now and not in New York?"

Thomas asked why.

"I figure that anything as slow-moving as I wouldn't live long in the city. I would have been hit by a bus or had a knife perforate my ribs. What do you think of that?"

Thomas shrugged noncommittally.

Lunch was a seafood salad. A bottle of chablis appeared. Zenger's mock belligerence was gone now. He and Thomas talked amiably. Zenger dwelled on how sorry he had been to hear of the passing of Daniels, Senior, a year earlier. But, of course, he excused himself, he'd been unable to travel and attend the funeral. Then Zenger asked about the law firm, wanting to know with glee who was suing whom and for what. Thomas gave him as much gossip as he could, but never mentioned the fire.

Gradually the old man's attention lagged. He gazed off away from Thomas and out the dining-room window. His eyes squinted.

"See that?" he asked.

Thomas looked. "See what?"

"The ocean," Zenger answered softly and almost affectionately. "Look as far as you can, across the waves, all you see is water." The eyes twinkled and the eyebrows were raised. He looked back to Thomas quickly. Daniels was considering the old man carefully, as if Zenger had gone soft for a few seconds.

"Someday, Tommy," Zenger continued, "someday soon, I'm going to take a long trip. Beneath the waves. And I won't be coming back."

"You look healthy to me," Daniels offered.

The old man scoffed. "Got nothing to do with it," he said. "When it's your time to go, you go. Simple as that. For me, I'd like to go beneath the waves." Zenger looked old in the afternoon light.

The housekeeper appeared. She cleared the plates and served coffee. At length, a different Zenger spoke. "Enough of the bullshit." His voice was upbeat now, a total change. "You didn't come up here for the salt air. You said something on the telephone about Victoria Sandler."

"That's right. I wanted to know about her. And the family."

"Know what?"

Thomas shrugged. "Everything. Whatever you know." Thomas saw a flicker of suspicion in Zenger's eyes.

"Why?" asked Zenger.

"The old woman just died."

"I know. We do have newspapers up here. But you didn't just come because you had a funny curiosity."

Thomas folded his hands together and remained silent while cream for the coffee was served. When they were alone again, he spoke.

"The firm used to handle the family business. You know that. If there's any question about a will, I'm going to need to know as much as I can."

"Uh huh," said Zenger without enthusiasm. "What about your files?"

"Incomplete." If Thomas had learned one thing from his father, it was never to reveal a position of weakness to another attorney. *Any* other attorney.

"Incomplete?" Zenger's wrinkled forehead formed a frown. "What the hell does that mean?"

Thomas shrugged innocently. "The material in the Sandler folder is sketchy. Leaves a lot of questions unanswered."

Zenger leaned back in his chair. He sipped the hot black coffee and looked Thomas in the eye. He let several seconds pass in silence.

"Sketchy, huh?" Zenger said. "That's a pretty vague term. What does it mean?"

"It means what I said it means," said Thomas. "It means—"

"It means I just nailed you for perjury," chortled Zenger.

Thomas was perplexed. "What?" he asked.

"Why don't you admit you got burned out," scoffed Zenger. "You don't *have* a Sandler file anymore. What you don't know is that you're God-damned lucky you don't."

Thomas could feel his mouth dry and open in unconcealed amazement. He felt just as many witnesses in past years had felt before attorney Zenger. Totally befuddled, caught off base by the unexpected assertion, the unanticipated declaration of the facts. Thomas tried to recover.

"You know more than I do," he said. "Why don't you let me in on it."

"Aah," scoffed Zenger, leaning back now and sipping coffee slyly. "There's nothing to let you in on."

"How did you know—?"

"About the fire? I read the papers, *damn it.* And even though my God-damned flesh is giving out, I have not lost the capacity for thought. Victoria Sandler dies. Your offices are demolished by arson. Your offices just happen to be where the files were on years and years of Sandler transactions. Well, what else am I to assume?"

"What was in the files? And who wanted it?"

Zenger shrugged. "I couldn't begin to guess," he said.

"Come off it!" Thomas's voice was sharp, his patience thinning. "I didn't come up here to play games. You may be having your cheap fun —"

"Calm yourself, calm yourself," cautioned Zenger patiently, waving a frail hand across the table. "You'll get your answers. In time."

"I want them now."

"You'll get them now."

Thomas gazed across the table in silence. "I'm waiting," he said.

"Yes. I can see that." Zenger paused. "Some people, young people mostly, don't know how lucky they are."

"What does that mean?"

"It means you're a very lucky young man. You have a great name to live up to. You have your youth. You have your freedom. And you have no knowledge of the Sandler family."

Thomas continued to stare at Zenger, having no idea at all where the old man was leading the conversation. Zenger continued.

"And you have a guardian angel. Before you could go to that file and involve yourself with it, someone burned you out. You owe the arsonist an eternal debt of gratitude. Maybe someday you'll find out who he was."

"Make some sense, damn it."

Zenger looked at the younger man in dismay. "I suppose," he said, "I was as naive and impetuous at your age as you are now. You want some sense made. All right. Here it is. The full knowledge of Sandler family transactions is enough to get you killed. I don't know everything and I don't want to know. The only person who'd want to live to be eighty-three is a man of eighty-two. I'm eighty-two. Have I made some *sense?*"

Thomas was thoughtful. He perceived a sincerity and almost a trace of fear in Zenger's eyes. "Some," he said. "But I'm not satisfied."

"Jesus," snorted Zenger in disgust, as he slapped the arms of his chair.

"I want to know as much as you know."

"You never will." The old man's voice was firm. "I won't tell you. Hot pincers couldn't get it out of me."

"Well," spoke Thomas Daniels in a controlled rage, pronouncing each syllable. "Then I'll find out myself!" He stood quickly.

"Tell me something," said Zenger, raising his hand to hold the young visitor. "Why is all this of such almighty interest to you?"

"In my position, wouldn't you be interested?"

Zenger pondered the hypothesis. "No," he said finally. "If a man with fifty years' experience in law told me that it could cost me my life to get involved with something, I'd take the hint. I'd lay off. That's why I can't figure you. No one with ten cents' worth of brains risks getting killed just because he's curious."

Thomas looked at Zenger carefully. "I have a client," Thomas said.

"What kind of a client?"

"A client."

"Oh, come on."

"You're not answering *my* questions."

Zenger thought for an instant. "So we'll exchange some information. Who's your client?"

Thomas sat down again. "A girl," he said. Zenger, unsatisfied, waited without replying. "I've got a girl who claims she's Arthur Sandler's daughter."

Zenger's face appeared frozen for several seconds. "Oh, Christ," he finally scoffed. "All this for some female fruitcake who turned up? My advice to you is take the pussy and run."

"I'm inclined to believe her claim," said Thomas.

"Why?"

"She has some documents. And I have a feeling. I think she's telling the truth. I suspect she *is* Arthur Sandler's daughter."

Zenger was already shaking his head. "Not possible," he said.

"Why?"

"Your father handled the Sandlers more than I did. But yes, I know a few things about the family. Arthur Sandler wasn't the type of man who ran around siring bastard children."

"She's not illegitimate."

"Well, then there's immaculate conception involved, because Arthur Sandler never married."

"Apparently he did."

"Bullshit!" roared Zenger heatedly.

"During World War Two. In England."

Now it was Zenger's turn. For an instant Thomas sensed that the old man was stunned by a revelation of truth. But, if he had been, he recovered just as quickly. He began to smile.

"That proves that it's a hoax," said Zenger calmly.

"Why?"

"The fact is that Arthur Sandler never left the United States during the war. Not for a single day. Being wealthy and being Germanic by extraction, he was afraid to leave."

"Afraid?"

"Some people, people with influential friends, knew what was happening to Japanese Americans. Sandler feared the same. He was scared that if he left the country he'd never be let back in. He'd be stripped of his fortune and his citizenship in one neat little swoop." Zenger, feeling his case winning, allowed himself a calm smile. He added, "And I can prove this."

"How?"

"I have an old friend in the passport office in Washington. I can arrange a visit for you. You can go down there yourself and inspect the old passport records."

"You make it sound very simple."

"It is."

Thomas pondered it, then shook his head. He fingered the cold coffee cup in front of him. "No, it's not," he said. "I took the liberty of making some telephone calls."

"Jesus Christ," snapped Zenger. "Who'd you call?"

"England."

"Who in England?"

"A bureau of records in Exeter. And the borough clerk's office in Devonshire."

"And?" asked Zenger coldly.

"The marriage certificates and the birth certificates check with what's on official record. Everything checks, right down to the signatures on both certificates. Now, if necessary, I can have the handwriting analyzed. I can also go to England and try to trace down the people who witnessed the marriage or birth. From there—"

"Holy Christ. Holy, holy Christ!"

Thomas looked across the table at the muttering Zenger. Zenger's face was ashen and his hands were shaking. His face started to sink to his palms, but Zenger caught himself and looked across the table. "You know too much already," he said. "You sit around with a telephone and play detective, but you don't really understand what you're fooling with." The old man leaned forward. "Thomas. *Don't get involved. You'll get everyone killed.*"

"Everyone? Who?"

"You!" snorted Zenger in a mocking voice. "You! Me! This girl, even if she is a hoax."

"In that case," said Thomas evenly, "you'd better tell me what we're dealing with. Because I'm going on with this case until someone convinces me that I shouldn't."

The old man's frail hand was shaking slightly. He picked up a linen napkin from the table and dried his palms. There was anxiety in his eyes as he looked at the younger man across the table.

"I used to think that your father was the shrewdest lawyer I could ever imagine. I might have been wrong." He paused for a moment. "I said hot pincers couldn't get this story out of me. And they wouldn't. But you're going to get your damned story." Zenger looked Daniels in the eye. "Promise me you'll drop the case when you leave here today."

Thomas shrugged, knowing he didn't have to bargain. "I can't make any promise," he said. "I haven't heard anything yet."

Zenger shook his head. "God help you."

He struggled to his feet, again needing the cherrywood cane. "I made a tactical error here today. I should have pretended that my brain had failed, too."

Zenger struggled back toward the leather armchair in the sitting room. Mrs. Clancy appeared, to clear the table.

"Follow me," he said to Thomas. The old man coughed violently as he walked. "If I'd known how long I was going to live," he said, "I'd have taken better care of myself."

"Above all, you must remember two aspects of Arthur Sandler. First, he had a consuming sense of family honor, very much a nineteenth-century German tradition. And second, you must bear in mind his brilliance. Brilliance," explained Adolph Zenger, "far beyond simple genius."

Zenger's voice was weaker than it had been two hours earlier when Thomas Daniels had arrived. The old man was again in his worn leather chair, the blanket draped across his lap. Thomas sat across the cozy sitting room, bookcases to his right, the window overlooking the garden on his left. "What sort of brilliance?" he asked.

Zenger's frail hand was on the carved handgrip of the cherrywood cane. His eyes were sharp and spirited as he replied. "Brilliance in every way, Tommy," he snapped. "But particularly in the three fields that interested Sandler most. Chemicals. Finance. Engraving." Zenger could see that his visitor was mystified. "You have to understand the Sandler family, Tommy," insisted Zenger. "You must understand the family."

Zenger began to explain, citing William Ward Daniels as his onetime source of all information concerning the Sandlers.

The paternal grandfather of Arthur and Victoria Sandler arrived in a wide-open New York in the late 1850s. A young man at the time, and an immigrant from Hamburg, he quickly prospered by importing fabrics from Europe and reselling them to American sweatshops at a five-hundred-per-cent markup. Then Wilhelm von Dreissen Sandler quickly sensed the investment opportunities around him. He purchased land and property as fast as he could, living frugally and pouring every cent into either a building or a plot of land. Within ten years he was a millionaire through one enduring principle: rents.

He fell in love twice: once with a woman, once with a building. In 1864 he married and embarked on a European honeymoon with his bride. Touring through France, Sandler happened upon the country château of the Baron Alexis d'Artennes. Sandler madly coveted the home, a magnificent sprawling estate which had been in the d'Artennes family since 1730. Sandler attempted to buy the estate. The baron, insulted that the wealthy parvenu American would have the effrontery to make such an offer, would not even reply. Embittered, Wilhelm Sandler returned to New York, where he was more used to getting any building he wanted. There he would have his way after all. He commissioned a replica of the château to be built on a strip of land he owned in what was then a tree-shaded suburban section of Manhattan. And so by 1877, when construction was complete, Wilhelm Sandler had become the Baron of Eighty-ninth Street. There his lifelong frugality gave way to indulgence. He gained one hundred pounds in three years. He would have gained more, but in 1880 he dropped dead of a stroke.

His fortune and the family standard passed to his three children. Wilhelm II was an adventurer; he died in the ninety-day war with Spain in 1898. A daughter, Theresia, had been endowed with thick horselike features and was reputed to be the ugliest woman in New York society. She never married. Childless, she died in 1932, her share of the fortune reverting to the family.

The only other child, the youngest, was Joseph. Joseph led an otherwise normal and uneventful life for a man of his extreme wealth. His only quirk was—in the tradition of some wealthy European families—marrying his first cousin, Lora Nuss. They had a daughter and son. Victoria and Arthur.

"There's not too much to be said about Victoria that you couldn't already guess," said Zenger. He glanced to the floor, then back up at Thomas Daniels. "Her mind never progressed past age nine. Arthur? Arthur was just the opposite. As shrewd and cunning a son of a bitch as you'd ever imagine. He attempted to rearrange the family fortune."

"Rearrange?"

"Chemicals," said Zenger. "From the time he was a boy he had a genius for chemistry. In the mid-thirties he began his own chemical firm. Was doing extensive business between here and Europe. Don't ask where in Europe." Zenger grimaced.

"Where in Europe?"

"Spain. Italy. Germany. Portugal. Get the idea?"

"All of Fascist Europe," said Thomas. The sun outside was crossed by clouds. For a moment the room was darker.

"He was making money. There's no question about that. His profits were enormous. That's when he was investigated by the Federal government. He had got himself into some titanic currency and securities transactions with those foreign governments. It was alleged, and I repeat alleged, that he was in some sort of deal to help prop up the Italian lira. Back then the lira was worth more than it is now. But it was still shaky."

"What happened?" asked Thomas.

"Sandler was indicted for currency manipulation in 1939," Zenger explained. "The government had a massive case against him, with a couple of fraud charges tossed in for good measure. And since the charges implied dealings with Fascist regimes, Sandler's usual family lawyers wanted nothing to do with the court battle.

"Victoria was so far gone by this time that she had no idea what her brother was involved in. Arthur turned his full attention to staying out of jail. Family business was ignored, even the management of the household. Servants left and were not replaced. Then more quit. Arthur desperately looked for a lawyer who could defend him and win. Not just get him a light sentence, but *win.*

"Well," chuckled Zenger, "Arthur found one. A man just about as old then as you are now. After a several-month delay, Arthur Sandler appeared in court with a brilliant young lawyer out to make a name for himself. The young lawyer staggered the courtroom with his booming, explosive oratory and his mournful pleas to the jury in defense of 'solid citizen Sandler.'

"I don't think," said Zenger to his visitor, "that I need to tell you what the lawyer's name was."

"My father," said Thomas.

Zenger nodded. "He won an acquittal which defied logic. It wasn't for another year that anyone knew how he'd done it."

The next year was 1940. The major European powers were now all in the war. Increasingly, it appeared that the United States would be drawn in also. But meanwhile, the Federal investigation of Sandler had yielded an interesting fact. He hated the Fascists, but he was willing to enrich himself by doing business with them. Secretly he loathed them. This set certain minds to work.

No sooner had the first currency fraud case been dismissed than the government started building another one against Sandler. But this time they had no intention of ever taking it to court.

It was November of 1940. Sandler was on his way into his office building at Nassau and Wall Streets in lower Manhattan. He took one step up onto the curb one morning after crossing the street, when four men in civilian clothes surrounded him. The sleeves of his jacket were grabbed by a man on each side.

A few bystanders stopped to witness the scene. Sandler, dressed in a suit and carrying a briefcase, was physically picked up by two F.B.I. agents and slammed against the side of a 1939 Packard. He was stunned for a moment. His briefcase had flown from his hand. He struggled again.

The leader lifted Sandler by his lapels and smashed him against the side of the car so hard that his back shattered the window to the backseat. Another agent opened the car door and Sandler was thrown into the car on top of the broken glass.

An agent got in on either side of him. The two others were up front. One had his briefcase. All trace of Sandler had been removed from the sidewalk.

At the start, Sandler looked on it all as just another painful nuisance. But he began to be genuinely apprehensive when, instead of being taken to the F.B.I. offices on Duane Street, he was hustled into the back entrance of the United States courthouse on Cardinal Hayes Place. An elevator was waiting for him. And moments later he was pushed into a straight-backed wooden chair in a sixth-floor office. A chain-smoking, red-faced man in shirt sleeves sat behind a massive steel desk. The man's name was Archibald McFedries.

McFedries didn't exactly speak. It was a low tortured growl. "I thought I'd save you the trouble of calling your lawyer," he muttered.

Sandler was speechless. Seated silently and uncomfortably across the room *was* his lawyer, William Ward Daniels.

Sandler looked nervously to his attorney. Daniels obviously knew enough to keep quiet. When Sandler looked back to the huge desk in front of him he was aware of four dossiers in front of McFedries. McFedries looked back to Daniels. "Tell him why he's here," he ordered.

Daniels told him. Sandler had been brought to the office of a Special Assistant to the United States Attorney. While the U.S. Attorney was occupied with organized crime and rackets cases, McFedries headed a separate and more covert branch of the Federal prosecutor's office. McFedries's concern was espionage. There were scores of Japanese and German agents operating in and between New York and Washington. To some degree the F.B.I. had been able to identify and monitor them. But what they had been unable to do was infiltrate them at the highest level. That's why Sandler was there.

McFedries spoke of the Sandler family's place in America, the wealth they had accumulated and how, in the war that was now inevitable, certain Americans of "questionable" heritage might have to be interned and their possessions placed under state control. "America must protect herself," mused McFedries gently.

Arthur Sandler was now terrified. William Ward Daniels continued not speaking unless specifically asked a question.

"Do you know what these are?" McFedries finally growled. His fist landed on the four dossiers.

Sandler remained silent.

"Three new currency violation charges against you, Sandler," announced McFedries with obvious pleasure. "Plus probably an additional charge of treason."

Sandler's face went white. But as he looked imploringly toward his attorney, he was enough in control of himself to remain silent.

"Trading with Germany has been illegal since 1938," McFedries reminded the squirming Sandler. "Just because you've been doing it through a Swiss corporation doesn't mean you can get away with it."

"Absurd," whispered Sandler defensively.

"Think so?" snapped McFedries. "We also know how your friend here beat the last set of charges we had against you."

Again Sandler looked to his attorney.

"It's true," said Daniels. "They're planning to charge me—and you—with jury tampering."

"They can't prove any fucking thing," retorted Sandler, suddenly indignant.

But William Ward Daniels only shrugged nervously. "They're prepared to negotiate," said the attorney. "We should be, too."

McFedries actually chortled. "If you can rig a jury, so can we." He beamed. "I'd say we can put you away for thirty years, Sandler. Maybe forty. And your hotshot mouthpiece here will do seven or eight. In the bargain you lose your property and your crazy sister lands in a padded room. Think it over," he offered calmly.

Sandler looked at McFedries. "All right. What do you want?"

"Help."

"From *me*?" asked Sandler. "*You* want help from *me*?"

"You and your government are in a position to help each other," said McFedries slowly. "You know your way in and out of Germany rather well. You speak the language perfectly. You know German society. German business. Even the military."

"So?"

"So you are in a unique position," said McFedries. "You can contact

German agents within the United States. As an American with access to money and power, you can offer help to them. Eventually, when and if the United States becomes involved in Europe, you will choose to flee. You will return to Germany. And you will continue to work for this government."

Sandler sat there feeling the screws turn and wondering if it was actually happening. Then he looked at the four F.B.I. agents, his attorney, McFedries, and the locked door.

"You fucking bastards," he cursed in a low bitter voice.

McFedries sat down and hauled his feet up onto the desk. "I'm glad you see it our way," he said. "After all, it's us or prison. And when it's all over Uncle Sam will owe you a favor or two."

Thomas Daniels's legs were stiff from sitting and listening. The sun outside had vanished under an afternoon's worth of clouds. The Nantucket sky had changed from blue to gray.

"So thirty-five years ago Arthur Sandler was recruited as a U.S. spy," said Thomas. "And my father could have gone to jail for jury tampering. So what?"

Zenger smiled. "That's only half of it. Sandler turned out to be an excellent spy, far surpassing anyone's expectations. It's remarkable," he chuckled, "how the criminal in society is always so patriotic. But then again, Sandler didn't just have a lot to lose. He had a lot to gain."

"Meaning?"

"Sandler was, or is, a man of endless ingenuity. He could always emerge from a situation in a position of maximum strength. For example, within one year of the time he was recruited—"

"The end of 1941?"

"Yes. By that time he was the number-two German intelligence agent in New York. And he had the perfect cover. A third-generation American businessman with a chunk of the established order in America. But Sandler was never content in a subservient role. And yet he could only move up to be head of New York operations if tragedy should befall Karl Hunsicker, the number-one agent. So Sandler studied Hunsicker. He learned the man's habits. And he arranged the perfect accident."

Zenger cleared his throat. A slight smile crossed his face as he continued. "Hunsicker was a meticulously clean man who bathed before midnight each evening. Lived in a duplex floor through in an old apartment building at Eighty-fourth and Second. In the bathroom there was a large electric heater, equipped with a cone-shaped wire coil at its center. Sandler called on Hunsicker late one evening."

Adolph Zenger, apparently amused, toyed with the handle of his cane again. His eyes twinkled. "Hunsicker got his hot bath that night, all right. They found him two mornings later, still sharing his bathwater with the heater. But, hell. He was up to no good, that damned Nazi. Civic improvement."

"What happened to Sandler?" Thomas Daniels asked.

"He was moved up to number one in New York. Then about two months later things got hot for several Axis agents in the northeast. Several of them were recalled to Germany. Sandler went 'home' with them, traveling first to Mexico, where a submarine picked him up. Fine instruments, those submarines," he added parenthetically. Then he concluded, "Ultimately, Sandler drifted into German intelligence. Doing what, I don't know. He was a chemist, an engraver, a financier, and a pretty fair assassin. A man like that might have many uses."

Zenger hesitated, then actually stopped. His attention seemed to lag abruptly, his gaze drifting out the window to the ocean beyond.

"Funny thing about those submarines," he said. A slight pause, then, "Do you know that this island was blockaded during the war? Sometimes bathers could see smoke rising on the horizon. U.S. merchant boats torpedoed by Hitler's submarines."

The man's eyes were sad and distant.

"Fucking foreigners," Zenger grumbled. "Do you know what you can see from these windows *now*? Fishing fleets! Foreign fishing fleets, especially the Commie ones, catching everything that swims. Imagine. They come in here and catch American fish and we don't do a damned thing." He thought about it. "Ought to blow their fishing tubs right out of the water," he concluded. "Send out our Coast Guard."

"What about Victoria?" Thomas asked.

Zenger puffed his cheeks thoughtfully. "She got along. Thanks to estate management by Zenger and Daniels." The old man managed a sly grin.

"Naturally," said Thomas. "The money was there."

"Interesting point," said Zenger quickly. "The money wasn't there. No one had ever suspected, but the Sandler family had been almost flat broke."

Thomas frowned. "How could they have been."

"Taxes. They were land poor. Real-estate assessments were eating up the money as fast as Arthur Sandler could make it. After the war it was a different story. When he came home in 1946 he was loaded again. He had millions. And it couldn't have been through his companies. They'd stagnated."

"The government?" asked Thomas.

"Maybe," said Zenger. "But there's a darker possibility. Somehow he made a fortune during the war. The logical guess is that he continued to do it after the war." Zenger paused. The excitement was gone from his eyes. "Whatever it was, I didn't know then and I don't want to know now." Zenger looked at Thomas carefully, then added, "Your father knew. But he never told."

Thomas rubbed his chin thoughtfully. He got to his feet, stretched, and walked to the window. He watched the water in the distance as if in thought over how to phrase the next question.

"What about the man who was killed in 1954?" Thomas asked. "Obviously it wasn't Sandler."

Zenger shook his head, almost sadly. "No, of course not. Sometime after the war, early on in the fifties, some former members of Axis intelligence discovered that Sandler had sabotaged a major operation in Austria. There were a few old Nazis around North America and they attempted their retribution. Twice they came close enough to shoot at Sandler. Twice they missed. Sandler used his government contacts to gain time. He asked for a stand-in, someone to pose as him. He got one. And while the double remained in New York, Sandler traveled to Oslo, where he laundered his identity. A new name, a new life. Meanwhile he had a stroke of luck. His stand-in was murdered on the street one afternoon. And that seemed to satisfy Sandler's old acquaintances.

"The funny thing about it, though," concluded Zenger, "was that there was a rumor that said Sandler had been executed by British agents before the Axis people could even get to him."

"What sense does that make?" asked Thomas.

"None," said Zenger. "But Sandler had a new identity. He managed to vanish. He had his face entirely changed. Surgically."

Thomas let several seconds pass before asking his next question. "Is Arthur Sandler alive today?"

Zenger looked at him coldly. "Do you think that fire in your office set itself?" he asked.

Thomas was mystified. "How could a man in his late seventies be so dangerous?"

"I don't know. And I don't recommend finding out."

Thomas considered the blaze at his office. And he considered Leslie McAdam, struggling naked on a bed while her own father's hired killer attempted to murder her. "I have a client," he said.

Zenger was livid. "You also have sawdust between the ears if you take this woman seriously. First off, *she is an impostor.* Second, Sandler's not the type of man you'll want to try pinning a paternity suit on even if she's not an impostor. Third, you'll never collect a cent of inheritance. This girl will never be able to prove she's a real daughter of Arthur Sandler. And you'll never be able to prove that a man legally dead twenty-two years ago is alive today. You'd have to successfully trace a man who's been gone for almost a quarter of a century."

"It could be done."

"Thomas! Come to your senses! Do you think Sandler's going to let you and some girl pick through his wealth and his interlocked companies? Do you think he'd risk having his new identity exposed?"

"How is he going to stop me?"

"Listen, boy," said Zenger, shaking his head in disgust, "you don't want to live as long as I have, do you? I'll tell you how he's going to stop you."

Zenger paused and caught his breath. He was very weak, but his anger —or fear—kept him going.

"All I know is what I learned from your father. In confidence, in the years after the war. But when Sandler got a new face he also got a job in our government. High. Very high. So high that only two people knew who he was. Both were murdered in their homes within a week. Both the same night. Both with a wire."

Thomas Daniels practically bolted upright. "A wire?"

"A wire," said Zenger, elaborating in hopes of scaring Thomas off the case. "It was a trick Sandler learned in the war. In a hollow heel of a shoe he carried two brass rings with a piano wire strung between them. A makeshift garrotte. Always with him and damned effective. His favorite."

Thomas broke into a slow smile. Zenger cocked his head, looking at the younger man. "What did I say?" Zenger asked.

"You just proved that my client is telling the truth," Thomas said. "I'm sorry. I'm taking her case."

Thomas returned to New York the same evening. When he unlocked and pushed open the door to his apartment the white envelope was immediately conspicuous.

Thomas turned on the light, closed the door behind him, and tossed his travel case onto a table. He picked up the envelope and tore it open.

From it he pulled a yellow ticket. Second Promenade, the ticket said, Madison Square Garden. Hockey. Rangers vs. Boston Bruins. February eighth. Sunday evening.

It made no immediate sense. Then he unfolded a small piece of plain white paper that accompanied the ticket. It read:

> *Mr. Daniels,*
>
> *Please be there. And don't tell anyone.*
>
> *Leslie McAdam*

Thomas searched for a further explanation and found none. He crumpled the note and dropped it into a wastebasket. He walked to a bookcase that was so crowded that each shelf held two rows of books, front and back, mostly paperback. He withdrew a novel, third from the left on the middle shelf, inserted the ticket in the book, and returned the book to its place.

A few minutes later he was seated at the kitchen table, a cup of black coffee steaming in front of him, and visions of the cryptic Adolph Zenger dancing before him. Zenger was a sneak if ever a sneak had walked the earth. But had the retired attorney at least been forthright with his trusted partner's only son?

Thomas wondered.

The telephone rang.

He took his coffee with him, sat in an armchair in the living room, and took the call on the fourth ring.

"Find out anything?" a female voice asked.

For a split second he envisioned Leslie. But the voice was familiar. He felt a small tremor of disappointment as he recognized the caller. Andrea Parker.

"Let's say that I'm in hot pursuit of the facts," he said. "This Sandler mess is a can of worms. Walter Mitty's secret life was gossip-column stuff compared to this."

"I'm onto a good story, in other words," she said.

"Of course. Otherwise you wouldn't be calling so often."

"Don't be mean, Tom," she countered softly. "I've done some homework for you, too. Did you see Zenger?"

"Yes."

"Any help?"

"Some. He had some of the answers, but not all of them." He sipped the black coffee and listened to a guarded silence on the other end. "This whole thing recalls a lesson I learned in law school, working on a claims adjustment case."

"A *what?*" she asked.

"A woman came to me and said she'd been sitting in her parked car when a truck had bumped into her hard from behind. She was claiming damages to her car, plus personal damages for whiplash. She gave me her whole story. Then I talked to the driver of the truck. He said he'd been double-parked and so had the woman. Only she had released her brake and rolled back into him. Then I found two witnesses, a shopowner and a pedestrian. They told two other stories with even different details. Four different stories, none of them the same, all of them slightly suspect one way or another. Know how I got down to the truth?"

"How?"

"I sat them all down together and wrote down the few points in the story upon which none would argue. With a little pressing and a few concessions here and there, I came out with a composite story. That became the new 'truth' in the case. And that's what I finally went into court with." He sipped the coffee again. "The Sandler case is the same thing all over again, on a greater scale. You hear stories, the stories conflict. You check and double-check, you distill a composite truth from them. And that becomes the factual basis that you must work with."

"What did Zenger say?" Andrea asked. "Specifically."

"He said my client's a fake."

"Do you think she is?"

"I'm trying to be compassionate," he said, "as well as a realist."

"Evasive answer, counselor," she chided.

"So far, I believe her." He thought for a moment. "She has those documents. They look strong. Damned strong. If I went to England, say, and got more corroborating evidence for her . . . Well, she'd be in an even stronger position."

"Before you take any trips there's more you ought to know."

"Go ahead."

"With the help of some of our financial editors at the paper we've put together quite a bit on our favorite family. Interlocking corporations. Phantom ownerships. Trusts. Holding companies and such."

"In chemicals?"

"Chemicals and real estate. But that's not the point. It's mostly an odd assortment of smaller companies owned by slightly larger companies, equally strange. A merry-go-round of ownership, and no one can find where it started to spin."

"In other words," he said, "no one can find out where the money came from to start with. Sounds familiar."

"Right," she said. "And none of the companies do anything except hold wealth that seems to accumulate."

She paused for a moment. Thomas tried to conjure up an image of Arthur Sandler, the enigma at the center of the case. Sandler's finances were like the master himself, invisible but very much alive.

"What do you think it's all worth?" she asked.

"Zenger guessed twelve million. Tops."

"Try again."

"More?"

"We're figuring it conservatively and we've got it up to *fifty* million. That's five zero. And it's still growing. The more you trace, the more you find. It simply doesn't end."

"Jesus," he said with a low whistle and now, suddenly, an uneasy fearful feeling. "You could finance a small country with money like that."

"You said it, I didn't." There was a pause on both ends of the line. When she spoke again there was uncharacteristic concern in her voice. "Tom?"

"What?"

"You know you might consider dropping it. The whole thing's starting to look a lot kinkier than anyone realized."

"I should just drop it?" he scoffed.

"Maybe a different approach would be better. A newspaper exposé which then tosses it at the feet of the Justice Department. It's just a suggestion."

He could feel a headache begin. "It's not quite that easy after someone has fried your office," he said.

He pondered it. She, too, was thoughtful on the other end. "You have *no* idea who you're dealing with," she said. "None at all. If only you could take some sort of precaution . . ."

"Do you have any police contacts through the paper?"

"What sort of police contacts?"

"Someone on the force who could check fingerprints. On the sly."

She thought. "I don't know anyone. Wait! I know someone who does."

"Who?"

Another reporter, she explained, a man named Augie Reid. He was an older journalist who now worked Albany for the paper but who over the years had developed friends within the New York State Police. It was worth a shot, she suggested, to try him.

"The girl gave me a photograph," Thomas said, "of her father. If I give it to you first thing tomorrow morning will Reid see what he can do with it?"

"He'll do anything," she said, seeming confident. "He loves me."

He changed the subject. "What's happened about that mugging murder in front of my building?"

"What normally happens about muggings?" she answered. "Nothing. Why?"

"I got a note from some detective today. They're talking to everyone in the building. They want to see me." He shrugged. "The guy didn't even live in our building."

He could hear distant traffic in the background, and Mrs. Ryan's discordant piano was playing upstairs. Andrea continued to speak.

"You didn't tell me the end of the first story," she said.

"Which?"

"The automobile claims case. What finally happened?"

"I lost it," he said. "The woman who came to me was lying completely."

The afternoon of the next day Thomas walked down Third Avenue to the Nineteenth Precinct. He asked for Detective Aram Shassad by name and was shown through a large squad room cluttered with desks, chairs, and patrolmen in uniform. Then he was guided upstairs to where Shassad sat alone in the small space he shared with Hearn.

"I'm Thomas Daniels," said Thomas, offering his hand. "I received a note saying you wanted to see me."

"Seventy-third Street?" asked the harried Shassad.

"Yes."

"Of course. Sit down."

"I don't know how much I'll be able to help you," Thomas said. "I didn't know the victim."

"We're talking to everyone," said Shassad. "Formality really."

"I understand. I'm an attorney."

"I see," said Shassad. "Single? No wife?" Thomas nodded.

At that time Patrick Hearn entered the cubicle, drew up a chair and sat at his own desk. Shassad introduced his partner brusquely to Daniels. He also sought to dispel the inner dislike and distrust he had of lawyers. Lawyers and judges, to Shassad, were the people who kept the felons on the street.

Shassad briefly outlined the problem with which the police were posed. A homicide had been committed in front of Daniels's building. Was Thomas home that night or at that hour, they asked, and had he seen or heard anything at all unusual? They omitted mentioning that they had linked the dead man with a woman, and that the victim had stepped from Daniels's building just prior to being murdered.

"To tell you the truth," said Thomas routinely, "I left the building in the middle of the night."

Hearn's attention perked, as did Shassad's.

"Why did you do that?" asked Hearn politely.

Thomas explained about the fire in his office.

"Do you know what time it was?"

Thomas thought for a moment. "Yes, I should be able to recall exactly. Let me think." He pondered it for a moment, then answered assuredly. "Three forty-five."

Hearn and Shassad recognized the almost pinpoint time of the slaying. But they refused to even exchange a glance.

"Are you sure?"

"Absolutely," said Thomas, "almost to the minute."

"Why?"

"The night janitor at my office building. Kind of a cantankerous old character. He wanted to know exactly when I'd be going out the door or when I'd be there. He had the fire department there. I guess he wanted to know."

"So you think you left at three forty-five?" asked Hearn casually. Shassad was making notes.

"I *know* I did."

"But you didn't see anything in front of the building?" asked Shassad. According to Minnie Yankovich, two men had been lurking there for half an hour.

"No," said Thomas. "But I wouldn't have. I left by the back exit. It comes out on the avenue."

"Why'd you do that?"

"I was going to my car on Seventy-fourth Street. It's a shortcut."

"And you heard nothing?"

Thomas started to say no. But then he stopped in midsentence. "Come to think of it . . ." he began, having dismissed the incident in the travail of that particular night.

"Yes?"

"I heard someone come out of the apartment below me. Three C."

"A man or a woman?"

"I couldn't tell. I heard the voices of each. And frankly, I had other things on my mind. Hell, my office—"

"Did one of them go downstairs?"

Thomas thought. "Yes. There were footsteps. I waited till they were gone." He eyed both cops. "You know how it is. Middle of the night. You avoid strangers on staircases."

"Of course," nodded Hearn sympathetically.

"You never saw him? Or her?" pressed Shassad.

"No," answered Daniels flatly.

"Did you think it unusual that someone would be leaving that apartment at that hour?"

Thomas shrugged. "No," he said. "What's the nice way to put it? She has a lot of male visitors."

"Oh, I see," said Hearn. "She's popular, in other words."

"You could call it that."

"Do you know her very well yourself?" asked Shassad.

"No," said Thomas tersely. "Nor do I want to."

The interview finished amiably several minutes later. Hearn politely walked Thomas downstairs to the main entrance of the station house. Then Hearn rejoined his partner upstairs.

"What did you think?" Hearn asked.

"Intriguing, that one," said Shassad. "He's either lying or he actually heard the victim walking downstairs prior to getting carved."

"Not only that," noted Hearn, "but he practically put himself at the crime scene at the minute the stabbing took place. Think he was telling the truth?"

"Some of the truth," said Shassad. "I already know a little about him from others in the building. Know who his father was? William Ward Daniels."

"The shyster mouthpiece?" Hearn, like his partner, had little love for those who returned felons intact to the street.

"The same," said Shassad. "That doesn't speak too well for the integrity running through the family. And do you know what else?"

Hearn asked what.

"Our friend Daniels has a girl who spends nights there. Some girl who works for a paper or something. No big deal, except maybe she was there that night with Ryder, not expecting Daniels to come home. Daniels shows up unexpectedly and drives Ryder out, out into the hands of two goons he has waiting for him."

"In other words, Daniels sets up Ryder to be killed. And Daniels's girl is the girl Ryder was screwing."

"Well," shrugged Shassad, "it may be farfetched, but it's a workable theory. And Christ knows, the son of William Ward Daniels would probably know every kind of goon in the city."

"So?" asked Hearn. "We watch Daniels?" The question was rhetorical. He nodded in thought.

"We've got no one else to watch yet. Maybe he'll lead us to his girl. Then we might get something out of her." Shassad smiled faintly.

Chapter 9

Thomas arrived at Madison Square Garden at seven fifteen, fifteen minutes before game time, walked quickly among the scalpers and loitering boisterous teenagers on Seventh Avenue, and was in his seat by seven twenty.

She wasn't there yet. The seat next to his was empty. On the ice there were no players. The goals were being adjusted and the ice was being smoothed. He watched the minutes tick off on the electronic clocks at each end of the rink. Seven twenty-eight. Seven thirty. He wondered whether she'd be there.

The teams began to skate out onto the ice. The crowd roared. There was an inattentive hum as the recorded voice of Robert Merrill sang *America the Beautiful*.

Thomas was still looking around, more nervously now.

As the referee dropped the puck all eyes went to the ice. Thomas glanced down to the game as the puck was shot into the Rangers' end. Then he was aware of people standing to one side of him, allowing someone to enter the row. He turned his head quickly. Leslie.

She stepped past him and sat down.

"Welcome," he said.

"Thanks." She was slightly out of breath, still wearing her heavy overcoat. She quickly unbuttoned the front buttons. He raised his hand to help her with the coat. She motioned his hand away.

"You haven't missed anything," he offered.

She motioned indignantly toward the ice, toward the Ranger end. "They were damned fools to trade Ratelle and Park," she said.

"I didn't know you liked hockey."

"I don't. I hate it."

"Then . . . ?"

"We're here because it would be difficult to follow me," she said. "I bought the tickets from a scalper a week ago. If anyone followed me or you here, I'd hope the difficulty posed by the ticket takers would cause him, or them, to lose me."

"Clever," he allowed.

There was a roar as a Ranger shot hit a goalpost and flew back in front of the net. A rebound shot was deflected by the goaltender's stick and a third shot flew wide by a foot. The crowd was howling and Thomas turned to watch the play.

She spoke loudly, to be heard. "I didn't come here to watch grown men play a boys' game. What about the will?"

The puck flew out of bounds. Play stopped. The crowd quieted. He looked her in the eye.

"I don't have it," he admitted. "Not yet."

She stared at him coldly. "Why?"

He thought quickly. "It's taking time," he said. "My father kept important records very secretively. There were file references which only he could understand. I've got to go through everything to locate it."

She didn't appear pleased.

"Then we're at a standstill," she said impatiently.

"No." The play moved back to center ice. "I'm building a case for you. I'm looking for witnesses."

"What are you talking about?"

"I talked to Adolph Zenger, my father's former—"

"I know who he is. What did he say?"

"He told me the story of your father's background. The family. The activity during the war, or at least leading up to the war." He paused. She was nervously glancing around, looking down into the aisles through the crowd. He continued, "In a roundabout way, he confirmed a lot. It's slow, but it's progress."

She looked back to him, her dark eyes wide and extremely angry now. "Do you trust him?" she snapped.

"Who?"

"Zenger! Who else are we talking about?"

"I think so," he said.

"Who could he have talked to?" she snapped. "About me?"

"He never talks to anyone anymore. And we talked in total confidence."

"Well someone," she said angrily, pronouncing each syllable at a time, "has a big mouth. We're followed."

She motioned to the walkway down below them. Standing at least forty feet apart were two men, neither of whom was watching the hockey game. They were looking away from the ice, back up into the spectators. Directly toward Leslie and Thomas.

"The one on the left," she said, acting as if she hadn't seen them yet, "has a camera."

Thomas watched the man from the corner of his eye. The man indeed had a small concealed camera in his palm. It was aimed up toward the two of them.

"How," she asked him bitterly, "does a thing like that happen?"

He was speechless. "They can't do anything in here," he offered weakly. "Too many people."

"Mr. Daniels," she intoned, "you underestimate people." He glanced around again and couldn't tell if a third man was with the other two.

The crowd began to roar again as the Rangers worked the puck into the attacking zone. For those seconds they were fully in control, the Boston team only trying to knock the puck back to center ice.

"Obviously," she said, "we'll have to meet again at another time and place. Somewhere more private. Like your home office."

There was a scramble in front of the goal. The din had increased to such a point that he hadn't heard her.

The collective voice of the fans suddenly erupted. The red lights beneath the scoreboards flashed and the crowd came rudely roaring to its feet. Ranger goal.

Thomas looked to the far end of the ice to see the crowd of five white shirts in front of the enemy goal. The scorer was being mobbed. A dejected goaltender swept the puck out of the net. Thomas turned back to Leslie, began to speak loudly, to be heard above the din, and stopped short before speaking a single word.

An empty seat. She was gone.

He looked to her end of the row, knowing she hadn't crossed in front of him. He could just see her stepping away from the final seat in the row and moving back *up* the aisle between sections.

"Leslie!" he called after her. His voice was lost in the roar as the Rangers skated slowly back to center ice for the next face-off. Those around him took amusement from the fact that his "girl" had seemingly walked out on him.

He called after her again, then pursued. He pushed rudely through the row, more aggressively as she disappeared through a gateway and from his sight. He was jostled in return by those whom he struggled to get past.

At that moment, the eyes of the men who'd followed them returned from the ice. They saw that she was gone. They saw that Thomas was leaving. Quickly, the three of them followed.

He ran back up the steps and knew that she was way ahead of him now. He ran to the escalator, craned his neck over its side to see two flights below, and saw her running down. He called again to her. She only moved faster.

He tore down the escalator behind her and momentarily was aware of the three heavy sets of feet behind him, pursuing him just as he ran after her. Thomas couldn't believe how fast she moved.

She was out the Eighth Avenue entrance to the Garden. He had no idea which way she'd turned until fifteen seconds later when he ran out the same exit. He looked each way. He saw nothing. But he knew that the three men were not many seconds behind him.

He looked north again, south again, in desperation. Then, through the traffic, on the opposite side of Eighth Avenue, he saw her to the south. Still running, passing bemused pedestrians and attracting the leering catcalls endemic to that section of the city.

Thomas looked at the traffic. The light was changing. He saw the traffic south of him, given a green light, start to move toward the center of the block where he stood. He heard the men behind him reach ground level. Thomas ran out across the avenue as the lead car screeched its tires and its horn shrieked its complaint. Other cars screeched their suddenly slowing tires into the asphalt and other horns blared their disapproval.

Halfway across the avenue his left foot caught a pothole. His arms waved wildly as he tried to catch his balance. Then, quickly steady again, he continued. One car roared in front of him and he darted in front of another which abruptly slowed. He crossed the last lane of the avenue and was on the sidewalk of the opposite side, in front of the Thirty-third Street post office, its giant steps and columns. Neither rain, nor snow . . . Everywhere, the Federal government intruding.

He looked south. He saw her enter a building beneath a yellow sign with giant blue letters. P-A-R-K. Leslie McAdam had escaped, if that was what she was doing, into a five-story self-service parking lot a block and a half away.

Thomas ran after her. When he crossed Thirty-second Street he was aware again of the three men on the opposite side. They were waiting for the traffic to allow them to cross. They had Thomas in full view and they followed him southward on the opposite side.

The green WALK sign had changed to a flashing red DONT WALK. In fifteen seconds they, whoever they were, would be on his side of Eighth. One of them carried something black in a thick fist.

He fled into the parking lot, stood at a frenzied halt at its entranceway, and looked in every direction.

Nothing.

He looked to the man behind a glass, the man whom a driver would pay on the way out. The man's face was quizzical as he watched Thomas.

"Did you see a girl?" Thomas called frantically.

The quizzical expression creased into a knowing grin.

"I seen lots of girls!" The accent was singsong and Jamaican. "This Eighth Avenue, mon!" As if that explained everything.

"A woman ran in here ten seconds ago!"

The man laughed and nodded toward the only stairwell. "She go upstairs, mon. Happy evening!"

Thomas listened. He could now hear the footsteps of someone running one flight up. Leslie! But he could also hear the footsteps pursuing him.

He turned. The men who were chasing him burst into the parking garage. They froze, staring at him. First three men, then a fourth.

Thomas Daniels recognized Shassad, the last to arrive. He whirled again and ran not upstairs but straight to the rear of the garage to a door marked EXIT.

Two of the plainclothes policemen pursued Thomas. Two others slowly took the stairs.

Thomas reached the exit door and pushed it open, stopping, looking out onto Ninth Avenue, and calling Leslie by her first name.

He stood in the exit staring at the empty avenue, as if searching for her. There was no Leslie running in either direction. Shassad and Hearn were next to Daniels. Hearn was breathing hard, Shassad wasn't.

Shassad stepped past Daniels and looked up and down Ninth Avenue. He looked back to the attorney and spoke sourly. "Where is she?"

"You got a hell of a nerve! Where's who?"

"Don't get smart-assed," Shassad grumbled. "Where is she?"

Thomas Daniels was incensed. "It's *you* who owes *me* the explanation! You frightened away an important client."

"My ass, we did!" snapped Shassad.

There was the sound of a mechanical voice. A walkie-talkie. Thomas heard the voice say, "Sergeant, we might have something. Second floor."

Shassad smiled slightly. "Not so smart after all, are you?" he said.

Hearn held up and answered the walkie-talkie. "We'll be up." The detectives walked quickly upstairs. Thomas Daniels followed.

There was no woman to be seen anywhere in the second story. Just an assortment of parked cars, plus one car for which the owner had arrived. The car, a long dark-blue Pontiac, was at the top of the second-floor ramp. Its owner, a tall, conservatively dressed man in an overcoat, was standing beside the car. He'd been confronted by the first two detectives.

"We looked on every other floor," said one of the detectives to Shassad. "She's not in here."

"This guy wants to take his car out," the other cop told Shassad. "I asked him if he'd open his trunk and he wouldn't."

Shassad looked the man up and down. The man had been the first to appear who wanted to remove a car from the premises. The car owner looked ordinary enough, but Shassad was laden with suspicion. He asked the man again if he'd open the car's trunk. Thomas Daniels studied the victim of the harrassment.

"I'm sure you're only trying to do your job, patrolman," said the man, "but—"

"De-tec-tive," corrected Shassad, pronouncing all three syllables succinctly.

"—but, yes, I do mind."

The two other detectives casually stepped up and down the sides of the car, eyeing it as if they could see through it. The back seat and interior had long since been looked into.

"Why do you mind?" pressed Shassad, buying time.

"Because," said the man with growing annoyance, "I don't like being treated like a criminal. My trunk's empty," he said caustically. "You have my word."

The man's key was in his hand. He opened the door on the side of the driver's seat and began to step into the car.

"Suppose I insisted," said Shassad angrily, placing a hand on the man's shoulder.

Thomas, observing, spoke, "Couldn't an officer get a pretty severe reprimand for 'insisting'?" asked Thomas. All five heads turned to Thomas. "For insisting without a warrant? In front of a witness who also happened to be an attorney?"

Shassad removed his hand from the man's shoulder. He looked at Thomas Daniels bitterly.

When he stepped from the cab on Seventy-third Street, he looked both ways, a habit he'd developed in light of recent events. Daniels entered his building and climbed the stairs. He was still somewhat preoccupied with the events of the evening. He noticed nothing conspicuously unusual as he unlocked the double lock on his apartment door and entered.

He had already turned on the dim light in the entrance hall and had taken two steps forward into the living room. It was at that time, from the side, that an unseen hand turned on the living-room light and Thomas whirled to see a stunning second presence in the room with him.

In that immeasurable short lapse between realization and recognition, a thousand fears flashed through his mind. Not the least of which was that this was how people were murdered.

"Well," he said, fumbling with the words. His heart left his throat and tumbled back to where it belonged in his chest. "Life is filled with surprises."

He eyed Leslie appraisingly as she stood by a light switch in the living room. He was close enough to see her eye movement, close enough to notice that she was checking to be sure he was alone. Satisfied, she stepped away from the light switch. With a graceful, feminine gesture she swept her skirt under her and sat down on his sofa.

"You lied to me," she said. "At least three times."

"I? Lied to *you*?" he repeated. Both anger and confusion marked his words. He tried to fathom her statement.

"Yes," she said flatly, as if it made no difference. But of course it did.

He pulled off his coat and tossed it onto a chair. He sat down a few feet away from her across an open space of room. In one of the tributary channels of his mind it occurred to him that his door had shown no signs of tampering. How had she gained entry—magic?

"Lie number one: You told me you had an office here. You don't. Two: You said originally that you had access to the will. You haven't. And three, you said we were speaking in confidence. You've broken that confidence. Those men tonight were police."

"You're right," he conceded.

"Well?" she asked impatiently. "Aren't you going to offer an excuse?"

"Should I bother?"

"I wish you would."

He drew a deep breath and let it out slowly, acting just as a witness must when trapped with perjured testimony.

"My offices were completely destroyed by arson. You saw what was left. The arson may or may not have had to do with this case." He looked at her carefully, trying unsuccessfully to see how the story was being received. "When you came and presented your story, I believed you. I wanted to take your case and retain you as a client. So I misrepresented my files as being intact. I needed time."

"What about the police?"

"I had to account for my time on the night of the fire. They were questioning me on another matter."

"And the will?"

"I don't have it?"

"Where is it?"

"I don't know."

"I'm grateful for the benefit of the doubt," he said heavily.

Her left hand played with a strand of brown hair by her shoulder. "What worries me," she said thoughtfully, "is how proficient you are at lying. Tell me, is it hereditary?"

He let a moment pass before answering. "I might ask you the same thing."

Her hand was still. "Excuse me?"

"A lot of people maintain that you don't exist."

"They're all lying," she said with a stiff smile.

"In fact," he continued, "you're the only one who maintains that you exist. That's something of a minority opinion."

"What about you?" she asked. "Do you still believe me?"

He allowed a few moments before answering. "Yes," he said finally. "But I wouldn't mind an answer or two."

"Such as?"

"For starters, how did you get out of that garage?"

"I can't tell you."

He looked at her with a pained expression.

"I'm sorry," she said firmly. "If enough attempts are made on your life, you'll always have a few escape tricks ready, too. Next question."

"How did you get past those locks?" he asked, motioning toward the apartment door.

She smiled. "Your mistake is with your reasoning," she said. "The way you phrased the question precluded outside possibilities. I didn't use the door." His gaze was skeptical. "Look in the next room," she said.

Thomas was hesitant to take his eyes off her. But he stepped into the bedroom and glanced around. The small pane of one of the windows was broken inward. She'd climbed the fire escape from the outside, broken the glass, then unlocked the window and climbed in. "Pretty fair job of breaking and entering," he said without admiration. "Have you had practice?"

"I needed to get in," she said. "I was frightened."

"Of what?"

"Of those men!"

"They were merely local police. Detectives. From a homicide investigation." He grimaced slightly and sat down again. "I don't think running away from them made them any less suspicious. And the vanishing act. *That* will have them working overtime."

"I'm very selective about whom I trust," she said evenly.

"I consider myself honored." He was about to ask why he'd been so chosen as a recipient of trust. Then the telephone began. It rang twice loudly.

"It was ringing when I came in, too," she offered. "Someone's been trying to get you."

He looked at her as he picked up the receiver. "If I'd known you were going to be here I would have had you take a message."

Thomas picked up the telephone and heard the voice of Andrea Parker on the other end. To say she was angry would have been to understate greatly. "What the hell are you trying to do to me?"

"What are you talking about?" asked Thomas.

"The fingerprints," snapped Andrea, not assuaged a bit. "Did you level with me about them?"

"Completely."

"The one thing I don't need is a hassle."

"You're rambling. Tell me what you're talking about."

"The fingerprints," she said icily.

Thomas turned and looked at Leslie. She was still seated across the room on a sofa, now leafing through a magazine. But Thomas got the impression that she was listening to his end of the conversation very intently.

"Go ahead," said Thomas noncommittally.

"Okay," said Andrea, calming slightly. "Augie Reid sent them to the State Detective Bureau. Nothing. Then, automatically, they went into a

New York Police Department computer at One Police Plaza. From there, when nothing turned up in N.Y.C. records, they went through a computer linked to Washington. It took a couple of hours."

"And?" asked Thomas calmly.

"Nothing turned up in New York. But in that Federal computer the lights must have started flashing from here to hell and back."

"Oh, really?" asked Thomas with guarded evenness. He watched Leslie as he listened. Her position on the sofa was now subtly seductive. Or perhaps it was the angle from which he was watching her.

"I had a visitor this afternoon," said Andrea. "A Fed."

"A what?" He'd heard it properly the first time, but wanted to be sure.

"A Fed. A pricky career Treasury Department type named Hammond. Paul Hammond. Name mean anything?"

"Nothing. Should it?"

"Secret Service," crackled Andrea as Thomas Daniels listened without replying. "Those prints blew a fucking gasket on the Federal computer. Not only were the prints classified as to identity, but this Hammond prick was God-awful anxious to find out where I'd gotten them."

"Did you tell him?"

"No. But I might have to."

"Why?"

"I told him they were from a minor piece of evidence in an article on a case I was working on. Not important at all."

"What did he say?"

"He told me I was a liar. Which I was."

"Then what?"

"Then I told him I wasn't telling him anything else. I told him I had the right to protect my source of information. He cursed my God-damned ear off and told me I'd be getting written orders from the nearest Federal court to tell everything. Then he stalked out."

Thomas put his hand slowly to his head, as if to welcome an enormous headache. He was still looking at the woman who, in some way, had begun this. "I'd love the publicity of a court fight," she added, "but I don't have the stomach for it. Not now. And I doubt that this is the end of this."

"No, I doubt it, too," Thomas said with resignation.

There was a pause on Andrea's end. "Tom," she finally said, "this is my first brush with Feds and I'm not looking forward to the next one. But . . ." she added slowly, "I did ask around a little bit."

"About what?"

"Fingerprints in that category. The classified category."

"And?"

"One gets two words of advice on any investigation involving prints like these."

"Go ahead."

" 'Drop it!' It's more than either of us bargained for."

Thomas slowly placed the telephone back down on its hook. He could feel a thin film of sweat on his face and he felt slightly hot. He also thought he felt a sensation he'd not felt for a long time, and never in such a circumstance. Fear.

He turned to the woman in his apartment.

"What was that?" she asked.

"Really want to know?" He smiled.

"Sure."

"A girl friend," he said.

"I'm glad I didn't say anything," she said. "I might have made her jealous."

He smiled weakly and searched uneasily for the proper words. "Look," he said, groping. "This is all getting very much out of control." He paused. "If I've betrayed your trust, I'm sorry. But I've been trying to put things together on this case as best I can under the circumstances." He hesitated. "Maybe that's not very good. Maybe what you need is a bigger firm with more power to represent you. Why don't we both think things over for a day or two? Then you can decide whether or not you wish to continue with me. And vice versa."

She peered at him. He had the distinct impression of being transparent.

"You're trying to get out of the case. Aren't you?" she said.

He wanted to say no. But so far, lies hadn't been successful. "Maybe," he said, wondering how his father might have played the hand.

"All right," she said. "You think about it. And I'll think about it. But . . . you won't have to go very far to find me."

"What do you mean."

"I'm not leaving here tonight," she said politely. "There's no way I'm stepping out on the street."

"What are you talking about?"

"I can't take the chance that your police friends have found where I was staying. Not in the dark, anyway. So," she said casually, "I didn't think you'd mind if I installed myself in your study. The sofa looks comfortable."

"The final word in lawyer-client relationships," he mumbled. But then, uneasily, he was convinced he had to agree.

The sound of the bedroom door opening made him turn over on his mattress. He was instantly awake. The light in the room was dim but there was no doubt what he was hearing.

He suddenly felt sweaty. He tried to think of something to take in his hand as a weapon. But there was nothing.

The door opened fully. He sat up quickly. In the dimness he saw her hands. They were empty.

"I'm sorry," she said very softly. "I couldn't sleep."

Relieved, he leaned back against the headboard. "What's wrong?" he asked.

She moved forward. There was light from the other room now. She moved to the edge of his bed and sat down. She looked at him. Her manner was totally different now, as if she were a different woman. No longer the toughened woman used to defending herself. Now she was nine-year-old Leslie, defenseless and threatened.

"I'm worried," she said.

"What about?"

"You."

"Me?" He was baffled. "Why?"

"You're hesitating," she said. "I'm afraid you're going to drop my case."

"Jesus," he thought to himself. Here he was half scared of her. And now she was upset that she'd be dropped as a client.

"I'm sorry," she said. "I've trusted you this far. I've trusted you with my story, with my claim, practically with my life. I was speaking rashly before. I was upset." Her hands were folded in her lap. The thin nightgown, one of Andrea's, clung snugly to her legs and body. "I don't want to start all over with someone else," she said. "I want you to continue."

She sat sideways to him. He could see the nightgown's low neckline. Her face in the soft light was even more delicate and alluring than it was by day. He knew he was being manipulated. She established eye-to-eye contact, but he broke away from it, looking down her trim arms to where the hands and fingers were folded in her lap.

"That telephone call earlier," she said. "It concerned *me*, didn't it?"

He didn't speak.

"The truth," she said evenly.

"Yes."

"You don't trust me anymore, do you?" she asked. "You think there's something wrong."

"I took your case for two reasons," he said softly. "One, I needed money. Two, I believed you. I believe in simple justice under the law, you see." His smile was pained. "You appeared with a credible, interesting story. You had been wronged. You had documented proof and a certain amount of apparent sincerity. I felt you deserved your day in court."

"But something has changed," she observed.

"Why are your fingerprints in Washington?"

For a moment her eyes were angry. But they softened quickly. She calmed herself. Her body was motionless. The question hung in the air.

"How long have you been checking on me?" she asked. "From the start?"

"I do background on all my clients," he said.

"You believe in simple justice and the honor of the individual," she said, mocking slightly. "But with a security probe tossed in for good measure."

"I'd feel a lot better if you'd answer my question."

"Beneath it all, you're as cynical as the next man." She looked away. "But you do deserve an answer."

"I'm waiting."

Again there was a pause. "My father," she said.

"I'm afraid nothing's obvious."

"Arthur Sandler was a spy. You've confirmed that for yourself. He's still alive and he still knows the proper people in United States intelligence. He doesn't want me alive," she said bitterly. "*Of course* my fingerprints are on file somewhere. And if you've been good enough to trigger that central computer, it's only a matter of time before my father comes looking for me again."

"If you're claiming his estate, it's only a matter of time anyway."

"True," she said. She fell silent, reflective. "Consider Arthur Sandler. For every minute of his life that you've been able to account for already, he's wielded power. Every day, from every angle. In whatever identity he has now, he knows I'm the one person who might give him away. Do you need any further explanation of why my fingerprints would be on file?"

Gently, with a certain defensiveness, she was resting her case, leaving her story open to his judgment. She waited for a reply.

"What I need," he said slowly, "are photocopies of your documents. Your birth certificate. The marriage certificate. May I?"

She broke into the first natural, calm smile he'd seen from her. "All right," she said, and nodded enthusiastically.

"I'm going to disappear for a few days. I want to build a case for you. Will you be able to take care of yourself for a week?"

"I've taken care of myself for over twenty years," she said.

Her self-assurance was back. They'd reached an understanding.

She looked at him for a moment, then, in her excitement, leaned toward him. She embraced him as a friend would, then slowly she felt his strong arms around her shoulders. Her own arms responded in the same manner. She pulled away from him slightly.

"I'm glad we finally trust each other," she said. "It was lonely in the next room."

Understanding, yet mystified, he watched her as she stood up for a moment. Gracefully she reached to the front of the nightgown. The light was dim, but he could see every bit of her perfectly. She slid the two short sleeves away from her arms. He was almost speechless.

"Leslie . . . ?" he stammered.

"It's my decision. Don't say no."

The thin gown slipped away, sliding to the floor. She stood before him, slim, delicate. He was no longer conscious of the scar across her throat. His eyes were elsewhere as she moved onto the bed.

He hesitated. "I thought . . . ?"

"I changed my mind," she said spiritedly with her gentle British accent. "Now. No more discussion."

As his anxious arms reached for her, her own hands, the hands that had left the fingerprints on the photograph, reached to him and formed an embrace.

PART THREE

Thomas Daniels arrived at London International, otherwise known as Heathrow, at nine P.M., London time. He rented a car, stayed overnight in nearby Windsor, and the next morning drove southwest.

North Fenwick, where Arthur Sandler had married Elizabeth Chatsworth a third of a century earlier, was a quiet rural township of four hundred inhabitants. Much of the twentieth century, other than electricity, telephones, and automobiles, had been resisted. The air was clean, though damp and very cold that time of year. Houses were stone and had thatched roofs. Smoke from peat or wood rose from most chimneys. The atmosphere was rural without being provincial. The brown-stone church by the town hall dated from the fifteen hundreds.

The church, St. George's Chapel, was open. Thomas parked his car on the village green and walked into the church. The interior was barely warmer than the outside. The pews were dimly lit, as the stained glass allowed only modest amounts of light to filter across the old wooden pews, the center aisle and its stone floor, and the deep plum-colored cushions on the wooden benches. There was one hymnal per row.

But before even approaching the aisles or the pews, Thomas Daniels was struck dramatically by a large marble catafalque to the rear left corner of the worship hall. He approached it, as its contours resembled that of a human body.

He stood before it. There he looked upon a marble tomb, that of the chapel's founder, a sixteenth-century cleric named George Lorrick. Within were the remains of Lorrick, bones turned to dust over four centuries' repose. And along the top of the tomb, according to the custom of the day, was the likeness of the minister wrought in heavy iron. Head to toe, cap to boot, the iron image of the minister. Along the side, beneath the man's name, were his earthly dates: 1470–1545.

Thomas gazed into the metal image of the face, wondering whether the death mask did the man justice; whether or not the image of the rural parson revealed or concealed anything of the soul of the man sealed within. The graven image told only what the man had looked like on the exterior. It said nothing of the man behind the facade. A side notation was more helpful. Lorrick had founded the chapel, it said, in 1501. Stone after stone, by hand. In 1847 he'd been canonized.

Thomas moved on. He looked around both curiously and anxiously: curious whether he'd happen upon the pastor, and anxious as he looked forty feet ahead of him to the altar. There Leslie McAdam's parents had been married, the barmaid and the spy, during a dark hour of the Second World War. Thomas walked slowly and inquisitively up the narrow center aisle until he stood where Arthur Sandler and Elizabeth Chatsworth must have. He looked around the chapel from that spot. Receiving no special inspiration, he turned and walked again toward the two heavy front doors.

In the vestibule he stopped, examining plaques on the wall. A pair of plaques remembered the sons of North Fenwick who'd fallen in the world wars. Another, smaller and older, plaque bore two lonely names, a pair of long-forgotten souls who'd died for a long-forgotten cause under the command of Lord Kitchener. Transvaal. 1901.

Thomas turned and examined the opposite wall. There, engraved on stone, was part of what he'd been seeking. A listing of rectors of the chapel. From 1501 to the present.

His eyes stopped on Jonathan Phillip Moore, 1937–1949. A small cross by the name indicated that Reverend Moore, whose name appeared on the wedding certificate shown to Thomas by Leslie, had died while still the rector of that small parish. Another man had served from 1949 to 1957. Another from 1957 to 1968, and still another, Moore's third successor, from 1968.

Thomas went next door to the town hall. An old woman with grayish-white hair, a wrinkled face, yellowed teeth, and two heavy wool sweaters allowed Thomas to examine the town records, the official entries of births, deaths, and weddings.

Thomas turned to 1944. He sat at a long table and felt the old woman watching him from across the small town clerk's office. Thomas ignored her as best he could. He was on the page that included October in the heavy, leather-bound ledger. He ran quickly down the page with his finger.

Then he froze. Simply noted, no more than a single line, was: MARRIED —ARTHUR EDWARD SANDLER, New York, United States—ELIZABETH ANN CHATSWORTH, Tiverton, Devon. October twenty, ten A.M.

Thomas examined the page of the book. Without question it was the original page. The entry was legitimate.

Thomas looked up and found the old woman watching him. "Where would I find deaths?" he asked.

"Deaths?" She nodded toward him with a rasping voice. "Same ledger."

"But by specific names?"

She looked at him strangely. "What names?"

Thomas removed from his pocket a photocopy of Leslie's parents' marriage certificate. He read the names of the two witnesses. After a cross-reference procedure in which the old woman consulted a different town ledger, Thomas learned that both of the other witnesses to the marriage were also deceased. The most recent had died in 1953.

That evening Thomas drove back toward Exeter, Leslie's alleged birthplace. The town clerk's office was closed by the time he arrived. He stayed overnight at a small hotel and examined the town's registry of births that next morning. As expected, a baby named Leslie Sandler had been born at Altingham Hospital. July 30, 1945. A strange urge fell upon Thomas. He wished he'd asked her more about her girlhood in Exeter. He would have liked to visit her old neighborhood, see her former home, if it still stood, or perhaps the pub where Elizabeth Chatsworth had toiled during the war. But he hadn't asked.

He returned to London by car. He was trying to piece together a life that had been spent in the shadows. Or was it two lives, actually? George McAdam, Leslie's foster father, could piece together some integral pieces of the puzzle if he could be found. If he was still alive. It was worth a try.

From his hotel in London, Thomas contacted an international operator. He was connected to directory assistance for Switzerland. He first tried Vevey, the town Leslie had described. No George McAdam listed there. Then, using a map in front of him, he tried the larger cities in French Switzerland—Montreux, Lausanne, Geneva—and then the smaller towns surrounding Vevey.

It took fifteen minutes. Finally at 16, rue de Paudax in Lutry—the same small wine-producing town east of Lausanne on the Lake of Geneva where

Leslie had met her would-be assassin while working in a boat basin—Thomas uncovered a possibility. A listing for a "G. McAdam." Thomas obtained the number and asked that the call be placed.

He waited, quickly rehearsing his lines. Care *had* to be taken. McAdam was the only living man Thomas knew of who could confirm Leslie's story.

He heard the telephone ringing. Twice. Three times. Four, then five. Thomas cursed quietly.

Then the unmistakable voice of an Englishman answered on the other end. Thomas was almost tongue-tied for a moment.

"George McAdam?" asked Thomas.

The voice snapped, "Who's this?"

"You don't know me, sir, my name is Thomas Daniels. I'm an attorney from New York City." Silence on the other end. "I'm a friend of Leslie's," he tried.

There was a painfully long silence. Then McAdam replied quietly, "What do you want?"

"I need to speak with you. About your foster daughter. There's a legal proceeding in the United States involving—"

"I don't want to hear it," said McAdam coldly. Thomas groped for the proper response, but McAdam spoke next. "If you're trying to make money off my daughter," the voice said bitterly, "I'll have no part of it."

"I'm trying to help her. I represent her."

"*'Represent'?*" The voice was sardonic, bemused, scoffing.

"It's a matter of utmost importance," Thomas insisted. "Not so much for me. But for her."

"For *her?*" the voice said. There was definite sarcasm, a mocking tone to McAdam's voice, as if he both disbelieved and distrusted. "Poor Leslie," he said. Thomas began to speak, but McAdam interrupted sharply, asking where the call was originating.

"London."

There was silence as McAdam seemed to be thinking. "I won't talk about it," he repeated. Thomas was prepared to argue, but McAdam continued. "I suppose, whoever you are, there's not much you can do to me now. I won't talk about it, not on the telephone. Are you coming to Switzerland?"

"I can."

"You have my address, I assume," he said bitterly.

"I do."

"Be here day after tomorrow at ten A.M. If you have something to talk about, I'll see you then."

Thomas was about to thank McAdam, but the other end went dead. McAdam had put down his receiver.

Slowly Thomas hung up his telephone. He was exultant in finding McAdam. But his overwhelming feeling was one of uneasiness, of suspicion. McAdam wasn't doing him a favor. McAdam was trying to discover what Thomas was doing. There'd been something important unsaid in that brief conversation. Whatever it was, it was worth a flight to Switzerland to discover.

Chapter 12

Sixteen, rue de Paudax was a moderately sized stucco villa behind a large white brick fence and a large black iron gate. The rue de Paudax criss-crossed a large hill on the northern side of the Lake of Geneva. Had houses of similar size and design not been on the southern side of the *rue*, Thomas would have been afforded a fine view of the Lake itself and the French Alps on the opposite shore behind Evian.

Thomas stopped at Number 16. He examined the house and the iron bars of the gate. There was no name anywhere identifying the resident. The mail slot in the fence was unmarked. There was no bell to ring, perhaps a strong hint that the resident did not wish to be disturbed by outsiders. Perfect anonymity, thought Thomas, for a Swiss businessman or an Englishman who doesn't wish to be found.

Thomas examined the iron gate, fumbled with the interior of the latch, and forced an inside handle upward. The latch clicked grudgingly. The gate opened.

Thomas continued along a flagstone path toward the villa. He was halfway between the gate and the front door when he first heard the snarling dogs.

There were two of them. Brown, gray, and black with upcurled lips and raging white teeth. Two of the largest German shepherd guard dogs Thomas had ever seen. He stood in the path, transfixed with fear and afraid even to run. The dogs charged him. The walls around the villa were too large to scale. He was too far from the gate. Running toward the house would only incite the dogs further.

They were no more than fifteen feet away from him. His feet were rooted to the ground as they charged. Then Thomas and the dogs both froze when they heard the sharp commanding voice of their master, George McAdam. A one-word command had stopped the animals.

Thomas looked back to the villa. The solid front door was wide open now. A large, graying, heavyset man stood in full view. He wore a brown herringbone jacket, white shirt, and regimental tie which was slightly crooked.

"You're Daniels?" asked McAdam.

"Yes." Thomas alternated his gaze from the animals to McAdam and back to the German shepherds. He felt an incipient resentment at having been needlessly menaced. But he said nothing.

"You're alone?" McAdam asked.

"Absolutely."

"You'd better be telling the truth." McAdam glared at him as he studied his visitor. "Walk slowly toward me," he instructed. "Be gracious enough to hold out your hands slightly. About the height of your armpits."

Thomas obeyed, aware that the dogs were following closely behind him. "What the hell's this all about?"

"I'm planning to frisk you," said McAdam. "You may stop right there." Thomas was six feet in front of Leslie McAdam's foster father. "I assume you have no objection."

"I'm hardly in a position to have any objections. I hate dog hair."

"I have my enemies," said McAdam. It was in no way an apology.

I'd never have known, Thomas thought. But he didn't say it.

McAdam stepped forward, a severe limp now discernible. He was balding slightly and had mean gray eyes. His face, like his body, was thick and solid. Then, with agile hands which knew what they were doing, McAdam thoroughly frisked Thomas. The hands moved up and down Thomas's trouser legs, the belt, his jacket, torso, and sleeves.

"Lucky for you," said McAdam when he was finished. "You passed."

He stepped backward into the foyer of the villa. Thomas was instructed to walk in front of him. The dogs followed.

Thomas was directed to a small library to the left of the foyer. He sat on a small sofa while McAdam assumed a position behind a desk. As McAdam was seating himself, Thomas glanced around the room quickly. The furnishings were sparce. Books were in most of the shelves but other shelves were completely empty. On one wall, too far away for Thomas to examine carefully, there was an engraved certificate, an official document of some sort from the British Empire to George McAdam. Meanwhile, the dogs had settled tranquilly but alertly directly between the two men. Thomas got the message very clearly: Even if an intruder had gotten this far with a weapon, he'd not be able to get a shot off at McAdam without being torn apart immediately afterward. The Alsatians were still facing Thomas. He shuddered slightly.

"Talk," said McAdam.

"I wanted to talk about your foster daughter."

"I thought of her as my daughter," McAdam countered.

"Your daughter then," said Thomas. "And I didn't come to tell you anything as much as to ask you a few questions."

"I've never seen you before in my life," he said. "What makes you think I'd give you the time of day?"

"If she's your 'daughter,' as you phrase it, I'd think you'd want to help her."

"*Help* her?" he snapped. His face was a very belligerent scowl.

"Does that sound so strange?"

"It's beginning to."

"Why?"

"Daniels," chafed McAdam. "*You* are in *my* home. I'll ask the bloody questions!" He glared at the younger man. "Why are you here?"

"Your daughter is in New York at this moment. She is trying to collect a multimillion dollar inheritance which may justifiably belong to her."

McAdam continued to glare for a few moments. Then his hands closed before him and he rubbed his palms together. His gray eyes softened slightly. "You don't say?"

"You sound as if that's impossible."

"I want to hear more."

"Your daughter happens to be the biological daughter of a wealthy American. Arthur Sandler. A man who is legally dead, but—"

"I know who he is," McAdam said sharply.

"I know you do. And I know all about you, also. Retired from British Secret Service. Wounded in Suez, vacationing in Majorca when Leslie killed the Italian."

"Who told you all that?"

"Leslie, of course."

"Leslie," he muttered. "Certainly," he added coldly. "You see her often, do you?"

"She's my client. I'm representing her in her claim against the Sandler estate."

"Ah. I see," he said. "Money. You bloody Yanks."

Thomas felt himself starting to boil. He looked at the dogs and thought
better of it. "I'm here because she told me her story. Who she is, how
she came to live with you, how she went to Canada. I want you to confirm
it or deny it."

"Proceed," said McAdam cautiously.

Thomas began, repeating Leslie's story point by point as well as he
could remember. Then, barely breaking stride, he launched into an explanation of Arthur Sandler, of Sandler's fortune and Sandler's participation
in Allied intelligence work. Thomas concluded with an explanation of
how a young woman claiming to be Leslie presented herself in New York
with full documentation and asked Thomas to represent her. He omitted
any mention of the fire.

McAdam listened intently, but his reaction to a ten minute summation
baffled Thomas. There was very definitely something unsaid in the air,
some central and crucial detail still missing from the picture.

"You say you're a barrister?" was all McAdam would say.

"I've explained all that."

McAdam eyed him coyly. "So you have," said McAdam. "And against
my better judgment, I'm beginning to believe you. You're not a lunatic,
I can see that. You may be here in all good faith."

"What about the story I just told you?"

"Substantially correct. As far as the details of Leslie's past are concerned, your story is wholly factual. How's that?"

"What's *not* correct?"

"Have you been to London recently?"

"What?"

"I said, have you been to London recently."

"I just came from London. You know that."

"I think you should make another trip. I think you'd enjoy it."

"Cut the riddles."

"I'm offering you Arthur Sandler. Do you want him or not?"

The proposition seemed so tidy and easy that Thomas was immediately
suspicious. Why an unexplained giveaway after initial hostility?

"Well?" pressed McAdam. "Yes or no?"

"Why don't you explain for a change?"

"Oh, it's very simply, Daniels," scoffed McAdam. "I suspect you *are*
a New York lawyer. You look like one. And I think you very well may have
a client going by the name of Leslie McAdam. And I think," he concluded, "that a return journey to London would be of enormous interest
to you." He almost smiled. "Do you sense my meaning? I'm going to send
you to someone."

"Who?"

"A man named Whiteside. Peter Whiteside."

Thomas frowned, trying to recall.

"Yes," McAdam answered to the unspoken question, "I'm sure your Leslie mentioned him. Her Majesty's Secret Service. Peter Whiteside placed Leslie with my late wife and me."

"Of course," said Thomas, remembering.

McAdam reached to a pad of paper on his desk. He scribbled a name and address on the paper and slid it across the desk.

The dogs lifted their heads quickly as Thomas rose. McAdam spoke to the animals soothingly. Thomas was allowed to step gingerly past them and retrieve the paper. He glanced at it quickly, saw a London address he didn't recognize, folded it, and placed it in his pocket.

"Does he—?"

McAdam's hand rose, the flat of his thick palm extended rudely toward Thomas. "Absolutely not!" he snapped, shaking his head. "I can't tell you another thing!"

There was silence. McAdam got to his feet, struggling slightly on the bad leg. "Your questions will be answered in London as best they can be. Now, sir . . ." He motioned to the door with his head.

Thomas remained seated, contemplating the man before him. "One final question," he said quickly. "It has nothing to do with Leslie."

McAdam eyed the younger man in silence.

Thomas spoke. "Was it worth it? I'm just curious."

"Was *what* worth it?" McAdam asked defensively.

"Your career," said Thomas. "Here you are, a man in his final years. You hobble around from a twenty-year-old wound, you live alone with no one close to you, and you're so damned scared that someone's going to come and get you that you surround yourself with a brick wall and attack dogs. This is where all the 'For Queen and Country' stuff has gotten you. I was just wondering. Was it worthwhile?"

"Daniels," he replied without changing his expression, "you have fifteen seconds to be out of my sight. Thirty to be off my property. After that, I unleash the dogs."

Thomas was on his feet instantly. The heads of the dogs were upraised and the alert eyes and ears were pointed in his direction. In twenty-two seconds Thomas was on the sidewalk outside the iron gate, closing the latch firmly behind him.

British Airways Flight 012 from Geneva to London touched down on Runway 7 at two thirty, London time. The day was brisk and damp, but clear. Thomas enjoyed the long walk from the debarkation ramp to Immigration.

Thomas waited for his suitcase to reappear on the round conveyer belt bringing baggage in from the airplane. Then, with his bag in his hand, he waited for several minutes in the non-Commonwealth line through passport control. It was not until he handed his passport to the young uniformed immigration officer that Thomas sensed something amiss.

The young man studied the passport for a moment. "Your name?" he asked, loud enough to be heard by others nearby. He'd asked no one else that question.

"Thomas Daniels."

"Place and date of birth, sir." The young man's eyes glanced almost imperceptibly to the left.

"New York City. October 14, 1943." Now Thomas was aware of a thick, pudgy man in civilian clothes moving casually toward him. The man was bearded, wore a bowler and an overcoat, and had a round, moon-shaped face on top of a thick ursine body. Two uniformed policemen walked behind him, cautiously and slowly, each looking every bit of six and a quarter feet tall. A show of force, obvious yet not excessive.

The young clerk whacked Thomas's passport with an inked stamp.

"Enjoy your stay in the United Kingdom, sir," he said. The passport was pushed back into Daniels's hands. He was moved along from the immigration booth.

"Mr. Daniels?" said the thick round man, moving directly alongside Thomas. The uniformed policemen stood discreetly behind them. They were far enough from other travelers so that they couldn't be heard.

"Yes," said Thomas.

The man's thick squat hand disappeared quickly into his inside pocket. Out came a small card and a badge. "Rogers Hunter. Metropolitan Police Department."

"I'm innocent," said Thomas.

Hunter managed a forced smile.

"I'm here to accompany you to Mr. Peter Whiteside."

Distrusting, Thomas eyed Hunter quickly up and down. The two police in the background were watching him.

"I have his address," said Thomas. "I think I can find him by myself."

Thomas started to step away but an incredibly powerful hand grabbed his right arm just above the elbow. Hunter stopped Thomas in his tracks. "I insist," said Hunter.

"I don't need help." Thomas tugged his arm but the grip remained.

"I see," said Hunter reflectively, not put off in the slightest. "Am I to assume that you'll not be coming with me voluntarily?"

"You may assume what you like."

"Very well," said Hunter, releasing the arm gently. He turned and nodded to the two uniformed officers, then looked back to Thomas. At the same time, the two policemen moved with remarkable speed for large men.

"In that case," said Hunter with a sly smile of appreciation, "I'm placing you under arrest. I'm terribly sorry."

Thomas resisted slightly. Then it was nothing more than a blur as he was separated from his suitcase and shoved roughly against a concrete wall. By the time he looked down to his wrists there were handcuffs in place.

Chapter 14

Thomas was led from the immigration area and placed in the backseat of an unmarked dark-blue Rover. His luggage was placed in the trunk. He pulled slightly at the cuffs on his wrists and shuddered at the feeling of freedom diminished. He saw that the backseat of the car, which was separated from the front by a wire screen, had doors that could not be opened from the inside.

One of the uniformed men drove. The other stayed behind. Hunter sidled into the front seat in front of Thomas, his expansive shoulders filling practically half of the front area. The Rover pulled away from the curb.

"Where are you taking me?" asked Thomas.

Hunter turned to face his prisoner. "Are you worried?" he asked. Thomas didn't answer. The porcine bearded face slowly creased into a grin. "I wouldn't worry," grunted Hunter. "You're going exactly where you wanted to go. You really had very little choice about it. Mr. Peter Whiteside wants to see you himself."

The Rover was on the motorway heading toward London. Thomas looked out of the car apprehensively. "How did you know where I was coming from?" he asked.

"Oh, come now, Mr. Daniels," said Hunter in a baritone chuckle.

"George McAdam?"

"We could have picked you up in Switzerland if we'd liked. But that might have been sticky, as well as unnecessary. Thank you for flying British Airways."

Thomas settled back in the seat, calming slightly and seeing no alternative. "Why couldn't I have gone to see Whiteside myself?"

"Because you have a nonexistent address," growled Hunter. Thomas looked at the back of Hunter's neck, a neck that must have measured eighteen inches in circumference. "Really, Mr. Daniels, you're horribly naive."

The car traveled through the bleak working-class neighborhoods surrounding London. It passed through several unrecognizable sections of the city. Then Thomas recognized Victoria Station before the Rover turned left and within three more minutes was pulling to a curb in front of a Belgravia townhouse.

Hunter stepped out and quickly unlocked the back door. Thomas stepped from the car and looked into Hunter's drooping eyes. Thomas held out his captive wrists. "Are these still necessary?" he asked.

"You don't think I'm letting you run away now, do you?" asked Hunter harshly. "They weren't necessary at all. But you insisted." He took Thomas by the elbow and moved him toward the unmarked front door of a solid sandstone townhouse. "Come along," Hunter said absently.

Thomas allowed his overcoat to be draped across his wrists. Hunter pressed a thick finger to a doorbell and the townhouse door opened seconds later.

A plainclothed security guard surveyed them. The guard obviously recognized Hunter. Thomas was led inside as the driver from the Rover carried in his luggage.

They entered a small white rotunda where still another security man stood. A colored institutional portrait of the Queen hung on one side of the round room, a Union Jack stood on a standard on the other side. Thomas was led down a hallway which was carpeted with thick maroon runners. He recognized that he was within a gracefully aged Edwardian townhouse which had been converted to Government offices of some sort.

Hunter stopped him before a door. "Now," asked Thomas's bear-shaped keeper, "you're not going to do something foolish if I unlock you, are you?"

"Certainly not," said Thomas flatly. "I'm so happy to be here."

Hunter hardly batted an eye. He unlocked Thomas's wrists and then let Thomas into a small office off the hallway. Thomas's instructions were to sit down and wait, which he did, as Hunter closed Thomas in and stood outside.

Thomas seated himself on a comfortable sofa in a small plain room with no window. The room had an empty wooden desk, an armchair, sound insulation, and a few perfunctory decorations such as the British coat of arms on the wall behind the desk. The room offered very little other than privacy, of which it offered an abundance.

Thomas remained seated as an austere, elegant older man in a dark classically tailored pin-striped suit entered. The man was in his midseventies, but his body was trim and moved easily, giving no indication of its occupant's age. The man's eyes, as he glanced at Thomas Daniels, were sharp, blue, and alive. His hair had resisted grayness and was instead a yellowish white. In earlier years this had obviously been a remarkably handsome man, lean and athletic, a man to whom flabbiness of flesh would have been as repugnant as flabbiness of thought.

His movements were epicene. He offered his hand to Thomas. "I'm Peter Whiteside," he said. "Did you enjoy your trip?"

They shook hands. Thomas was still cautious. "From Switzerland to London? Or from the airport to here?"

"No matter. Either." Whiteside sat in the armchair and studied the younger man. He sat with his legs crossed and both hands on the top knee.

"Was that your gorilla who picked me up?" asked Thomas.

"That's not very kind of you at all," said Whiteside, "attributing bestial characteristics to my associate, Mr. Hunter."

"Why am I here?" Thomas asked.

"Because you wanted to be," laughed Whiteside. "Good God, man, you were in Devon a few days ago asking leading questions, badgering the hall of records and trying to scare up the dead. Now don't tell me you don't want to be here where you can ask questions about Arthur Sandler and Leslie McAdam."

"Then let's begin," said Thomas. "I don't like being held prisoner."

"You're not."

"I'm not under arrest?"

"You're free to leave at any time," said Whiteside. "There's the door. I'll escort you to the street if you prefer."

Thomas studied the door and wondered if he sensed a trick.

"However," said Whiteside, "you'll find it rewarding to stay. We can have a most interesting conversation."

"All right," said Thomas. He settled back on the sofa.

"Intriguing," said Whiteside absently. "How something like this crops up after twenty-some years."

"Excuse me?"

Whiteside's gaze shot back to Thomas. "I'm retired, Mr. Daniels," he said. "As far as the Foreign Office is concerned, I don't even exist anymore. But this Sandler-McAdam problem was in my lap back in 1954. Nasty problem, really, though I don't expect that you know the half of it yet. My 'section,' shall we call it, was within M.I. Six and linked with the Chancellery of the Exchecquer. Or Treasury, as you'd term it."

"Money, in any language."

"Currency, if you like," said Whiteside. "That's how I became involved with Arthur Sandler."

"Currency manipulations again?"

Whiteside smiled. "You *are* a barrister, aren't you? The incisive question quickly and succinctly. No matter. You'll have a few of your answers presently." The smile disappeared. "The trouble is, sir, for you, there will be other questions. Maybe you'll help *us* with those."

Thomas opened his hands to indicate that he had no idea of what Whiteside was speaking.

"Ah, yes," Whiteside continued, "you're owed a few explanations. Shall we start with Arthur Sandler?"

"I'd love to."

"You know him as an industrialist and a financier, I would think," said Whiteside. "And with a bit of chemistry added in. Correct?"

"Reasonably correct."

"Ah, yes. Some of the espionage nonsense, too. You know about that." Thomas nodded.

"What you don't know about is Sandler's greatest singular skill. The nice word for it is engraving."

"Engraving?"

"And the not-so-nice word for it is forgery. Or counterfeiting, if you prefer."

Thomas offered no reply. He merely sat there in puzzlement until Whiteside spoke again. He studied the intense acerbic man in front of him, a man with a Latin teacher's face and voice combined with the crisp assurance of a major in infantry.

"Daniels, either you're an actor of inordinate skills or you know nothing about this. In either event, I assume you would like to hear more."

"I would."

"Have you ever heard of Operation Bernhard?"

The two shrewd eyes watched Thomas as he thought. Thomas shook his head.

"What about Sachsenhausen? Name mean anything?"

Thomas shrugged.

"How innocent the young are," commented Whiteside sardonically. "What about Helmut Andorpher? Or Heinrich Kinder?"

"Nothing," said Thomas.

"It's time we added to your education," said Whiteside. "Allow me to graphically transport you back to 1943. As you may have learned from the history books, there was a bit of a conflict going on in Europe."

Thomas was silent, watching and listening as Whiteside folded his long narrow fingers into a steeple on the desk before him.

"Germany had several different phases of its war against Britain," Whiteside continued. "Not all were military. There is more than one way to destroy a nation. Militarily is one way. Economically is another. Operation Bernhard was of the latter."

"A plan of economic destruction?" asked Thomas, his eyebrows lowered into a frown.

"Operation Bernhard was a highly secret German project," explained Whiteside, leaning forward and speaking with more intensity now. "The operation was to counterfeit British currency, specifically the five-pound note but also tens and twenties. This was the brainchild, as it were, of an SS colonel named Helmut Andorpher who conceptualized the project in 1940 and received approval directly from Hitler in 1941. The intention was quite simple. Inflate the pound sterling so catastrophically that its value on the world market would be destroyed."

"Brilliant idea," conceded Thomas.

"Not at all original," sneered Whiteside dourly. "Andorpher was a student of history." Whiteside cleared his throat and allowed himself a thin smile. "During your War of Independence our General Howe counterfeited Continental dollars to undercut their worth. With considerable success, I might add. The only distinguishing quality separating the original from the facsimile was that the counterfeit was a better product."

"But we won," said Thomas.

There was a silence. "Yes. I'm told you did. In any event, Andorpher headed Operation Bernhard. He was a formidable stategist and an excellent soldier. What he was not was an engraver."

Thomas nodded.

"What he needed to make his operation work was the *homme indispensable*, the indispensable man who could engrave the plates and who could duplicate the paper. The man who could turn out the unquestionably perfect counterfeit product."

"And he found him. Within German intelligence, I'll bet."

"Very good, Daniels," nodded Whiteside. "Of course he found him. A man very intimate with international finance and currency. A German intelligence officer named Heinrich Kinder." Whiteside allowed himself another meager smile. "A *nom de guerre*, of course."

"Of course."

"Arthur Sandler," sighed Whiteside. "Our dear, dear American double agent." Pensively, he continued, "Well, our friend Herr Sandler straightened out the Huns with their printing presses. It makes sense. He was a chemist, remember? He concocted a bleach that positively lifted the ink off old one-pound notes. Then he reduced the paper to pulp, reprocessed it to accommodate five pound notes, meticulously reengraved the plates and began running off five-pound notes as fast as the presses could roll. Damned nice of our American cousins to supply the enemy with the essential man for their Operation Bernhard. Don't you think so?" he concluded with bitterness.

"How much damage did they do?"

Whiteside broke his hands apart and rubbed the palms together. "During the war, surprisingly little. The saving factor was that an operation such as this took enormous time to get underway. Kinder—or Sandler— was given his workshop in Sachsenhausen concentration camp. He had labor there to run the presses, but there were logistical problems getting all his material and engraving tools to him. By the time everything was fully underway and by the time the presses were rolling at full speed, it was late 1944."

"And the war was almost over."

Whiteside nodded. "The German armies were in retreat everywhere. And the channels in Switzerland, North Africa, and South America which could pass the money were limited or impaired. It was somewhat like the V-2 rockets, Daniels, or the atomic bomb. Time ran out on the Huns before they could shove it down our throats." Whiteside spent a moment in quiet reflection. "Bloody Jerries," he muttered.

Thomas sensed that Whiteside might be given to more candor than he'd intended. He pressed the questioning.

"You haven't even told me the real problem," said Thomas.

"Sorry?"

"You said Operation Bernhard did surprisingly little damage. Your own words. Yet it was important."

"Yes, it was."

"Why?"

"I said it did little damage *during the war*. What we're leading up to is 1945. Early on in the year."

Thomas thought quickly. It was just before this period that Arthur Sandler had stepped out of the life of Elizabeth Chatsworth.

"The fate of the Third Reich had been decided by the beginning of 1945," said Whiteside. "No question about that. Again, it was a matter of time, closing the noose, choking off the armies, and reaching Berlin."

Thomas listened intently. His eyes drifted to the coat of arms on the wall behind Whiteside. The Lion and the Unicorn, *Dieu et Mon Droit.*

"The Reich was drawing in upon itself," said Whiteside. "Hitler had retreated to his *Alpenfestung.* He was on the dark side of insanity by now, of course. He was ordering children into combat, sending out commands for battalions which had long since been decimated. And he ordered his counterfeiters to keep working. Right up till the end."

"Did they?"

"Yes," he said with a pained smile. "And beyond. When the Bolsheviks got to Berlin, the counterfeiters packed it in. They—Sandler, Andorpher, and whatever help they had—tried to escape with all the equipment, heading south toward Austria. They travelled by truck. That essentially is how we know what they were up to. The main truck, bearing most of the equipment plus crates and crates of freshly printed pound notes, broke down on the escape route. They couldn't bury it, it was too big. And they couldn't abandon it, it was too valuable. So they tried to hide it. Sandler released the brake on the top of a hill. They let it roll down until it splashed into a lake. And there it sank."

"Forgotten?" asked Thomas with obvious sarcasm.

"For a few weeks. Then the crates broke open. Millions of pounds worth of notes came floating to the surface. Fives, tens, twenties, and fifties. Need I say, the locals had a fine time. Wringing out the money and hanging it in trees to dry. It was the first time Allied intelligence heard of it. Wasn't exactly the type of thing that could be kept quiet. It was the first time any outsider had any inkling about Bernhard." Whiteside's brow was furrowed. "There'd been suspicion for a long time, mind you. There were simply too many pounds circulating. But now we knew. Our sacred pound sterling, and our friends the Sausage Makers had been printing it."

"And Sandler?" asked Thomas, sensing the next chapter. "And Andorpher?"

Whiteside made a gesture with his mouth. It was half wince, half pained smile. "This is where it gets sketchy," he said. "But some basics are known. Andorpher, for example."

"Captured?"

"In a sense. He was found dead, seventy-five miles *east.* Not west, mind you, but east. He was lying in a ditch." Whiteside delivered the next sentence as casually as he might give a cricket score or a weather report. "Andorpher was lying in a ditch with his throat cut. Ear to ear. That left our friend Sandler."

"Alone?"

"Almost. When the trucks were pulled out of the lake we learned that he'd taken along some items for good luck. The plates. The engraved counterfeiting plates."

"Of course," said Thomas, almost inaudibly.

Whiteside looked at the younger man as if to judge him. Whiteside's eyebrows were slanting downward in a nervous frown; his teeth were clenched in concentration.

"Now," Whiteside continued, "let's see if Thomas Daniels is a man or a boy. Let's see if he can spot the fox in the thicket."

"Go ahead."

"You're obviously a clever young man, Mr. Daniels. Otherwise you would never have gotten this far. And if you're as sly as I give you credit for being, you'll have spotted something very wrong. There *must* have been something in the story I told you that struck you as odd."

"A certain detail or turn?" asked Thomas.

"Yes. What was it?" he asked challengingly.

Thomas didn't have to think. "*East* made no sense," he said simply. "In light of everything I know about Arthur Sandler, east makes no sense at all."

"Exactly!" snapped Whiteside with enthusiasm, bringing a fist down hard on his desk. He allowed a moment or two to regather his poise. "For twenty-two years, Mr. Daniels, east has made no sense. And now we'll discuss why."

"No bloody sense at all," continued Whiteside. "None! Here's a top American agent, a man who spent the war slipping back and forth across enemy lines, a man who moved around Austria and Germany with obscene ease, a man who knew the inner mechanisms of German intelligence for five years, and what does he do when the war is over? He moves one hundred eighty degrees in the wrong direction. Instead of returning to the Americans, he jumps into the Russians' laps." Whiteside shrugged disgustedly. "We know he was in Moscow for a month at least."

"There are possible explanations," said Thomas thoughtfully.

"Of course there are," huffed Whiteside. "Countless explanations. Want to know the best one, the one most popular at the Foreign Office? Here it is: The Yanks recruited a closet Bolshevik in 1941. Sandler, the theory goes, was working three ways from the middle, with his highest allegiance being given to Moscow."

"I don't follow," said Thomas.

Whiteside huffed slightly, as if mildly exasperated at having to explain. "A triple game, Mr. Daniels," he elaborated. "You Americans thought Sandler was your own spy acting as a double agent against the Germans. In a sense he was, but he was also a triple, selling out Washington to Moscow whenever he had the opportunity. That would have explained why he went east instead of west."

"Intriguing," said Thomas reflectively.

"Intriguing, yes," retorted Whiteside. "And possible. But it doesn't wash. Not all the way. We tried several theories on Sandler. We had to. Can you guess why?"

"It's obvious, isn't it? He had those plates. He kept using them."

"Brilliant," remarked Whiteside quietly from behind white teeth that were almost clenched in annoyance. "He kept printing our money."

Thomas suppressed a sudden smile as the incredible Sandler fortune, the one which had magically materialized after the war, flashed into his mind. Of course, he thought to himself. Of course, of course, of course!

There were muffled noises in the corridor outside the small room. They were voices. It broke Thomas's concentration and he glanced at his watch. He had been alone with Whiteside for almost an hour.

"From there we lost track of Sandler. We thought the Russians had him. But then he turned up some way in New York. How he got from one place to the other I've never known. All I know is that he did. And his plates were with him."

"In the United States?"

"Where do you think all those pounds were being printed, damn it," snapped Whiteside. "In your citadel of democracy. Our pound was being sabotaged unmercifully. It was happening on United States soil and nothing was done to stop it."

"Maybe . . ."

"Washington knew," said Whiteside flatly. "They knew and did nothing." After an annoyed pause, he added, "It strengthened the dollar, you know."

Thomas felt a tinge of embarrassment. Whiteside knew it and played the moment to its advantage, letting several seconds pass before speaking again.

"So you see, we knew that our currency was being sabotaged by counterfeits, we knew who was doing it, and we knew it had to be stopped. Your Uncle Sam wouldn't help." Whiteside sighed. "We don't like to do things this way, really we don't. But it became incumbent upon us." He paused. "We ordered him 'put down.' "

"Is that what you call assassinated?" Thomas asked. Whiteside nodded. "Sounds like the mercy killing of a horse."

"Term it anything you like," said Whiteside. "Men are much more vile than animals anyway. Call it killed. I gave the order myself. Personally. In 1954. And in case you're wondering," he added without hesitation, "I'd order it again today."

"You might have to," Thomas said. "You missed the first time."

"Yes," said Whiteside. "I know. Sandler was up to the challenge, as usual. He had a double. Imagine," mused Whiteside pensively. Then his expression brightened. "But in any event, the forgery of pounds stopped soon thereafter. So the put-down of the double may have accomplished its purpose in a roundabout manner. Maybe it drove Sandler farther underground. Maybe it genuinely scared him, though I doubt it. Or maybe he was plain ready to graduate to other things. Who knows?"

Both men were silent in thought for a moment. Whiteside spoke next. "All I know is that the forgery of British pounds sterling stopped within weeks. That was all I was ever concerned with."

"No, it's not," Thomas reminded him gently. "Not all. Not by a long shot."

"Ah, yes," he said, remembering. "Leslie."

"You certainly took steps to protect her. But why after all those years did Sandler feel that he had to come back and kill a wife and daughter? That makes no sense, either."

"Vaguely, it does," said Whiteside. "But only when considered from a certain angle, and conceding that with Sandler one isn't always dealing with a rational man."

"Can you elaborate?" asked Thomas.

"This is merely speculation, but maybe we never knew the full story of the postmarital breakup. Perhaps there was a good reason why Sandler never returned to her after the war. Thus he could have been infuriated that she'd claim part of his 'estate' after he was 'dead.'"

"Maybe," said Thomas. "But why wait so long?"

"She initiated the contact," Whiteside said. His hands were busily working a small Canary Islands cigar out of a compact gold case. He took the cigar in his lips, lit it, and was enshrouded by a mild white cloud of smoke as he continued to talk. "Perhaps Sandler had believed her to be long lost and forgotten. Or perhaps he thought she'd been killed during the war. Maybe he doubted that the daughter was his." Whiteside shrugged. "I don't know," he said. "And from my standpoint, it's not all that important."

"Not to you, maybe. But there's something big that's still missing."

"Granted."

"He loved Elizabeth Chatsworth enough during the war to want to provide for her in the case of his death. Then—suddenly—after the war he's totally oblivious to her. British and American intelligence knew he was a spy and helped cover him up. Right?" Whiteside nodded absently. "Then this same man wants to come back and kill his wife and daughter nine years later." Thomas was shaking his head. "There are large pieces of this missing," he concluded.

Whiteside managed a pained smile. "Larger than you imagine," he said. "Particularly in view of this woman who has come to you in New York."

Thomas frowned. "Meaning what?" he asked.

Whiteside rubbed his hands together gently, then flicked a small tip of ashes into an ashtray. He stood. "Come along," he said. "We're going for a ride. I want to show you something."

Thomas stood and let Whiteside lead him to the door. "Should I bother to ask where we're going?" he asked.

"This should be of interest to you," he said. "I'm taking you to see Leslie McAdam."

The car was still at the curb in front of the stone townhouse. The tall, austere Whiteside stepped from the building first and immediately the driver slipped back into the car. The Rover began moving through congested London traffic. A few minutes later the windshield wipers were turned on and silently kept a fine rain from obstructing the driver's view.

Twenty minutes later the Rover eased to a stop in a subdued neighborhood bordering Earl's Court and Kensington. Whiteside and Thomas stepped from the car. They were on a quiet street with little traffic, trees, clean sidewalks, and a small church.

"The Chapel of St. Michael the Redeemer," said Whiteside. "Peaceful, I suppose, though I've never much cared for Presbyterians." The driver remained with the car. "Come with me," said Whiteside to Thomas.

They walked through a side door to the small, modest neighborhood church. The rector saw Whiteside and the two men exchanged nods. No word was spoken. Thomas reasoned that the church might have a small group of Anglo-Scottish parishioners. But he was only guessing.

They walked through the chapel, up the aisle, and then past the altar. Whiteside led Thomas out another side door which led into an old churchyard with weather-worn tombstones, a few ornate but most of them modest. The headstones marked the resting places of humble working people from the neighborhood. There was a steady cold drizzle now.

"I was always very fond of Leslie McAdam," Whiteside said in a moment of unconcealed candor. "A frightened little girl most of her life." He looked at Thomas as the rain fell on his angular face and dripped down to his beige Aquascutum raincoat. He wore no hat. Whiteside's hair was matted and soaked. "Man to man, old boy," he said, "I guess I saw in her the daughter I would always have liked to have had. Are you married?"

"Divorced."

"I see," he answered, as if suddenly enlightened. He added as an afterthought, "I was never of the temperament to marry." His smile was wry. "A bit of a public-school vice, you understand." He motioned to a modern tombstone in the newest section of the churchyard. "Here we are," he said.

Thomas looked down and stood absolutely motionless as he read the inscription in gothic letters:

LESLIE MCADAM
1945–1974

He stared at the stone disbelievingly, then lifted his gaze back to the older man. Whiteside was studying his reaction, conscious that he'd just thrown his trump card. Several moments more passed before Thomas spoke. "What's this supposed to mean?" he asked.

"It means that a man with counterfeit money also has a counterfeit daughter," said Whiteside. The rain continued to fall on his face. His expression was twisted in confusion also. "Albeit," he added, "as usual Arthur Sandler's counterfeit is, well, perfect."

"Perfect?"

"The story you told George McAdam in Switzerland. It damned well made poor old George's blood go cold. The story was perfect. Not a word out of place. Every detail. Things that only Leslie would have known. Your girl in New York. She knows them all. I'll be bloody well struck dumb before I can figure out how that's possible."

Thomas looked down at the headstone again, at the wet grass growing around it and the long convex mound of earth upon the grave. "How do I know that there's anything really under there?" he asked.

"You don't. But I do. And I'd have no reason to waste time lying to you. Would you like to see the coroner's report? I could arrange it for you. It's a fitting day for it."

"Are you sure you buried the right girl?"

"Yes," he said flatly. "May of 1974. The real Leslie McAdam is dead."

Thomas squinted slightly from the rain. "Sandler?" he asked.

"We think so. She was in London visiting and about to return to Canada. She was staying in a flat in Bloomsbury. Protected by the Foreign Office, yet. Found with her throat slashed one morning. Shall I go on?"

"Only if you want to," said Thomas.

"Well," huffed Whiteside, pulling his overcoat closer as the drizzle thickened, "from our point of view there's an awful lot still at stake. There's the murder of this girl and a still-unsolved murder of her mother from 1954. Unfinished business you might call it, not of the highest priority but important nevertheless."

As Whiteside spoke, Thomas was silent. He pictured Leslie McAdam in New York. Someone—if not everyone—was lying mightily.

Whiteside continued. "This whole thing is bloody perplexing and the fact that Arthur Sandler is involved is what makes it so. What was so important that he find this girl, a daughter whom he might never have even seen? Something is still happening and we don't know what it is. Our government is rather curious. If Sandler can be found, we'd like to have a go at him, too."

Thomas was shaking his head, still looking downward at that headstone. "He's got to be seventy-six years old," he said.

"Unless he's been reincarnated some way," said Whiteside in half-serious tones.

"What?"

"Well, let's face it. We're rational men standing here in cold daylight in the middle of a very real world. But this Arthur Sandler is defying natural law, one would think. Rather spry for a man of his age, wouldn't you say? We should all be treated so kindly by time."

Thomas didn't reply. But the answer was yes.

"Consider your problem, Mr. Daniels," said Whiteside. The two men turned. Whiteside placed his hand on the other man's shoulder as they walked around the churchyard, through the rain.

"You have a man who's alive who claims to be dead. And you have a girl who's dead who claims to be alive. I don't envy you. And I'm not at all certain you'll ever be able to resolve this to everyone's satisfaction."

They passed back through the small stone chapel. Thomas was reminded of the church in North Fenwick. The image of the marble tomb flashed before him, the Devonshire priest entombed beneath his own likeness in iron. Thomas couldn't shake the image.

He was aware of being watched. Two old women were in the pews, one with wrinkled lips moving above a prayer book, the other silent and motionless on her thick, aged knees. The parson watched Thomas with more than transient curiosity. Thomas glanced back at him and had the distinct impression that the man's face evoked Central Europe—perhaps the Alps or the Tyrol—more than the island of fog, Dickens, and gin.

Whiteside spoke again when they reached the wet sidewalk. "Tell me, are you planning to pursue this affair?"

Thomas looked into Whiteside's cunning eyes. "I've come this far, haven't I?"

Whiteside was thoughtful as they approached the Rover. "This is just a suggestion," he offered, "but you might give some thought to discovering who was running him."

"Running him?"

"Yes. Who was controlling him." Whiteside looked to Thomas and realized he was drawing a blank. "An agent might operate for totally self-centered reasons," he elaborated. "Money. Sex. Power. But he doesn't operate by himself. Sandler had to have had a case officer, a superior in control who was, as we say, running him. Has that occurred to you?"

Thomas shook his head. "No, it hasn't."

"It should have. Give it some thought." He paused, then added as the chauffeur unlocked the Rover, "If you're able to arrive at any conclusions, do let me know. Her Majesty's Government should be most grateful."

They reentered the car and it slowly pulled away from the chapel, moving toward Westminster. Thomas was deeply in thought. The only words on the return trip were Whiteside's after another long pause.

"I like to think of myself as a career servant with unimpaired honor, Daniels. So trust me on one further point. There's a further aspect to all this. But I'm absolutely forbidden by ethics, English law, and propriety from divulging it at this time. Terribly sorry."

Daniels looked at Whiteside, as if to see within the man. He couldn't. "Does it affect my . . . my search?" he asked.

"Not in essence," said Whiteside. He sighed, as if he wanted to say more. Thomas had a slightly disgusted look on his face. He was thinking of the graveyard as much as anything. Whiteside read him perfectly.

"This whole thing has a rather repellent smell, doesn't it?" asked Whiteside. "Killing young girls, and all that." His smile to Thomas Daniels was bittersweet. "People genuinely stink. Myself included."

PART FOUR

At first he thought the letter was from Leslie, or rather the woman who claimed to be Leslie. Then Thomas Daniels recognized the blue personal stationery of Andrea Parker.

Tom, dear,

I tried desperately to get in touch with you. I wanted you to know I'll be out of town. A fabulous, fabulous man and I are going to Martinique for a week of sun. Please don't be jealous. I am sure you'll live a lot longer than he will, anyway. I'm thinking of you always.

Love, love,
Andrea

Such expertise. He crumpled the blue paper in one fist and sent it airborne toward the kitchen garbage can.

He kicked the door shut behind him and stalked into the bedroom, still in thought. He tossed his suitcase onto the ragged bedspread, stood there a moment, returned to the kitchen, and retrieved the crumpled blue paper. It had been beside a dustball at the base of the stove.

He pulled the note open and looked at the date on top. The note was already a week old. He tossed it to the garbage can, accurately this time, where it could now remain.

Augie Reid. He'd suspected it all along. Well, he reconciled himself, at least today was Sunday and the week in the sun was over. He wouldn't have to think of it while it was still in progress.

Eight months earlier his wife had left him. Now Andrea, traveling her own road with a new companion. To lose one woman is a tragedy. To lose two in a year is plain carelessness. Was that Oscar Wilde?

Carelessness? Or a form of failure?

He tried to push the thought aside. He hated the word *failure*, hated it because it slipped into his thoughts so often. Besides, law hadn't been *his* chosen profession. He'd been pushed, seduced. By his father. His only real failure, he told himself, was not having gotten out sooner. Better late than not at all. And soon it would be over, years wasted on a career he hated. Better mere years than a lifetime.

By ten that night he was gloriously tired, his body still on European time. He fell asleep on the living-room sofa, reaching up and turning the light out, too tired to move. His last thought as he drifted off concerned the last woman to have come to his office:

If she wasn't Leslie McAdam, who *was* she?

What she was was punctual, among other qualities. Thomas had spent most of that next day looking at the clock, often noticing that only a few minutes had passed since he'd looked last. He was anxious to see her, or at least to see if she'd be where she'd said she'd be. Eighty-ninth Street and Madison Avenue, appropriately across the street from the aging Sandler mansion, that sealed mausoleum of a house in front of which *someone* had been murdered in 1954. Why, Thomas wondered as he stood across the street at two minutes to four, looking up at the shuttered windows, the corroded green roof, and the impregnable brick walls, did appearances have to be so deceiving?

He glanced at his watch. Then he looked down the street. He saw her rounding the corner from Park Avenue, walking boldly toward him, dark glasses shielding her eyes and a scarf surrounding her scarred throat.

She was smiling. So he smiled, too. Sure, his better instincts told him that Leslie McAdam was in a churchyard in London. But he was glad to see her anyway.

He let her walk all the way to him before he spoke, and even then it was simply "Hello." He reached out and took her hand.

She looked at him oddly, as if to correctly sense his hesitancy. "For God's sake," she chided, "we've been in bed together. You're allowed to kiss me."

He leaned forward and did kiss her. And against his better judgment
—or against any kind of judgment at all—he felt himself drawn protectively toward her. Never get involved personally with a client, his father
used to tell him. Never. Oh well, he thought, a lot of good the old man's
advice had done for him so far.

She looked away from him for a moment, taking his hand and removing
her dark glasses. Her gaze was on the bulwark of the building across the
street. Her brown eyes were appraising, almost scheming and plotting.

He, too, glanced to the house. He thought of those fortress walls and
the secrets they surrounded. Within, doddering old Victoria—too frightened of water to even bathe—had entertained her succession of dogs
named Andy, had interred them, and had doted with equal fanaticism
upon dollar bills. Similarly, this had been the very house from which
Adolph Zenger had emerged in 1955, changed and shattered, a shell of
the man he'd once been. "A different man," as William Ward Daniels
had described it to his son.

"How can we get in there?" she asked.

"In the Sandler house?"

"Is there any other house under discussion?" she asked impatiently. Her
mercurial smile was already gone and the affectionate greeting had given
way to a businesslike sense of priorities.

"With burglar tools," he said.

"Fine."

"*What?*" he asked.

"I said fine," she persisted.

"I'm afraid I wasn't serious," Thomas said.

"I'm afraid I am." She withdrew her hand.

"That house is sealed by law." He saw her grimace distastefully as he
spoke. He could practically feel her disapproval. "The state closes an
estate upon the death of its owner. It would take a court order for us to
get in. The fact is, I could file a motion for—"

"You disappoint me," she said softly.

"I disappoint a lot of people." He shrugged. "But I won't break the law
to win a case. I warned you already. I'm a lousy lawyer. Maybe that's the
reason."

She glanced back to the mansion, then to him, dark eyes probing. Then
the tension on her face melted. She took his arm and said, "I'm sorry.
Let's walk down Madison Avenue."

They turned the corner, putting the Sandler mansion at their backs.
The icy wind swept uptown toward them and blasted them head-on. With

one arm she held her coat close to her and with the other held his. He could feel her warmth contrasting with the cold in the air. He wondered again who that warmth was and what she wanted.

"Tell me where you've been," she said, as casually as an old friend might. "You've been away. Was it for me?"

"Partly," he lied. He told a fabricated story of interviewing old contacts and associates.

"But did you discover anything important?" she asked. "About my father? Or yours?"

"No," he said.

She shrugged. "An honest answer, at least," she said. He glanced sidways at her and saw not the slightest hint of sarcasm on her lips. Only a sudden smile as she looked ahead.

"Look at this," she said, "an art gallery."

"Madison is loaded with them."

"I never knew that," she said. She stood before a large plate-glass window in which the Anspacher Gallery announced a showing by an American impressionist named Gerald Detweiler.

A smile crossed her face now. She was like a small girl beholding a toy store two weeks before Christmas. Her grin was impish, girlish, and excited, and she turned to him warmly now and asked as a child might ask a parent, "Can we go in?"

"It's a free country," he said.

"Come on," she said, sprightly, her clipped British accent slightly more noticeable. "I never tire of other people's artwork." She pulled him along and they entered the crowded gallery. It was opening day of the exhibit. The gallery, which occupied the lower three floors of a converted brownstone, was packed. She seemed to feed emotionally on the enthusiastic bustle of the gallery, as if it excited her and allowed her for a few minutes to put Arthur Sandler out of her mind.

She led him from one canvas to the next, canvases which rendered impressionistic interpretations to northeastern-American landscapes. Factories by the sides of rivers, crowded beaches bordering empty oceans, dry-docked pleasure boats tied up beside foreboding dark lakes. "Always man bordering nature," Leslie observed, moving from painting to painting. "Bordering by confrontation. A standoff, really," she said. "Do you go to galleries often?"

"I've never had much time for it," he admitted, wondering why she perceived so much on canvases where he saw so little.

"A shame," she said. "You should make a point to go more often." He vaguely resented her tone of voice, as if she were gently talking down to him.

"Maybe we should talk more about your father," he suggested. "I have some questions."

She either didn't hear the question or chose not to hear it. She stepped close to a canvas, examining closely the texture of a Maine landscape dominated by pastel blues, greens, and yellows. "Look at those brush-strokes," she said. "Detweiler studied Monet. You can tell. Sorry?"

"Your father," he said. He was slightly jostled by a stout dark man with a cigar pushing to get past, accompanied by a hard-faced woman with silver-blond hair.

Leslie's face twisted into a slight frown. She had forgotten about Sandler. Thomas had reminded her. "What about him?" she asked, sounding as if the subject were an intrusion here. He began to sense an evasion, an unwillingness to discuss the very topic that had initially brought her to him. Why had she brought him into an art gallery, he wondered. To divert his attention?

"I'm trying to discover as much about him as possible," he said.

Her eyes glimmered and she gave him a smile. "That's good. But you probably know more than I do already."

"Why do you say that?"

"Why"—as if it were self-evident—"you knew one man who knew him very well. Your *own* father."

Strange, he thought, how she constantly turned each question, putting him back on the defensive. He would have expected it from another attorney or an investigator of some sort. But not from a scholar and aspiring artist.

"My father never talked to me about Arthur Sandler," Thomas answered, jostled again from behind by a large balding man jockeying for position near a painting. Thomas took Leslie's arm and led her to a less crowded section.

"Never at all?" Her eyes were sharply probing.

He considered it briefly and seriously. "No," he said, searching his memory. "Other clients from time to time. But never Arthur Sandler."

"I see," she said thoughtfully, as if his words had been meaningful.

They began to examine other paintings, more absorbed in their discussion now than in what they viewed. He tried a different line of questioning. Every once in a while he would look at her, want to believe her, and see the tombstone in the London churchyard.

"What about the British government?" he asked casually.

"Labour," she said. "Unfortunately, I support the Liberals."

"That's not what I mean, as I'm sure you know."

"Sorry," she apologized. "I don't mean to be flippant. But what's the question?"

"Your foster father," he said. "Or that man you said you knew in British Intelligence. What's his name?"

"Peter Whiteside?"

"Yes," he said. They were walking in the general direction of an elevator which led upstairs. They politely edged their way through the assemblage. Thomas was conscious of no one in particular other than the man with the cigar who'd bumped him once before. The man was now waving a checkbook at the gallery's manager and loudly trying to bargain on a price. "McAdam and Whiteside. What help would they be?"

"None at all," she said. "They're both dead. Shall we go upstairs?"

"Dead?"

"Dead," she repeated. "It's a condition that sets in as soon as the heart stops."

"You never told me Whiteside was dead."

She looked at him curiously. "You never asked," she countered, frowning. "Why? Why is it important?"

He shook his head. "Dead since when?" he demanded.

They stood by the elevator and waited. All three of them were dead, Leslie and the two others, depending on whom one asked. Funny thing was, they all looked healthy. He studied her carefully, just as he'd study a witness on the stand, trying to discern not just whether she was lying. "Dead how? And why?"

"My God, you're persistent," she said, irritated. "I thought we could relax and look at a few paintings."

"You *hired* me. Remember?"

"Sorry," she said. He saw that she twisted her hands nervously for just a moment. Then she seemed to catch herself. She held her handbag, covering her anxiety. "It's an unpleasant subject," she said. "They were the only two men I could trust. I'll explain."

"Please," he said.

The elevator arrived, returning from upstairs with six aboard. It was a small elevator, the sort one finds added into narrow older buildings. Two steel doors opened, sliding each way from the center, to disgorge the passengers. Thomas and Leslie waited for the six to step out, then boarded the elevator themselves. They were followed by two meaty businessmen who pushed past them within the small elevator and stood behind them. Leslie eyed them nervously. One man carried a brown woolen scarf in his thick hands. The other leaned across and pushed the button for the top floor.

Thomas pushed the button for three. The door closed. Thomas looked at Leslie and she exchanged a glance with him, one that said they'd continue their discussion outside the elevator. Thomas gave a slight nod and the elevator passed the second floor.

The elevator rattled as part of its standard operating procedure. Then it jerked to a hesitant halt at three. The steel doors jolted open quickly. Thomas allowed Leslie to step out first.

Thomas stepped out of the elevator. Then, at the same instant that he heard the doors start to close, the brown scarf suddenly looped downward over his head.

It caught him around the throat and yanked him backward toward the elevator.

He gagged and fell against the closed door of the elevator, his hands and fingers digging at his throat.

The scarf, tight as a hangman's noose around his neck, was still being held from within the elevator, but was also being clutched within the steel doors. The elevator began to rise.

He kicked and banged. Leslie whirled, gasping. The scarf was pulling him upward. In five more seconds his neck would be crushed. He flailed with his feet, but it was no use. He was being lifted off the ground. He could sense his death.

From the corners of his bulging eyes he could see Leslie, frozen where she stood.

She didn't scream. She didn't panic.

What the hell's she doing? he thought. Standing! Watching! She drew me here for this!

Suddenly she bolted toward him, tearing open her purse.

He saw something flash in her hand, and he saw it was a blade.

Her hand went to his throat and the knife dug—not into his flesh, but behind him. The blade practically knicked his ear, and he could hear it bite at the steel door.

She slashed. Once. Twice. A third time and he was falling, awkwardly pinning an ankle beneath him.

He gasped and coughed violently. She'd cut the scarf, slashing him free. His throat felt as if it had been run over by a truck. Her hand was on his back, making sure he could breathe. Tears were on his cheeks. His eyes, which had felt as if they were going to explode out of his head, were flooding.

He could later remember his first thought. Not of fear, not of perverse exhilaration at having been nearly killed. It was fury. Those two men. He wanted to grab her knife and charge after them, using the stairs to corner them on the floor above.

He tried to rise.

"Easy, easy," she said, holding him. He still tried to stand. But his legs were rubbery and he couldn't get up. He continued to cough, almost retching with each convulsion of his windpipe. She clicked the knife closed with one hand and shoved it into a coat pocket with remarkable dexterity. No one else had seen it.

No one, in fact, had seen anything.

"Yes," she said, almost in a whisper. "You're all right." Her voice was as soft as the hand on his shoulder. "Let them go. They failed. Don't go after them."

He was still coughing. A horrified crowd was gathering, asking what had happened. A man in a dark suit, in charge of the floor, pushed his way through and asked if he could help.

Leslie explained. "His scarf caught in the elevator," she said. "It's all right now."

There were gasps, mostly from women. "Careless," Thomas heard a man's voice mutter. "Ought to be more careful." Thomas tried to rise. His legs were still unsteady and disobedient. He continued to cough violently and uncontrollably. And the one voice which he continued to hear was Leslie's, close by his ear, in a protective English whisper, repeating soothingly, "It's all right now; take your time. Wait till you can breathe comfortably and for God's sake don't say anything."

He was happy he could still breathe. Talking could wait.

Chapter 17

They were at a corner table in the rear of a small dimly lit pub on Madison Avenue, a quiet, genteel watering hole frequented by the well-heeled clientele of the East Side neighborhood.

There was draft beer in mugs on their table, accompanying half-eaten steaks. Thomas's throat hurt when he swallowed, a nagging cough persisted, and he wondered whether or not he needed a doctor. Food was one thing he *did* need, he admitted, though the incident at the Anspacher Gallery was not the sort that triggered hearty appetites.

He sipped the beer.

"How's it feel?" she asked, apparently sympathetic.

"The throat?"

She nodded, concern on her face.

"Awful," he said, his voice catching and irritating as he spoke. "But at least it works. Air goes in and out. What more can I ask?"

"You were on the verge of asking many things," she reminded him.

"So I was."

She worked on her steak with a fork and knife, holding the utensils European style, and eating with what he took to be a great deal of calm —unlike himself, he noted. He was still shaken.

"It's rather shattering," he pondered aloud. "Someone trying to kill you."

"It is," she said.

He studied her. "Of course," he said. "You'd know, wouldn't you?"
She nodded.

He glanced at the razor-thin scar across her neck, barely visible in the dim pub. He was conscious of the soft pop voice of Judy Collins from the jukebox. "All in all, my throat got off better than yours." He paused. "Who were they?"

"I don't know," she said definitively. Her voice was brisk and authoritative. Not the voice of the aspiring artist, but rather that of the woman who carried a knife in her purse.

"You must have an idea," he said.

"None at all. You're closer to the answer than I am."

"Me?" He coughed. "Why do you keep coming back to me?"

"Because that's where it begins," she insisted. "It's not just *my* father. It's Arthur Sandler's connection to William Ward Daniels."

"Lawyer and client," he answered.

She was shaking her head before he was finished.

"More than that," she insisted, eyes flashing. "Much more."

"How can you be so certain?"

"Very easily. My aunt dies, bringing the family to an *apparent* end. Her death means a will, a search for heirs. That means that the family's dirty laundry will have to be public. Old files opened, examined. What files burn? Yours. Your father's, more specifically." She motioned at the air with both hands, palms open. "Something was in those files. More than a will. Maybe the key to where my father is. Or *who* he is. Or maybe there's some indication that *I* exist."

"But it's twenty years after the fact," he said, perplexed. "Who'd care now?"

"My father," she offered quickly.

"How do you even know he's alive?"

"Maybe this proves it," she said. "You know as well as I do that the scarf around your neck was no accident. Maybe you know something," she pressed adamantly. "Maybe something crucial which might not seem so important to you, but which—"

He was shaking his head, every bit as insistent as she. "Nothing," he said. "I know absolutely nothing about the Sandlers. Only what you tell me. And what's public record."

She fell silent, looking down at her plate in thought. "Whom did you go see?" she asked. "When you were away?"

He weighed the question and knew it was one he didn't yet want to answer.

"No one important," he said.

"Zenger again?"

"No one important," he said. Only people who insisted she was an impostor. No way he was delving into that yet. Someone in a well-tailored female form existed. He knew because she'd just saved his life. When she'd come through in a moment like that, how much else could he hold against her?

"All right, don't tell me," she said sourly and with evident disappointment. "But someone you've seen has betrayed you. Someone thinks you know too much already."

"Me?" he posed. "Why not you?"

"They wanted to kill you first," she said. And she smiled with gloriously sweet sarcasm, letting her point rest.

"True," he admitted.

A waitress cleared the table and brought coffee. He was silent as he tried to put events in order and find the pattern. He glanced at her and felt helpless. There *was* no pattern.

Damn her, he thought, she was perfectly calm. She was asking better questions than he, and for that matter was running a damned fine interrogation. Maybe she should have gone to law school in his place, he thought. He'd learn how to paint.

He sipped the coffee. Its warmth soothed his throat slightly. He broke the silence, seeking to change the drift of the conversation at the same time.

"You know quite a bit about art," he said.

"Very little, actually."

"What about forgeries?"

Her coffee cup hesitated between the saucer and her mouth, then returned to the saucer untouched by her lips.

"Forgeries?" she asked, as if seeking a further elaboration of the word. He nodded, his turn to be calm.

"Art forgeries?" she asked. He nodded again. "I know they exist," she said. "Usually a counterfeit is made of a painting that actually exists. Then a transfer is made, gulling people into believing that the bogus one is the original." She frowned. "Why?" Her voice was suspicious.

"Think that could be done with people?" he asked, leaning back slightly. Damn it, he had to cough slightly.

"Counterfeit people?" she asked.

He nodded as they considered it.

"An imposter for the original? Is that the question?" She was pensive and his impression was that she was not acting. But he couldn't be certain. "I suppose it could be done," she said. "Why?"

"Just a theory."

"I'd *love* to hear it," she said, leaning forward with obvious interest.

He shook his head. "I told you, I discuss facts, not theories. Sorry. When I have facts I'll be glad to—"

"I save your life and this is my thanks?" she inquired, gently chiding and not really challenging him. If he didn't want to tell her now, she seemed to be saying, he didn't have to.

So he changed the subject. "That reminds me," he said, "that wasn't an emery board you cut me down with. Do you always carry it?"

"A girl needs protection."

"It's against the law, you know."

"Law?" She looked at him disbelievingly and laughed. "I'll take my chances," she said with a certain bitterness. He didn't ask how she'd become so proficient with it. Instead he had the sense of having said something silly.

Again he changed the subject. "Let's go way back before the elevator," he said. "You were about to tell me about George McAdam and Peter Whiteside."

There was an uneasy silence for a moment. She pursed her lips, as if wondering how much to say, then folded her hands on the table before her, pushing the plate away. She looked him in the eye as if to speak from the soul.

"Yes, of course," she said absently. "You should know. I should have told you already." It was as if an eloquent debate were taking place within her, conflicting urges to tell the truth against an impulse not to reveal too much. Clearly she was struggling with it. She looked up at him and saw him studying her. She perhaps realized that she appeared evasive. So she blurted out the truth. "George McAdam was a 'sandhog.' "

"A what?"

She looked perplexed, as if to wonder, "You mean you don't even know *that*? Are *you* lying to me, or are you just plain ignorant?" But she said nothing other than, "Let's go for a walk. I'll tell you about it."

They were on Lexington—as usual she was choosing the direction. They carefully watched around them, nervously paying attention to each car that passed and anyone walking too closely behind them. She chose to walk uptown on an avenue that came downtown, so that they could see traffic approaching. No mistake. She knew the tricks. More than he did, he was reminded, and it was a good thing she did. She'd saved his life once already. But then again, it was his sudden involvement with her that had almost cost him his life in the first place.

Or so it appeared.

"Sandhogs," he said.

"A nickname." She walked beside him, close but not holding his arm. Her coat was pulled tightly around her and her hands were thrust protectively into her coat pockets. She watched ahead and didn't look at him as she spoke.

"Keep going," he said.

"It was the nickname given to agents within a certain branch of the S.I.S."

"S.I.S.?"

She glanced at him quickly, then looked away again. "Never heard of it?" she asked. He wasn't sure if there was suspicion in her voice.

"Never."

"Sorry. Secret Intelligence Service," she said. "British, of course."

"Continue."

They walked northward.

"In this branch were the agents who had a certain sort of expertise," she said. "You already know my foster father was in the Middle East when he was shot. What comes out of sand?"

It took him only a moment. "Oil."

"Oil," she confirmed. "I pieced it all together over the years, just as I pieced together who I was. The sandhogs were the British agents in oil intelligence. Long ago the British government realized that it was burning more oil than was healthy. Great Britain is an island, dependent on its imports. As long ago as the fifties any intelligent observer could have told you that England could be brought to its knees if its petroleum imports were cut off. There's never been any secret."

He listened intently as they walked.

"I have no idea what the sandhogs were doing. All I know is that he, McAdam, was back and forth in different parts of the world. Standard cloak-and-dagger stuff, I'm sure. It was on one of those intrigues that he got shot in the hip in 1953. Before he retired and took me on as a daughter."

He nodded. The icy wind made him pull his coat collar tight.

"Well," she continued, "some men can never retire. They miss the excitement. Or maybe it's just the violence and the blood they miss. My foster mother died in 1968. That left my foster father in Switzerland, limping around in an empty house staring at the lake and longing to be back in the service."

"At his age?"

"At his age. And as it happened, S.I.S. were willing to take him back.

They had an operation in a different part of the world that needed sorting out. An area where no one would know him, they thought. Venezuela. South American oil instead of Middle Eastern." She smiled. "It all gives off the same stench when it burns."

They turned another corner and were now on a side street east of Lexington Avenue. "Can I ask where we're going?" he said.

"See that sign down there?" she asked, pointing halfway down the block to a sign saying READER AND ADVISER, MADAME DIANE. *"That's* where we're going."

They walked. She continued to speak.

"My foster father had contacted another man in the Service. The man in Whitehall who was his immediate superior and to whom he would be reporting once his new assignment began. They planned to rendezvous in Maracaibo. They did, in fact. Then they went on to Caracas. Eventually they were heading north to the United States. There might have been a meeting with some U.S. intelligence service. I don't know. I only know they never arrived."

"Why not?"

They stopped short and stood immediately beneath the READER AND ADVISER sign.

Leslie glanced at the vacant doorway to the gypsy's parlor.

"The airplane blew up an hour after takeoff," she said. "A Caracas-to-Miami flight. June 14, 1971. Sabotaged. And it wasn't an accident that they were on it. I suspect it was sabotaged for them expressly. After all, there are agents from the 'other side'—as my foster father used to call it —who are actively seeking the oil down there. And with one well-placed bomb, the top British sandhog and his superior were eliminated from the region." She looked at Thomas, studying him for his reaction.

He listened to her story with compassion and sympathy. He believed her just as he had on the first day she'd come to his office. And just as he'd believed the man in London calling himself Peter Whiteside.

"And that, Thomas," she said in softer tones, "is why my foster father can't be of help anymore."

"What about Peter Whiteside?" he asked.

Her smile was pained. She shook her head. "Sometimes you can be very slow," she answered.

He looked at her quizzically as if to ask what she meant.

"Who do you think his superior was?" she asked. "The second man on the airplane."

There was a long pause and he felt a tumbling sensation in his stomach. "Naturally," he finally muttered.

"You've learned a lot today," she said. "Now I'll teach you one thing more. The defense of the rabbit. The fleet escape. Never go into a place which you can't get out of in at least three ways. Follow me in five seconds. You'll see what I mean."

She leaned forward and was no longer a teacher, but rather a woman and a lover. She kissed him on the lips and had him so starved for her physical affection that he tried to pull her closer by drawing him into her arms.

But she'd have none of that. It wasn't time. No sooner did he try to draw her closer than she resisted firmly and pulled back.

"I'll be back in touch," she said. "Remember. Follow in five seconds."

He stood there completely mystified as she briskly went up the stairs beneath the sign of Madame Diane. Thomas watched from the sidewalk, then followed after a slow count to five.

He went quickly up the stairs, reached a dingy hallway at the top, and heard nothing. There were four alternatives. More steps leading up. A corridor to the right, a corridor to the left. Back stairs leading down. All four marked with exit signs.

She'd known this place, which thicket could best confuse the hounds. She was gone. Had anyone been following them, she would have led the pursuer here and easily slipped away.

Her lesson had been well illustrated. He'd learned it.

For himself, he chose the corridor to the left, the one leading past Madame Diane's emporium of guidance. He passed down a side stairway into an alleyway between buildings.

He thought of sandhogs, alive and dead, on his way home, men whose lives and jobs orbited the three spheres of blood, sand, and oil. McAdam and Whiteside. Men or mirages? And what about Leslie? A cooperative client in desperate need of help? Or a treacherous conniver?

Or both?

During the long walk through the icy wind, he wondered who was real, who was imagined, and who lay in the murky area somewhere in between.

He pulled his coat close to him. Each shadow he passed on that cold night, each stranger coming near him on the sidewalk, represented a multitude of fears. In the same way, the empty apartment he would return to represented a certain loneliness which, at his point in life, he no longer wished to face each night.

He wished that she were coming home with him. But he had no idea where she was, much less who she was.

It had never escaped Shassad's thoughts that the slaying of Mark Ryder had been done with such surgical precision that it had the mark of professionals. Similarly, what Minnie Yankovich had described had sounded more akin to an elaborately disguised execution than a mugging.

Shassad looked at Mrs. Ryder in her moment of most acute grief. He knew what his job was.

No, she said, she hadn't seen her husband since the morning he'd last left for work. No, he had no enemies that she could think of, nobody to whom he was in debt, and she knew of no one whom he might have been seeing whom he didn't approve of. Shassad gallantly refrained from asking the next obvious questions: Did she have any idea where her husband might have planned to spend the night? Did she have any idea that he was seeing another woman? The answers were obvious.

On the morning following Ryder's identification Detective Patrick Hearn had arrived at the offices of Bradford, Mehr & Company, where by five minutes past nine he had obtained a photocopy of Ryder's employment records. Subsequently, Hearn interviewed Ryder's co-workers, none of whom could suggest anyone harboring a grudge against the deceased. To those who seemed to have known Ryder best, Hearn posed one further question: "Do you happen to know if there were any women in addition to his wife?"

Invariably the answer was no, clearly and simply, except in one instance.

A young man of Ryder's age, an executive trainee named Durban Hayvis, balked perceptibly before also answering no.

On a hunch, Hearn spent an extra hour going over address lists of company employees, hoping one—a female one—might read 246 East 73rd Street. None did. The closest address was 316 East 94th Street, the address of Mr. Hayvis. No immediate significance.

However, Hearn did much better two hours later.

He had gone to the Seventy-third Street building itself, and sought to interview the remaining tenants. He finally managed to locate the most elusive, a single girl, early twenties, going by the name of Debbie Moran. Hearn had been seeking her since Daniels had first mentioned the nocturnal activity in her apartment.

Debbie lived in Apartment 3-C, on the floor below Thomas Daniels. She invited the detective in and sat demurely on a large white vinyl couch with large plush cushions, her legs folded under her in tight jeans. The detective sat across the room and questioned her.

Debbie Moran puffed a cigarette carefully and spoke politely with a hint of a New York accent. She gave her profession as a part-time actress and part-time model. Her hometown, she said, was St. Paul, Minnesota.

"Actress, huh?" asked Hearn with interest. "Maybe I've seen you in something. Broadway? Off Broadway?"

"No, probably not."

"Movies?"

The "no" was hesitant. Her eyes lowered to the ashtray. Hearn glanced around the room. The furniture was both modern and reasonably expensive, centered around a large comfortable sofa. The adjoining bedroom, which Hearn eyed when he asked if he could use the washroom, was dominated by an expensive waterbed. The apartment was designed, in its way, for comfort, for satisfaction, and as a den of voluntary seduction. Under further questioning Debbie Moran admitted that she just remembered what her last acting job had been. "A series of TV commercials on the West coast," she volunteered. "It's not being shown no more."

Hearn reached to an inside jacket pocket and handed her a picture of Mark Ryder.

"Ever seen this man?" he asked.

She glanced at it. "No."

He watched her for a moment, studying the facial features and expression.

She handed back the photograph.

"You're sure?" he asked.

"I'm sure."

"That man was murdered in front of this building," he said.

"How awful."

"He was visiting someone in this building."

She shrugged.

"What we're interested in," he said, "is what time he left, not what he was doing here."

"I live in the back of the building," she said. "I sleep soundly. I didn't see no one or hear no one. I go to bed early."

And often, thought Hearn. All the way back to the precinct he cursed her.

Hearn found Shassad sitting at his cluttered desk on the cramped second floor. Behind Shassad was his bulletin board on which, in addition to items of more importance, there were two small posters. One pictured a blue-uniformed police officer guarding a school crossing, set in an idealized suburban America of the mid-1950s. The caption read, "The Police Officer is your friend. Trust him." The other, hand-lettered by an anonymous precinct-house philosopher, proclaimed simply, "God loves Negroes. That's why there's so many of them."

"I found the girl," Hearn said.

"Apartment Three-C?"

Hearn nodded. "A high-priced hooker," he said, "unless my eyesight is failing. What I don't know is whether she's doing bar pickups or whether she has a little black book. There's no other female in the building who Ryder would have been on top of."

"Did you show her Ryder's picture?"

"She recognized it. And she wouldn't talk."

"Okay," said Shassad casually but with satisfaction. "We know what's next."

By the next morning, Shassad had obtained four extra detectives, two teams of two, to aid in the Ryder case. A surveillance unit in a panel truck was placed on Seventy-third Street to observe Debbie Moran. At four fifty that afternoon she emerged from her building, hailed a yellow cab, and led two detectives in a plain car to Gypsy's Bar at Fifty-fifth between Sixth and Seventh avenues.

Ten minutes later an undercover detective from the Midtown Anti-Vice Squad (known in the police vulgate as the "Pussy Posse") entered the bar. The detective's name was Samuel McGowan. His partner was a policewoman named Theresa Duchecki, better known as Saint Theresa for reasons which were clear to anyone who'd met her. McGowan was wired.

McGowan spotted Debbie sitting alone at the center of the bar. He approached the bar and seated himself at the far right end. He watched the clock until twenty minutes past five. Then, certain that she'd been watching him, he initiated an aimless conversation.

Several minutes passed. Debbie wanted to know if she was wasting her time. "Look," she finally purred, leaning slightly forward so that McGowan could look down her dress, "what do you say we cut out the talk and have some fun?"

"I'm having fun right now," he said.

"Come on, sugar," she intoned, "I have a nice apartment where I'm all alone."

"I don't know," he said, fidgeting with his drink.

"You look like the type of guy who'll pay to have a super evening."

"Pay?"

"Don't you like what you see, sugar?"

"Sure," he stammered, "but, uh, well . . . How much?"

"A hundred and fifty dollars," she whispered, never suspecting that the cigarette case in his pocket contained a microphone and no tobacco. "You get whatever you want twice. And I have to be back here by ten o'clock."

"Let's go," he said.

They went, but not to Seventy-third Street. They were no farther than the sidewalk when they were joined by Saint Theresa. They didn't have to tell Debbie she was under arrest. She knew immediately.

"We've pegged something wrong somewhere," Hearn said, sipping lukewarm coffee from a plastic container. "Maybe they *were* a pair of standard muggers dressed up in good coats."

"No way, Patty," said Shassad, his dark eyes narrowing. "You saw those knife wounds. A surgeon couldn't make better incisions."

"Then what's wrong?" asked an exasperated Hearn, heavy circles forming beneath his eyes.

Then finding no method to the crime, Hearn sarcastically answered his own question. "Maybe they got the wrong man."

Shassad, in thought, said nothing. But his eyes were wide. "Jumping Jesus," Shassad then said softly. "Of course. The wrong man."

"What?"

"Debbie Moran and her rent-a-muff had nothing to do with it. Try this: Her customer—Ryder—had the luck to walk out the building at the wrong second. Two professionals were there waiting for a hit. But not Ryder. No one cared about him. No, sir. They were waiting for someone more important who was supposed to step out precisely the same time. *And who nearly did.*"

Hearn twisted his face, half in enlightenment, half in skepticism. "Daniels?" he asked.

"Yeah," said Shassad, opening his hands expansively. "Yeah, why the hell not?" They paused and considered it. "He said himself that he was coming out right at that same time."

Shassad paused a few seconds between sentences, stopping to think as he spoke. "How big is Daniels? Five ten? Five eleven?"

"Approximately."

"Same as Ryder, right?"

Hearn nodded.

"Coloring? Hair? Build? All similar, right? Similar enough to be mistaken by people who were waiting for a man they'd never met before? Waiting on a rainy night in January when they knew their victim would be coming out of that building."

"But they'd have to know right down to the minute in order to jump to a conclusion like that?"

"Of course. They *did* know. Don't you see?"

"Sorry. No."

"The janitor wanted to know almost to the minute how soon Daniels would be leaving. Remember?"

Hearn's face was assuming a slow glow.

"And sure," said Shassad, getting to his feet excitedly and slapping the back of an open palm into his other hand, "one of the men on the street was back and forth to the telephone. That's how *they* knew when to look for Daniels. They were tipped from Thirty-first Street. Huh? What do you think?" Shassad folded his arms against his chest, as if in summation of his case.

"I like it," answered Hearn slowly. He was thoughtful. "Ryder goes out the front door while Daniels steps out the back. Poof. Ryder gets carved in Daniels's place. Now," he added with an almost imperceptible pause, "who wants Daniels dead?"

"Only one possibility in the world so far," said Shassad. "Jacobus!"

"Why?"

Shassad poked at the air with a forefinger. "That's what we find out next."

Jacobus was the thin thread which stitched Shassad's theory together. Like the slaying of Ryder, Jacobus also made little sense.

Shassad had reassigned two support teams of detectives. No longer did they shadow Thomas Daniels in hopes that the young attorney would lead them to the missing woman. Instead, Jacobus was now under twenty-four-hour surveillance by three different two-man detective teams. After three days, the accumulation of information on Jacobus had been a genuine team effort. No one had discovered anything.

Shassad and Hearn were plainly worried. Jacobus's house in Astoria had been watched; no one unusual had come or gone. The night custodian had been followed to work as he drove his dented aging Ford from Queens to Manhattan and left it in a metered parking place on Thirtieth Street off Park Avenue South, a similar location each night. He'd been under intense scrutiny for several days and Shassad's theory of his link to the Ryder murder was fading quickly. "Just another stiff in another crummy job," had been Shassad's recurrent thought after observing the man. "Just like the rest of us."

Jacobus's thumbprint had been taken from his home mailbox and had been sent downtown to the crime laboratory for a fingerprint analysis. A police photographer, concealed in the office building across the street at 460 Park Avenue South, had taken thirty-some telephoto snapshots of the man. And Shassad had made arrangements to visit Jacobus's bank to peer into his financial status.

But as the two detectives sat in Hearn's car on lower Park Avenue, surveying the entrance of 457 Park Avenue South for the third consecutive night, the possible involvement of Jacobus as a homicide conspirator seemed less and less likely. By night, no one came or went from the building in which Jacobus worked. And the only occasional company the detectives had in the nocturnally quiet section of Manhattan was that of the large white sanitation trucks which prowled the streets picking up refuse.

On the third night of their stakeout, three A.M. passed quietly. Then three thirty.

Hearn nudged Shassad sharply, taken by surprise himself. "Hey," he said excitedly. "What's this?" He motioned with his head and indicated an activity halfway down Thirtieth Street. He raised the binoculars to his eyes.

The two detectives had been ignoring the side street. They'd become sleepy and their attention had lagged. They didn't even know where the dark green Chevy Nova on Thirtieth Street had come from. Nor did they know how long it had been there. What they could see was that the car had double-parked next to Jacobus's battered old Ford. And the driver of the Nova was a busy man.

The man stood behind his own car and unlocked the trunk. He opened it slightly, but didn't raise the rear hood. He moved directly behind Jacobus's car and seemed to fumble with something small.

"What is it? What is it?" asked Shassad.

"Keys," Hearn said. "He's got keys to Jacobus's car."

"What the hell . . . ?" asked Shassad rhetorically. He was totally perplexed now, the odd scene on Thirtieth Street making no sense yet. "Get his license number."

The rear hood of Jacobus's car went up. Then the man left Jacobus's trunk wide open and stepped quickly back to his own car.

He opened his own trunk. Then, with obvious effort, he reached in and picked up a large canvas bag, the size of a post-office mailbag or a sack of flour. He pulled it out, hoisted it over his shoulder, stepped with a slight wobble to Jacobus's trunk, leaned forward, and as best he could eased the bag into the Ford.

Then with one hand he reached in and picked up another sack. This one was much lighter, though the same size. It was bulky, but obviously not nearly as heavy.

The man hoisted the second bag over his shoulder, stepped back to his own car, and dumped the bag almost carelessly into his trunk. He then slammed down both trunks, and hurried back to the wheel of his own car.

"I don't get it," said Shassad. "Not at all."

The lights of the Nova went on. The engine started. Hearn was still staring through glasses.

"You're going to love this part," he said.

"What?"

"It's a DPL license, New York State." Shassad almost gawked at his partner. Diplomatic plates. The car was registered to an embassy or consulate within New York City. Since when did diplomats play musical trunks with janitors? The unmarked police car moved slowly to the corner.

"I can't stand it," cursed Shassad. "See whether he goes straight or turns."

Hearn leaned forward, barely able to keep the binoculars focused on the Nova. The car was moving now, approaching the red traffic light at the end of the block at Lexington and Thirtieth.

Hearn watched the car ease to the corner, never halt completely, and turn.

"He ran the light," said Hearn.

Shassad could stand it no longer. "A *red* one?"

Knowing what his partner was thinking, Hearn nodded the leprechaun grin he saved for moments of special joy.

"Let's go fuck him," said Shassad.

The red beacon was still flashing on the dashboard of the unmarked police car. The Nova had been pulled to the curb on Lexington Avenue. Shassad and Hearn approached it from different sides.

The driver of the Nova, sitting with his arms folded, looked through the window at Shassad.

"Lower that window or I'll punch it in!" snapped Shassad. "I want a license and registration out of you!" He banged the window twice with his fist.

Hearn watched the driver and inspected the Nova from the other side.

With deliberateness that was meant to antagonize, the man at the wheel slowly rolled down the window. "What seems to be the problem?" he asked calmly in foreign-accented English.

"You! License and registration."

Grudgingly the driver handed both documents to Shassad. "I'm a member of the diplomatic corps," he said.

Hearn eyed the trunk of the car. Then he walked around to join Shassad.

Shassad glanced at the man's license. André Corescaneu, an attaché of the Romanian delegation to the United Nations. Shassad knew he couldn't touch him with a motor-vehicle violation. He also knew he couldn't tip his hand and let Corescaneu know that Jacobus, whom the Romanian obviously knew, was the subject of surveillance. There was no other choice. The detectives would have to slip into their act. It called for a temper tantrum.

"You see?" said Corescaneu. "Diplomat. You cannot—"

"Get out."

"What?"

"Get *out!*" roared Shassad. "Get out of that car before I haul you out!"

Apprehension showed on the diplomat's face. "You can't—"

"The rules are off, fella," barked Shassad, glaring into the car. "I'm doing whatever I want tonight."

Corescaneu was flabbergasted, not knowing how to react.

"Come on, come on," Hearn said. "Calm down." He put his hand on his partner's shoulder.

"No, fuck it!" screamed Shassad. "I've had it with these frigging foreigners. I'm writing him up!"

Hearn looked at the man in the car. His expression was one of compromise. "Look. My buddy's in a real bad mood. Step out and we can all calm down."

Corescaneu looked at Hearn carefully, then complied.

"I'm running him in," said Shassad. "Fuck his diplomatic immunity. I'm arresting him!"

"You can't ar—" began Corescaneu.

"Don't tell me what I can't do!" snapped Shassad, his eyes raging. "Don't you know what a red light means?"

The Romanian shook his head.

"Liar," snarled Shassad. He looked down at the license and registration. "How do I know this is you?" he asked.

"Of course it's me," said Corescaneu defensively.

"Prove it."

Indignantly, Corescaneu did what Shassad wished. He produced a passport. Hearn noted the number.

Corescaneu was obviously concerned now. Not by any legal trouble that he'd be in, his diplomatic status would protect him. What he feared was harrassment from an enraged local police officer. Shassad paced up and down beside the car, looking for something wrong.

"I say this is a hot car," he finally decided.

"Hot?"

"He means stolen," Hearn offered.

Corescaneu kept looking around, feeling trapped and in danger. "Is not a stolen car," he said.

"Prove it."

He pointed to the registration.

"That don't mean nothing," sneered Shassad.

"Hey, Aram, take it easy," said Hearn.

"I want this fucker fingerprinted. I want the car searched." He looked back to the diplomat. "What's in the trunk?" he asked.

"Nothing."

"Bullshit," Shassad said. "I'm having you towed in."

Shassad went back to his car, as if to use a radio, which he didn't have. Corescaneu protested heatedly.

"Why don't you let him look in the trunk," suggested Hearn. "That'll cool him down. If he's convinced you haven't got anything, he'll let you go."

The diplomat looked back and forth between the two cops. "All right," he finally said. "There is nothing."

With amazing eagerness, convinced that the detectives would never understand the implication of what they were looking at, Corescaneu opened the burlap sack and pulled out one dozen empty film cans, cans used to store movie film, the size of reels used for a standard professional projector.

"What's all this for?" Shassad asked.

Corescaneu explained. He pointed to a name tag on the sack. He had a friend who worked for a Romanian film company, Rota Films, located on Varick Street. The friend didn't own a car. So Corescaneu, good Samaritan that he was, was helping his friend move the dozen empty film cans.

"I just picked up the bag down on Varick Street," the diplomat offered.

"Is that a fact?" mumbled Shassad, apparently appeased.

"See?" said Hearn to his partner, appearing to grow bored with their captive. "He's just a wild foreign driver. But there's nothing in his car."

Corescaneu nodded eagerly. "Is nothing," he said.

"Come on, Aram," said Hearn. "Let's have some coffee and forget about it."

Shassad shot Corescaneu a withering look. "Get those cans together and get out of here," he said. "And if I ever see you run a light again, I'll run you in for reckless endangerment."

"You can't," said Corescaneu without thinking. Shassad's eyes blazed. The diplomat quickly turned, fumbled the loose cans together, closed the trunk and hopped back into his car before Shassad could change his mind.

Shassad and Hearn sat in the warmth of their car.

"I got a hunch," said Shassad, perfectly calm, lighting a cigarette. "I say we scored. I say now we snoop around Rota Films."

Chapter 20

He looked at her from across the city newsroom. Andrea was seated at her desk, leaning back in her chair. A man two decades older than she, a professorial-looking man who'd gracefully entered his later years, sat on the edge of her desk and engaged her in a subdued but intense conversation. Even before they saw him, Thomas Daniels knew who the man was. He had a sense of intruding.

"Thomas," she said with animation when she spotted him. She leaned forward quickly, then stood. "You're just who we were talking about."

She embraced him fondly. "I'm sure you were," he said flatly.

The older man was on his feet now. He was standing uncomfortably, waiting to be introduced.

"This is Augie Reid," she said. "He covers Albany and the idiots in the state legislature for us."

"I know," Thomas said. "I've seen the by-line." The two men extended their hands in a chilly, if nonetheless civil, greeting. "Don't let me interrupt anything," Thomas said, perfectly pleased that he had interrupted. "If you're having an intimate chat, newspaper work or otherwise, I could come back."

"Not a chance," Andrea said, leaning over and pulling a chair from a neighboring desk. "Sit." A woman with an insatiable appetite for gossip or argument, she wanted to see the two men faced with each other. Thomas knew it.

"I was just leaving, anyway," offered Reid politely. His pipe went from his left hand back to his mouth. A thin stream of smoke drifted upward.

"Maybe all three of us should talk," Andrea suggested. Thomas looked at Reid with thinly veiled displeasure. Reid shook his head mildly to Andrea.

Thomas sat and threw a jaundiced eye upward toward Reid. "Do we have something to talk about?" he asked.

"Oh, I doubt it," offered Reid amiably. "Maybe your father."

Daniels was quick to frown and pursue the point. "What?" he asked, a suggestion of anger in his tone. Everywhere, *everywhere*, William Ward Daniels.

Reid offered a smile. "Met him once," said Reid, teeth clenched on the pipe. "The man impressed me. Only reason I mention it is my older brother knew him well." Reid perceived that Thomas was annoyed at something. "No offense intended," he said.

"None taken," said Thomas slowly. "Where'd your brother know him?" The question was cautious, exploring the territory.

"City College," said Reid. Thomas could see that the reporter was studying him as he spoke. Daniels disliked people who seemed to look through him when conversing. He'd seen too many of them. "They were classmates together. Prelaw." Another puff of smoke was launched toward the ceiling. "Knew each other *very* well there, in fact. Debating team. Political Science Union. Chess Club. My brother," added Reid, changing pace just slightly, "he died about two years ago—"

"I'm sorry."

Reid shrugged, as if this were the accepted course of things, and continued, "my brother said that your father possessed the most overpowering intellect he'd even met."

Thomas shrugged in noncommitment. He'd heard it all before, too many times.

"Only one thing puzzled him. Mind if I tell you?"

Andrea took in the exchange greedily. She loved it. Reid waited for a response and when Thomas acquiesced in silence, Reid continued.

"City College back in the thirties," the reporter said. "Well, I'm old enough to remember a bit of that myself. Great ideologists. Reaction from the Depression. Reaction to capitalism. Know what I'm going to say?"

"No," said Thomas. He didn't. But he was hooked. He watched another puff of smoke rise. The reporter knew how to draw someone into a story. Reid held the pipe in his hand.

"All the great intellects were left wing," he said. Shaking his head, he added, "Understandable. That's where the intellectuals were. With the great 'Russian Experiment,' as they called it. They hadn't had to excuse the Stalin purge trials yet. But that's aside from the point. The point is, my brother was always puzzled by your father. He was *the* intellect of his class. *The* intellect. And he went the other road completely. The *other* wing. And all that jingoistic nonsense."

Thomas shrugged slightly as if to ask what that proved.

"Well," said Reid, recovering slightly, "human beings do things for reasons. Other human beings try to figure out why. How could your father have come out of that same environment and been *so* different politically?"

"I have no idea," said Thomas flatly.

"Ever wondered?"

"No," he admitted.

"Mmmm," hummed Reid. "People are people, I suppose." He was thoughtful. "He flirted with socialism for a while, my brother used to tell me. Sold socialism to other freshmen, then dropped it himself."

"Who?"

"Your father," said Reid with a slight smile. "For a few months as a freshman. You act surprised."

"I am."

Reid offered a pensive and perplexed expression as if to say, "What does it mean? I don't know." He said in closing, "Well, guess it doesn't mean much now. See you again sometime."

He offered his hand. Thomas took it without resenting it. He didn't dislike Reid as much as he'd wanted to. For some vague reason, he didn't dislike him at all.

Reid nodded to Thomas and Andrea, made an awkward halfmove—as if starting to lean forward to kiss her, then thinking better of it—then turned and left. Thomas sat by her desk in silence for a few moments watching him leave.

"They're getting older all the time, aren't they?" he asked.

"Who?"

"Your new beaux," he said. "Aren't you afraid you might give him a heart attack?"

Her eyes narrowed and focused on him sharply. "I could ask you to leave for a remark like that."

"I'm sure you could. We'll start again. How was your trip? 'Your' in the plural sense."

"Profitable."

"Profitable?" he asked, exploring the use of the word.

"I enjoyed myself. I'm getting to know Augie very well."

Thomas shrugged. "I have eyes. Why do you have to tell me?"

"Because this is partially for you."

"For *me*? What is?"

"Augie," she said, as if in revelation. "And the Sandler case. It all fits together."

"Not for me it doesn't. The power of instant and devastating insight was not one of the traits my father passed on."

"A shame," she said. "Perhaps that's true. So I'll explain. Augie's a political historian in addition to being a reporter. Political and social."

"So?"

"And his particular field of expertise, if you want to call it that, is intelligence services. Nineteen forties and fifties." There was a pause as Thomas sat there unmollified but now interested. "The fact is," she continued, "that he was an intelligence officer in the war." She smiled with a mixture of smugness and self-efficiency. "I've been plying him with questions," she said. "Questions beyond the routine ones."

"What are you talking about? The Sandler case?"

"Of course. Espionage systems." She nodded to the direction in which Reid had disappeared. "That man is a walking compendium of the various intelligence systems. He taught a course on it at Columbia in the early sixties, before interest in such things went out of vogue. But," she explained further and again that smile returned, "I have ways of getting him to talk even more than he would to his class. A man will answer any question when his mood is properly arranged."

He looked at her with an attitude that bordered on disbelief. An instinct for the jugular was one thing. But here was an instinct toward a more remote artery, the secret unspoken recesses of a man's memory. His father would have loved it.

"You're incredible," was all he could mutter. "Is that all you see in him?"

She opened her hands as if to say maybe, maybe not. "He's an attractive man in his own way. I enjoy his company. I enjoyed being away for a week with him. Pleasure with business, you could call it."

"There are a lot of things you could call it."

"Call it anything you prefer," she said. "I love this Sandler story. You're breaking into a terrific story. I want to understand it piece by piece as you uncover it. I have to understand it." She raised her eyebrows. "You promised it to me, remember? I promised to help you as much as I could. In return, the story's mine."

He nodded. "That was the agreement."

"What brings you here today? It's Sunday."

"The *Times* files."

"What about them?"

"Can you get me access to them?"

She pondered it for a moment. "Yes. Why?"

"I want to find out about an airplane crash in 1971," he said "Then I want to go farther back. I want to read everything in the newspaper files pertaining to two men."

"Who?" she asked. "Sandler's one, obviously. Who's the other?"

He hesitated only slightly before answering. "Who were we just discussing?" he asked.

"Why not?" she answered. "Let's go."

The microfilm was both the easiest and the most logical place to begin. Left by Andrea in the archive room of the rambling old building on Forty-third Street, Thomas wandered for several minutes among the rows after rows of catalogued and categorized files. Occasionally, at random, he would open a drawer and superficially eye the contents. Obituaries of the remote and long-forgotten. Clippings and news stories of events, important and otherwise, which no living person could remember.

Then, for the time, he moved on to the microfilm room. He obtained a spool for June of 1971 and anxiously cranked it to the fourteenth of the month.

Then to the fifteenth.

He scanned page one. He saw nothing of the airplane crash which Leslie had mentioned. Nor was there anything on page two or three.

He scanned to the index and saw nothing there. Then, meticulously, he began again at page four, ready to read every headline on every item in that day's edition. At the bottom of page eight, in a quarter-column story hidden in a corner, he saw it. **CARACAS TO MIAMI FLIGHT MISSING**, read the small headline. **39 ABOARD.** Thirty-nine lives, relegated to page eight. The story gave virtually no details, nor any list of passengers.

Thomas moved quickly to the next day's edition.

There, this time on page twelve, he found a further elaboration. The Avianca flight had crashed sixty minutes after takeoff, going down in clear weather into the Caribbean. The final sentence of the short article implied that sabotage had not been ruled out as a reason for the crash.

Thomas anxiously cranked the microfilm spool for the next edition's coverage. But there was none. Nor was there any further mention of the crash in any succeeding day's *Times*.

He sat there for several minutes trying to draw some implication from

the way the story had evaporated from the newspaper. Then he returned
the spool and prowled through a microfilm index and directory until he
found what else he wanted.

The Miami *Herald.* For the same dates.

In the Miami newspaper the crash had made the front page, since
several Florida residents were lost in the crash. On page two of the *Herald*
of June 16, Thomas found what he'd been seeking all along.

A passenger list.

Anxiously he read down. It was alphabetical. He quickly skipped
through to the middle. To the M's. Then he saw it.

McAdam, George F., Kilnwick, Surrey, England

Of course, he thought to himself. An English address instead of a Swiss
one. He skipped to the end of the list—the last name in fact. Leslie
McAdam, or at least the young woman whom *he* knew as Leslie Mc-
Adam, was as good as her word. It read:

Whiteside, Peter S., Oxford, Oxfordshire, England

Thomas then scanned the list more carefully. He saw no other names
he recognized. Nor were there any other British subjects on the flight.

Thomas removed the spool of microfilm and for several minutes sat
before the viewer with the spool of microfilm in his hand. He said nothing
and barely moved. Mentally he tried to sort details, to find a flaw in
someone's version of the story. He'd met a credible George McAdam.
And he'd met a Peter Whiteside who, if not genuine, had to be part of
a hoax of staggering proportions.

And Leslie McAdam? The woman he had encountered in the charred
skeleton of his office, the woman who'd raised goosebumps on the back
of his neck when she'd related her story, the woman with the savage scars
across her throat?

She, too, was credible. Every bit as credible as the other two. Yet at
least one side was lying outright. Someone was dead, someone else was
alive. And like the elusive Arthur Sandler himself, who was alive yet
couldn't possibly be, each side was a ghostly contradiction of the other.
In a world where everything had to be black and white, Thomas was
dealing only with emissaries of the gray regions.

Thomas returned the spool of microfilm that he'd held in his hand.
Then he proceeded to the biographical files. And from there, over that
afternoon and the entire next day, he withdrew every available shred of
material on two men.

Arthur Sandler. And Thomas's own father.

He hid himself at a remote table in an isolated corner of the archives. He examined even the most infinitesimal details of two lives. He sought, above all, any crosscurrents he could detect, hidden, salient, or otherwise. He sought corresponding patterns to their lives, public or private.

He waited for some great truth or revelation to leap out at him, for something unseen to become abruptly visible, for something long overlooked to become suddenly and stunningly understood.

Instead, nothing. Only the ordinary.

Arthur Sandler, the industrialist. William Ward Daniels, the attorney. Linked together in only the most obvious manner, a client-lawyer relationship.

Or was it?

On the third day, a Tuesday, Thomas returned to the *Times* archives. He searched for implications: He would examine not what he saw, but what he didn't see. And slowly, a small portion of the darkness lifted.

1954, frozen for eternity on microfilm. Thomas could remember the year. His eleventh birthday had been in October and he could remember *the* catch Willie Mays had made off Vic Wertz in the World Series. Eleven years old. He recalled the family home in Westchester County. Back then, William Ward Daniels was still a certifiable hero to his only son. So what that in that year Daniels, Senior, was defending a sleazy character named Vincent De Septio? The boy never knew about it. Until now.

The name De Septio rang a distant bell for Thomas. Somewhere he'd seen the name before. Recently. Very recently. Within the research of the previous two days.

He began the paper chase again from the beginning. And he was well into the afternoon when he rediscovered where he'd first seen the name. De Septio had been a client in 1938, 1939, and 1940. Each time he'd been arraigned on various charges involving currency violations. Just as Sandler had been, thought Thomas as he reread the scant, undetailed mention of Vincent De Septio, a Runyonesque underworld character who, for his imitative talents with pen and voice, was known as Vinnie the Parrot. Thomas muttered to himself, wishing those extensive files which had been destroyed by arson could some way be reclaimed from their ashes. Who was De Septio? What could his father's files have told Thomas?

He pondered it for a moment. Then, quickly looking back to notes he'd made on the life of Arthur Sandler, he posed to himself another unanswerable question. Why, he wondered, did it happen that De Septio was a client at the same time as Sandler? What was the connection, if any, considering they were operating in the same realm of criminal activity?

Thomas returned to another file in the *Times* archives, his palms wet with anxiety now, and withdrew a meager file on a middle-echelon crook named De Septio.

Once again, the file spoke through what it left unsaid.

A brief biographical sketch traced De Septio's birth to Palermo in 1920. He entered the United States with his parents two years later, settling in New York City in an ethnic enclave around Mulberry and Canal. By the late 1930s De Septio had earned himself a solid police record, yet, unlike that of many of his peers, nothing touching on physical violence. De Septio's art was that of the swindle or, by 1940, the skillfully forged check.

Everything was predictable enough, Thomas noted. Then, after recurring legal trouble which threatened to set him on the gloomy side of prison walls, De Septio happened upon an attorney who could work miracles. William Ward Daniels represented De Septio. And William Ward Daniels somehow managed to get three separate indictments dismissed.

Dismissed not in court, Thomas noted with increasing incredulity. But by a special prosecutor. A man named McFedries, the special prosecutor for espionage cases, the man before whom the F.B.I. agents had once dragged Sandler.

Then a gap. Nothing in the biography accounted for the years after 1941. No deportation order, no armed forces. Nothing.

Then De Septio surfaced in the 1950s. He'd been indicted. He'd gone to William Ward Daniels for help. And apparently he'd received it.

The year was 1954 and again De Septio had involved himself with bogus money. In the autumn of that year his case had gone to court. And, according to newspaper accounts of the day, William Ward Daniels had managed to stall the trial date into November.

Then something had happened, though the newspapers and chroniclers of the day were unable to tell exactly what.

On November eleventh, Armistice Day, court had not been in session. On the twelfth, the court had never convened. And on the thirteenth, Vincent De Septio's case was dismissed.

Thomas sat down slowly in a wooden chair in the archives and tried mightily to grapple with what he was reading. What he saw before him was clear, yet carried no explanation. It was self-explanatory, yet was wide open to so many potential interpretations. And both stories, the De Septio story and the Sandler story, had been almost side by side within the same day's newspaper. November 12, 1954. But with no apparent link.

On that crisp day in November, some twenty-one years before Thomas Daniels sat in a grim quiet newspaper archive piecing together forgotten events, a man thought to be Arthur Sandler—who, like De Septio, had been a counterfeiter in his day—had been gunned down on a fashionable Manhattan side street.

On the day thereafter, De Septio had been issued from Washington, D.C., a pardon exonerating him from all crimes past and present, thus ending his problems with the local Assistant U.S. Attorney.

And even more cryptic, noted Thomas Daniels, was what followed.

Nothing. A gap which extended to the present.

After the thirteenth of November, 1954, Vincent De Septio was never seen or heard from again.

Without question, the Vincent De Septio affair was the major case before Zenger and Daniels that year, perhaps their most important case in the 1950s. But Thomas would never have drawn the De Septio connection at all had it not been for one word, one forever-unproven charge which drifted like a phantom through the accounts of the case.

Counterfeiting.

Chapter 21

An eskimo, Thomas thought to himself. She must think I'm a God-damned eskimo.

He shivered against the railing to the Brooklyn Heights Promenade. His back was to the massive brutal skyline of Manhattan and he looked both ways, waiting for her. Waiting for Leslie at eight P.M. that next evening. And the winter wind, sweeping across the unprotected Promenade, was freezing him.

Each time he breathed, the cold breath he drew in almost hurt his lungs. And the flesh of his face was stinging—actually stinging—from the cold. He looked up and down the Promenade again, seeing only one isolated stroller and another man crazy enough to walk his dog in such weather. Thomas envied the dog its fur coat.

What was wrong? The note he'd received had given this location, the Promenade just off Pineapple Street, at eight P.M. Where *was* she? What had happened? Yes, he admitted, he was worried about her. Worried about her physical safety. He began to walk up and down the Promenade again, four hundred yards down and back, just to move around and keep warm. Keep warm and think.

The man with the dog, a German shepherd, passed him, white clouds of frosty breath appearing before the man's face and the dog's jaws. Holy Christ, it was cold out there!

He'd like to build a fire, Thomas thought. Yes, that was it. He agreed with himself, a nice big raging log fire in a six-foot fireplace. And he'd curl up in front of it with . . . with . . .

Well, yes. With Leslie.

He'd surprised himself. *Leslie? It used to be Andrea, the prime candidate for accompaniment at a cozy fireside.*

He couldn't stand the wind in his face anymore. He turned and started walking the other way, up the Promenade now, with the wind at his back and with his gloved hands clenched into fists and shoved uncomfortably into his pockets.

Leslie? Well, yes, damn it! Of course he cared about her. Personally. How could he not? *Bad, bad, bad,* he told himself, shivering and now convinced he would freeze to death out there overlooking the cargo docks and the mouth of the East River.

Bad, real bad. First thing his father ever taught him: *Don't get personally involved with a client. It blinds you, Tom. Might just as well gouge your own eyes out. You stop seeing.*

His head was down against the cold and he continued to walk. Then he saw feet. He raised his head quickly and saw a figure fifteen feet in front of him.

And then all worry about her safety or his own personal involvement with her vanished.

"Leslie," he said.

"I'm sorry. I'm late." She was clad in a dark coat, and the fair and lovely face was masked partially by a wool scarf.

"It happens," he shrugged. He didn't mind the cold so much for a few moments. His instinct was to go to her and embrace her. But he refrained. She was, after all, a client.

"You weren't worried, were you?" she asked.

"I figured you'd turn up. I just put my mind to waiting."

He moved the final few steps next to her. They began to walk, following the railing and with Manhattan at their sides. Manhattan's lights glittered.

"I could have picked a warmer place," she conceded.

"You couldn't have picked a colder one."

"You've never been to Quebec in February," she said. They were walking close by each other's side now.

"You win. I haven't," he said, turning to look at the woman within the shrouding scarf and bulky coat. "This is a business meeting," he said. "Would a warming arm around your shoulders offend you?"

She looked at him and laughed, one of those rare times when he'd seen her smile.

"My God," she said. "Don't be silly. No arm offered at all is what would offend me." Her British intonation disappeared into a faint, short laugh and his arm around her shoulders held her tightly.

"I discovered something important, I think," he said. He could still feel her shivering. She said nothing so he continued. "Vincent De Septio," he offered.

"Who?"

"Vinnie the Parrot?" he persisted. "The name means nothing?"

She shook her head and looked at him. She reached to her scarf and rearranged it slightly. "Who is he?" she asked.

"I wish I knew." He paused for a moment, then began. "I've found a lot on your father. Yes, he was a spy, just as you say. But everything he did also seemed to advance his own position monetarily. You know about the currency speculations. Chances are he was into counterfeiting, also."

"I wouldn't doubt it," she said calmly.

"De Septio was a much younger man. Chances are he could still be alive. He was in the same rackets as your father."

"You're sure?"

"Yes," he said firmly. "But that's about all I know. That and the fact that my father successfully defended him several times."

"Your father and my father," she noted wryly. "Strange how the two of them continue to crop up together. What's the French phrase, 'For a good cat, a good rat'?" She paused for a moment. "Thomas," she asked, "tell me honestly. How well did you know your father?"

"How well did I know my own father?" he asked with incredulity.

"Yes."

"I knew him well," he said with a tone of exasperation, as if the answer were so self-evident that it hadn't deserved being asked.

"Very well? His beliefs? Do you think you knew his innermost thoughts?"

His face twisted into a scowl. She knew she'd have to retreat slightly. "What kind of grilling is this?" he asked.

"It's important," she said. "Everything is your father this, my father that. First it was the link between us and the will. Now it's the link between De Septio and us. Doesn't that strike you as curious?"

"Suspicious as hell," he allowed.

"Does it trigger anything in your memory? Anything at all that you haven't told me yet?"

He searched his brain, desperately trying to think of one time, however many years ago, when his father might have mentioned De Septio. But no, there hadn't been a time. Not once. He shook his head no. She seemed disappointed.

She glanced to her left. Then quickly to her right.

"Did you come alone?" she asked, looking back to him.

"Of course."

"We're not alone now."

And they weren't. Naturally it was Leslie who'd been the one to notice.

"Walk with me," she said. "How did you get here?"

"By car."

"I'll get us out of here," she said. "Then you lead us to your car."

There were two men again, but different men this time. Different from at the Anspacher Gallery, one in each direction. One seemed like an older man; he walked as a man in his seventies might. Lean, intent, shadowed by the overhead lights. The other was thick, wrapped in a bulky parka and hood, but wore a beard which for a fleeting second Thomas thought he'd recognized.

But no, it would be impossible.

She pulled at his arm and steered the two of them toward the lean older man. The wind was whipping into their faces, lessening Thomas's chances of seeing either man clearly. He only knew he wanted to be out of there. Whom had they followed, he wondered, him or her?

Nearing the lean man, Thomas kept his head down. The man's hat remained a cover for his face. Then, as Thomas was about to look up at the man, she yanked his arm and pulled him.

"Come on! Run!" she yelled.

She sprinted ahead of him and he followed. He was aware only of the fact that the tall man didn't run and the shorter, thicker one with the beard did.

Thomas could hear the footsteps becoming more distant. She led him up an exit from the Promenade and onto Columbia Heights. There he yanked her hand and pulled her to the left toward his car two blocks away.

They sprinted the two blocks, turning down the block at Pineapple. They heard the running footsteps behind them. The windy street was otherwise quiet. As they ran and as they panted from the sprint, the cold air seared their lungs.

"Hurry, hurry," she said quietly. He motioned toward his car.

He fumbled a key with his hands. He pulled his glove off to get a better grip. But his fingers were so cold that they were almost numb. The metal key didn't wish to obey any more than the fingers did.

He tried to force it into the lock on the door.

At first it wouldn't turn. The lock was frozen.

"Hurry!" she said again, an excited, shrill whisper.

The door opened. She climbed in quickly, turned, and grabbed his wrist, preventing him from going to the driver's side.

"No time!" she snapped. "Get in! Get down!"

Again, she knew the tricks as well as, if not better than, her pursuer.

She pulled him onto the front seat and continued to instruct him. "Down," she said excitedly. "Stay down!"

She slid her own body down beneath the steering wheel. He held himself in the leg room on the passenger side of the front seat. The street was dim, shadowy.

"It's too late to try to drive," she explained. "He'll have to be tricked into thinking he's lost us."

"Who is he?" he asked.

She put a finger upraised to her lips to silence him. He stayed perfectly still, listening, wondering, feeling his heart pounding and thinking that there was no way he'd ever catch his breath. The car was worse than freezing. It was an icebox. He fought back the urge to cough as he panted for the frozen air.

The bearded man stood on the corner, confused and baffled. He knew the direction the man and woman had gone. He also knew they were out of sight.

Turned another corner? he wondered. Escaped into a house? There were low fences on the block. The man started walking down Pineapple Street toward Thomas's car, holding something ominous in a hand beneath his coat.

He approached the car, close enough so that the shadow from his head and hat fell across the interior of the car. No more than three or four yards away; the light came from a street-level apartment window.

He stopped.

Thomas thought his heart would stop, too. He saw the shadow moving. He glanced at Leslie, almost afraid that the movement of his eyes would be too loud. Her face was intense, studying the situation and deciding what their next move would be.

Their move, Thomas thought. Did they have one? Did *she* have one? Thomas knew *he* didn't.

The gunman turned toward the car, his hand beneath his overcoat.

All he had to do was look down.

The shadow approached. We're screwed, Thomas thought. Within his gloves, his hands were soaking wet.

The gunman turned completely, examining windows and fences and gates. Not a movement on the street. Nothing. Then two teenagers appeared at the end of the block on the other side of Pineapple Street.

The gunman began to move. He walked back toward the Promenade, slowly examining the situation.

Leslie allowed a minute to pass. Then slowly she raised her head, looking in each direction. Thomas watched her, marveling at her composure. She held a hand to him to indicate not to move. "Not yet, not yet," she said.

More seconds passed. She was convinced the man had drifted a safe distance from the block. "We can't make a mistake," she said. "If he sees you pulling out he'll shoot your tires out."

"Terrific," mumbled Thomas.

"All right," she said. "Quickly."

They switched positions in the car, Thomas climbing into the driver's seat and pushing the key at the ignition slot until it slipped in.

Then he turned the key, waiting several long, painful seconds until the engine laboriously turned over. He stared in the rearview mirror the entire time, waiting for the bulky man in the overcoat to reappear.

He gunned the engine. "Where to?" he asked.

He backed the car jerkily until it touched the car behind him. Then nervously he allowed the front fender to scrape the car parked ahead of him. He pulled out.

She seemed to consider the question. "My place," she said.

"Yours?" He had never seen it, nor ever had any indication where it was.

"We'll have to," she said. "Yours isn't safe anymore. Take the Brooklyn Bridge back to Manhattan."

He turned off Willow Street, heading for the Bridge. "You know your directions pretty well for a foreigner," he noted, the remark being a remote form of accusation.

"I learn quickly."

Several seconds passed. He was still perplexed by what had transpired. "Who were they?" he asked at length.

"Your latest troublemakers," she said. They were on the Brooklyn Bridge. From the corner of his eye he could see her admiring the Manhattan skyline. An overloaded car cut across the solid line into the lane in front of them. Standard bridge etiquette. "You're a popular man," she added. "You now have two competing sets of goons after you."

He gave her a long, hard, and inquisitive look, removing his eyes from the road, also standard bridge etiquette. "How do you know *that*?"

She fed him a cryptic smile. "Call it my artistic temperament," she said. "Or attribute it to the fact that I've spent my life as Arthur Sandler's daughter. I can sense it," she declared. "I *know.*"

He was without a reply since obviously she was not a woman to reveal one iota of unintended information. They neared the exit ramp in Manhattan. He continued to study his rearview mirror as he asked, "Where to next?"

"We're going to West Thirtieth Street," she said. "Between Tenth and Eleventh Avenues."

He looked at her as if to ask whether or not it was a serious request. "Yes," she answered, "I'm serious."

The block of Thirtieth Street on which she lived met Thomas's expectations and surpassed them. It was a dark, heavily littered street which even during a bright afternoon would be worth a detour. There was an all-day garage which had closed at six, two vacant vandalized store fronts which had been Spanish grocery shops, and in a row toward Eleventh Avenue were three decaying warehouses. Across the fronts of these iron grates and metal grills had been pulled, protecting the interiors from becoming nocturnal discount centers for shoppers armed with crowbars.

Nestled among these establishments were several old brick tenements, walk-up buildings in various stages of repair and disrepair. In better days the block had been a Lithuanian enclave. Now the newer immigrants from the West Indies and Central America populated the streets. The newer immigrants plus Leslie McAdam.

The only sign of life on the street was a tawdry bar close to the corner, outside of which several flashy models of Detroit workmanship were double-parked. A Rheingold sign flashed in the bar's window.

They walked by it quickly, just long enough to see two large black men fondling an equally large black woman at a window cash register. There was boisterous activity at a bar farther into the noisy dimness.

Leslie explained that she lived one flight above it, and that she was in the habit of moving quickly past the bar and into her doorway, key in hand, of course. "One night I was followed in," she said. "They thought any white girl on the block had to be selling herself."

Thomas closed the front door behind him. The alcove and hallway reeked embarrassingly. They climbed the dimly lit staircase, the noise from the bar thundering on the other side of the wall.

"Aren't you scared?" he was going to ask, but didn't, because obviously she wasn't. Not in relation to the more direct threats on her life, those she'd lived with for so long.

Then he was struck from nowhere by a more invidious thought. Was this all part of a trap? Why was he—defenseless—being lured to a roach farm in the west thirties. He didn't know why he thought of it. After all, he trusted her—*didn't he?*—but there was something macabre, out of place, about this setting. Suppose he was being taken here for his throat to be perforated? More than one person had insisted that she was a fraud. This was exactly the type of building in which a body would be found two weeks after the fact and the murderer would never be apprehended.

He was on his guard as she unlocked her apartment door, stepped through it, and allowed him to follow.

Then the thought of a physical threat to him eased away as he observed her surroundings.

"What's the old axiom?" she asked. "Be it ever so humble . . . "

The chairs were overstuffed and threadbare, the floorboards worn and creaky when walked upon. The walls were of a gray plaster which might have been a pale green in better days but which had passed many years since last being on familiar terms with a paintbrush.

The kitchen was narrow and cramped. It featured a single fluorescent light overhead. The stove was old-fashioned, the sink basin curiously stained with green, and the linoleum worn almost to the underlying woodwork.

Thomas took it all in as he sat gingerly upon the settee, half waiting for a spare spring beneath him to barge upward.

"It's not Versailles, is it?" she said with an apologetic smile.

"I suppose it's comfortable," he said. "If you have to make do."

There was noise from the sidewalk below where two sodden revelers were engaged in a heated and profane discussion with the fat woman from the cash register. Leslie went to one of two windows and pulled the shade down. Thomas glanced to the next room, a bedroom which was even more sparse than the living room. A simple wooden dresser. A narrow single bed which had a dingy brown cover over its concave middle.

Thomas watched Leslie return from the window and sit down beside a dim thirty-year-old lamp beside the sofa. Here was a woman of grace, charm, and youth in a setting of gloom and despair. Here, within gray walls that were despairing, amid furniture which could better serve as firewood, and above a watering hole where man's primordial instincts took their last stand, the putative last of the Sandlers lived in exile. In a world removed from the faded elegance of the mansion on Eighty-ninth Street, she sought and awaited what she claimed would be her rightful restoration.

Her hands were in her lap. She was clearly embarrassed to be seen in such surroundings.

"No one will ever accuse me of squandering my inheritance in advance," she said, forcing a slight smile.

"How did you find this"—he seached for the word—"place?"

"I needed something fast," she said. "This is what I could afford."

The noise from the bar increased with profane shouts. There was the sound of a television and jukebox below. Thomas could hear footsteps on the floor above him.

"How safe is it?" he asked.

"How safe is anything?" she said. "This is safer than most. Four escape routes. Kitchen window, bathroom window, front door, back fire escape to the neighboring rooftops, six different escape routes from there."

"You've got the angles figured well," he said, admiring her inventiveness as a latter-day Houdini.

"There's no particular brilliance involved. Just self-preservation."

She glanced around the drab room, focusing on the empty, dirty walls. She slipped out of her shoes and undid the top button of her blouse, aspiring toward whatever small comfort she could find.

"I suppose what bothers me most," she said with a half sigh and as if in response to a question, "is the unimaginative squalor of it all."

"Sorry?" he asked.

She turned to him, her arms folded as if stepping back from an easel to study it. "The apartment," she said. "Maybe I should invest in a few cans of wall paint."

"Another color might help," he offered in agreement.

"You miss the point," she said. "Not *one* other colour. Several. I could do a mural." She glanced at the bare walls, as if conceptualizing her project. "Wouldn't that please the landlord?"

"Maybe it would," he said, "if your work became valuable someday."

"Of course," she mused, imitating a carnival barker. " 'Come see the mural of the modern-day Anastasia, the claimant to the Sandler chemical fortune.' " She uttered a low bitter laugh and continued. " 'Spent years trying to collect what was rightfully hers. Never collected a penny! Died young and broke! But out of this life of torment came *art*. Real *art!* If you don't mind walking up one flight on Thirtieth Street.' "

She glanced at him, then quickly turned away. A cynical smile was melting. It took him several seconds before he knew she was hiding tears.

"Leslie," he said, rising and going to her.

He took her in his arms, her back to him. Her hand was at her face.

"I haven't cried in years," she said. "I don't want you to see me. It's weakness, I know."

"I won't look," he said with sincerity.

A moment or two passed. She turned to him, face to face, her eyes slightly red but dry already.

"I'm sorry," she said. "You deserve better than having a weepy female on your hands." She didn't allow him time to answer. Instead, she added, motioning around her, "It's this place," she said. "It's abysmal. It depresses me."

"I understand," he said. "Honestly, I do."

She nodded appreciatively. "Did you think of anything else?" she asked. "About De Septio? De Septio and your father? Or Arthur Sandler?"

He shook his head again, wondering how they'd traveled back to that subject so abruptly.

"There *has* to be something important," she said. "How can we possibly find out?"

"The only real hope," he said, "would be that Zenger would remember De Septio."

"Zenger?"

"My father's former partner."

"Of course," she recalled.

"I'd suggest that we go see him immediately."

She seemed startled. *"We?"*

"Do you object?"

There was a silent moment within the room while she considered it. "No," she said. "But I don't see why it's necessary."

"It's *not* necessary. But it might be a good idea. You could question him yourself if you felt like it."

"He won't want to see me," she said. "I know that in advance."

He nodded. "I know. He won't know until you arrive at the door. Then he'll have no choice." He could see again that she was pondering it, her mind examining the many facets of his suggestion. "He's expecting me tomorrow," Thomas said. "Instead of just me, he'll get *us.*"

"Tomorrow?"

"I already telephoned," he said. "I said I'd be there sometime by evening tomorrow. There's an Air New England flight—"

"No airplanes." Her voice was firm.

"The alternative is a hell of a long haul by car and ferry."

"That's preferable."

He weighed it, then gave in. "Have it your way," he said.

Pensively she broke from his embrace. She went to the second window in the living room and pulled down a shade, sealing off the outside just as she might seal a secret within her soul.

Thomas Daniels watched her graceful movement as the noise intensified from the bar below. No place at all for a princess, he thought. A woman who conveyed elegance and breeding, who said she was the last of a once-dignified family, deserved better than two and a half tacky rooms above a cheap red-light bar. "You'll stay with me tonight, won't you?" she asked.

Deserved better, he thought. But would she ever have it? What could he honestly do to help? "Of course," he said.

She turned from the window, speaking brightly now, her entire mood radically changed and elevated. "I'd be worried about you returning to your place," she said. "They'll be looking for you again."

Whoever "they" are, he thought.

"You're precious," she concluded. "I'll make you as comfortable here as I can."

"Considering the events of this evening," he answered, "tomorrow will be a good day for a trip."

PART FIVE

A cold rain was lashing the entire East Coast that next morning. Thomas and Leslie left Manhattan very early by car and drove northward through Connecticut, Rhode Island, and the southwestern tip of Massachusetts. The drive was torturous, with gusts of rain and wind battering the car and with the windshield frequently immersed by sheets of water kicked up from passing trucks.

They arrived at Woods Hole at three in the afternoon. The rain still fell relentlessly. They waited at the gloomy colorless depot until the boarding of the late-afternoon steamer to Nantucket, the second and last boat out that day. The ferry encountered a severe squall crossing Nantucket Sound. On board, the storm felt even more intense than it was.

"Where are we going to stay tonight?" she asked, two hours out from Woods Hole. She sat beside a large plate-glass window that looked out on gray sky and water.

He shrugged. "It won't be a problem," he said. "There are a few places open year round."

She snuggled close to him, her softness and warmth a comfort on a genuinely unpleasant voyage. "Let's find an inn for the night," she said. "The least we can do is have some fun." She gave him a soft kiss on the cheek, then, noting his sleepiness, disappeared for a few moments.

When she returned and again filled the empty space next to him, he was looking out the window, lost in thought about Sandlers, forgers, and claimants to unfound wills.

"I brought you something," she said. He looked at her.

She pushed toward him a steaming white styrofoam cup. "Tea," she said. "I got one for each of us."

He took it, the tag to the tea bag hanging out as the steam rose aggressively.

He smiled. "Tea, huh?" he said amiably. "Even in North America you can't take the English out of an Englishwoman."

She shook her head and sipped. "What's inside someone, what he or she is born with, doesn't get scrubbed out," she said. She sipped again. "My mother used to tell me that when I was small. I didn't understand it then."

"But now?"

She looked at him as if to nod, her eyes soft and more relaxed than he'd seen them before. Some of the tension was gone from her face, even on a nerve-wracking journey like this, even when about to face Zenger. Maybe a voyage on salt water, however short or rough, did that for someone. Maybe in the future, he caught himself thinking, they could take a voyage together. Just off somewhere. No destination to speak of.

He caught himself. What the hell was he thinking about?

"What would you do with it?" he asked.

"Do with what?"

"The money," he said. "All that Sandler money."

She smiled. "Even if we win, it's years away."

"But eventually if you got it. Even if you got a small portion of it. That's still a lot of dollars."

She appeared pensive. "Go off somewhere, I suppose," she said. "Stop worrying about my father. Never worry about money again." She let a few more seconds go by. "Maybe continue my education." She looked at him with a sly smile. "Want to hear something even funnier?"

"What?"

"I might even want to have a family someday," she said. "Who knows?"

He returned her smile, then was abruptly aware that her smile had vanished and the tension had returned to her face. "I'll never have any of it while my father's alive," she said. "Never. This can only end in one of two ways. Him or me."

He placed his hand on hers, which were fidgeting in her lap. "We're doing all right," he said. "So far. The machinery of justice moves slowly, but it does move."

She glanced up at him, looking him squarely in the eyes. "I want to ask you something," she said. "And I want an absolutely honest answer. I won't be hurt, no matter what it is."

"Go ahead."

"Do you believe my story?" Several seconds passed. "As you sit there," she said, "looking back at me, can you honestly say that you believe that everything I've told you is the truth."

"The honest answer?"

"Yes."

He hesitated slightly, choosing his words with an attorney's care. "At first I believed you maybe because I merely wanted to believe you. But when you first told me your story, that day back in January, I accepted it. Then I began to doubt and question. I couldn't help it. I was trying to examine your case rationally. I've trained myself to question, not to accept what isn't readily provable."

"But today?"

"I've come to grips with my doubts. I believe you're who you say you are. I believe you completely."

Her eyes fell to her lap for a moment. He studied her and watched her lips move nervously for a moment. He was aware that she was huddled near him for warmth, her legs folded beneath her against the dampness. He thought of the warm body huddled inside those extra layers of clothes. He thought of the protectiveness he felt toward her, despite the fact that he knew she could probably protect herself better than he could himself.

She leaned to him and kissed him softly on the cheek. "I'm glad you believe me," she said. "Mr. Zenger's going to say I'm an impostor. I wanted to know if you would stick by me. No matter what."

"I'm unshakable," he said.

She hugged him suddenly, almost spilling both cups of tea. On the other side of the grimy gray window, with rain spattering into small rivers on the opposite side, the outline of Nantucket harbor was slowly becoming visible through the fog.

Then she pulled away for a moment. "And what would you do with it?" she asked.

"With what?"

"The money. Your share if we win?"

"I'd go off and get lost," he said. "With someone I liked."

Their car had emerged from the hull of the ferry, had driven to the remote southwestern end of the island, and had pulled to a halt before the stone domicile of Zenger.

The hour was late, well past eight in the evening. The windows of the stone house blazed warmly from within. Thomas and Leslie walked up the flagstone path as the rain, carried on sweeping easterly winds, continued to pelt them.

Mrs. Clancy, the housekeeper, was gone for the evening. So when Thomas banged the brass knocker on the solid oak door, almost two full minutes passed before there came any response.

Then the door slowly opened and the light from within flowed out in a sudden wedge.

"Thomas," rasped Zenger, standing in the alcove, holding the door ajar. "I've been expecting—"

His eyes hit Leslie, unseen until that moment.

"Good evening, Mr. Zenger," she said with both civility and charm.

Zenger recoiled rudely, stepping backward two steps into a darker spot in the hallway. His eyes were in a shadow and Leslie stepped forward with some effort to see him.

He reached to the breast pocket of his maroon robe, pulled from the pocket a pair of heavily tinted glasses, and seemed to study her through them. Thomas observed him with rising suspicion and dislike. She, in turn, returned the scrutiny, looking him up and down and trying to see past the glasses to his eyes.

"Yes," said Zenger slowly, as if in appraisal. "This is the woman you spoke of last time." He glanced to Thomas, then back to Leslie with disdain. "The one calling herself Sandler's daughter."

"It's not a matter of what I call myself, Mr. Zenger," she said flatly. "That's who I am."

"Young lady," he said with condescension, his expression tightening with distrust and dislike. "I'm an old man. It's late in the evening. I'm not fair game for a lengthy argument." His eyes, behind the tinted glasses, flashed with anger. "You're welcome to your opinion, your claim, and your day in court. But within my own house I'm entitled to voice my own view." He looked back to Daniels. "I know a fraud when I see one, Thomas. Why did you bring her here?"

"It's important that we talk," said Thomas.

"Who's 'we'?"

"All three of us." He paused, then asked, "May we come in?"

"Looks like you already are," he grumbled. Zenger spat on the porch.

He stepped back and held the door open. He was walking without the use of the cane. "Come on," he said. "Come in. Let's have it out in the open."

They hung their soaking coats in the front hallway, then followed the frail little man into his sitting room. The light there was dimmer than in the front hall. The embers of a fire smoldered in the fireplace and wheezed out an occasional spark or crackle. Outside the rain continued to pound against the square windows.

Zenger eased himself into his favorite leather armchair. A half-consumed brandy was on an end table beside him.

"If you wish, either of you," he said, "a drink to warm you," he motioned to a bar across the room, "help yourself. I'd serve you myself if I were twenty years younger."

Leslie declined. In silence, Thomas helped himself to a bourbon from the bar. He returned and sat down across the room from Zenger. The older man's eyes were scrutinizing his two guests. Zenger finally turned to the younger man.

"Well, Thomas," he said with concession in his voice, "I'm alone in this house. You have me at your complete mercy. What is it this time?"

"I came to you as an old friend and the son of a former partner. I need help. I need it badly."

"What kind of help?" he snapped. Leslie studied his eyes.

"I need answers," said Thomas. "And I know you don't talk on telephones."

"I've told you everything I know."

"Impossible. Who was Vincent De Septio?"

Thomas could see the reaction immediately, though Zenger did his best to mask it. It was a moment's hesitation, an infintesimal jump on the part of Zenger. The old man replied by merely saying, "What?" Thomas knew he'd struck close to something.

"Vincent De Septio. I'm sure you heard me the first time."

"He was a client of ours, your father's and mine, once upon a time many years ago." The old man sipped his brandy calmly and shrugged, leaning back to relax under questioning. "Nothing important about De Septio. Why?"

"I suspect he's very important."

The old man shrugged again and gave Thomas an innocent smile. "Suspect anything you like. It's a free country."

You old bastard, thought Thomas, knowing he was being lured into the usual verbal chess game. If Zenger had ever given an immediate straight answer in his life, Thomas had never heard it.

"Let's talk about money," said Thomas.

"All right. Let's."

"Counterfeit money."

Zenger was silent.

"Ever defend a counterfeiter?" pressed Thomas.

"Not to my recollection."

"You're perjuring yourself, counselor!" snapped Thomas caustically. "You know God-damned well what I'm talking about. De Septio and Sandler were in the same business! Weren't they?"

The old man shrugged complacently. "If you say so," he intoned calmly. And he sipped his brandy as if bored.

Thomas bolted upward from his chair and leaped at the older man, charging with fury across the small room. He smashed the end table away from Zenger's chair and sent it crashing against a wall. The lamp upon it shattered, its bulb bursting with a flashing pop. Thomas grabbed the brandy snifter from Zenger's hand and furiously, with one motion of the hand, hurled it crashing against the back of the fireplace.

The old man's eyes were wide with surprise and fright now. The brandy whooshed into flame.

Almost before Thomas knew what he was doing, he had picked up Zenger by the lapels and was shaking him.

"*God damn you! God damn you!*" roared Thomas over and over. "Are you going to talk to me or do I have to beat it to hell out of you?"

He shook Zenger mercilessly, forgetting totally about Leslie, who sat calmly to the side and watched the scene as it transpired. She studied the two combatants as dispassionately as one might watch a dull movie.

The old man's voice could be heard screaming over the younger man's. "All right! All right!" he was yelling.

And then, with a hand that was suddenly more agile and dextrous than it had previously admitted being, Zenger reached to the cane beside his chair. As the shaking stopped and as Thomas threw the octogenarian back into the leather chair, Zenger swung the cane around and caught Thomas with it. Daniels was able to raise his arm slightly in defense, blocking the blow partially and catching the brunt of it on the left of the skull.

The force sent Thomas staggering backward a step or two. His left hand rose quickly to where he'd felt the impact. The side of the skull was pounding and when he lowered his hand he saw blood on it.

But he was almost glad it had happened. The old man, defending himself like a cornered frightened animal, had literally knocked Daniels back to his senses. Thomas wondered if he otherwise could have killed the old man in a blind rage.

"Just like your father," muttered Zenger, bitterness and perhaps even a dash of hatred creeping into his voice. "A hothead."

Several seconds passed as the two men stood glowering at each other. Zenger sat in his throne of retirement, bitter, frightened, but composed.

Thomas stood in the center of the room, a thin trickle of blood on the side of his head, panting for breath with arms hanging at his side.

Zenger finally spoke.

"Sit down, young fellow," he said in a labored, sarcastic, and mock avuncular voice. "You'll get your cursed answers. You'll get everything you deserve. And more." Zenger continued to glower at the younger man. He glanced past Daniels to Leslie. "Both from me and your fraudulent friend here." He motioned his head contemptuously toward her.

Thomas didn't move until he felt Leslie beside him. One of her hands was on his left shoulder, the other on his arm. She was telling him to calm down, to sit down, and she offered him a handkerchief for the cut on his temple.

He nodded to her and eased into the nearest chair. She sat behind him and watched Zenger from over Thomas's shoulder.

"Isn't this sweet?" asked Zenger.

"De Septio," Thomas repeated. "I want to know about Vincent De Septio."

"He was a counterfeiter."

"*Was?*"

"Was. A good one, too, but he got careless. Your father got him off the hook twice."

"What did De Septio have to do with Sandler?"

Zenger hesitated slightly. "They knew each other."

"Well?"

"They were friends."

"Did they work together?"

Zenger answered with silence.

"*Did they work together!*" screamed Thomas a second time.

"*Yes!*" roared the old man. "*Yes! Yes! Yes!*" He was seething with anger but had no choice but to respond. He shook his head violently from left to right. "Boy," he said in calmer tones, "you don't know the half of what you're asking. Yes, damn you, they worked together! For a short while, very closely."

"What did they do?"

Zenger's face took on a dyspeptic look. "What the hell do you think they did? They made money. Take that literally."

Thomas eased back in his chair slightly and massaged the side of his skull with his hand and Leslie's handkerchief.

"What about the war?" Thomas asked. "World War Two."

"The Allies beat the Axis."

"I'm talking about De Septio."

"He was in the army."

"That's not a good enough answer. De Septio doesn't have an army record."

"He certainly does," said Zenger quickly, in a response that Thomas believed. "But maybe he was a little embarrassed to tell anyone about it." A faint smile returned to Zenger. He laid his cane aside. "Know what his job was for five years?"

"That was my next question."

"*Trash collection,*" said Zenger casually. Thomas voiced no response, so Zenger, almost merrily, repeated. "That's right. Trash collection."

"I don't understand."

"Of course not," said Zenger. "There's nothing *to* understand. De Septio collected trash for five years in the army. Imagine. Pearl Harbor. Iwo Jima. The Bulge. Berlin. Stalingrad. And Vincent De Septio was busy picking up trash." The old man laughed like an elf.

"Something's missing."

"You don't believe me?" Zenger's eyebrows shot upward, as if recoiling from an affront.

"No," said Thomas crisply.

"Then you can ask Mr. De Septio yourself."

Leslie leaned forward, as if suddenly absorbed in what Zenger was saying. Thomas noted her movement.

"What do you mean?" asked Thomas.

"That was your next question, wasn't it? You've done your homework, I can see that. You were going to ask me where De Septio went after 1954, weren't you? You wanted to know why his case got tossed out and where he went. Didn't you?"

Humbled slightly, Thomas replied, "Yes." Zenger had jumped ahead of him again. They both knew it.

"Do you know anything about patriotism, Thomas?"

"Patriotism?"

"No," scoffed Zenger. "Of course not. The younger folks don't even know the word anymore." Zenger's eyes burned at Daniels. "Vinnie De Septio, whatever else his faults, was a patriot. That's why, despite his transgressions, the government chose twice not to prosecute him. Patriotism, Thomas," Zenger continued in lofty tones and after a slight pause. The old man glanced at Leslie. "That's what this is *all* about." He raised a finger and stabbed it at her. "That's what *she's* all about. Remember that, you young moron. You heard it here first."

Thomas let the insult pass. "Where's De Septio?" he asked.

"In a town in Pennsylvania. A town outside of Scranton. It's called

Barnstable. De Septio retired from crime in 1954. Out of gratitude, the government gave him a new identity, a new name, and a new start in life." Zenger was philosophical. "I've always liked that phrase, 'a new start in life.' "

"What's his new name?"

"New? We're talking about twenty-one years," taunted the old man. "But the name is Jonathan Grover. He's easy enough to find. He's the only one in town by that name." Zenger smiled. "Runs a stationery story. Get it? He prints stationery now, not money. And he will have been undisturbed for many years until you darken his doorstep." Zenger paused. "Anything else?"

Thomas shook his head. The left temple still throbbed. He felt Leslie's hand on his shoulder and glanced at her to see if she had any questions for Zenger. She shook her head. She didn't.

"That's all," Thomas said.

"You better hope so. You're never getting into this house again. If I ever see you or expect you again, I'll have our local gendarmes waiting. The police like me here," he added with cynicism.

Thomas motioned toward the door to Leslie. Without speaking they rose from their chairs and returned toward the front door. Thomas could feel the old man's icy gaze on his back the entire time and he somehow felt, though he'd gotten the answers he'd come for, that the old master had ended with the upper hand again.

That feeling was reinforced as Thomas opened the front door to leave.

"Hey Tom, boy!" called the old man from the next room. Thomas looked to his left as he felt the rainy night before him through the open door. Down to his left through the alcove he could see into the sitting room. He looked squarely at the old man, seated merrily again in his chair despite the broken table and lamp beside him.

"Tom, boy!" Zenger called. "There's something else. As long as I'm in the business of shattering images this evening, I've got something else."

Daniels stood in the doorway, saying nothing but waiting to hear. Leslie stood outside, struggling to put up an umbrella against the rain.

"Do you know what your own old man did during the war? Big brave Bill Daniels? Remember all those high command stories he told you when you were a boy? A younger boy?"

Thomas listened, waiting.

"A pack of lies, Tommy. A mound of bullshit," shouted the old man enthusiastically. "You can check it for yourself, but Bill Daniels sat on his cowardly ass in New York for the whole war. He was a *recruiting sergeant.* Get that? Too chickenshit to go out and pull a trigger himself. So he lined up other people to do the fighting. Ask De Septio what a 'recruiting sergeant' is, if you live long enough to find him!"

The old man had a rattling, cackling laugh like that of the Devil himself. The laughter resounded in Daniels's ears until he quickly bolted forward into the rain and closed the door. He took Leslie's arm and huddled with her very closely beneath the protection of the umbrella. Mercifully, it took only a few steps before the maniacal laughter from the sitting room was drowned by the fury of the cold rain. Moments later, Thomas and Leslie huddled into the chilly car.

He was angry, disgusted. Her mind was flashing, inquisitive. "How well do you know him?" she asked.

"The more I see him, the less I think I know him," he answered, starting the car and gunning the engine. He glanced at her, frowning slightly and seeing her face illuminated dimly by the house lights. "I've seen him only a few times in my life," he admitted, "even though he was my father's partner. Why?"

"*He* says I'm an imposter. *I* say he's lying," she explained briskly and incisively. "I wanted to know whom you're inclined to believe."

He started to pull the car away from Zenger's isolated driveway. "My father gave me a few pieces of good advice in his lifetime," he said. "One tidbit was, 'Never trust the lawyer for the opposition. Assume he's lying.' "

She smiled, satisfied. "Good. That answers my question."

Upon her insistence, they registered under false names at an old guesthouse, the interior of which recalled and celebrated the glorious slaughter of the great whales. They parked the car for the night in an isolated spot near the center of town, but nowhere near their guesthouse. "I don't want anyone to be able to find us tonight," Leslie explained.

Thomas didn't ask why.

Chapter 23

It all began with water, the paleontologists maintain, with life beginning in small tidal pools beside prehistoric oceans. On the next morning in Nantucket, however, as Thomas Daniels and Leslie McAdam drove toward the ferry depot, there seemed a chance that all would end in water just as easily.

Great sheets of water, ripping across the island. It wasn't a hurricane, nowhere close according to the natives, and the dauntless ferry, the *Islander*, planned to make its very-early-morning crossing as scheduled.

Thomas wondered whether the ferry ran through Yankee ingenuity or Yankee stubbornness, or perhaps an ingredient of both. There were few passengers, no more than fifteen or twenty, although Thomas and Leslie weren't close enough to any to see their faces, and the ferry ran with a skeletal crew of four. Nonetheless, they were both grateful when the ship left at its appointed hour.

Having their virtual run of the ship, Thomas and Leslie sat on an upholstered bench on the port side. Both were silent, Leslie having fallen particularly untalkative since the previous evening. "Something's bothering you," Thomas had insisted.

"No, not actually," she'd said.

"Something about Zenger."

The statement was followed by silence, then a girlish shrug. "He gave me the creeps," she'd said.

Already, he thought he knew her better than that. She was a woman, not a girl, and was given not to irrational "creeps," but to thoughtful observation and conclusion. "Creeps" was the girlish disguise she liked to crawl into. It was a mask for something else, something more disturbing.

But what? He didn't know.

Thomas closed his eyes for a moment, asking if she minded. No, not terribly, she said, and if he wanted to nap, she might take a walk around the boat.

"Walk? To where?"

"I like to explore," she said. And she left it at that.

"Try to stay on board," he kidded. "I hear it's hell to turn these tubs around."

"Just for you."

He closed his eyes and an hour passed. He was awakened by the sound of two children whose mother thought nothing of letting them run up and down the aisle between seats. Not surprising that the kids should wake him, he thought, blinking awake. Enough noise to wake the dead. He looked next to him and she was gone.

The ship was rocking perceptibly. Torrents of water continued to pound it and lash the windows. Thomas looked around, pulling himself up in his seat. Leslie was nowhere to be seen.

All right, he thought, he'd have a walk, too. There were only so many places, indoors or out, where she could have gone.

He spent fifteen minutes looking. Indoors, outdoors. Above on the wet deck, down below near the cars. Under cover, in the rain.

She was gone. Damn her, he thought. Always games. Games? He was beginning to be concerned. A vision of her being washed overboard flashed before his mind. But he quickly shook it. She was far too careful for that. His mind raced to a murder case his father had once been in. A man had pushed his wife overboard on an otherwise joyful Bahamian cruise. Not guilty. The body of the deceased, the court ruled, had been sodden with alcohol before being immersed in the deep. Accidental drowning. William Ward Daniels had been *proud* of that one.

Thomas walked through the interior sitting rooms of the ferry. He passed the fire station, with its extinguishers and axes. With each minute that passed he became more anxious that something was wrong. He prowled the rear of the ship, finally stepping outside onto the extremity of the main deck farthest to the rear.

He looked around, bracing himself against the wind and sheets of rain by holding firmly to a deck railing. He looked around. No Leslie. He heard a noise.

He turned, leaning against the railing, and saw the door closing again, the same door he'd come through. A wide man in a city raincoat was approaching him. A hat shielded his face from the rain.

Thomas noticed the sign near him. No PASSENGERS BEYOND THIS POINT. A crew member, Thomas thought, coming to tell him to stay out of that area. It was dangerous. No one anywhere else on the ship could see that section of the rear deck. Why, someone could fall off and never be . . .

Thomas froze with the sudden realization. His mind was instantly off Leslie. He wanted to be out of there, preferably back inside.

Thomas started to move, but his worst fears were suddenly realized. The man grabbed him by the arm, pushing him back to the rail.

Thomas tried to push the man's grip away, but heard his voice. "I want to talk!" the man said, shouting to be heard above the elements.

The men came eye to eye. The coldness Thomas felt beneath his clothes was not from the wind and water. This was one of the men in the elevator at Anspacher Gallery. This, in fact, was the man with the scarf.

"Where is she?" he said.

"Get your hand off me," Thomas countered.

The gloved hand released his arm. A gesture of good faith? "Where'd she go?" he asked.

"I don't know what you're talking about." A bold lie, which didn't betray the fact that Thomas's heart was pounding so fiercely that he could feel it throughout his chest.

The man's face, thick with vaguely Eastern European features, broadened into a wide grin. "I'll help your memory a little," said the man. And as if on cue, with the end of the sentence, the inquisitor's fist smacked into the center of Thomas's stomach.

Thomas was completely unprepared for the shot to the solar plexus. He winced violently and doubled up, gasping and taking in half a mouthful of rain.

The strong hand went to his shoulder and straightened him into an upright position.

"Does that help you think?" asked the man. "Maybe now you know."

Thomas coughed. He tried to gasp, "I don't know." The man shook him and said, "Answer me. Answer me!"

"I don't know!" Thomas barked again, sputtering the words through the rain. His face and head were soaked.

"Bet you don't know how to swim either."

Thomas was shoved hard against the rear railing. The ferry's diesel engines ground noisily below. The water swirled.

"I'm telling you," he insisted angrily and fearfully, "I don't know! She disappeared! Maybe you already tossed her overboard."

"Maybe," gloated the man. "But not yet. She came on the boat with you. I want her!"

"So do I." A moment passed as the assailant seemed to decide his next move. Thomas's throat and stomach still pained him. He spoke, playing for time. "How'd you find us? Zenger?"

"Assume whatever you like. Where's the girl?"

"Then it *was* Zenger. What'd you do? Fly up last night, knowing we couldn't get off by boat until today? Then you watched the ferry depot until we showed up? Right?"

"You're smart," he growled. "Not as smart as your father. But smart." The man had a trace of a middle-European accent. German? Polish? Something. "How's your throat? Hurt?"

"I like my throat. I like swallowing with it."

"Like to swallow some water? A whole ocean of water?"

Thomas felt the grip go tight on his arm again. The man would have little trouble forcing him over the rail. Little, if allowed to strike first. Thomas reached into his coat pocket and gripped his car keys.

"I'll make you a trade. The girl's life for yours. Where is she? Otherwise you both go overboard and—"

Thomas's free arm streaked for the man's face, a Volvo key gripped like a blade between forefinger and middle finger, braced by the whole fist.

A strong forearm flew up to block Thomas's thrust. But it wasn't quite in time. The key savagely slashed into the thick skin beneath the left eye. It dug and it tore and the man bellowed with pain and anger. Blood was already streaming from the jagged deep cut.

Thomas tried to dig the key into the man's eye. He failed. A forearm smashed Thomas's fist so hard that the key, Daniels's only defense, flew across the wet deck. The man's eyes were crazed. Both hands clutched Thomas around the neck and throat.

Thomas knew. He was to be killed. He'd had his one chance and he'd failed. Thomas kicked at the man's shins, trying desperately to dislodge the grip upon him.

But the hands were at his throat. Then only one hand as the man pulled back a fist and slammed it into Thomas's stomach.

Thomas winced and doubled again, feeling as if he should crumple to the ground. He staggered and tried to stay up. But he was absolutely no match for a man schooled in violence. A savage chop to the back of his neck, and Thomas went down to the wet deck. He wasn't fully conscious. The man tried to pick him up. Thomas tried to stay down. Thomas tried to crawl away. Over the railing would be the next stop. Thomas knew it.

He heard a remote noise in the background.

The man leaned down and grabbed him by the coat, hoisting him up. Thomas was blinded by water in his eyes and pain all over his body. He was coughing and trying to break the grip on him. But he kept being lifted, lifted. No matter how much he struggled to stay down, he was being forced upward against the railing until he could feel half his body being forced over it.

Only a matter of seconds now, for the other half to join the first.

He was hanging on with one leg and one arm, looking up blearily into the face of his killer, fighting the rain, the wind, and a man twice as strong as he. He was almost over.

Then abruptly the man let out an unearthly bellow. A howl. A scream of anguish that belonged in a slaughterhouse. The iron grip melted. The power in the hands was gone.

Thomas blinked rapidly and peered through the rain. The man's eyes were bulging, inflated in the most undiluted anguish. He staggered and turned.

Thomas, clinging to the railing, gawked, almost sickened at the sight.

The broad back had been hacked open. Blood poured from a huge seven-inch gash that formed a diagonal cross against his upper backbone. The man staggered, trying to reach with his hands behind his back, trying to get to the source of the pain.

But he couldn't. He could only lurch.

Then Thomas saw. Leslie.

She was standing several feet from him, the fire ax gripped defiantly in her hands, hatred—and perhaps fear—in her eyes. Blood, washed by rain, dripped from the blade of the ax.

The man howled obscenely. Thomas was transfixed by what he saw, almost forgetting to pull the part of him that was not on board back from over the rail.

The man lunged at Leslie, cursing her. She held the ax like a spear, thrusting the blunt handle end forward and thumping it with a loud crack against the man's upper chest bone. Then, slashing with the wooden end, she crashed it against his head, sending him down against the wet floorboards.

She dropped the ax. She extended a hand to Thomas and pulled him back from the railing. His mind was a mass of confusion, his body still anguished in several parts.

"Help me," was all she said.

Help *her*? he wondered.

The body was still writhing, still alive but bleeding profusely.

"Help me," she repeated.

He didn't understand. He didn't know what she wanted.

She went to the body, lifted the struggling assassin by a shoulder, and motioned to Thomas. Motioned to the man's other shoulder. And motioned to the rear of the deck.

He stood there. He knew what she wanted. He couldn't.

"Do it, damn it!" she screamed. "He tried to kill you! Don't you understand? *Twice* he tried to kill you!"

He grabbed the other shoulder, and with a quick motion across ten feet of wet deck they ran the man to the railing, using their momentum, the man's momentum and the ship's to send him hurtling against the railing, then up and over it.

Thomas expected to hear a splash.

He didn't. The rain, the wind, and the engines covered it.

They were both soaked, of course, and Thomas knew he was going to be sick. He looked at the wide wake left by the boat and tried to see the body.

He couldn't. The indeterminate mixture of sea and rain covered everything with gray. The man was gone. No visibility on Nantucket Sound in a squall. Fifty feet at best.

He turned and faced Leslie. She was surprisingly calm, as if it were all in a day's work. She looked at him inquisitively as if to say "My, wasn't that close." Then she picked up the ax, carefully holding it by the handle, and glancing around to assure herself that they remained unobserved.

Then she flung it in a twisting, spinning arc over the rear railing, perhaps to act as a tombstone for the nameless man they'd buried.

Again, they heard no splash.

She took his hand. "I wouldn't trust Zenger again," she said in a most appalling understatement. "He's not on our side. Shifty eyes." She gave his hand a pull. "Come on," she said. "Let's get dry." She gathered his car keys for him. Some women think of everything.

He pulled back and shook his head. "Not yet," he said. He motioned to the rail and indicated the turbulence in his digestive system.

"Ah, yes. I see," she said. She paused. "Well, when you're finished come inside and we'll have some tea. It will make you feel better."

He nodded. She disappeared inside and he spent a sickened moment at the rail, alone this time, looking at the gray sea behind the ship and marveling how nature covers everything.

He turned. The rain washed across the floorboards of the deck and the runoff joined the sea. A moment ago the floorboards had been pink with the suggestion of blood. But within another half minute all traces of blood were gone and the color of the deck was a glimmering green again.

He went inside to where the two children were running up and down a different aisle now, shrieking and playing pirates.

Chapter 24

He watched through the drawn front gate of the ferry as the vessel neared land. Occasionally he glanced in his rearview mirror, half expecting the car to be surrounded by police. "Who was the man you threw over the side?" they'd ask him. "Why'd you kill him?" they'd demand. *"She* swung the ax," he'd answer. And they'd never believe it. Was *that* her game? He chided himself. She'd saved his life twice and he'd caught himself still being suspicious.

"I've never been involved in this sort of thing," he mused absently. He could feel the jitteriness in his stomach. He was shaken.

She looked at him sternly, almost inquisitively. "Your father was in plenty of them. Wasn't he?" It sounded like a probe.

He turned to her, frowning, sensing an implication but unable to grasp it. "What makes you say that?"

Her face softened and she gave an innocent shrug. "Just that I've heard your father's reputation," she said. "A fairly well-known criminal lawyer, wasn't he?"

"The word *criminal* is a noun, not an adjective," he said. "My father's got nothing to do with me."

She laughed slightly, raising her eyebrows. "Oh, come now," she said. "He has *everything* to do with you. *He* drew you into this."

He searched her face, begging for more. "If you know more than I do, I'd love to hear it."

"Of course I don't," she scoffed. "All I'm saying is that if you search your memory—"

"I don't know one bit more than you do!" he snapped at her quickly, tension and a vibrating headache getting the better of his nerves. "How many times do I have to tell you that?"

She lowered her eyes demurely, not challenging him, but rather embarrassing him. He sighed. "I'm sorry. I don't mean to yell at you." He tried to smile. "I owe you too much, I guess."

She returned his smile. She could forgive as easily as she could sketch or dispose of a body.

They were no more than a hundred feet from docking now. The buildings of the Woods Hole wharf were visible through a misting rain and a gray fog.

"Ever paint seascapes?" he asked.

She wore a fleeting smile, her artistry being recalled to her. "Occasionally," she answered brightly. "I went to the Gaspé in Quebec for a summer. Fabulous land- and seascapes up there. You should see it sometime. Breathtaking."

"I should," he agreed, though his breath had been taken often enough recently to last far into the future.

Her smile vanished. "I don't think I could do a seascape again for a while though," she said.

He asked why, as she knew he would.

"I'd become involved with the water," she said. "I'd see the man we just buried."

He looked away. So much for changing the subject. The boat docked with a sudden grinding of the engines and a resonant thud. Moments later they drove from the ferry and picked up the route northward to the bridge to the mainland.

They drove for the entire day, stopping only for a meal late in the afternoon. In the evening they crossed from New Jersey into Pennsylvania. By nine o'clock that night they were in the town of Barnstable, where they checked into a motel which featured Magic Fingers, loud televisions in every room, and every other drearily functional detail expected of such places. In spite of it all, or perhaps because of it, they were asleep by midnight.

The light sliced across the motel room, crossing the bed where Thomas's head was. He felt the moonlight on his eyes.

At first, in his sleep, he held a forearm across his face. But the light disturbed his rest. He found the brightness an intrusion, one which he could not immediately avoid. Blinking, his eyes opened.

He was aware of movement in the room.

For a moment he lay there in stark fear. He would not move.

He focused his eyes on a mirror. Then he could see. The room was easily bright enough for him to see the figure of a nude woman moving before the dresser.

Gently he rolled over. He was now aware that he was alone in the bed. He kept his eyelids close together so that they'd appear closed. He watched her. She was doing something which she did not want him to see. She stood there completely naked, facing him, watching to make sure that he was still asleep.

He didn't move.

Quickly she dressed. She grabbed her coat silently from a closet.

But instead of immediately leaving, she returned to the dresser. There she began picking through the coins he'd taken from his pockets before going to bed. She was putting together a handful of change.

Carefully she took the key from the top of the dresser. She looked back at him to assure herself that he still slept. She reached the door.

His instinct was to sit up quickly and demand to know where she was going. He glanced at a bedside clock. It was three A.M. He said nothing. She disappeared out the door.

Immediately he sat up and pulled on his clothing. He was just lunging for his coat when he heard her footsteps outside his window. He edged close to the curtain and looked out.

He saw her.

Leslie was in the parking lot in front of the motel. She was trotting quickly toward the center of the lot. He couldn't see what was attracting her there. Then he realized. She was going to the telephone booth.

He watched her. She glanced around as she entered the booth. She looked carefully back toward the motel. She saw no one. She put two coins into the pay telephone.

He could see that she was not speaking. She was waiting for her coins to get her a dial tone. But something was wrong.

He watched her press the coin return and repeat the process of dropping coins. Then she struck the telephone with the flat of her hand. A second time she hit it. She pressed the coin return and tried a third time. The telephone was out of order. It wouldn't work for her.

Disgustedly she stepped out of the booth. She looked in all directions, obviously realizing that the only telephone nearby was out of order. She was only about fifty feet away from him. He could see the expression of displeasure on her face, an expression of anger that he'd never seen on her before. She began to walk back to the motel.

He quickly pulled off his clothes and dived back into the bed. He resumed the same sleeping position he'd been in before she left. Seconds later, the door quietly opened.

She undressed quickly, laying each article of clothing exactly where it had been. Then she stood in the middle of the room, naked again, now with the moonlight cutting a ribbon of white across her.

She climbed back onto the bed, a bare knee first. She started to ease beneath the covers.

He sprang up, surprising her so that she began a slight scream. He grabbed her shoulders with both arms and pushed her back down onto the mattress. An image flashed into his mind as he saw the scar across her throat: the image of the Italian youth who'd tried to kill her.

He lay on top of her, pinning her down playfully and trapping her between himself and the mattress.

He began to laugh, showing her that everything was all right.

"Did I scare you?" he asked.

"Half to death," she said, her British intonation sounding particularly indignant.

"What's wrong? Restless?"

"I couldn't sleep."

"No?" He gently slid off her and sat up, propping a pillow against his back. She sat up with him, the sheet falling away from her and resting across her lap.

"I went out," she said. "For some air. I took some change from your dresser," she said.

"The air is free," he offered.

"Of course," she said. "I was looking for a soft-drink machine. I was thirsty, too."

"Find it?" he asked.

"Yes," she said.

He smiled, watching her closely and seeing that she was perfectly at home with a lie. "I guess customs are different here from in England," he said.

"Sorry?" she asked, cocking her head slightly and not knowing what he meant. He studied her carefully in the soft indirect light. He could see all of her, from the delicate features of her face to where the sheet lay motionless and slightly rumpled across her lap. "Customs?"

"Yes," he said. "Over here, people don't normally get sodas out of telephone booths."

There was a moment's awkward pause, as if she'd been slapped suddenly, not expecting it at all. Then her mouth flew open, not in defensiveness, it seemed, but in resentment.

"Why, you spy," she charged. "You *sneak!*"

"*Me?* It wasn't me who was skulking around in the dark."

"Might just as well have been," she ranted indignantly. She folded her arms across her breasts so that he could see them no longer. She pulled up the sheet and held it to her. "You're a wicked, distrustful man," she declared.

"I know this trick," he said. "You learn it in the first year of law school. Put your opponent on the defensive. Don't try it with me." She looked away from him in disgust. "Tell me who you telephoned."

"No one," she said, abandoning her initial tactic and now playing the hurt little girl. "The booth was out of order."

"I could see that much. Who'd you *try* to call?"

She reached to him and took his hand. His hand resisted slightly, indicating to her that he wanted truth, not affection, not at that moment, anyway. Her face appeared confused, as if torn between two confessions, neither attractive. Then she spoke to him with feeling, the same sincere voice that she'd first used to lure him into her case weeks earlier.

"The truth will hurt you, I suspect."

"Not as much as the goon on the boat wanted to hurt me, I hope."

Her voice was quiet, appearing to come from the heart as much as from the scarred throat. "No," she agreed with a weak smile. "Not *that* much." She paused and then gave it to him, as if to thrust a dagger quickly to get it over with. "I already have a lover," she said.

The bluntness of it took him aback. He could not find words. She could.

"In point of fact," she said slowly, "I was living with a man in Montreal. Before I came down to see you. When this is over I plan to go back to him. I love him."

He sensed a certain deflation within his chest, a sensation of hopes tumbling. He knew he had no right to her, no claim, other than a professional and theoretically dispassionate one. She too, like Andrea, like his ex-wife, was another man's woman. He had no right to expect otherwise.

"I've been thinking of him," she said. "Each time I've been in bed with you . . . Shall I go on?"

"Why not?"

"Each time I've been in bed with you, I've thought of him. At least part of the time. I wanted to hear his voice," she said, still holding his hand. "Even if only for a few minutes. That's where I was. That's who

I tried to call." She watched her words sinking in and watched his expression, which he tried to maintain without change. "I'm sorry," she said.

"Sorry? Why?"

"I thought you might be hurt," she explained. "Most men like to think they're the only ones."

"I suppose they do," he allowed, the sullenness in his spirit carefully disguised. "*Some* men. I won't make that mistake. As long as we understand each other."

"I think we do," she said. She kissed him affectionately, not as a lover might, but as a good friend would. She was very tired, she explained further. She settled down onto her half of the twin beds and pulled the covers closely around her body. She slept.

He understood. He knew what she'd been trying to tell him and he accepted it, her story, at its face value. It fit perfectly into place. Women like her *were* always taken, or so it seemed. He eased into his half of the sleeping accommodations.

He wanted to turn to her. He wanted to ask more about the other man. Thomas disliked him, having never met him, and wanted to know about him, perhaps to be able to find a chink in the man's armor, a character weakness which she'd never noticed.

He lay there in thought, feeling very lonesome, feeling quite left out from something he wished to share. He wanted to wake her and join her on her side. But now, because he'd asked about the telephone call, he couldn't. He wondered why he couldn't have kept his suspicions to himself. At least for one more night.

They checked out of the motel and drove across Barnstable, passing through a strip-mining area and then by a coal-processing plant. They easily found the white split-level home, surrounded by bare trees, which had the name J. GROVER on the mailbox before it.

When Thomas pulled his car to a stop at the curb before the house, he noticed a long blue car already parked in the driveway. A young girl, school aged and appearing to be about ten, played on the front walk.

Thomas turned off the ignition of his car. "Coming with me?" he asked Leslie.

"If you want me to," she answered.

"You don't have to."

She pondered it for a moment. "Tom," she said, "it's upsetting to me."

"What is?"

"To have to look at this man. An associate of my father's." She hesitated. "I know I come across as pretty cold-blooded sometimes, but other times . . . well, I *am* human, you know."

"Apparently."

"Is it acceptable if I wait here?" she asked.

"I don't mind," he said.

She smiled with a certain sheepishness, as if embarrassed over revealing a weakness. She leaned to him quickly and kissed him on the cheek. "Thanks," she said. "I do appreciate it."

He pushed her away slightly. "No big show of affection here," said Thomas. He was looking at the door to the Grover house. A man was leaving. Thomas studied him closely.

It was a tall erect man with a briefcase, a man in a gray suit covered by an open topcoat. He gave a stark smile to the young girl on the flagstone path and the girl responded perfunctorily, without emotion.

The man walked toward the blue Pontiac.

Thomas stepped from his own car and called to the other man, calling him by Grover's name. Thomas studied the other man intently as he called. Thomas was ignored.

"Do you want my father, mister?" a small female voice asked. The young girl couldn't understand why the visitor had mistaken someone else for her father. She was quick to correct the error.

Then she led Thomas to her front door and into the house, calling for her father as she turned and saw the second arrival, the woman, sitting in Daniels's car.

Thomas heard a man's deep voice saying, "Yes, sir?" He turned to see the portly stationery-store owner emerging from a swinging door which led from the kitchen.

"Hello," said Thomas mildly. "You're Jonathan Grover?"

"I am," said Grover cautiously. A woman in an apron emerged from the kitchen behind him. Elaine Grover stood behind her husband.

"My name is Thomas Daniels," he said, and getting no response he added after a moment, "My father was William Ward Daniels."

Grover looked at him blankly, then broke suddenly into a broad smile. "I'll be God damned! Of course," Grover said. "You look just like him. Same face, same hair. Remarkable. Same profession, Mr. Daniels?"

"Similar."

"I see," answered Grover with a trifle of hesitation. "Well, then, I don't know what brings you here, but if you'd like to step in for some coffee, we'll chat."

Thomas followed, leaving Leslie in the car behind him, completely out of his view.

Thomas Daniels found himself seated at a long walnut dining-room table. Why a family of three would have such a large table, at which eight could comfortably fit, was a small transient mystery to Thomas. Grover moved to the other end of the table, walking with a slight waddle, and wedged his suet-laden frame into a captain's chair. He folded his arms before him on the table and, by his presence and his very corpulence, seemed to be a man who'd spent many happy hours in that location.

Elaine Grover served them coffee. And a cinnamon cake. Grover took two ample pieces and Elaine offered the rest to their guest.

Thomas declined with a smile.

"No, no, I insist," said Grover, his mouth full and speaking with a voice muffled by pastry. "It's excellent."

Elaine hadn't moved the cake from where she held it for Thomas. Thomas, reassessing his decision, took the smallest piece offered. Grover took another piece as it passed by him again and was working on that third piece when he began to speak.

"Damned good, isn't it?" he said.

Trying to be sociable, Thomas agreed.

"I'll get you another piece before you leave," Grover said. "Elaine will wrap it. You can take it with you." His lips smacked as he spoke, punctuating his sentences.

Grover continued for several minutes, dipping into a monologue on his wife's baking. "Married, Daniels?" he asked, not waiting for an answer. "Marry a woman who can cook. A wife's got two jobs to do. Cooking's the other one." He continued, moving on to the comparative merits of the bakeries of lower Manhattan. "The French think they're the bakers," he postulated between gulps of coffee. "French don't know crap about pastry. Show me a great baker and I'll show you an Italian."

He allowed himself a satisfied smile. Thomas returned it. Grover was no fool. He'd just admitted who he was, his origins around Mulberry Street. "How's the city?" he asked. "I never go there no more."

"It's still there," said Thomas.

"It's a great town," Grover said, as if reminiscing. "But it's a young man's town, don't you think? I had myself some times there." He looked over his shoulder to the door to the kitchen. As if on cue, Elaine reappeared with coffee and more cake. Thomas received more without asking.

When Mrs. Grover disappeared again, Thomas spoke, put at ease somewhat by the large man's informality. "I was afraid I'd have difficulty with you," he said. "You wouldn't want to admit, you know, who . . ."

"Who I am?"

"Yes."

Grover stretched his expansive shoulders. "What's there to deny? I don't shoot my mouth off around this town. But you? You're your father's son. Why would I lie to you? You probably know more about me than I do myself," he chomped.

"I doubt it," Thomas conceded.

"I'll tell you something," said Grover, leaning forward slightly as if to share a secret. "I don't say 'I'm sorry' for nothing I ever done. Nothing." Behind the conspiratorial smile were hard eyes. "The neighborhood where I grew up was a cesspool of robbing and stealing and knifing. I done what I did to get out of it."

"I'm sure you did," said Thomas, anxious to strike a point of agreement. And equally anxious to move on to more pressing matters.

"I'll bet you would have done the same."

Thomas shrugged, without indication either way.

"You wouldn't have?"

"I don't know. I wasn't in your situation. A man never knows what he'll do in a situation until he's in it." A good response, Daniels congratulated himself. He was certain now that the cagey Grover was trying to manipulate the conversation.

"Good point," allowed Grover. He nodded in thought. "Your Dad used to say something similar. What was it?"

"I'm not sure."

"Have some more cake," he said with a rising laugh. "How many times do you live?"

"That's hard to say."

"Excuse me?"

"Some people manage to lead two lives," Thomas suggested. "Yourself, for example. Take that as a compliment." Grover nodded gratefully. "Maybe some other people, too."

"You're losing me," said Grover curtly, the wide grin gone.

"Really? It concerns you. Indirectly."

"I'm surprised that there's still anything that could concern me," he said, obvious annoyance beneath his flat tone of voice. He was licking his fingers, making soft smacking sounds, then with slight nervousness working on a thumbnail with his teeth.

"It's nothing for you to be worried about," said Thomas. "It affects a client of mine."

"Oh," said Grover, shaking his head warily and speaking louder, "but I *do* worry. I worry about everything. You know, under normal circumstances I'd tell you absolutely nothing. I'd want you to prove who you are."

"I could if you wish."

Grover held up a hand. "No need. You wear your identification. I can see your father all through you."

"I understand you were pretty good," said Thomas.

"Good?"

"As a forger."

The rotund man's eyes twinkled. "A man takes a certain pride in his work," he allowed. "No matter what that line of work is."

"I understand you were very good."

A smile crossed Grover's face. "Want to know the truth, Tom, if I can call you that? I was excellent."

"Would 'unsurpassed' be the proper word?"

"Maybe," he conceded. His deft fingers drummed on the wooden table in front of him. He paused and Thomas remained silent, sensing that Grover, out of pride or nostalgia or both, would say more. "I'll tell you how good I was," he added, his eyes twinkling. "I would forge a man's signature to a check, then take the check to the bank it was drawn on. I'd present it to the teller for payment, but I'd say to the teller, 'Please. Take a close look at the signature. I don't know the man who signed it. I want to be sure it's genuine.' "

"And?"

"The teller would compare my forgery against the real thing. Then I'd be informed that the check was fine. No problem."

"And that always worked?"

"Never failed. Look, would I try to sell a product that wasn't perfect? I told you, I have my pride."

"You also had your legal problems."

"For that I had your father," Grover recalled fondly. "One way or another, when push came to shove, Bill Daniels would get me off."

"Like before the war?"

Grover's eyes narrowed slightly and he was less given to elaboration. "Correct," he said.

"And in 1954."

"Correct again."

"Can we talk about the war?"

"I fought in Europe."

"What's 'trash collection' mean?"

"I have a cousin who's in refuse hauling. That's all it means to me."

"That's not what Adolph Zenger said."

"Whatever Zenger said," said Grover calmly, "I wouldn't put too much faith in it. You must know yourself that he's an old liar." Grover's thick brow furrowed. "Did *he* send you here?"

"What about Arthur Sandler?"

"What about him? He's dead."

"No he's not."

Grover gave Thomas a look which seemed to convey genuine surprise. He was thoughtful for a moment. "No," he said. "I saw the body myself. I was his friend for a while, you know that, I'm sure. I viewed the body after he was shot. It was him."

"What would happen," asked Thomas slowly, "if I told you I thought you were lying?"

Grover's tone became more grave. "You'd be halfway out of here," he said. "Look, Daniels. As you probably noticed, I'm a respectable member of this neighborhood. For the first time I've got things people can't take away from me. Nobody except my wife even knows who I was. I plan to keep it that way. I'm not burrowing into the dirt of twenty or thirty years ago. I paid my debt to—"

"How? You never spent a day of your life in jail."

Grover's eyes were angry. "Why don't you look in your old man's files."

"They were torched."

"Pity." Grover glared at Daniels. "All right, I'll tell you anyway. I agreed to be an informer. I'd inform on a man the Feds wanted. I'd get a pardon, they'd arrest their man. Trouble is, the man they wanted got shot first. I still got my pardon."

"Sandler?"

"You're brilliant." He glanced at his watch. "I have a store to open in fifteen minutes. Saturday's my big day." Then, unable to resist a parting shot, he added, "Not all of us were lucky enough to have a wealthy lawyer for a father. Some of us have to work." He rose rudely from the table, pushing his chair back, and trying to end the visit.

Thomas spoke, without rising. "How many governments did Sandler work for at once?" he asked doggedly.

"What?" He looked at Thomas as if the attorney had won an uncontested divorce from his sanity. "*What?*" he repeated.

"What about yourself?"

"What *about* me?"

"*Everything* about you, right down to your current cloak of piety. Sorry," he said, starting to stand, "but I'm innately suspicious of a man who disappeared in 1939 and surfaced immediately after the war. The real problem with you, what bothers me the most, is that you have no loyalties other than yourself. You sell to the highest bidder. I wonder how many people you sold to."

Grover shook his head, calm and listening, and sensing no serious threat. "Your old man never trusted anyone either." He looked Thomas up and down. It wasn't a glare. Thomas had seen the look before. It was contempt, the contempt of the street-wise kid for the private-school boy, the dislike of someone who thought he'd had none of the breaks for someone else who seemed to have had them all. "Tell me something," said Grover. "You come busting in here bothering me, stirring up skeletons and asking me questions. Now you tell *me* something." It was posed as a challenge. "Who's this client of yours?"

"Arthur Sandler's daughter."

Grover looked at Daniels as if to wonder whether or not Daniels was serious. "Don't give *me* any crap," Grover warned, "or I'll rearrange your dental work."

"I'm serious."

"Arthur Sandler didn't have a daughter. Or a son."

"What would you say if I told you she was in a car in front of your house?"

"I'd say you needed glasses."

"Be my guest," said Daniels. He motioned with an open palm to the dining-room door.

Grover walked through to the living room and stood at the window, looking out. Thomas stood to his side, watching not the car but Grover's expression.

Grover's expression was unyielding for a second or two. Then for an instant the eyes seemed to go wide, as if in rude recognition, and the tight lips seemed to drop slightly. Almost as quickly, Grover gathered himself. But a man wears the face he has earned. Grover's expression now betrayed mystification, not hostility. Yet Thomas sensed that a full and complete story was not yet ready to be told.

"She's a fake," he said softly and calmly. "Where'd you find her?"

"She came to my office. Looking for help."

Grover took a deep breath, almost a sigh of resignation. He looked up and his puffy eyes glared into Thomas's.

"I'm going to do you a favor," he declared briskly. "I'm going to tell you the truth." From Grover, it seemed a major pronouncement.

"Will it be at odds with everything else you've told me?" asked Thomas with evident sarcasm.

"You know," said Grover, "the only thing worse than a smart-assed lawyer is a dumb-assed lawyer. Want to hear it or not?"

"Sorry," said Thomas with conciliation. "Go ahead."

"Yes, Sandler had a daughter," Grover said. "And no," he added, motioning toward the car, "that's not her. Sandler's real daughter is in London. Dead. Buried. And you'll be, too, if you don't get away from that little cutie out there."

Thomas searched the face of his father's one-time client, a man whose credibility vacilated between total and zero from minute to minute. Thomas could picture the rainy cemetery in Earl's Court. He could picture Whiteside. He could picture the tombstone.

He could picture the scar across Leslie's throat.

"Who's going to kill me?" Thomas asked.

"*She* is," said Grover simply.

"Would it surprise you that she's *saved* my live twice?"

"Not at all," he said. "Perhaps she's biding her time."

"Waiting for what?"

"For the right time. For you to reveal some piece of information that she wants. Or for you to lead her to something. Bet she questions you all the time about your old man's relationship with Sandler," he suggested with a grin.

Thomas was silent, not wishing to admit that Grover's guess was accurate.

"See?" Grover said.

"Why should I believe you?" Thomas asked.

"You probably shouldn't. But if you're lucky, you will." He glanced at his watch. He motioned to the time with utter sincerity. "Now, really, Mr.

Daniels. Please believe me. I *do* run a stationery store and it *is* Saturday."

Daniels looked at Grover and looked at the door, thinking of the woman in the car waiting for him. Waiting? For what? He was torn between leaving and staying to badger Grover with further questions, just as he was divided over whom to believe. Him? Or her? Whiteside or Leslie?

"Why would—?"

"Please," said Grover quickly, raising a fat palm and shaking his head. His double chin shook gently, too. "I've told you everything I can. Really, I have."

Their eyes met. "Please," said Grover again. He motioned to the door and a tone in his voice suggested that the next request would not be as polite.

Thomas was halfway down the flagstone path when he passed Susan Grover. The little girl was in a buoyant mood. She'd been talking to the lady in the car, she said, and her daddy could talk just like that.

"What?" asked Thomas, hardly slowing his step. Leslie sat in the car, facing away from the house.

"Daddy can talk just like the Queen," said Susan. "The Queen of—"

"Susan!"

Grover stood at his front door and bellowed at his daughter. "Susan! Get in here!"

The little girl was frightened. She turned and ran toward her father, not knowing what she'd done wrong. She'd never seen him like this. A man of many voices and faces, both voice and face now denoted one emotion: anger.

Grover glowered at Daniels. "Get off my property, mister," he said. "When we meet again it will be on *my* terms." The fat man raised his hammy forearm to his face and bit savagely into what appeared to be a muffin. He glared and chewed simultaneously.

Thomas turned and walked to his car. Leslie had witnessed the scene on the flagstone path. She'd heard Grover, but not his daughter.

Thomas slid into the driver's seat. Leslie appeared disappointed. "Your exit didn't look friendly," she noted wryly. She had a pad and pencil in her hand and was drawing an oval on it, an oval which, as the basis of a sketch, would form a head.

Thomas glanced away from the pad, back to the house where the door was slamming.

"He wouldn't talk," said Thomas, turning the car key in the ignition slot. "It's back to New York."

She nodded.

They drove through miles of wooded forestland in northeastern Pennsylvania. Leslie continued to sketch, even in the moving car. He marveled that she could do it and occasionally glanced down at her work. A man's face was appearing on the paper. Thomas recognized it. Grover. De Septio. "Why are you doing that?" he asked.

"As you Americans would say," she said, " 'for the hell of it.' "

She continued. A strange sense was upon Thomas; miles had passed before he recognized it.

He'd been here before. Not in Grover's house, and never within Grover's company. But the section of the country, along the highway, he recognized from his early teens.

On bitterly cold autumn mornings, when brown leaves crunched underfoot and formed coiled, hissing whirlwinds with the breeze, his father had taken him deer hunting. "Bag a buck before Christmas," William Ward Daniels had told his boy rhetorically. "Hunters built America." Daniels, Senior, had been a lethal shot. "Learned how to shoot in the war," he'd always explained. His father had never even seen a combat zone. But he'd taught his boy how to shoot. "It could save your life someday," opined the father.

"Like when?"

Daniels, Senior, thought. "Like when a buck is charging you," he suggested.

No buck ever charged them. Most of the bucks had wanted no part of them at all, but some had managed to fall within rifle range. For his part, Thomas was rooting for the deer and often missed his shot on purpose until quickly his father began to suspect. "You're as good a shot as I am, maybe better," the older Daniels concluded one day. "Now kill something, damn it!" he ordered.

Thomas brought down his next deer, a clean kill through the shoulder and heart. The father was elated. The boy could shoot. Proficiency with a rifle, marksmanship that was accurate at hundreds of yards, had to be learned young. Then it would never be lost.

"I hate blood sports," Thomas said absently to her as the car passed out of the wooded regions into farming land.

Leslie looked up from her pad, closed it on the likeness of Grover, and glanced at Thomas with interest.

"Hunting?" she asked, mystified.

He nodded.

"You know how to shoot?"

"I suppose," he said. "I haven't for a long time."

She let it drop and the next two hours of the drive were passed in silence.

Lincoln Tunnel brought them into Manhattan at Tenth Avenue and West Thirty-eighth Street. Thomas turned southward. Five minutes later he'd pulled his car to a halt in front of her building. The shabby block was remarkably quiet in the early hours of a Saturday afternoon. She realized immediately that only she would be getting out of the car.

"You're not coming up?" she asked.

He shook his head.

"Why not?" Her question was sympathetic, not challenging. She knew the answer. The other man in her life, the one she'd revealed the previous night.

"I don't think it would be a good idea. I need perspective."

"Perspective on what?"

On you, he thought, but he didn't say it. "On the case," he said to her. "Lawyer-client relationships," he said, "shouldn't be at the mercy of personal relationships."

She seemed nonplussed, a little hurt, and certainly surprised. "I . . . I don't understand the problem," she stammered, apparently more upset than she'd been when disposing of a body off the stern of the ferry. Or when slashing Thomas loose from strangulation in an elevator door.

"The problem," he said, "is you. I'm emotionally involved. And I shouldn't be."

"Ah," she said, her accent apparent even with that single sound. She lowered her eyes as if embarrassed. "I see," she said.

"You didn't know. Until now?"

She shook her head. "I hadn't been thinking. Not about that."

"Of course," he said, as if in resolution. His tone changed. "I have to get into my apartment anyway," he said. "I have papers there. Briefs. Books. I have motions that have to be filed for you. Right away, if possible." He let a few seconds pass. "In other words," he said, "I'm still working for you. No matter what."

"Be careful," she said. "In and out of your apartment, I mean."

He nodded.

"You're precious," she said. She leaned to him and kissed him on the cheek, a gesture of both affection and gratitude.

He watched Leslie McAdam disappear into the shabby building. He waited until she raised the window shade upstairs, signaling that she'd passed through the odorous hallway uneventfully.

Then he drove back uptown, wondering if this last case in his legal career would ever make any sense. By Fifty-seventh Street his thoughts were drifting. He wondered how Andrea Parker was getting on with Augie Reid. How long could a man in his fifties hold her? New York was a *young* man's town, he tried to convince himself.

PART SIX

It was quarter past six when Hearn returned to the Nineteenth Precinct from the downtown headquarters at One Police Plaza. He strolled casually through the squad room and continued upstairs to the cubicle where he and Shassad shared two desks.

His red hair was disheveled. Half of his thoughts were on his nine-year-old daughter who had the measles. The other half were on the contents of a manila envelope which he carried under his arm.

He arrived at Shassad's desk, found his partner present, and tossed the envelope across the desk, where it nearly knocked over a paper cup holding dark lukewarm water and a tea bag.

"Tea?" Hearn asked, seeing the untouched cup.

"It's that idiot in the deli," answered Shassad. "I ordered coffee with milk. He gives me tea. Tea!" he repeated, playing with the word and trying to sound like an English butler. "He must think I look like a fairy." He picked up the envelope. "What's this?"

"Drop a coin in the slot and see what you get," said Hearn. "Or send down a pair of thumb impressions and see what comes back." Hearn's expression was anxious, yet sober. Shassad instinctively knew that the folder within the envelope contained something new on the Ryder case. "It's the fingerprint readout for our buddy at 457 Park Avenue South," added Hearn, sitting down on the edge of his own desk. "You'll like it. I promise."

"It's about time," Shassad answered. He opened the folder and frowned slightly.

"It took a while, they told me," Hearn continued, "because they had to go to a back-date file. The guy who belongs to that thumb died in 1965. Supposedly."

Shassad examined ten different fingerprints on the master chart returned to him, ten small black-and-white squares enclosing mazes of gray lines. The left thumbprint matched Jacobus's.

But the name? The name on the file was all wrong. "I can't even pronounce this crap," said Shassad.

He read. *Sergei Sholavsky.*

"What the hell's this Sholavsky bullshit?" Shassad mumbled to his partner. "Jacobus's real name?"

"In a sense," said Hearn. "Yes. I think it is." He paused as his partner glanced through the printout with considerably increasing fascination. "Aram, fella," he said, "do you get the idea about what we're getting into?"

Shassad looked at the front and side profiles of the man named Sholavsky. Then his eye skipped to the text below.

Sholavsky, it read, was Russian by birth. Born in Minsk a few years after the First World War. A dedicated Communist, he'd served in the Red Army through the forties, distinguishing himself as an artillery captain in Germany.

After the war, Sholavsky had been promoted, a lateral promotion as opposed to an upward one within the army. He'd been assigned to the KGB, whereupon he'd been assigned to Soviet Consulates in Oslo and Paris, in the guise of a clerk.

"See the fine print at the bottom?" asked Hearn. "It says that Sholavsky died of illness in Turkey in 1965. And evidently someone somewhere believes that because these prints were among those of the dead."

"But they gave them to us anyway?" asked Shassad flatly, not yet realizing the proper implications.

"Yeah," said Hearn. "They said, 'Hey, you idiots, cut the clowning. Stop wasting our time with old prints. Cut the shit.' And just to show us that we'd taken the wrong print off the mirror, they gave me these. The print boys wanted to *show* us how wrong we were."

Shassad eyed his partner coldly. "But we're not wrong, are we?" he said.

Hearn reached into his pocket. "Here are the pictures we took," he said. "I picked them up at forensics on my way uptown."

Hearn laid out the prints taken of Jacobus through the telephoto police lens. Side view next to side view, full frontal next to full frontal.

The picture of Jacobus next to the deceased KGB agent, Sholavsky. Jacobus was ten pounds heavier, balder, and wore more lines around the eyes. Otherwise, the conclusion was clear.

"It's the same man," said Shassad. "The same man."

Hearn and Shassad exchanged long stares. They were both exhilarated and perplexed by their discovery. Yet they were simultaneously put off by it, too. What were they doing? After all, they were New York City homicide detectives, not counterespionage agents. They were investigating a murder on a sidewalk, not a spy ring.

And yet. And yet . . .

One aspect of the case, formerly so inexplicable, now made sudden, brutal sense. The two men on Seventy-third Street, the pair who'd slain Ryder. Shassad had always thought they were professionals. But his theory had made no sense. What business did a janitor have dealing with trained killers and alerting them when to strike a designated victim? A janitor had no such business. But an alien agent? A man long since thought to be dead, masquerading for years as a night custodian? Professional assassins fit perfectly to a man like that.

After several moments of pause, Hearn spoke. "Aram, look," he said. "We've got to make a decision. This doesn't look like our turf. We could wrap this up as is and dump it on the Feds. Matching fingerprints, pictures, the corpse, everything. We'd never see it again, which might suit us fine."

"Yeah," said Shassad, hesitantly and thoughtfully.

"You don't like that, do you?"

"Hell," said Shassad. "What do we get paid to do? Solve murders, right? We run with it. I don't give a flying fuck where it takes us."

Hearn's face radiated with a smile. "I knew you'd see it my way," he intoned.

"Have some tea," said Shassad. He held up the cardboard cup as if to throw it at Hearn. "Come on. Let's do some digging."

And dig they did, assisted by the two other teams, McGowan and Duchecki, Grimaldi and Blocker. Within two days, Shassad and Hearn were in possession of new and perplexing details which contributed to the background of the Ryder murder case. The developments were disjointed and obviously unconnected to Ryder himself. Yet somewhere there was a covert connection. Shassad wanted it. They *all* wanted it. Was it through Daniels? Shassad continued to work on the "wrong man" theory, postulating that the victim had no link to the crime except bad luck. The most unorthodox murder case he'd ever encountered, Shassad admitted to himself in his most private thoughts.

And, *unorthodox?* How about Rota Films?

The stated business of the company was the import and export of films; commercial American films purchased for viewing abroad, and documentary films about North America shot by Rota employees. Many Rota films were clearly nonpolitical studies of wildlife and geology. All of their original films were returned in sealed cans to Romania for developing and processing.

Such activities appeared innocuous enough on the surface. What bothered Aram Shassad about Rota Films was what was left unsaid, the unseen factors lurking beneath the surface.

Little things, for example. Like the full-time armed guards who protected their Varick Street offices against "burglaries" around the clock. Or like the bank their checks cleared through—the same bank that Jacobus used.

Then there were the big things.

Rota, for example, owned no modern film equipment. They employed no professional camera operators. They had not purchased an American film for Romanian distribution since 1973. They had no apparent income and should have been losing inordinate sums of money for the past several years. Yet they were unquestionably solvent, maintaining two entire floors of office and "production" space in a sturdy—and recently reenforced—warehouse at the base of Varick Street, in the bowels of Manhattan.

And then there was the factor that piqued Shassad the most. Despite the fact that Rota produced few films and purchased fewer, they were a hornets' nest of activity when it came to export. Exposed films to be developed were constantly being shipped back to Europe. And therein lay an apparent sweetheart deal with the Romanian government.

So that the sealed film cans would not be "accidentally" opened and exposed, Rota Films managed to send their products home via the diplomatic pouches, therefore at no time under the scrutiny of any Customs service. The pouches, and the sealed film cans therein, flew a triangular route between New York, Washington, and Bucharest. Then, once arrived on the other side of the Atlantic Ocean, Rota products would drift into oblivion.

Shassad called a meeting of all five detectives assigned to the Ryder case for ten A.M. on a Monday. Five weeks had passed since the murder of Ryder. He reviewed all information previously assembled and anything new any detective had to offer. "Think of a dirty word that starts with an 'F,'" he then suggested obliquely.

In unison, three of the other detectives made a four-letter suggestion, the presence of Saint Theresa notwithstanding.

"No," answered Shassad, "the word I'm thinking of has *five* letters." He looked expectantly from face to face. His dark eyebrows were raised slightly, his thin lips pursed in anticipation. When there were no takers after several seconds he offered the answer. " 'Front,' " he said. "Rota Films is a front for something. Any ideas what?"

Again, silence.

"Well," said Shassad, his playfulness turning into annoyance, "I don't know, either. I don't know how it's connected to Jacobus and I don't know how it connects with Thomas Daniels."

"Daniels?" asked Grimaldi.

"Of course," scoffed Shassad. "For Christ's sake, his old man was as dirty as they come when it came to a sneak operation. I got a gut feeling about Thomas Daniels. I say the only difference between him and his old man is that the old man was five times as smart."

Shassad glanced at the other faces in the room. There was no disagreement.

Chapter 27

The note arrived late in the afternoon while Thomas was out. One odd aspect of it, in retrospect, was that he'd only been gone a short time. It was as if she'd made a conscious effort to avoid him. The other odd aspect was that it was typewritten. Where had she obtained a typewriter? And why, suddenly, was she now using one?

He attributed those two concerns to her idiosyncracies. The important thing was that the note was signed Leslie and she was summoning him to another late meeting. Midnight, this time. But tonight they'd be hiding in plain sight. She gave as a meeting place a discotheque named *Suzanne's* on East Fifty-second Street. He had no choice. He would go.

Suzanne's, at midnight, was simultaneously colorful, loud, garish, and crowded. Thomas arrived a few minutes before the hour, entered and waited at the end of a long, dim bar which afforded a look at both the front door and the dance floor. The bar and the dance floor were ringed by mirrors. Some enterprising proprietor had had an inspiration in dry ice and a thin, filmy cloud floated around everyone's feet. Reds, yellows, and greens dominated, mostly in plastic, neon, and then more neon. Cramped tables lined the outer reaches of the dance floor and tobacco smoke wafted around the sound system which hung from the ceiling. On the dance floor, gaudily clad youths moved dispassionately to the blaring music. *Suzanne's* was, Thomas Daniels observed, either a dream or a nightmare, depending on one's perspective; the kind of a place which makes one want to dress up or throw up. Again, depending. There were no laws against bad taste, Thomas reminded himself.

Thomas remained at the end of the bar, studying alternately the dancing area and the entrance. Watching, waiting, growing impatient. No Leslie.

He was aware of movement next to him. He glanced at a man he'd never seen before, then looked away.

"Looking for some action?" The words barely carried above the sound of rock music. When the man repeated the words, Thomas knew he was being spoken to by someone with a vaguely British accent.

"I'm waiting for someone."

The man smiled. "Sure," he said.

Thomas looked away, attempting to ignore his new acquaintance. The man elbowed him and continued to talk. "Plenty of unattached ass here," he proclaimed. "Won't find it on a bar stool, though. Got to make the move over there."

The man pointed toward the hustling figures in the larger room. Thomas turned toward him.

"That's not what I'm looking for! All right?" he snapped, raising his voice to be heard.

The man raised his open palms in mock surrender, as if to apologize. He was silent for a moment, then, also shouting to be heard, announced, "I know what you *are* here for."

Thomas studied the entrance and the dance floor again, then checked his watch. It was twelve ten. He felt the elbow against his arm again. He looked back and the man was holding his hand open, a small glass vial in his palm.

"What the hell's that?" asked Daniels, annoyed.

"It's what you want."

"Get lost."

"You snort it, man. It's terrific. It'll get you a rush like—"

Thomas glared into the man's eyes. "I said, get lost! Can't you hear me?"

The man only smiled. "Your name's Daniels, isn't it?" he asked. "And you're looking for my friend Leslie?"

Thomas froze. He studied the man intensely. The man's palm closed on the vial, but the small glass object was not put in a pocket. "Where is she?" Thomas asked.

"Let's sit down," the man said amiably, pointing to two empty chairs at a table toward the opposite end of the bar. "It's important."

Thomas didn't know whether to trust him or not. But again, he had little choice other than to follow events.

They sat at a small table, leaving their drinks behind. Daniels figured he'd give the man two minutes to make sense. Otherwise he'd consider the typed note a hoax and leave. He looked at the man carefully again as they sat. He was about to speak when he became aware of movement behind him, two figures emerging from the fury and sound of center stage at *Suzanne's*.

Daniels attempted to whirl and get to his feet since the two faces were familiar. Instantly he knew why he'd been drawn here. And by whom.

But as he tried to rise, four hands seized him and jammed him roughly back into the wooden chair. He cursed at them and tried to flail with his arms.

But Grover held him on one side. And the bearded Hunter had him pinned steadfastly on the other.

Then as Daniels struggled, amidst the noise and flashing lights, his nose was accosted by a repulsive smell which made his entire head jerk backwards. His eyes glazed, but through the red and yellow and green he could see enough to know what was happening.

The man from the bar was leaning forward. The cap had been removed from the vial and the small glass container was being jammed beneath Daniels's nose.

He tried to move his head away, but someone was gripping him by the hair. He tried to hold his breath, but his lungs gave out and he gasped.

Then he coughed violently, gasping again, taking in large gulps of the chemical being forced upon him.

The will to resist left him. He felt his limbs growing weak and the fight was gone from his arms. It all seemed better now, the noise and these men around him. Within the dull blur they seemed less menacing. Another gulp and he was almost unconscious, not struggling at all.

The next thing he knew he was walking, or being helped to walk. His legs were wobbly and his senses were askew. But Grover had him on one side and Hunter on the other. They were walking him out, taking him from the cigarette-stenched air of *Suzanne's* out into the cold night.

He remembered hearing Hunter speak to the man at the door. "Our friend's had too much to drink already," Hunter said. And Daniels could hear distant laughter. He tried to talk, but the words came out garbled. More laughter.

He was aware of being pushed into a car and feeling both dizzy and sick in the backseat. Then everything was blackening and he remembered thinking that if this was dying, it certainly was easy.

Chapter 28

Voices. Distant voices, becoming louder.

Thomas turned over on the bed and was slowly conscious. He saw the dingy ceiling and stared at it without comprehension. He saw sunlight streaming in from behind drawn venetian blinds and he saw the bare branches of a tree beyond the blinds and the window.

He sat up in the bed, still hearing the voices, men's voices, in the next room. Voices with English accents. One American accent, too. He was suddenly dizzy and his head was aching, a headache beyond comprehension. He slipped back onto the pillow and thought.

Where was he? He knew his mind was working slowly, but he simply couldn't figure it out. Where *was* he?

Then he realized. He recognized nothing because he had never been in this room before. And the last thing he remembered was that Knight of the Nightlife accosting his nostrils with that stinking vial.

He lay there until he thought he could walk. He could not discern what the voices were saying. But if he could make it to the window and peek beyond the blinds, well, maybe at least he'd have an inkling of where he was.

He tried to stand.

He wobbled and took a step.

Then the dizziness was upon him and he swayed. One direction, then the other. He groped for the bedpost and missed by several feet. He tumbled forward, knocking over a wooden chair and banging noisily with a thud onto the floor.

The voices stopped. Moments later the door opened.

Hunter stood there, watching him from that round face with the puffy relentless eyes. Hunter turned and addressed the men behind him. "He's up," he said.

Thomas wanted to say something, but was still too woozy. Then he heard footsteps. Three men were walking toward him from the doorway. Hunter was the first, Grover the second.

The third was an older man.

Thomas's vision was blurred. He squinted and glared at the third man and was struck by the idea, the sudden flash of excitement, that this could indeed be Arthur Sandler. At last. It was in fact an older man. Tall, lean, and graceful. Meticulously dressed in a dark Saville Row suit. He stepped past Hunter and Grover and stopped, looking down at Thomas and flanked by the two henchmen.

Thomas tried to focus on the face. It was familiar. He had seen it before.

"Whiteside," he muttered. And he let his cheek touch the floor again.

"Yes," said Whiteside thoughtfully, as if in response to a question. "Yes, it is." He turned to Grover and Hunter. "Wake him up, damn it," he ordered crisply. "He didn't even welcome me to America."

Thomas felt the footsteps coming, then he felt the hands on him. He was sat up and shaken, then stood up. The two men began to undress him and warned him not to resist. Stripped to his undershorts, and allowed to keep them in the interest of decency, he was walked to the bathroom adjoining the bedroom. He managed to see out a window. He was in a house in the country somewhere and it appeared to be midmorning.

"Your morning bath, sir," Hunter grunted with obvious enjoyment. Hunter's hammy fist reached into a shower and turned on the frigid water full blast. Then, with no further introduction, Hunter and Grover shoved Thomas into the jet of water.

Forty-five minutes later, Thomas had been permitted to dry himself and dress in fresh clothes. He was seated in the living room of a small apparently rural house. He was on a sofa sipping a lukewarm cup of black coffee.

Grover was to his right. Hunter was to his left. Both were seated. Whiteside was seated in an armchair in front of him. Whiteside was talking.

"From what I hear," Whiteside purred amiably, leaning forward a trifle for emphasis, "you made my associate, Mr. Hunter, do a little wrestling." He stared at Thomas primly and blankly. "Rather nasty of you, I should think."

Thomas set down the coffee on the table, wondering absently what was in it. He could imagine battery acid which would taste better. But then the English were cognoscenti of Asian leaves, not South American beans.

"Where am I?"

"Safe," offered Whiteside, as if giving a benediction. "Quite safe, I should say."

Thomas's eyes drifted to Grover, then to Hunter. "Safe?" he asked, indicating the latter. "With this ape here?"

Hunter smirked.

"Mr. Hunter is a paragon of delicacy and fine manners," said Whiteside. "I have no doubt whatsoever that if Mr. Hunter used force to bring you here, it was because you provoked him. Is that not the case?" he asked, turning to Hunter.

Hunter nodded soberly.

Whiteside allowed himself a slight smile. "As I suspected," he intoned softly. He looked back to Thomas. "I'm not at all surprised that he subdued you. Mr. Hunter was always a bit of an athlete. Tried out as a midfielder in 1952 for, which was it, Arsenal or Sunderland?"

"Southampton," mumbled Hunter with obvious satisfaction.

"They're all the same," snorted Whiteside.

"Maybe he should have tried as a defender," offered Grover, slipping into an impeccably working-class accent from northern England. "For Newcastle. Or maybe Leeds United."

Grover broke into a genuine laugh as Hunter shot him a half-annoyed glare. "For Christ's sake," snapped Thomas angrily and in confusion, "what the hell are you talking about?"

The room was quickly silent as the three men knew Thomas was now thinking properly and able to reason.

"You don't understand our terms, is that it?" asked Whiteside.

"No."

"Well," he answered expansively, drawing out the word, "in point of fact, that's why you're here." He rose from where he was sitting and explained further. "Terms," he said.

"Terms."

"Trash collection," said Whiteside. "You know all about it. Except what it is."

Thomas eyed each of the three men.

"And how about your dad?" asked Hunter. "The 'recruiting sergeant'?" There was a trace of hostility in his voice.

Thomas looked at the three men suspiciously. He answered in a calm even voice. "I don't even know what you're talking about."

"Well then," said Whiteside, his voice now barely above a whisper. "It's high time you learned." Whiteside turned his graying head and addressed Grover. "Tell us, Mr. Grover," he said, "take us back to 1938. When exactly did you go into trash collecting?"

"It was that year," said Grover.

"Maybe you could give our friend here a few of the details," Whiteside suggested, easing himself back into his chair. "Bring him up to date."

Grover looked at Thomas with some surprise. "You don't know this story, huh?" he asked.

"How would I know anything about you?" answered Thomas huffily.

"Your old man," said Grover, speaking again in an American accent, this time almost with New York street intonations. "He sure kept his lips tight."

"What's trash collection?" Thomas asked.

"Disposal of waste material," said Grover. "Getting rid of the garbage. Human garbage. Got it yet?"

"Not quite."

"From the start, Mr. Grover," said Whiteside in civilized tones. "Briefly, but from the start."

Hunter leaned back in his chair, tilting back on the chair's two rear legs. His thick arms were folded across his barrel chest. He alternated his gaze back and forth between his captive, Thomas, and his associate, Grover, who was starting to speak.

"I'd had trouble with the law off and on through 1938 and 1939," said Grover. "Small stuff. Checks. Bank books. Shit like that."

"Mr. Grover was a forger, Mr. Daniels. A *very* good one. As you know," commented Whiteside.

Thomas nodded.

"I don't like to be boastful," said Grover humbly, "but—"

"But he could look at a signature once and reproduce it," said Whiteside. "The endowments of an artist, in a sense."

"I know about his criminal career," said Thomas. "What's it have to do with garbage?"

"Trash," Grover corrected him, quickly and gleefully. "Trash collection. You see, in 1940 I was in trouble. Very serious trouble with the United States government over a bit of artwork I was doing."

"Forgery?"

"Certain signatures," said Grover innocently. "On a set of Treasury bills." He shrugged. "The signatures themselves were perfectly done. Using the wrong name did me in."

"What did it have to do with Sandler?" asked Thomas.

Grover smiled. "Very good," he complimented the younger man. "You figured that right away." He paused, glancing at Whiteside. "I was a forger, not an engraver. Does that answer it? It should."

Thomas assessed him coldly, wondering what was within or outside of the bounds of credibility. "But Sandler could engrave," he suggested, half a question, half a statement.

"Could?" he laughed, his eyebrows shooting skyward. "*Could?* Do the frigging birds sing in the morning? Best damned engraver who ever lived. Give him the right tools and he could reengrave Cleopatra's needle so that you couldn't tell his from the original. Hell," he laughed, "he could reengrave Cleopatra."

"So you were his associate. I already knew that. So what?"

"Trash collection," smiled Grover, warming to his reminiscences. "The government arrested me for forging Treasury bills. They were all set to really stick it to me. I figured that I was ready to sit out the next twenty in the jug. But then," he added slowly, "they offered me a deal. Mind if I smoke?"

Grover reached to a pack of cigarettes within his pocket. No one was inclined to object.

"The government told me there was a lot of trash in the country and abroad," he said. "They knew I was Italian and knew I spoke Italian fluently. Like a native. They asked me," he said through a cloud of smoke as he looked Daniels squarely in the eye, "how I'd feel about killing."

"Killing who?"

"Killing whoever they told me to," he said. He drew on the cigarette. "We came to an agreement. Four assignments. Trash assignments, they called them, and I'd be the collector. Foreign spies against the United States, they assured me." He blew the smoke out through his nose. "Well, I'm as patriotic as the next guy. Even more so, if it keeps me out of prison. *Capisce?*" he winked, with an exaggerated gesture and an Italian-peasant accent. "One murder in New York, another in south Philadelphia. On the third they sent me to Calabria in 1944. I scored."

Thomas wondered about the fourth assignment and was about to inquire when Whiteside spoke.

"So there's what a trash collector is," said the Englishman. "Now you know."

"Sure," said Thomas. "But that can't be all of it."

"Perceptive, perceptive," grinned Whiteside. "Of course there's more. How could there not be? After all, there was more than simply my friend Mr. Grover involved. There was also Arthur Sandler. *And*, of course . . ." He offered his hand forward expansively, soliciting the missing word from Thomas.

"My father."

Hunter and Grover both smiled. Whiteside eased back in his chair, apparently quite pleased.

Whiteside spoke more rapidly now, as if to cover a great expanse of time as quickly as possible. Mr. Grover, he explained, had entered the war in Europe as a man of many principles. But the foremost principle was that of flexibility.

Through an underground route of partisans, Grover, after assassinating a German counterspy in Calabria, was whisked by boat and railroad to Gibraltar. There he contacted a man named Lester Gregory. Gregory was a captain in the British Army, stationed "on the rock," as they called it, since Hitler was still trying to entice Franco into entering the war by attacking the British at Gibraltar. Captain Gregory also had another function. He was one of the top M.I.6 agents on the rock.

Through joint Anglo-American intelligence reports, Gregory knew both the function and the assignment of the man whose real name was De Septio. Gregory, however, acting on orders from London, sought to raise Grover's self-awareness to a higher level. Grover, accepting cash as compensation, agreed thus to become a British operative within the United States, unknown to his American superiors.

" 'Spy' was too strong a word, of course," said Whiteside. "An 'eye and ear' man would be more like it. Nothing treasonous, since it concerned Allied nations. He'd just report on anything interesting he'd seen or heard."

Thomas eyed Grover during Whiteside's explanation. The logical conclusion for wartime capitalism, he thought; allegiances bought and sold. He looked back to Whiteside. "So?" he asked.

"So," retorted Whiteside quickly, "there are two aspects of this for you to remember. One, Mr. Grover—*né* De Septio—was a trash collector for the Americans while he was a lower-echelon informant for us. Two," he continued, "you should have noticed a parallel between this man and his erstwhile associate. Sandler."

"They were both recruited as spies," said Thomas.

Whiteside fought back a smirk. "Yes," he said. "Now, in reference to whom have you used the word 'recruit' recently?"

It took Thomas a long second and then he blanched. Recruitment. His father's involvement. The recruiting sergeant. Of course! So painfully obvious all along. In retrospect so clear.

" 'Recruiting sergeant' was a term used for a certain type of man," Whiteside began forcefully. "A man like your father. Whatever his reasons, he sought to avoid the military, to not partake in any of the actual fighting. Know how he avoided it?"

"Go ahead," said Thomas, defensiveness in his voice.

"By recruiting. As a barrister or attorney, particularly *his kind*, he had ties to criminal society. Such as Mr. Grover. Or the slightly more re*spect*-able criminal society, such as Arthur Sandler. He also knew an important Federal prosecutor named McFedries. He used one to please the other, saving his own tail in the process. Ingenious, really. He'd take on as clients men like De Septio and Sandler who were facing extremely stiff Federal prison terms. Then he offered them up as bait. He would recruit them as U.S. spies, taking advantage of their own special skills. He would tell them it was prison or a few years in intelligence work. Wasn't much of a choice, I should think. The criminals got out of their jail terms, your father got out of the military, and your government got its spies."

Thomas, almost nonplussed by Whiteside's discourse, let it sink in for a few moments. "Did Zenger know?" he asked finally.

Whiteside laughed. "That conniving little twerp? God, yes! He was doing the same thing. Only not as well."

The four men sat there in rude silence, three men on one side, one on the other. None was inclined to speak. Thomas tried to measure the other three men, seeking somewhere to find a reason not to have to believe them. The trouble was that their whole story fit together so well.

Or *did* it? A thought came upon him.

"Let me ask you something totally unrelated," Thomas said.

"Ask," said Whiteside generously.

"What would you say if I wondered who you really were? What if I questioned whether the real Peter Whiteside were actually dead."

The man before him smiled. "I would say," said Whiteside, "that some unknown person has been filling your head with lies. Probably told you some rubbish about a plane crash leaving Caracas."

Thomas felt a sinking feeling in his stomach, a sense of having been made very neatly into an imbecile, though he wasn't at that moment certain by whom.

Whiteside knew he'd hit the mark. "Yes, of course," he continued. "That impostor girl told you that, didn't she?" When Thomas gave no answer, Whiteside knew he was correct. "I'll explain," he continued. "George McAdam was a 'sandhog,' which means he—"

"I know about that part," said Thomas. "I know what he did."

"All right," said Whiteside, "old George and I were in Caracas on a little expedition. We were scheduled to leave for Miami on an Avianca flight. At the last moment we changed our plans. Fortuitously for us, don't you think? Well," he smiled, "there was no reason to disappoint the folks who thought they'd blown us into the next dimension. We simply had the nice people at Avianca, after a little arm-twisting, add our names to the list of passengers. Simple, really. George and I were legally dead. Confused the living *hell* out of the KGB people in Venezuela." Whiteside's smile was enormous. "So if a little bird whispers in your ear that I'm dead," he said in conclusion, "don't believe her."

Grover interjected. "That's also why she wouldn't come into my house the other day," he said. "Afraid I'd call her a liar right there."

"Why should I believe that? Maybe she wasn't in the mood to look at a petty criminal who'd been her father's partner." Thomas furrowed his brow and added anxiously, "Yes, how about that? When did you stop being De Septio and start being Grover?"

"November 12, 1954," said Grover with a grin.

"After the Sandler stand-in was taken down on Eighty-ninth Street," said Whiteside. "Thanks for reminding us. That's important."

Important both now and twenty-two years earlier, Whiteside explained. Sandler's unorthodox actions after the war—fleeing east instead of west, staying east and then slowly coming home—had long baffled his superiors in American intelligence. But gradually the suspicions around the man grew. His revivified fortune after the war and his steady reaccumulation of wealth were every bit as bizarre and perplexing as, say, his sister's doting on dogs named Andy and one-dollar bills.

"Gradually, the conclusion became irrefutable," said Whiteside.

"Somewhere along the line Sandler had been recruited as a Soviet agent. Nobody knew when or where or by whom, but the case against him was even stronger than the one against Rudolph Abel."

"So why wasn't he arrested?" asked Thomas.

"Because things aren't that easy. Hard evidence, the sort admissible in an American court, was at a minimum. What we had were the accounts of agents, men and women whose identities could not be compromised in a trial. And," he added boldly, "we had a perfect set of crosscurrents."

"Crosscurrents?"

"Yes. The British wanted him for his counterfeiting of pounds. The Americans wanted him for espionage. Both would be a lot happier with him dead than on trial. Add to that the situation of Mr. Grover, here," he said with a nod. "Grover had been arrested again. Your father then began to guide the direction of the case. William Ward Daniels reminded all concerned that Grover had been a trash collector during the war. He'd made three assigned collections, but had never been assigned a fourth. Another deal was proposed. Sandler would be the fourth, in exchange for a new identity and immunity from all charges past and present."

"I agreed quite readily," said Grover. "And I told them I'd do it my way, with my own assistants."

"There were three assassins," said Thomas. "I learned that much myself."

"Well," said Whiteside slowly, "I gave British approval from London." He paused, then said softly, "And I partook in it personally. I wanted to see it done."

Thomas stared at Whiteside for several seconds. "Of course," Thomas mumbled. "You would have."

"And even then," said Whiteside, "I worked with my current associate." He nodded toward Hunter, who smiled broadly through his beard.

"We put more than a dozen bullet holes in him," Hunter grunted softly.

"You killed the wrong man," said Thomas slowly.

"And whose fault is that?"

"Your own."

"Wrong!" interjected Whiteside. "Whose *idea* was it originally? Who did I say nurtured the plan and sold it to two intelligence services? Need I remind you?"

Thomas was again silent, almost struck dumb by the implication.

"Never really had a heart-to-heart talk with your dad, did you?" chided Grover.

"He got the wrong man killed intentionally," said Whiteside casually, though Thomas had already gotten the message. "He was protecting his friend and client, protecting him so well that for twenty-one years everyone was convinced that Sandler was dead."

"Then a Treasury agent came to my door one morning," said Grover. "He'd tracked me down. A man named Hammond. He showed me a stack of money which was indistinguishable from real U.S. currency." He shook his head. "Only one man who could make counterfeits like that. Only *one* man."

"So Mr. Grover reported back to me," said Whiteside. "Our old eyes-and-ears network back at work after twenty-some years. He convinced us that Sandler had to still be alive. Or at least the man last known as Sandler. In one form or another, in one identity or another."

"Somebody must have known where Sandler went," said Thomas.

"Of course," said Whiteside. "There were four possibilities. But as the U.S. counterfeits began, the four possibilities closed. Victoria Sandler, crazy as she was, may have had an inkling. She died. Your father must have known. He died. His files—*your* files—might have held certain clues. They burned."

"Forget any smokescreen about a will being destroyed," offered Grover. "Sandler's identity today. *That's* why your files burned."

"What's the fourth? Zenger?" asked Thomas.

"No," said Whiteside. "His involvement with Sandler didn't run to the level of your father's. The fourth possibility—and it was only that, a possibility—was the other person who would have been reviewing those files after your father's death. That person could have happened upon something."

"Me," said Thomas softly.

"And you were marked for death, too," said Grover. "Trouble is, a mistake was made. Some poor bloke named Mark Ryder happened to look like you at the precise time and date when you were supposed to be leaving your building. They bought him instead."

Thomas sat reflectively in silence for several moments. It was all so neat and uncomplicated once the pieces fit together. Thomas had the sense of having watched his father wear a mask for his entire lifetime, Thomas knowing the man yet not really knowing him. If these three people, confessed killers, could be believed.

Hunter was at the window, Glover fidgeted with his fingers, and Whiteside stared relentlessly at Thomas.

"Who'd want to kill me?" Thomas Daniels finally asked almost rhetorically. He could see Hunter smirk. "I knew nothing about any of this."

"You're blind," said Whiteside. "Who'd want to kill you? You've been stalked for weeks now." Whiteside's features twisted into a scowl. "You mean you really don't see it?"

"Leslie," Thomas said, half as a question, half knowing the answer.

"They'll have you under a microscope," snorted Whiteside. "They'll examine you from every angle. Find out what you know or whom you might have told. Then when you least expect it, wham!" Whiteside slapped his palms together for emphasis. A resounding clap filled the room. "Wham," he said, "you'll be at your own funeral! I don't believe that you can't see it for yourself."

Thomas's ashen appearance indicated the answer to Whiteside. No, Thomas didn't see it for himself.

"Women are lethal in games like this," said Whiteside hatefully. "I suppose she's arranging for a nice hot bed for you at night. Keep you on *her* side," he said. "Keep you tired and busy at nights so you can't start thinking. As long as she's got you locked in between her legs, your brains will be on vacation."

Thomas looked at the three men who surrounded him. He wanted to stand and attack them, rise up and strike out at them, just as they had struck out at his father and Leslie. But how could he disbelieve them?

"Cute little bird, too," grunted Grover. "Probably a nice warm one on the mattress, all right. Seems a shame. But we're going to have to wring that little bird's neck." Hunter plainly relished the thought.

"There's one other thing," said Thomas, directing his attention back to his tormentor, Whiteside.

"Do tell us."

"The last time I saw you," said Thomas, "in the churchyard in London, you left me with a suggestion."

Remembering, Whiteside allowed a coy grin to cross his face. "I told you to give some thought to—"

"—to whoever was running Arthur Sandler. If Sandler was a spy, you said, he had to have had a superior."

"That's right," said Whiteside. He let a moment pass as he gathered the proper words. "I've *always* known who the superior was. The question was," he intoned slowly, "whether *you* knew. Or whether you could find out."

"My father," said Thomas coldly.

Those two words hung in the air for what, to Thomas Daniels, seemed like an eternity. He felt the six other eyes on him, almost X-raying him. And he recognized now their attitude toward him all along. In their own way, they'd been as perplexed with him as he'd been with them. They'd had his father pegged as a spy, of which sort Thomas still didn't know. But what the men in this room had wondered all along—and probably still wondered, Thomas concluded—was how much the spy father had passed on to the attorney son.

Whiteside finally chipped the silence. "What you lack in speed, Mr. Daniels," he said, "you regain in diligence. Of course, the question we now must ask is *the* question."

"Sorry?"

"We *know,*" said Whiteside with feline smugness, "that your father was a spy. A specialist in recruitment, at that. What we must know is, *for whom?*"

"For whom?" Thomas repeated in perplexed tones. "*What* for whom?"

"Do you speak any Russian, Mr. Daniels?" asked Hunter flatly.

"*What?*"

"How about the Cyrillic alphabet?" asked Grover. "Know it?"

"Where would I have learned it?" asked Thomas angrily.

All three men shrugged. Whiteside, his eyes fixed on Daniels, spoke bluntly. "At your father's knee, perhaps?"

Daniels was shaking his head, failing to comprehend. "What are you angling at?" he demanded. "What the hell are you people after?"

Whiteside sighed. "The extent to which we've been compromised," he intoned. "That's what we want to know. That's what you have to tell us."

"You're not making sense."

"Oh, no?" Whiteside shot back, the white eyebrows rising quickly. "Here, then!"

He explained.

Many of the most enterprising intelligence networks of the Second World War, said Whiteside, had been joint Anglo-American endeavors. That was thirty years past, of course, and such past history would hardly have mattered were it not for one simple fact: "A proven network is a proven network," Whiteside pontificated, "and good, sound alliances aren't tossed away for the fun of it. They're kept intact. Sometimes for twenty or thirty years. Even longer."

Thomas listened, uncomfortable under the gaze of Hunter and Grover.

"Do you see the 'problem'?" inquired Whiteside. "Your father was a recruiter. He headed a network. The network functioned through the war, into the postwar period, and was intact at the time of his death."

"Intact?" asked Thomas, almost incredulous.

"Yes, intact," said Whiteside intensely, his voice low and serious.

"Intact, but very, very rotten from within. Sandler was no friend of Great Britain, you know that by now. Ergo, he was no friend of the Anglo-American alliance."

"I follow."

"He was a double, damn it!" Whiteside erupted. "And we want to know who else was running him. Maybe the Huns themselves recruited him after the war. Maybe our friends the Bolsheviks to the East, or maybe he was a double cross by some moralistic cowboys in Washington. In any event, he wasn't on our side in any way. Yet he was in a network we took part in." Whiteside nodded toward Grover, his own free-lancer. Whiteside drew a breath and concluded. "We find out who Sandler's ultimate allegiance was to, and we find out how much our postwar networks have been compromised."

"That simple?" asked Daniels, knowing it wasn't.

"Almost," responded Whiteside with equal cynicism.

"Aren't you missing something?"

"What?"

"You're more concerned with finding Sandler's control than with finding Sandler. Why?"

"Last time we spoke," Whiteside reminded him, "I said there were things I couldn't tell you. Not yet. That answer is one of those things. At the proper time, you'll be informed."

Daniels grimaced. "And yet Sandler, if you found him, could answer your questions for you."

Whiteside shrugged noncommittally. Thomas frowned. "Perhaps," Whiteside offered, his gaze squarely upon the younger man before him. "But someone else, *someone in this room*, might also be able to answer a key question, something which might tuck it *all* in place."

Thomas felt the gaze of the three other men upon him. "What are you implying? I don't know a damned thing."

Whiteside sighed. "No," he said, "I don't think you do. But if you take the question with you from here and examine it, maybe the solution will appear." He paused. "This is why you're caught up in this, naturally. It's the whole match, for our part. Your father might have said something, *anything*, at one point or another."

"Like what?"

"Like what side he was *really* on. Like whom he was really controlling Sandler for. And why." Whiteside rubbed his chin in reflection, then hissed his final words with restrained anger.

"Your father headed a network," he declared, "a damned *good* network. But *whose* was it? The Huns'? The Bolsheviks'? The Cowboys'?"

Another uneasy pause, then, "Take your pick, Mr. Daniels. Because it *had* to be one of the three!"

Thomas stared at Whiteside for several seconds, weighing the question. "How could I ever know any more than I know now?" he asked.

"Very simple," scoffed Whiteside. "Ask the girl. Before she manages to kill you."

It was eight thirty in the morning. Jacobus, returning home from a night's work, was as concerned as he was tired. After all these years in the United States, after obtaining employment in the proper building, after carrying through years of planning without the slightest impediment, there were hints of trouble.

Corescaneu had been stopped by a city policeman, or what appeared to be a city police officer, and made to open his trunk. And then a night later another officer had been prowling around Rota Films on Varick Street.

Jacobus had been given a red light. Nothing new to do until an all-clear signal was given. He slid the key into the door of his home, the upstairs apartment of a two-story house. He slammed the door behind him as he entered. He cursed to himself in Russian, a language he hadn't spoken aloud since his entry into the United States. Next thing he knew, he cursed, he'd be under surveillance.

He dropped his black metal lunchbox in the front hallway and hung up his red-and-black-checked overcoat. He walked into the living room and froze.

He had a visitor, quite uninvited and equally unwelcome. The visitor sat in an armchair in a far corner to his extreme left, the only blind corner in the room. The only place where he wouldn't have seen someone immediately.

He cursed again to himself. He'd worried about that corner for years. Now every worry was confirmed. The visitor held a small snub-nosed pistol aloft, pointed right at the center of his chest.

"Hello, Sergei. Please don't move."

He glared back. "Who are you? What do you want?" he asked. "I have no money. If you wish to rob me—"

"Be quiet," was the command. "You're an Eastern European. Hold still. You should like classical music."

A gloved hand went to a radio by the armchair. The radio was turned on and the volume turned up. The music grew louder and, by chance, the crashing end of an orchestral piece neared.

"*Firebird Suite*. How perfect. I'll bet you're a Stravinsky fan."

Jacobus could read the intruder's intentions. He'd been on the other side of such confrontations in his life. He knew how they worked. He knew also that loud music masks the sound of a pistol. He wondered if Stravinsky had known that. He wondered if he could jump back and be out the door before the trigger could be pulled.

The sound of drums and cymbals arrived much too quickly. Jacobus whirled and leaped toward the hallway but at the same instant the pistol erupted.

The bullet caught the night custodian in the center of the chest, shattering his breastbone as the shot tumbled upward through the flesh and bone of his body.

The second shot, fired a quarter second after the first, crashed into a rib bone on the left side, traveling into his body straight thereafter and ripping into the right ventricle of the heart. All Jacobus felt was the sudden searing pain in the center of his chest, an intense stabbing sensation, and he understood that he was going to fall.

But the fall itself was experienced only by his body, not by the man who'd inhabited it. His huge frame tumbled against the wall and sprawled over a table and an umbrella stand before rolling onto the floor and landing on its side, one arm outstretched and the other pinned beneath the body.

Gradually the volume of the music was lowered until, as the suite ended seconds later, the radio was turned off. Jacobus, dead before he'd even hit the ground, was motionless, his eyes still open in terror.

The assassin carefully tucked the small pistol into an overcoat pocket. The body on the floor was inspected gingerly and turned over with a deft toe. The intruder knelt down and delicately felt the wrist for a pulse beat. There was none.

The telephone rang at a few minutes past nine A.M. Thomas was sitting alone in his apartment, submerged in thought.

Whiteside's accusations—the suggestions and implications—unnerved him. They challenged the very foundations of truth which Thomas had always accepted: his father's identity. The unswerving, unrelenting patriotism of William Ward Daniels. How could a lifetime of jingoism possibly be questioned?

And yet . . . Thomas thought. And yet . . . ? The questions wouldn't go away.

Examined from another angle, studied in a different light, William Ward Daniels might have seemed a different man altogether. And yet it was ridiculous, Thomas concluded. How could a fastidious and dedicated man like Whiteside be so far off?

Then again, was Whiteside Whiteside? Or was Leslie Leslie?

The bell of the telephone jingled a third time. Thomas answered it and recognized Leslie's voice immediately. It was a voice which he now greeted with both attraction and anxiety, strong feelings pulling in two directions.

"I'm glad you called," he said. "I filed two motions in probate court for you yesterday. I also filed photocopies of your birth certificate and your parents' marriage license. It's the first step toward—"

"Listen to me very carefully," she said. "It's vital."

"You sound upset."

"Not upset. Just concerned."

"What's wrong?"

"The people who are after me," she said. "They may be very close."

His mind drifted back to rural Pennsylvania. The man in the blue car. Grover. Neither of whom she'd face. He received her words with a certain skepticism that remained unspoken.

"Why so suddenly?" he asked.

"There are reasons," she said. "I can explain. Believe me, Tom, I can explain any questions you have, but not now."

"Why are you calling?" he asked.

"I want you to get out of your apartment immediately," she said. "This minute. Close it and prepare not to return for several days."

"What are—?"

"Just listen to me," she said steadily. "I'm in a telephone booth. Neither you nor I have much time."

"Keep talking."

"Leave your apartment and make certain that no one sees you. Go somewhere for the day, places you've never been, places where no one who knows you would look for you. Then tonight you have to meet me."

"Where?"

"Anywhere," she said. "But it must be someplace deserted. What's the most deserted part of the city after midnight?"

"I suppose Central Park at four A.M.," he said jokingly.

"Perfect."

"What?"

"Perfect," she reiterated. "What part?"

"You can't be serious."

"I haven't much time! What part?" Her voice was strident and agitated, as he'd never heard it before. He could hear the sound of traffic behind her, horns and automobile engines. She was indeed in a booth.

"Do you know where the Great Lawn is?"

"I can find it."

"There's a rock formation off from the Great Lawn to the east. Between Eighty-third and Eighty-fourth Streets," he said. "I can be in that area."

"I'll find you," she said intensely. A recorded operator's voice sounded on the telephone and he heard her drop another coin into the slot. "Now do as I've asked. Get out of your apartment. Prepare not to come back. Don't be seen by anyone you recognize until you see me tonight."

"Can't you tell me what—?"

"It's your life I'm talking about," she snapped. "You can either believe me or you can risk getting killed. The choice is yours, Thomas. Trust me or not. That's all I can say."

"But—"

"I have to ring off."

He heard the sound of the receiver being quickly hung up. Then he was hearing a dial tone.

He sat there stunned with the telephone still in his hand. He set it down and looked around the apartment. Trust her or not, he thought to himself. It all came down to that. Was she saving his life or luring him to an isolated section of Manhattan where he'd be as easy a murder victim as the unwitting Mark Ryder had been?

He glanced around his cluttered apartment and made his decision.

Shassad stood in the hallway looking down on the body. A photographer from the Medical Examiner's office aimed his camera, flashed a pair of shots, and moved into a different position.

Detective Jack Grimaldi looked at Shassad from the other end of Jacobus's corpse. "We blew it," he said.

Shassad looked at him with genuine anger. "I'll say you blew it, all right," he snapped. "You've got this guy under surveillance and he gets killed under your fat noses. What the hell are you, cub scouts?"

Grimaldi, looking for a hole to crawl into, said nothing. Nor did his partner, Detective Ed Blocker.

Patrick Hearn approached the area where Shassad stood. Behind Hearn detectives from forensics dusted the room for fingerprints.

"They find anything back there?" asked Shassad.

"Some prints," offered Hearn. "But they're probably his." He motioned to Jacobus.

"Christ," muttered Shassad. He looked at Grimaldi with contempt. "Okay," he said, "run through it again for me. From the top."

Grimaldi drew a breath and measured each word. He retraced the events of that day.

Grimaldi and Blocker, working twelve-hour shifts, had replaced the previous team assigned to Jacobus. The assignment had begun at six A.M. on Thirtieth and Park. Grimaldi and Blocker had then followed Jacobus home by car at eight o'clock that morning, watching their mark disappear in the front door of his second-story home.

Aside from Jacobus's murderer, the two detectives had been the last to see the custodian alive. But they had perhaps seen the killer, too.

"We parked out front about a block away," Grimaldi explained. "We watched the house from there. Then about five minutes later Ed went around back."

"Back where?" Shassad asked.

Detective Edward Blocker replied. "There's a patio behind these row houses," he said. "It's visible from the side street. I took a stroll down the side street and took a look. I saw a girl."

"Girl?"

"Yes, sir," said Blocker. "I think it was *the* girl."

Shassad looked at him coldly. "*What* girl?"

"The one we chased out of the Garden that night," he said. "The one at the hockey game. The one we lost in the parking garage."

"Where the hell was she?" demanded Shassad. Hearn leaned on the hallway wall and studiously looked into the vacant eyes of the corpse. He listened intently and was completely expressionless.

"She was coming down the back staircase from Jacobus's apartment," said Blocker. "They have an outside back entrance."

"And?"

"And she looked around when she got down. I was about a hundred feet from her. She turned and saw me standing there and quickly turned and started the other way."

"Were you wearing a sign?" asked Shassad. "One that said, 'I am a cop'?"

Blocker looked at his feet, as if waiting for permission to continue.

"Yeah? Then what?"

"I tried to follow her, but there was a fence in the way. She picked me up right away. Saw me trying to get past that fence immediately. That's when she really started to move."

"Yeah? So? Where'd she move to?"

"I don't know. She might have disappeared into a store and waited for me to disappear. For a second I thought she'd slipped into this blue car."

"Get the plate number?"

"Out of state. That's all I know."

"Marvelous," sighed Shassad. "Tell me, why do you come to work without your dog and your cane?"

"An expert," offered Grimaldi. "Had to have been an expert the way she got loose."

"I ran to the end of that block and I looked in every direction. Gone. Not a sign of her. No one had seen her. I circled back to the car where Jack was," he nodded to Grimaldi, "and she hadn't gone past him."

Shassad listened bitterly. "You were right," he uttered. "You blew it."

"*Must* have been an expert," Grimaldi suggested. "Had different escapes all planned."

"The trouble is," retorted Shassad, "you gentlemen are supposed to be experts, too."

Shassad looked imploringly to Hearn, employing his best how-did-they-let-them-get-out-of-the-police-academy expression. Hearn brought Shassad up to date on the subsequent developments.

Grimaldi and Blocker, Hearn explained, had then spent the rest of the day on their stakeout. But toward darkness, in the early evening, Jacobus had failed to show for his twelve-hour night shift. The day manager of the office building had telephoned him. No answer. Eventually, the owner of Jacobus's home, the man who lived downstairs, was telephoned. The landlord agreed to go upstairs and ring the front bell. No answer to the bell. But when the owner glanced inside, the light in the front hall was still on. And the body of Jacobus was plainly visible, even the details, like the pool of blood he lay in.

"Ta-rif-fic," Shassad grumbled. He had a terrible headache. He had counted on Jacobus to help put together the pieces of the Ryder-Daniels case for him. So much for that.

He glanced at his watch. It was twenty minutes past six. "Know what we do now?" he asked Hearn.

"Daniels, of course."

"Damn straight," said Shassad with disgust. "The girl's our suspect, he knows where the girl is. At least he's got to know who the Goddamn girl is. Material witness. We pick him up."

Grimaldi looked at his superior. "Do you want us—?"

"You two head back to the One Nine," he said. "We'll find Daniels."

"If we can," added Hearn. Shassad looked at his partner as if to ask what *that* meant. "I doubt that he'll be home," suggested Hearn.

Thirty-five minutes later, Shassad and Hearn knocked on the door to Thomas Daniels's apartment. Predictably, there was no response from within.

For Thomas Daniels, there had only been one decision. Whether it was insanity, risk, bad judgment, or simply a lethal brand of curiosity, he planned to meet Leslie McAdam. He was too deeply involved in the case, emotionally and professionally, to sidestep her. Facts, simple facts, were what he wanted. Positive identifications of the players and their rightful teams, that was what he needed—what he *had* to have—more than anything. There was only one way: maneuver Leslie face to face with Whiteside. Force them to identify each other . . . or call each other's bluff. It was the most fascinating case of his life, coupled with the most intriguing woman he'd ever met. Stay away? He couldn't. Trust her one final time? He'd have to. Accept her warning and stay away from his apartment indefinitely? Well, yes. He'd do that, too.

Following her agitated telephone call, he quickly packed a small bag with a few changes of clothing. He set it by his door. Then, pondering his venture into Central Park eighteen hours hence, he considered his own safety. He was not trained in any form of self-defense. And unlike other attorneys he knew, he owned no handgun.

Foolishly perhaps, but swept away somewhat by his predicament, he opened a kitchen drawer and pulled out a steak knife. Feeling over-dramatic and even a bit silly, he wrapped the knife in a thin cloth and taped it to his left calf. Then he left his apartment.

Killing a day in Manhattan, when one is ill prepared for it, is not the easiest of tasks, particularly when cold blustery weather hampers any enjoyment of the outdoors.

He checked his valise at Grand Central Station. Then he considered his alternatives. Kill the day, but go nowhere near where anyone would expect to find him. Go nowhere where he'd ever been before.

It's your life I'm talking about, she'd said. *Trust me.*

He considered the reading room of the Public Library. Worth hours anytime. But he'd been there before, scores of times. A library. He went to a branch library on the Lower East Side. There he killed the morning. At lunch he ate in a nearby dairy bar.

In the afternoon, he considered a movie. But not necessarily one he'd wanted to see. He went to a second-run house on the Upper West Side, then, tiring from the vacant hours he was seeking to fill, went to another second-run house a few blocks away. He nearly dozed off. He fought to stay awake.

Then evening. An hour walking around the city. Then dinner at a Broadway cafeteria. Another movie.

Tired, anxious, and beginning to question the necessity of what he was doing, Thomas found himself in the East Forties at nine thirty. What was he hiding from? Whom was he avoiding? He wondered. More than six more hours to kill. He was sleepy and getting sleepier.

He decided. He would go back uptown to his home block. He would cautiously try to reenter his apartment. He would then nap with the light off and go to the park at the prearranged time.

He took the subway to Seventy-seventh and Lexington. Then he walked on Seventy-seventh Street all the way to First Avenue. Then he approached his own block from the east, rather than from the west, the route he normally traveled. All this, he thought as he walked, as an outgrowth of his father's wartime business. He was marching around on a cold Manhattan night thanks to events of twenty to thirty-five years ago.

He stopped short before coming to Second Avenue. On the avenue, parked by a fire hydrant, was a car occupied by two men. They were sitting, waiting and watching. Staring toward the entrance to his building.

One of them began to turn his way. Thomas whirled quickly. He fought back his instinct to run. He resisted looking back.

Instead he walked briskly, turning again as soon as he reached First Avenue. But he knew that if he'd been spotted—by whoever it was he was avoiding—the area would be alive with people looking for him.

He hailed a taxi. He gave an address in the East Fifties. Andrea Parker's block. Why not? He had to be off the streets. He watched in the rear window of the taxi but was unable to recognize any specific car following. He had the strong sense of being pursued, but his pursuers were faceless.

Arthur Sandler? How could anyone be afraid of an septuagenarian who was legally dead?

The taxi dropped him on the corner of Fifty-first and Second. Andrea lived nearby, on the twelfth floor of a new white high rise. Thomas hurried into a telephone booth and dialed her number. She answered.

"I have to come up," he said.

"Tom?" she whispered.

"Yes, it's me," he said almost breathlessly. "I'm on your block. I have to come up and see you. Now."

She laughed coyly and calmly, as if to convey a message. "Oh, no," she said, without calling him by name. "Not *now.*"

"Andrea, please. I'm begging you."

"It's awfully late," she hinted.

He glanced around and saw no one he recognized. He spent another plaintive minute, arguing with her. Begging. She refused.

"Look," he finally said, "you don't understand. It's crucial. There are people after me. I've got to get off the street. I just want a place where I can curl up in a corner for two hours and then go back out."

He could hear her putting her hand over the mouthpiece of the telephone, speaking to someone with her.

"Thomas," she began. "Please understand . . ."

"You're 'entertaining,' aren't you?"

"Yes."

"I don't care," he said.

"My other guest does," she said.

"My aging nemesis Augie, right?" he asked.

"It's immaterial," she said. It was Augie, that proved it.

"The best development of the whole Sandler case," he said, throwing it out as bait. "Happening right here, right now. You either let me come up or so help me you'll never hear a word of it."

She was slow to respond. She was thinking it over. "Thomas," she then began, speaking with a deliberate but negative tone. "I—"

"Look," he said. "We'll compromise. I'll come to the doorman downstairs. He'll ring you. You tell him to send me up. I won't go to your apartment. I'll go to the roof gardens for two hours. I want to be off the street."

There was silence on the other end. Then the recording in the telephone began.

"Please!" he begged. "I don't have another coin. Decide!"

"All right," she gave in. "But if you come near my door, I'll call the police."

The police, he thought. Lovely.

"Agreed," he said.

He hung up and turned. He jolted to a halt. Two men were completely blocking his way out of the booth. He thought his heart would leap out of his chest. Or stop.

How could he have been so careless? How had he let them close in on him?

"Who were you talking to, Mr. Daniels?" the larger one with the Irish face asked.

"A lady, maybe?" asked the smaller, darker one.

Hearn and Shassad, respectively.

"If you'll excuse me," said Thomas, trying to push his way past.

Hearn's arm was up quickly and blocked Thomas's route, keeping his back to the telephone booth. "I'm afraid we can't excuse you," said Shassad. "We'd like to talk with you."

"How about tomorrow?"

"How about now?"

Thomas grimaced at Shassad. "You're forgetting," he said. "I'm an attorney. I know my rights. Unless you have a specific—"

"Your janitor friend Jacobus was murdered this morning," said Hearn, "in case you didn't know." Thomas's eyes were riveted on the wiry man with the gaunt, sad face. "Your girl friend, the one who's the hockey fan, was seen leaving Jacobus's home. You know who she is. You may even know *where* she is. That makes you a material witness. If not an accomplice."

Thomas searched their faces, recalling Leslie's words not to talk to anyone familiar, not to trust a soul. Just trust her, just once more.

"I don't believe you," he said.

"Want to see a body? Jacobus should be at the Medical Examiner's right now. We'll take you."

"Sorry," he said. "I'm not going."

Shassad grinned. "Yes, you are. Unless that was your girl friend you were just talking to. If you'd like to take us to see her, we'd appreciate that, too."

Thomas looked at both men again. "All right," he said to settle them. They relaxed slightly and Thomas bolted.

It was hardly a race.

Thomas had traveled no more than fifteen feet when Shassad grabbed the back of his jacket, slowing him enough for Hearn to grab him by the arm. Hearn chicken-winged Thomas's left arm and shoved him against the side of the building. Before Thomas knew what was happening, he was being frisked. They found the knife.

"What the hell are we carrying this for?" demanded Shassad, as Hearn pulled out the knife and handed it to his partner. "In case a steak floats by?"

"It's a dangerous city," said Thomas. He was permitted to turn and face the detectives.

Shassad's face began to break into a sly smile. "Some attorney you must be," he said. "A second ago you were a mere witness. Now you're under arrest. Concealed weapon." He gave a low whistle of satisfaction. "That's serious stuff, Daniels. You know that?"

"I'm an attorney," Thomas said sourly. "You don't have to remind me."

"Seems I heard a saying once," said Hearn. " 'The lawyer who pleads his own case has a fool for a client.' "

The son of William Ward Daniels resisted a response. He was taken to the Nineteenth Precinct, pondering whether his client, the woman who'd be waiting in vain for him in Central Park, had a fool for a lawyer. It was ten fifteen.

Thomas Daniels sat with his arms folded in front of him. The lighting was abrasive in the stuffy small room with grim avocado walls. Patrick Hearn sat at one end of the table, Daniels at the other. Shassad was more prone to being on his feet. As Daniels listened to him, circling back over the same subject matter an uncountable number of times, Shassad was also more prone to anger.

Thomas looked at his watch. It was one thirty in the morning.

"All right," said Shassad, "we'll start again from the top. Where were you at eight o'clock this morning?"

"I've already told you. Home in bed. The answer hasn't changed."

"No witnesses?"

Daniels glared at him cynically. "Unfortunately no."

"When did you hear from your 'client' last?"

"This morning at nine. She telephoned me," he repeated grudgingly.

"Why did she call you?"

"To discuss her case. I filed motions for her yesterday."

"Where is she?"

"Damn it, Shassad," retorted Daniels, "the answers aren't going to change no matter how many times you ask. I've told you everything I know.

Shassad turned quickly and angrily, leaning forward on the table, pushing his contorted face to within inches of Daniels's. "Damn it!" he roared. "*What's her name?*"

Daniels was silent, Shassad's eyes fiery and inches away from his own.

"*Where's she live?*"

Silence again.

"*Where is she?*"

More silence.

"God damn you!" he roared. He turned over two chairs beside the table and sent them crashing against a wall and a filing cabinet. "Son of a bitch! Trying to be the hotshot like the old man, huh? Fuck the cops, huh? All right! You wanted it!"

Shassad burst from the room and was gone for less than ten seconds. He returned with the steak knife taken from Daniels earlier. The knife, tagged as evidence and now shielded in a plastic bag, was flung down on the table in front of Daniels.

"See that?" roared Shassad. "*See* it? That's something your old man was never dumb enough to do! Concealed weapon. You won't cooperate with me, I don't cooperate with you. How'd you like to go out to the desk sergeant and be booked for that? Huh? That can mean jail, you know. You want that?" Shassad was leaning forward on the table again, above the knife, shouting.

"Lawyer-client relations are confidential," said Daniels placidly. "I don't expect you to understand a tricky philosophical concept like that." He glanced at his watch. "That's why you're a cop."

Shassad moved back slightly, changing his tone of voice. "What's the matter. You catching a train or something?"

"What?"

"Nothing," said Shassad.

"If you want to book me on a weapons charge, go ahead," said Daniels. "I'll have bail posted before you can get back to your car."

Shassad grabbed the knife angrily. "Fuck it!" he spat violently. He stormed out of the room and didn't return.

Hearn was expressionless as he sat in silence across the table. He made a final attempt at his role of arbitrator. "Hey, look," he said at length, "why won't you cooperate with us? My partner there's under a lot of stress. Can't you give us a break?"

"How can I?"

"You *must* know where she is. How about if you bring her in, let her talk to us. You can be here. If she's innocent, if she was in trouble, we'll listen. She must have had a reason to have been there."

"I don't know a damned thing about it," said Thomas. "What else can I say? That's the gospel."

"I'm sure," intoned Hearn blankly.

Thomas looked at the detective, a man who was as tired and disgusted with his job as Daniels was. He felt a strange affinity toward the man, then wondered absently how many hundreds of times his father had been in similar situations, hauled into police stations to spend the night lying to the local constabularies. Thomas felt diminished in his own opinion of himself. He'd never been in this situation before. Yet having arrived, he found it easy to . . . well, to lie.

He glanced at his watch. Two ten. Hearn was watching him. Shassad reappeared, nasty as ever.

"Go home," said the detective.

Thomas looked at him. "What?"

"You don't understand English now? I said go home. Patty," he said, turning to Hearn, "tell him in Gaelic or something. Tell him to get his ass out of here. It's my good deed for the day. Plus I don't want to go to night court."

Thomas looked with puzzlement and a touch of suspicion to Hearn. Hearn shrugged as Shassad departed.

"The knife, we keep," said Hearn. "You can go, but you'll have to stick to soft foods for a while."

"I own another knife," Thomas offered.

"Try leaving it in your kitchen," suggested Hearn. "Go on. Get out of here. You'll hear from us again."

It was two thirty when Thomas walked out the doors of the precinct house. He was painfully tired and the first steps he took were in the direction of his apartment.

But then he stopped. Leslie's warning had been clear enough. Were the police the people he was to have avoided? Or were there others? He glanced at his watch again and conceded that one more hour, killed at the end of a quiet bar, might not be so painful.

He marked an hour at a Second Avenue bar. Then he exited the bar at three thirty and began walking toward Fifth Avenue and the park. The streets were reasonably quiet as he walked crosstown. Twice, then a third time, he looked behind him. Always there was someone, about a block and a half away. He was at Seventy-third Street and Park Avenue when it dawned on him. He hadn't been released through goodness, kindness, or even chance.

The detectives had seen him glancing at his watch. Figuring he was concerned about the time for a reason, they'd decided to let him lead them to Leslie. They were following him. Thomas had no idea how many there were. But he knew, since two deaths were already involved, there had to be several.

He continued to walk uptown, stepping up his pace. He had twenty minutes to elude an entire squad of experienced detectives and get to the park. And with so few people on the street, he was that much easier to tail. If only he had Leslie's experience, he thought.

Leslie's experience? Of course!

He led the pursuers farther norhtward, then toward Madison Avenue. Then he cut back toward Lexington, as if hoping to have thrown them. He led them to Seventy-eighth and Lexington where, halfway down the block, he saw the sign he wanted.

READER AND ADVISER, MADAME DIANE. It was almost four A.M., but Madame Diane's lights were still on and her door was still open. The early-morning hours were ideal for those disturbed souls needing tea readings and advice.

Thomas walked halfway down the block, then quickly cut into the gypsy's street-level door. He darted up the steps and through the corridor, receiving a surprised look from the Madame herself, who stepped into the hall and shouted at him.

Then he heard footsteps on the stairs where he'd entered. His pursuers. Thomas was down one of the back stairways and out into an alley moments later, just as Madame Diane was asking the detectives if she could help them. No, she hadn't seen anyone, she told them, but if they cared to brew some tea, maybe . . .

At the end of the alley, Thomas climbed over some abandoned wooden crates and over an iron gate which was closed at night. He jumped from the top of the gate onto the sidewalk, nearly skidding on an icy patch.

But when he looked around, no one was anywhere in sight. He ran northward two blocks, then started in a half run toward Central Park. It was already ten past four. He hoped she'd still be waiting. Against every bit of good judgment he had, he wanted her to be there.

He entered the park at East Eighty-first Street. He walked northward toward their chosen rendezvous point. He would have liked to walk slowly and cautiously, not knowing what else might be lurking in the shadows on even the coldest of nights. But he was already late.

He neared his destination, the rock formation which was shrouded with shadows a few hundred feet from the Great Lawn. An ideal place for a covert meeting, yes. Equally serviceable for a murder. He imagined the headlines the next day. **"MAN ESCAPES POLICE SURVEIL-LANCE, KILLED IN PARK."** Would they say that a mugger had done it? (Like Mark Ryder?) Or would the mystery woman be suspected?

Was he crazy? he wondered. Would his father have come here? Maybe he should have let the police follow him? Or had they anyway? No, he'd definitely lost them. *Definitely.*

He neared the rock formation and squinted through the darkness. There was no sound, no movement. All he could see before him was his own breath, a ghostly cloud each time he exhaled. He tried to allow his eyes to accustom themselves to the dimness.

He was staring straight at the rocks. Gradually they took shape through the shadows. He took a step closer and continued to stare. His eyes focused and he felt his heart jump for an instant.

A human form. Dead? Alive? Male? Female? He took a step closer. "Tom?"

He nearly jumped at the soft intonation of the voice—it was as if it called in hushed tones from a cemetery. But he recognized it.

"Leslie," he said. "Thank God."

"Are you all right?" she asked, implying that there'd be some surprise if he weren't.

"Yeah. Fine. I've had a day, let me tell you," he said.

"I have, too."

"I'm not surprised," he said.

There was a pause. He stepped closer to her, standing just a few feet away now. She stepped to him and gave him an affectionate kiss. He said nothing, not knowing where to begin. She sensed his unease immediately.

"Something *is* wrong," she said.

He could see her face now, clearly enough to recognize her. "I'm afraid my client owes her counsel a lot of answers," he said.

"Meaning?"

"Jacobus," he said.

There was a hesitancy, then "What about him?"

"You should know," he said. "You killed him. Whoever you are."

"Tom," she said, acting hurt but shocked. "What are—?"

"No, no," he said, his voice rising, "no more of the double talk. No more of the deception. I want the truth out of you. For once. I'm still your attorney and I'm still on your side. But I'm tired of being the dumb sucker in the middle."

"I've never lied to you," she said defensively.

"Not true."

"Why?" she retorted sharply.

"It's not what you say, my dear," he said caustically. "It's what you don't say. Right now, for example. You still haven't denied shooting Jacobus."

She didn't answer. She took one step away in the darkness, making him squint to see her.

"A nice little old man," he said. "Eccentric, maybe. Quarrelsome, at times. But you killed him, didn't you? Why?"

"All right," she said, turning toward him. "Yes. I did. So what?"

"So what? You shot him and you say 'So what'?"

"He was trying to kill you," she said. "He and some others."

"Oh, brother," he said with disbelief. "Tell me a better one. Explain the man in the blue car."

"You'll know eventually. Soon, in point of fact."

"Yes, sure," he said. "That's what I mean. You never lie completely, just omit the truth. The man at Grover's house a few mornings ago was the same man who was in the parking garage the night you disappeared. Correct?"

"Correct."

"And yet at Grover's you wouldn't even look at him, much less admit that you knew him. Correct?"

"Correct again."

"And you *do* know him. He's a . . . how shall I phrase it? An 'associate' of yours. He got you out of the parking garage. You were in his car. The trunk, I'd guess."

"Very good," she allowed.

"And Peter Whiteside and George McAdam," he pressed. "They're alive, aren't they? As alive as you or I."

"Of course," she admitted. "Their names on the Avianca passenger list was a hoax. I've always known that."

"Then why—?"

"I didn't want you seeing them."

"And the reason is that they could identify the real Leslie McAdam," he suggested. "Correct?"

She nodded.

"What about the real Leslie?" he pursued. "Arthur Sandler's daughter. Dead or alive?" He waited. When she didn't answer, he thought he knew. "Dead?" he concluded. "Right?"

She took a step or two away again. His attention was riveted upon her. He half expected her to make a run through the darkness. Or pull a weapon.

"Well?" he said. "I came here for answers. Before I do one more thing for you, I want answers. And you know where you can start? With your identity. I want to know who you are and what you want."

"You'll know soon enough," she said, turning again.

"When?"

"Soon," was the calculated reply. But the voice was not Leslie's. It was a man's voice and came from behind Thomas. "Now, in fact." The accent was American. Thomas Daniels spun around in terror, his vision clouded by his own breath.

But he could see well enough to discern the features of the man before him. The man from the parking garage, from the blue car, from Grover's front porch. The man was standing fifteen feet away and holding out before him the unmistakable form of a pistol, a long-nosed weapon with a thin mean-looking barrel which strongly suggested the presence of a silencer.

"Please," said Paul Hammond, hesitantly and mustering courage. "No heroics."

Thomas looked at the two of them, bitterly and with exhaustion. He was freezing. He'd been awake for twenty hours. He was too tired and cold for heroics. "Damn you both," he said bitterly. He looked at Leslie, the most fascinating woman he'd ever met. "Damn you in particular," he cursed. How could he maneuver her now?

"It's all been necessary," she said. That soothingly sweet voice again, the cultivated accent of royalty. "If you've been frightened or inconvenienced, I'm truly sorry."

"Inconvenienced?" He looked at the form of the gun. "And you're *'sorry'?"* He looked back and forth again. "If you're so damned sorry, why did you bring me here?"

"Because, Mr. Daniels," said the gunman, "your time has come."

Leslie spoke next. "You're going to disappear," she said sweetly but authoritatively. "And I assure you, no one will *ever* find you."

PART SEVEN

Shassad grabbed the telephone impatiently as it jangled on his desk. An amateur like Thomas Daniels, a lawyer no less, had managed to slip away from a professional surveillance team. Shassad was sore. Genuinely angry. It not only confirmed that Daniels was every bit as shifty as Shassad had thought, but also that the Department was promoting imbeciles to the rank of Detective. Daniels had now been missing for two days.

"Sergeant Shassad?" asked the exuberant voice on the line.

"De-tec-tive," Shassad grumbled, already recognizing the caller. "What is it now, Gary?"

"This is your favorite Keeper of Kadavers," said Gary Dedmarsh, speaking by reason of vocation and avocation, and buoyant enough to refer to himself by the title he'd newly self-bestowed. "Guess what I've got for you."

"For Christ's sake, Gary," implored Shassad, "I'm not in the mood for games. What do you want?"

"I've got a floater for you. Someone you knew."

Shassad was silent for a moment, looking absently up at a clock, rubbing his chin and wondering who the hell had been fished out of the water.

"A pair of kids were playing on the waterfront near East Houston Street," explained Gary excitedly, "when they saw this hunk floating in the Hudson. Well, the hunk was a male in his early thirties, maybe, and he'd been floating for about thirty hours." Gary, knowing how to deliver a punch line, paused before adding, "The floater had a piece of paper with your name and telephone on it. I was wondering, Sergeant, if you wanted to come down and give him a peek?" Another pause and then, "He's all puffed up and waterlogged, but the features are intact and—"

"Save it, Gary," said Shassad. "We'll be down." Jesus, what a perverse kid, Shassad thought, setting down the telephone. There ought to be a law.

Shassad left Hearn at the precinct and drove down to the Thirtieth Street morgue. Gary was seated at a desk, waiting for him feet up and reading a racing newspaper. "Got here fast, Sarge," said Gary, genuinely marveling. "Must have been afraid he'd float out of here again before you got to view him. Want a look?"

"I didn't come for the conversation," said Shassad. "Where is it?" For some reason Shassad always referred to corpses by the indefinite pronoun.

Gary Dedmarsh had a cute act of forgetfulness, reserved for such occasions. "Let's see now," he asked. "Where'd I put him? Where'd he go?"

Shassad grimaced as if to say, Come on Gary, I'm not in the mood for comedy. He wasn't. Gary led him into a colder room, then down a corridor where the refrigerated drawers were kept. He looked for the proper number.

"Took a bullet right there," offered Gary, as if trying to interest Shassad in an attractive piece of merchandise. "Must have been high caliber. Made a real mess. Right in the center of the chest. Then after it had floated long enough, it all puffed up and—"

"Just show it to me, just show it to me!" Shassad snapped, already envisioning the bloated features of the missing attorney.

Gary glanced at the detective. Hurt was on his face. "Jeez," he said slowly, "I didn't know you was in a bad mood."

"Just show it to me."

"I won't say nothin'."

Gary unlocked the small door in the wall, pulled out a second panel, and pulled out the long slab. He unzipped the plastic bag. On the flat board rested the puffy remains of a human body. Male, early thirties, just as Gary Dedmarsh had advertised.

Shassad looked into the swollen white face. He blanched slightly. It was not the face he'd expected, not at all the features of Thomas Daniels.

"You looked surprised," said Gary soberly.

"I am."

"Know him?"

"I recognize him," said Shassad. "He was a guard at a Romanian film company on Varick Street. I met him once. He caught me prowling around his building. I had to give him my card and number." Gary looked at the detective, then back to the corpse, trying to decide whether there was significance to what Shassad said. He found none.

For his part, Shassad was completely silent, clearly envisioning Thomas Daniels, but not even wishing to utter the missing attorney's name.

Chapter 32

"So you see, Daniels," Hammond said drily and without a smile, explaining for the sixth time, "if we hadn't assumed the guardian-angel role you'd probably be dead right now. Throat cut. Drowned. Strangled," Hammond suggested as if the method made little difference. "Maybe even shot, unoriginal as that is. Coffee? You look like you could use it."

Thomas raised his hand, squinting uncomfortably through reddish eyes, and shook his head to say no. His nerves were frayed and his patience was wearing thin. He'd been taken quickly from the Park to a small Federally financed apartment on East Ninety-second Street. He'd seen the sun rise twice and set twice. Now it was evening again. Leslie sat on a nearby sofa and watched Daniels and the U.S. Treasury agent. There were circles beneath her eyes, too.

"You don't have to *drink* the coffee, you know," Hammond persisted, again without a smile. "We could give it to you intravenously. Are you certain you won't have some?"

"I'm sure, damn it," snapped Thomas. "I'm also sure that I want to get out of here."

Hammond sighed, shaking his head and making a tsking sound with his tongue. "Lawyers," he muttered with earnest dismay. "Always asking the impossible. Never considering how things really work in the flesh-and-blood, kill-and-be-killed real world. Well, if you won't join me . . ."

His voice tailed off. He poured a tin saucepan's worth of lukewarm water into a cup where he'd already piled three teaspoons of instant coffee. He added saccharine, then a powdered creamer.

He sipped, he winced.

Leslie looked away, gagging and almost able to taste it herself.

"I've been a coffee drinker all my life," announced Hammond. "And I can't understand why."

Thomas didn't completely understand, either, but it had nothing to do with the coffee. They had made him "disappear," but had given only a sketchy explanation why. He was well treated, but a prisoner. Not under arrest exactly, but sequestered. For the time being, as Hammond put it, William Ward Daniels's son was being "protected."

He was owed an explanation; the debit remained outstanding.

"Protected from what? From whom?" Thomas had asked repeatedly during his first day in captivity. "Give me specifics. Facts. And tell me how long you're keeping me here."

"For as long as necessary," was Hammond's unyielding reply, as if the answer were obvious. Two armed guards in the next room, which served as a living room, enforced Hammond's ukase. And once he'd uttered in disgust, while pointing to Leslie, "Look. How many times does she have to save your life? There are people out there who don't *like* you. They want to *hurt* you. Hurt you so badly that you *pass away*. Get it now?" Hammond appeared tired, drawn, and badly unnerved. A career man experienced in sensitive situations, he was now driving himself all the harder, trying to compensate for his age and the inner fear that he was slipping.

Thomas had to look at Leslie, who appeared bored, then back to Hammond. "So how long is *that?*" he'd persisted.

"Until," said Hammond confidently, "the trash is completely collected."

"Grover?" Thomas cocked his head.

Hammond scoffed. "That wop is past history," he said. "Retired." Retired like I'd like to be, the Treasury agent thought idly.

That's what you think, Thomas reasoned silently. But he said nothing.

Hammond continued. "New men. Able men. They're getting rid of the garbage. I'll let you know when it's safe."

Toward evening, Hammond had been willing to expand slightly. "It's a counterfeiting ring," he'd said. "Run by foreigners. Their assassins tried to kill you and sliced up some other poor bastard instead. They tried again in an art gallery—"

"And again on the steamship from Nantucket," Leslie reminded him. "How's your throat feel?"

"A little dry," Thomas conceded.

"Then . . ." Expansively and with a midwestern smile, Hammond motioned toward the jar of instant coffee. Thomas winced. Hammond lost his smile. "Lucky you have a throat left at all," Hammond mumbled. "If it weren't for us, you wouldn't."

"You're using me for your own reasons," retorted Thomas. "We all know that."

A telephone rang and Hammond conducted a brief conversation which culminated in his smiling. Something about the trash having been picked up completely. Couldn't be the city sanitation men, Thomas thought. And then Hammond repeated something further about dropping the last bag of it under the Williamsburg Bridge. And letting it float. The call ended.

Hammond turned back to Thomas. "You want to know why?" he asked.

"Yes."

"Good. I'm ready to educate you."

And with Leslie's help, he did.

It had begun—as many things do—with money, Hammond intoned. Not his money, not the Treasury's money, not anybody's money. Counterfeit money. "Printed in Germany during the war. Nazi counterfeits," he elucidated, pronouncing it Nat-Z, "of British pounds."

So far, so familiar, thought Thomas. But as Daniels listened intently, the story swerved resolutely into darker regions.

"It was our man who was helping with the printing," said Hammond. "A man who was an agent for us. You know the name. Sandler."

"Of course," said Thomas.

"Recruited by—"

"My father."

Hammond glanced to Leslie, whose eyes told him to skip ahead, far ahead. Thomas knew the basics.

"After the war, in the late forties," Hammond said, "the counterfeits of the pounds picked up again. It was a crackerjack effort. The counterfeiter was bleaching one-pound notes, turning the paper back into pulp, re-cutting it and then reengraving higher denominations on the same God-damned paper. Soon it had increased from a brief flurry to an avalanche. The British were pretty sore about it."

"Can you blame them?" asked Thomas, trying to weigh the story at its face value.

"No," said Hammond. He raised his head, sipped the bitter coffee, and shook his head. "Don't forget, I wasn't in this case till recently. Don't blame me for past history."

"I wouldn't think of it."

Leslie settled into an armchair, folded her arms, leaned back, and listened. She was thinking of her girlhood, and how the circumstances of her life had led her to this room with these men.

"The English were tactful about it at first. Course, they had to be," Hammond smirked. "We won their God-damned war for them." Leslie shot him a withering glare and Hammond continued quickly before he could be interrupted. "They asked us for Sandler. We wouldn't give him to them."

"Why?"

"The United States does *not* turn over its agents," said Hammond, pride and jingoism in his voice. "Not to enemies, not to allies. We just don't do it. No matter *what* the agent has done." He let the point hang in the air, then disclaimed, "And besides, we didn't *know* that it was Sandler. Sandler left this country as a good engraver, not a *great* one. What's there to prove to us that he's flawless upon his return?"

"What was there to prove that he wasn't?"

"Lawyers," muttered Hammond, looking at the younger man with distaste. "We assume innocence in this country, don't we?"

"Some of us do. Continue," said Thomas. He looked at the Treasury agent and felt a surge of dislike welling within him. Not so much for the man, but rather for imperious attitudes, his representation of his department as flawless. It didn't become a man who was showing his years, slowing down, tiring, and, frankly, slipping.

Hammond went on. "For the next few years the British grew noisier and noisier about the Sandler matter. They claimed there were far too many pounds in circulation, so many that it endangered the exchangeability of their money. They attributed it to Sandler. In 1954 they got tired of complaining. They went out and killed him."

"Or tried to," said Thomas.

Hammond studied Thomas. "*Someone* was killed," uttered Hammond. "And Sandler disappeared. The bogus pounds stopped. You could draw any of several conclusions. We chose to believe that Sandler had been murdered, some sort of vendetta from the war."

"Still believe that?" asked Thomas, glancing at Sandler's self-proclaimed daughter. She was eyeing both men carefully, as if serving as a judge in a debate.

"No," admitted Hammond. "A few years ago the assault began on the dollar. Same assault, same technique. We investigated. The British had claimed all along that Sandler was still alive. He'd been trying"—he motioned to Leslie—"to kill his daughter, they said. So we started looking for him, too."

Leslie chimed in. "Convenient timing," she said. "Whiteside was forced into retirement. I lost my protection from the British government. I needed—" Her voice tailed off.

"A new protector?" suggested Thomas.

She replied with a nod. "I wanted to study. I wanted to live a normal life, either in an academic career or as an artist. I couldn't do it looking over my shoulder."

"So you agreed to help the Americans find Sandler," Thomas said, his best cross-examining voice, of course.

"Better than that," she said, her eyes blazing with hatred. "I wanted that man dead." Her voice hit the final word heavily. "I know how that sounds. . . . Call it a crime of passion. Or call it self-defense, a preemptive strike against the man trying to murder me."

Somehow, Thomas understood. When the man who'd tried to kill him had gone over the stern of the steamship, Thomas had been sickened. He'd thrown up from the sight; but he'd shed no tears. Simple physics: for an action, a reaction; for brutality, vengeance.

"A woman artist who packs a gun and a knife," reflected Thomas aloud. "Fabulous. Wait till the New York Women's Collective hears about—"

"That brings us back to your father," Hammond interrupted.

Thomas initially thought the Treasury agent was addressing Leslie. He wasn't. That left Thomas.

"*My* father?"

"Yes," Hammond said. "The great patriot. Our favorite flag waver in the legal community. A member of Intelligence during World War Two."

"What about him?" Thomas's voice was defensive.

"Well, quite a bit about him. He'd been a recruiter for our side, you see. He regularly lured some of his criminal clients, such as Sandler, into compromising legal positions, then put the shitty end of the stick to them. Told them jail was inevitable . . . unless they agreed to conduct intelligence work for us."

"I know how that all worked."

Hammond was pleased. That saved explaining. "Coffee's cold," he noted, setting his cup aside. He looked to Leslie, waiting for her to volunteer to reheat it for him. She sat tight. He sighed. What was wrong with women these days? Uppity ideas. Silently, Hammond suffered deeply.

"I'm afraid your father drew a zero on this one," said Hammond. "Couldn't help us at all. Not at *all.* Said he thought Sandler was dead. Said we had to be barking up the wrong tree if we were looking for him. Yet," he said, with rising eyebrows and an open gesture of both hands, "we *knew* we had to be looking for Sandler. There was no one else. Your father didn't *want* to help."

Thomas's question was so obvious that he knew the answer as soon as he asked. "Why didn't you open Sandler's grave? See whether he was dead or not?"

"Impossible." Hammond puffed on a freshly lit cigarette. The smell of the smoke annoyed Thomas. "Sandler was cremated. According to his wishes. Ever try to check the dental charts of ashes?" A few particles from the tip of his cigarette flicked onto the floor. He toed them into the carpet, then grinned sheepishly. "Not those ashes," he said.

Thomas felt his eyes becoming drearily tired. He rubbed them for a moment with his thumb and forefinger and looked back up at Leslie and Hammond, odd allies in an odder struggle.

"So now," asked Thomas, "everyone concedes that Sandler is alive?"

"Yes," said Hammond. "And we've traced the route of the counter-feits. A Romanian film company smuggles them in and out of the country in cans which are supposed to contain undeveloped exposed film. They finance U.S. intelligence work this way. Several of their employees are Russian KGB operatives. That's who tried to kill you."

"We've tended to them," said Leslie. "An eye for an eye. Spies are jailed. Killers are killed."

"And Jacobus?" Thomas asked, still with incredulousness in his voice, wanting to disbelieve but unable to.

"A KGB man, waiting for his proper chance to eliminate you. He was in with the two others who tried and failed."

Jacobus, thought Daniels, turning over the name in his mind, and envisioning the perennially cranky custodian. He recalled how surprised Jacobus had been when Thomas arrived safely on the night of the fire. Thomas shook his head. "I find it incredible," he muttered.

"Don't," said Leslie. "Who do you think *set* the fire." She let him consider it for a moment, then concluded jauntily, "Your dear custodian was the only one in the building. *Of course* he set it."

"What was he trying to cover up in the file?"

"Nothing. He was trying to lure you onto the street," Hammond said.

"Where your muscular neck could be perforated," mused Leslie, the expert on throats and the severing thereof.

Confused, he looked back and forth between the two of them. "But the Sandler file?" he asked. "It was gone."

Hammond looked at Leslie and the two of them shared a wide conspiratorial grin.

"You're a poor record keeper," she admitted. "*We* took it."

"Your office was burglarized about a year ago," Hammond said. "Right after your father died. The next day, in fact." He chuckled. "For an Ivy League boy you ain't got *all* the smarts," he mocked. "We took six of your files. You never noticed."

Thomas studied Hammond closely, trying to discern whatever truth or untruth was behind the man's eyes and words. Daniels's eyes moved a quarter inch and looked at Leslie.

She spoke, reading his questioning thoughts. "It's true," she said. "I suppose we can't make you believe it, but—"

"Why didn't *they* try to rob my files?" Thomas asked.

Hammond answered. "They probably did," he said. "Jacobus was akin to the keeper at the gates. The watchman. He had keys to all the offices," Hammond said. He ran his hand across his chin. "I suppose he went into your father's files, looked around, and didn't see what he wanted. That made them think that *you* had hidden everything. They figured that in time you could be pressed and would reveal where the files were. But then Victoria Sandler died. People would be going into that old mansion eventually. They had to act in a hurry. You had to be silenced, just in case. They couldn't *study* you any longer."

"*Study* me?" Thomas felt a distaste in his stomach, a sense of having been on the plate of a microscope without knowing it. Christ, how much of his private life had been prowled into? All of it?

"Of course," said Hammond. "We've studied you, too." He glanced at Leslie. "Essentially, that was her endeavor. Get as close to you as possible. Get inside you. Get into your brain. Find out how much you knew."

"About what, damn it!" roared Thomas. "Would you come out and say it. What were you trying to find out?"

"How closely you worked with your father," said Leslie bluntly. "How much of his business you knew. How much of his work you were planning to continue."

"His legal work?"

Hammond grimaced, as if Thomas were a slow learner. Leslie sighed.

Thomas's eyebrows were slanted downward in an angry frown, looking from one face to the other.

"Call it his *il*legal work," said Hammond flatly. "The espionage."

"I never knew a damned thing about it," he said sharply. "Not until" —he raised his hand and pointed rudely—"this fraud appeared in my offices and began to educate me."

"Evidently," muttered Hammond.

"I'm not a fraud," she answered.

Thomas looked to her with anger and was about to pursue the point when Hammond spoke.

"In any event," Hammond said, "we're forced for the sake of expediency to assume you had no knowledge of your father's activities. Miss McAdam here is convinced that you're innocent of any espionage activities."

"Innocent?" repeated Thomas. A bizarre terminology, he thought, from one of the bastards who'd send you out to do the spying. "What the hell are you implying?"

"I myself," said Hammond, standing, still rubbing a hand across his unshaven grayish chin, "I have my doubts about you. But there's no case against you, anyway." He seemed to weigh his next words in advance. "That's why we're taking you in with us," he concluded. "You might have a certain insight. You might want to help us help ourselves . . . to let us *know* your name is clear. Get my meaning?"

"No, I don't!" snapped Thomas angrily. "*In* what? Where are we going?"

Leslie smiled as Hammond explained with icy politeness. "Why, into the Sandler mansion," he said. "We've broken a wall beneath the streets. We're all set to go exploring." He let the words sink in, disbelief all over Thomas's face. "You *would* like to join us tonight, wouldn't you? Now that we've made it safe for you to step out the door?"

Thomas leaned back in his chair and felt the scratchy beard growing on his own face.

"Why are you breaking down walls?" Thomas asked. "What's the matter with the front door?"

"We don't wish to be seen," said Hammond icily. "By anyone."

Thomas looked at Hammond, then glanced back to Leslie. "The three of us? Tonight?" he asked.

"More, if necessary," Hammond allowed.

"I wouldn't miss it for anything," Daniels said. "It will allow me to answer several of my own questions."

"I had a set of electric trains when I was a boy," Thomas said reflectively at seven minutes past two the following morning. "And I ran them more efficiently than these trains."

The three of them, Thomas, Leslie, and Paul Hammond, stood on the downtown express platform at the Eighty-sixth and Lexington subway station.

The platform was not crowded, though not deserted either. A handful of early-morning stragglers waited for their late ride home. Thomas stood by the edge of the platform. He looked to his left, northward, into the black mouth of the underground train tunnel. In the distance he saw two headlights, gleaming like the eyes of an animal in the dark. A train was approaching.

"You're missing the point," said Hammond, large bags under the Treasury agent's eyes. "We're not waiting for a train to arrive. We're waiting for one to *leave.*"

"I'd almost forogtten," Thomas muttered. He, too, was tired. He considered the Christmas day when he was eight years old, the year his father had presented him with a four-hundred-dollar set of electric trains. An elaborate setup, it had been, three engines, passenger trains, yards and yards of track, two freight trains, mountains, cities, freight depots. Then what had William Ward Daniels done? With his usual sensitivity, he'd prompted his son to invite in the poorest kids in the neighborhood, the better for them to see what their own parents could never afford. Better for Thomas to realize that he had so much, and the others had so little.

He saw a uniformed transit patrolman and turned away, afraid that any police officer might recognize him.

Leslie studied her surroundings, particularly the graffitied walls and defaced billboards. "What a mess," she mumbled. "Are all the stations like this?"

"This one's cleaner than most," Thomas explained. She looked at him and was surprised to see he wasn't smiling.

The train arrived. They remained on the rear of the platform. They waited until the subway doors had slid shut and all passengers had either embarked or disembarked. Hammond tensely studied the surroundings. The transit officer was gone. Their platform was vacant and only a bent-over black woman with a shopping bag was on the opposite side on the uptown platform.

"Okay, now!" said Hammond tersely in a loud whisper. "Follow me! And don't touch the third rail or you're finished."

Kneeling quickly on the edge of the platform, Hammond eased himself down onto the tracks. He turned and extended a hand to Leslie, who followed. Thomas slid off the platform at the same moment and let himself drop between the two rails. "Hurry! Hurry!" Hammond urged.

With Hammond leading, they jogged northward as fast as they could, just short of breaking into a run. First one block, then a second. Hammond was obviously winded already. Leslie kept pace well while Thomas, anxious as well as excited, was starting to lose wind, also.

Two headlights appeared ahead of them, several blocks off. "Duck in here," Hammond instructed quickly. They stepped from the rails into a side booth, designed to protect workers on a track as a train passed through.

They waited, out of sight. "That one's early, damn it," snorted Hammond, panting slightly. "With the cutbacks they're only supposed to be traveling twelve minutes apart at this hour."

"Maybe the last one was late," Leslie suggested.

Hammond shrugged. The train passed. Thomas watched it disappear toward the illuminated Eighty-sixth Street station. Hammond then urged them on a final block of tracks. Then they cut through a side corridor and slid upward through a small crawl space under Eighty-ninth Street for at least fifty yards.

The passage was unspeakably dirty and sooty. Hammond led the way with a flashlight he'd produced from his coat. The smell was foul and suggested stale urine.

"Don't mind the stench," said Hammond. "We're above the sewer. Not in it."

"I'm grateful for the small amenities," Thomas retorted. He glanced at Leslie, who slid in front of him, between the two men. "No place to bring a lady," Thomas chided. No time at all to joke; Thomas was concealing his claustrophobia. All four walls were just inches from him on each side. He felt as if the walls would suddenly spring in on him in the shadows and darkness, gripping him and holding him. Apparently, it didn't bother Leslie. Compared with having your throat cut, he reasoned, it wasn't much, after all.

He saw light ahead. He was relieved.

Hammond had slid from the crawlway and was standing, proud that at his age he'd made it. Leslie followed. Thomas emerged third, coming up at the feet of the others in an illuminated chamber. He stood. There were two other men, both dressed in the blue work uniforms of New York City Metropolitan Transit Authority. Neither man was a subway worker. They stood beside a hole in a brick wall, a hole large enough to step through sideways and crouching. The underground chamber, illuminated by battery-operated lanterns, was against the pantry wall of the Sandler mansion. Thomas had traveled a city block underground since leaving the subway tracks. It had seemed like four blocks.

"Like I promised," said Hammond, trying to gather himself. "We're going in."

"Have you been in already?" asked Thomas.

"We've been waiting for you," said Hammond. "We didn't know whether you'd be able to guide us or not."

Thomas looked at the hole that had been chiseled through brick that was four feet thick. A less awesome entrance than the front door, he thought, yet having more dignity than the servants' entrance. His mind then traveled to Zenger, his father's partner. Zenger, one of the city's leading attorneys twenty years earlier, had entered this house through the front door and had reemerged, as his father termed it, "a different man." A recluse, a man who'd retired soon afterward.

"We had a quick look around the ground floor after we knocked through," Hammond finally admitted. "Now we'll have a more thorough look."

Hammond nodded to the two gatekeepers. He stepped through the hole into a dark pantry. Thomas followed, then Leslie. Each picked up a heavy-duty battery lantern on entering. Leslie drew her service pistol and carried it in her other hand. Looking for her father? Thomas wondered.

Thomas, like Leslie and Hammond, had the sense of having stepped through a corridor into another decade. Out of the seventies, into the nineteen thirties. The wallpaper, once elegant and colorful, was now faded and yellowed. Heavy, solid furniture was in each room, and the kitchen appliances were relics of the Depression. Sagging drapes, often threadbare near the floor, shut out light from the windows, and the carpets were worn where Victoria Sandler had made her daily paths. An ornate art-deco clock, capped with a cupid with bow and arrow, was stopped on a table. A mirror was thick with dust. The entire house smelled of both mildew and time. The interior of the mansion wore the years with a morbid pallor.

"Anything in particular you want to start with?" Hammond asked.

"Ground floor," said Thomas. "Then the basement."

Hammond nodded. The main floor was the first floor fully above street level, he explained. The ground floor, the one they were on, was almost completely below sidewalk level. Beneath was a basement. "Why the basement first?" Hammond asked as an afterthought.

"I'm sure that's where she kept the skeletons," said Thomas, sober-faced, then somehow managing a laugh. Hammond looked displeased, a don't-joke-at-a-time-like-this expression. Daniels couldn't be sure, but he thought Leslie, who was standing so close that their arms were against each other, shuddered.

Together the three explored a ground floor library. When Hammond expressed desire to glance through the second of the five floors, they separated. Leslie went with Thomas, both holding lanterns, she alertly holding the pistol. One never knew, though Thomas thought the armaments vaguely melodramatic.

"Where's the door to the basement?" Thomas asked.

She led him. He followed closely, realizing that she'd been there before, at least briefly and probably with Hammond.

Thomas pointed the lantern down the narrow stairs. The first step creaked and almost seemed to sag beneath his weight. He pressed gingerly with one foot, then the next.

The light shone ahead of him, a dusty maze of shadows and cobwebs. It occurred to him that Victoria Sandler might never have been down here any more often than she'd been in her bathtub. Which was to say, seldom in the last twenty years.

Followed by Leslie, he reached the bottom of the steps. He flashed the light around and saw nothing move, except for the shadows dancing under the beams of their two wavering lanterns.

They stepped forward, walking among the faded, forgotten belongings of two generations of Sandlers. They stepped through a large cluttered room, perhaps thirty feet by forty feet, crowded with dust-laden white sheets over unused or retired furniture. A walking space, such that it was, was along the wall, a wall lined with old portraits from nineteenth-century Germany. The forgotten progenitors of the Sandler clan.

Then from across the room a noise and two red eyes.

Thomas felt his heart leap and whirled with the lantern. "Leslie!" he blurted quickly.

But she'd already turned and the pistol was upraised. Two red glimmering eyes reflected back at them. A large rat sat on top of an old steamer trunk, the latter bearing stamps from voyages in the 1920s.

Brazen and defiant as any Sandler, the rat ignored the intruders into his domain. A second or two later he leaped to the floor and disappeared. Thomas began watching his own feet and ankles as he walked.

"You're jumpy," she said.

"This isn't my ordinary sort of legal work" he explained.

She flashed her light on ahead to a passageway. "What's that?" she asked aloud. The passage led to a separate room, one apparently clear of storage.

"Furnace room?" he guessed.

"The furnace room is behind the stairs," she said.

They neared the open doorway. He felt her hand on his shoulder. "I'll go first if you wish," she said, motioning with the pistol as if to indicate why. He shook his head. He expected nothing living past the doorway. Nor would he admit fear or hesitation.

"I'll go," he said.

He stepped through the passageway, followed quickly by Leslie. They found themselves in a mausoleum. There were plaques on the wall, marking births and deaths.

He screwed his face into a perplexed scowl. "What in hell is this?" he asked breathlessly.

She was more calm. There was a small altar before the plaques on the wall, complete with candles and the dusty remains of flowers which had faded and died innumerable years earlier. They both had the sense of having stepped into some bizarre medieval sacristy, a holy shrine of a small and perverse order. In a way, the sense was a proper one.

"There are names on the plaques," he said.

At once they stepped forward, examining the names. Each name was the same—only the dates differed on the small tarnished gold plaques.

ANDREW, read the first gold plaque, corroded with age, but still legible. 1932–1939.

And the next, ANDY 1939–1946.

And the next and the next, all the same, at various intervals until the last in 1975.

"The dogs," said Thomas. "It's where she interred the dogs."

Leslie shook her head incredulously. The room was a canine mausoleum, complete with a small bronze statue of a poodle on the opposite side from the altar.

"Incredible," said Thomas. "A crazy old woman. A fortune and all the time in the world. And this is what she does with it." He pondered the darkest recesses and warpings of the human mind. This was Victoria Sandler's other family. Her Andys. It was cold in the room. The lanterns moved from moment to moment and threw changing, disproportionate shadows on the walls. At one point Leslie's lantern shone directly upon the statue of the poodle and a giant shadow of the dog rose in stark black against a side wall. For a moment they could almost feel the presence of Victoria Sandler, of the mind of the recently deceased woman who had consecrated this most sacred part of her world.

The man's voice came suddenly from behind them, loud, casual, and totally unexpected. "Find anything?" it asked solemnly.

They almost felt their insides explode as they whirled in their tracks, both brandishing their lanterns and Leslie raising her gun to fire. A third lantern shone back into their eyes, blinding them.

"Sorry," said the man, filling much of the doorway. "Did I surprise you?"

He lowered the lantern. It was Hammond.

Leslie and Thomas drew deep breaths, neither completely willing to admit that Hammond, approaching without being heard, had set their nerves on edge.

Leslie eased her pistol downward, scared that she might actually have fired. The weapon had been trained accurately on the center of Hammond's chest. And her jittery finger had been squeezing. People had been accidentally killed for less.

Leslie conversed with Hammond, explaining what they'd found. But Thomas's attention was transfixed by what he'd seen quite accidentally in the shadows on the other side of the altar room. He might never have noticed it had he not had reason to whirl suddenly and shine the lamp the wrong way.

But there was a long convex section of the concrete floor. A section maybe nine feet by four feet, and unnoticeable to the eye in proper light. It had been uneven in the beam of the light, however, reflecting the shadow disproportionately.

"Wait a minute," asked Thomas as Hammond and Leslie were ready to dimiss the altar room altogether. "What's this?"

He motioned with his lantern, shining a beam up and down the length of the slightly convex area. At first they didn't see it, didn't realize what he was indicating. Then they both noticed also. The dirty gray concrete of the floor was ever so slightly higher in that small area than anywhere else in the basement.

Hammond stooped down and examined the area, looking first at the convex area, running his hand across it, then looking at the concrete along the wall. He compared the concrete there to the rest of the cellar.

"You've got a pair of eyes," Hammond said. "This floor's been refinished. It's anywhere from fifteen to thirty years old. The rest is original."

He studied it again. "The new floor's higher than the old, too," he concluded. "But not by much. Sharp eyes, all right, Daniels."

"I knew what I was looking for," allowed Thomas, drawing curious glances from both of them. Yet exactly what Daniels had been looking for was already evident. Hammond began nodding slowly. Leslie made no indication, though all three of them knew immediately what could be in a rounded section of the floor in an area of that size.

"A grave," said Hammond. "Maybe." He glanced up, searching the face of Thomas Daniels. "Did she ever have any large dogs?" he asked.

"No." Thomas was already shaking his head. "Not that I ever knew of."

"Figures," said Hammond softly, looking back and still holding his fingers to the concrete floor, as if to pick up sensations or intuition. "We'll have to chisel it up, won't we?"

"Chisel what up?" Thomas asked.

Hammond looked back as if to answer a silly self-evident question. "Why, the *floor*, of course," he said. He pondered it for a moment. "Can't bring a drill in," he planned. "Too much noise. Can't use electricity anyway." He paused, then concluded. "Have to use hammers and chisels," he said. "A lot of work. Muscle mostly." He rose. "Take us a while, probably," he said in conclusion.

"Us?" asked Thomas nervously.

Hammond smiled and Leslie managed a vague titter of laughter.

"Relax," said Hammond. "We have specialists. We can have the floor up in a few hours."

"How long is 'a few'?" asked Daniels.

Hammond eyed the concrete area intently. Thomas shifted his own gaze to the floor. He was reminded of the small church in Devonshire, where former parish ministers were interred beneath the stones of the floor.

"Eighteen to twenty-four hours," said Hammond flatly. "That's a guess, an educated guess."

Thomas looked back to Hammond, assessing him carefully now. "I want to bring someone else in here," Daniels said.

"*What?*" snapped Hammond. Leslie watched Thomas cautiously and curiously. Thomas repeated, though it wasn't necessary. Hammond dismissed it out of hand.

"You want to find out about Arthur Sandler?" Thomas asked. "You want to know about your damned counterfeit? You want to know where the espionage angle leads you? You'll let me bring two more people in here."

"Who are they?" asked Leslie, ready to negotiate.

"Doesn't matter," said Hammond quickly. "No—"

She held up her hand. "Who are they?" she repeated.

"I won't tell you. You'll refuse if I tell you."

"Then why should we permit it?"

"Because I can see everything starting to fall into place," Thomas explained. "*All* of it. Look. When you're an attorney you're trained to put pieces of a story together and form a whole story, something which becomes the functioning truth in a case. That's what I want to do. I want to link your story with another story. I want to eliminate the contradictions. Let me do that, let your mechanics chisel up that floor, and we'll be damned close to a solution."

Hammond was hesitant. Thomas looked to Leslie, then back to Hammond. "Your alternative is going back to Washington empty fisted," Thomas said to Hammond. "And you, Leslie, your alternative is not finding the man who probably still wants to kill you."

Hammond looked to Leslie.

"Trust me," Daniels said simply, preparing to rest his case. "With any kind of luck, I'll produce the missing man you're looking for. Alive. Within twenty-four hours."

Hammond was indignant. "I thought you said you didn't—"

"—know anything?"

"Yes."

"I didn't. But unlike you, I've seen both sides of this. I've figured it out."

A strange look came over Hammond, one of superiority or pomposity. Or was it challenge? "Including about your father?" he asked.

"I can't be blind forever. It's making sense."

Hammond sighed. He was tired and in a mood to concede a point if it would bring things closer to the point of resolution. Under normal circumstances, he conceded nothing. Everything was done his way. A man like Daniels would never be out of his sight. And he was as skeptical as he was tired.

"Where do you make contact with these people?"

"One telephone call. And I bring them in."

Hammond grimaced. It wasn't that he didn't like it; he hated it. He looked to Leslie. So did Thomas, seeing where the tie-breaking vote would go.

"Seems to me," she said with gentle intonations to Hammond, "that we might do well to trust him."

"All right," said Hammond. "It better work. Otherwise I'll find you again."

Thomas smiled. It would work. It *had* to! With all the pieces gliding together as they were, how could they *not* fit the way he wanted them? Then again, how had he not seen it earlier? How had he been so blind to a man he'd been so close to?

"Watch those damned subway trains when you come out of the crawlway," Hammond muttered, by way of send-off.

Thomas recalled. The crawlway. Dirty, dark, and evoking claustrophobia.

He shuddered.

Chapter 34

Thomas stood on the far end of the Eighty-sixth Street subway platform. He looked anxiously at his watch, seeing that it was ten minutes past five A.M. His eyes were stinging with fatigue. Two subway trains had come and gone. He looked up and down the platform and did not see the two men he awaited.

He'd been there half an hour. He'd reached them by telephone. They were late. What, he wondered, was wrong? Nothing? Everything. "Come on," he addressed them in their absence. "Arrive, damn it, arrive!"

A downtown express train rumbled into the station. A pair of transit patrolmen watched Thomas from within the end car, idly wondering why, if he was standing in the station, he wasn't boarding the train.

The train began again. One of the patrolmen reached to a walkie-talkie at his waist. The platform was clear again. A man dropped an early edition of the *Daily News* on a bench. Thomas glanced at a headline. A huge Soviet fishing fleet was in the North Atlantic off Massachusetts, it said. Thomas glanced away.

Hurry up, damn it, he thought again.

He wandered toward the far end of the platform. Then he froze in thought. Footsteps approached and he looked up. He saw the tall, lean man first, then the shorter, stronger one, the one with the beard.

Whiteside and Hunter.

"You look surprised," said Hunter.

"Not at all." Thomas glanced at his watch. "You're late. Punctuality is next to godliness. Didn't your keeper here ever teach you that?"

"Where's Sandler?" asked Hunter.

"And the girl?" asked Whiteside.

"Around."

"Don't be coy, Mr. Daniels," intoned Whiteside gently. "It doesn't become you." He shifted weight from one foot to another, cocked his head, and glinted at Thomas. "Why did you call us?"

"I told you," said Thomas, folding the newspaper beneath his arm. "I'm going to give you the 'new' Leslie McAdam, the source of the bogus British pounds, and Sandler in the bargain. In return, I want the entire background story on Sandler. *Every*thing."

"I already agreed," said Whiteside with cunning. "I agreed an hour ago on the telephone." Hunter glared at Thomas, then looked around the platform, clearly unsure of his ground.

"I just wanted to be sure that we understood the ground rules," said Thomas.

"Obviously we do," Whiteside snorted with impatience. "Otherwise I wouldn't be in this Godforsaken place at a bloody hour like this. Where do we consummate our arrangement? Here?"

Thomas shook his head. He glanced to the tracks. "It's my turn to take you into a tunnel," he said. "We wait for the next train to pass. Then we go underground."

Fifteen minutes later, three men slipped onto the tracks and moved quickly northward, then westward beneath the streets of Manhattan. When they came to the narrow crawlway, it was apparent that the older Whiteside would only navigate with a certain difficulty. And Hunter insisted that Whiteside travel first, followed by Thomas, then Hunter. It took another fifteen minutes to arrive before the broken brick wall.

Whiteside and Hunter stepped through the pantry, Whiteside vainly trying to wipe the dirt from his clothing. Hunter's gaze was all around him, nervously anticipating some sort of entrapment.

They passed on to the dining room. There, in the room lit by flashlights and scented by the mustiness of furniture, Whiteside stopped short. His expression froze.

"Well, Whiteside?" asked Daniels. "Yes or no?"

Hunter, in front of him, acting almost as a shield, stepped to the side, glaring at Leslie, glancing back and forth between Hammond and Thomas Daniels as well as the woman. His own expression, shrouded by his beard, seemed to demand an explanation, the explanation owed to his superior. "It's yes, isn't it?" asked Daniels.

"Yes. Yes, of course it is," said Whiteside softly.

"Hallo, Peter," she said. She grinned. "I guess you didn't get a good look on the Brooklyn Heights Promenade," she suggested.

"No," he said. "You made sure we didn't. I sensed it was the real Leslie when you turned out to be so elusive." He thought back. "That poor girl in London. We buried a girl who was the very image of you."

"The very image," suggested Thomas, "but not the original. That seems to be the type of game we're all involved in, isn't it? I may be slow sometimes, but I'm catching on."

"Sir?" asked Whiteside turning.

"A game of doubles," said Thomas. "Or double doubles, if you prefer. One side can play the same game as the other. And every bit as well."

"Perhaps," Whiteside said. He looked back to Leslie. "I wish I could have known what you were doing."

"There were leaks all over. By arrangement with the Americans, British security was to think I was dead."

Whiteside nodded pensively. "Perhaps now someone can explain how—"

"Not yet," interjected Thomas.

"I beg your pardon?"

"We're here to exchange information," said Thomas, "not to give it away. We have one half of the Sandler story. You have the other half. Now we're going to put them together."

"For what purpose?" huffed Whiteside with a certain hostility.

"You want the man who was printing pounds? You want the man who killed her mother, tried twice to kill her, then killed another girl in her place, the girl you were kind enough to bury?"

"I want him," said Whiteside flatly.

"Then tell us everything," pleaded Leslie. "We'll tell our half of the story, then you tell us the rest of yours."

"The part you always held back on," said Thomas. "It's critical, isn't it?"

"It's also classified British intelligence," said Whiteside with a sigh. "On my own, I have no authority—"

"Within another day the man we both want will have escaped from within our grasp," Daniels said. "You have your choice. Help us or he escapes."

Hammond looked nervously at Thomas, feeling left out of things.

"There are official regulations about releasing information," said Whiteside.

"Break them!" ranted Thomas.

"Please," Leslie begged.

Whiteside could see the scar across her throat, the one which had never healed. He glanced to Hunter, who offered no opinion or change of expression. "All right," Whiteside finally said. "Let's be genteel about this. Let's sit down."

Gradually the four men and one woman stepped toward an aged, dusty, dining table. The room was illuminated by a pair of dim kerosene lamps set up by Hammond. Shadows fell across the heavy, drawn curtains which dated from the 1920s. Three chairs at the oblong table remained empty. Whiteside seemed to study Leslie a final time, as if to test his senses.

She began.

"We finally all agree on who I am," she said softly, looking from eye to eye. "Good," she said. There was no disagreement.

She moved quickly over areas of common knowledge, her birth, the 1954 attempt on her life, her relocation with the McAdam family, the subsequent attempt by the Italian in 1964, and her return trip to England in 1974.

"It was about that time," she said, gazing at Whiteside, "that British intelligence washed their hands of me." Her voice contained residual resentment, not at all tempered by the passage of years.

"Decisions made higher up," he offered plaintively. "Leslie, dear, honestly, I had nothing—"

"You'll have your opportunity to speak, Peter," she snapped brusquely. "Allow me. Please."

He nodded. She went on.

"I wasn't considered important anymore," she said. "There'd been no threat on my life for several years, the counterfeitings of the pound by my father had ceased many years previously, I was considered . . . expendable."

Whiteside shook his head sorrowfully. Not expendable, he was telling himself. Merely lower priority. The Sandler case had been considered closed by M.I.6. But Whiteside was too well-mannered to interrupt again.

Thomas watched both of them. Silently. Hunter gazed at Hammond and Daniels steadily, his thick bulk wedged into the narrow dining chair once favored by Victoria Sandler.

Sounds of concrete chipping rose from the basement. To Whiteside, for a fleeting moment, the sounds conjured up an image of Verdi's anvil chorus. He, too, was tired. Physically and emotionally.

"It was at about this same time in 1974," she said, "that a man named Robert Lassiter approached me in London." Hammond's eyes came alive. He was the only one at the table who knew the name. "Lassiter said he was from the United States Treasury Department," Leslie explained. "He'd been dispatched by a man named Merritt, who was said to be the Director of U.S. Treasury Intelligence."

Whiteside frowned, perplexed. Hammond nodded. Hunter was impassive, Thomas so intrigued that he hardly breathed.

Leslie told her story.

Lassiter was completely familiar with her case, he'd said. He approached her in a London restaurant near Cheapside. He'd asked if he could make a "business" proposition to her, one which would guarantee her safety in the future. "After all," he'd said, "your father is still very much alive."

It had taken no more than those words, plus a convincing explanation of Lassiter's own identity, to move Leslie McAdam. The two memories of her father were like wounds which festered, pained, but never healed. There was always that threat, the deathly fear that he could always be standing behind her, going for the throat a third time.

Leslie McAdam, hater of violence, expert on impressionistic art, devotee of Brahms and Vivaldi, was practically obsessive on the subject of Sandler.

"What I'd like," she'd told Lassiter, "is seeing my father dead. Can you provide that?" she'd challenged.

His answer surprised her, astonished her, in fact. "With your help," he'd said simply, "yes. Can do."

Already notified that she'd soon be losing her British protection, Leslie had little choice. She'd leaped from British arms to American arms, desperate for protection and willing to take it from whatever quarter offered it. And none too soon.

The forces protecting Arthur Sandler made a rare mistake, but a fatal mistake for an innocent English girl. They thought that a stenographer who worked for the Foreign Office was Leslie under a different name. They came calling on her toward five A.M. one morning. The usual routine with the piano wire. They left her quite dead, her head almost completely severed.

"They never knew their mistake," said Leslie, "until I surfaced after Victoria Sandler's death."

"And that other girl was the body we put in Leslie's grave in London," muttered Whiteside. "We knew we weren't burying the real Leslie. We didn't have any idea where the real Leslie was. Not until just now. But back then, back in 1974, we took the chance that Sandler and Company had thought they'd executed the right girl. We wanted as many people as possible to believe that she'd been killed."

"Including me," said Thomas, thinking back to the churchyard.

"Of course," said Whiteside, his eyebrows raised. "We didn't know who you were. We only knew that you had bloody good information. No way in the world we wanted an enlightened stranger to think the real Leslie McAdam was still alive." Whiteside pondered it for a moment, then continued. "Similarly, Daniels, we've been following you ever since, which hasn't been easy. We wanted a look at your 'Leslie' before anyone else got too close a look."

"And equally you wanted me to think my 'Leslie' was an impostor," said Thomas.

"We didn't want you spreading the word that the real Leslie was alive," countered Whiteside tersely.

"I was thinking of attending the interment," Leslie backtracked sourly. "I was curious who'd care enough to come. But Mr. Lassiter insisted. I left the country the night the murder was discovered. I went back to Montreal. As far as everyone was concerned," she said, "I was dead." She reflected happily, "It was marvelous. For once no one was looking for me. If you're already dead, no one bothers you."

"Usually. Not always," said Thomas, arms folded, looking her in the eye. He could hear the chipping downstairs. The dead would rise in more ways than one before the next sunset. He was *certain*.

"Perceptive, Thomas," she answered. "You're catching on."

"It's about time, don't you think?"

Intense hammering and chipping rose from below.

Leslie concluded. "Months passed. Mr. Lassiter told me to live as quietly and normally as I could. What they were waiting for was a natural and infallible way to smoke out Arthur Sandler. They were waiting for—"

"Victoria to die," said Thomas triumphantly.

"May I continue?"

A portrait of Victoria from forty years earlier gazed down from the wall, a tart sneer of disapproval on her lips, the usual vacuity through the eyes.

"Continue," said Whiteside, trying to calm Leslie.

"They were waiting for Victoria to die," said Leslie. "They had a pretty good idea where these counterfeits were coming from, who was making the flawless engravings, and who had concocted a formula to provide the perfect paper. Sandler." She paused. "So when Victoria died, they asked me to come forward, to put in a claim against the will. That would force the Sandler estate, including this building, to be closed by the State of

New York. And, they hoped, it would force Sandler to come forward."

"In one form or another," said Whiteside.

"Correct," she said. "I was to lure the fox from the thicket. That was one role. The other was to get as close to Thomas Daniels as possible." She looked at him. "I was to discover how much collusion there'd been between him and his late father."

"And?" asked Whiteside, raising his thin white eyebrows, hoping for a revelation.

"I haven't uncovered any. Yet."

Whiteside appeared modestly disappointed. So did Hunter.

The chipping downstairs intensified. Thomas was so engaged in what he was hearing that he nearly leaned forward out of his seat to push the conversation onward. "That brings her to the present, doesn't it?" he asked.

Hammond nodded. So did Leslie. Thomas turned quickly to address Whiteside. "And it kicks the ball into your zone, doesn't it, Whiteside?"

Again the raised eyebrows, accompanied by a nod.

"You're going to have to cough up that one bit of the story that you've withheld so far, aren't you?" pressed Thomas, trying valiantly not to gloat. "You've got the one missing piece and you're going to have to put it in place for us now. Aren't you?"

"It won't be so painful," allowed Whiteside. "Not if you keep your subsequent part of the bargain. I'll tell you anything you want if you provide the man we're looking for." Whiteside wore the expression of a tournament bridge player about to reveal a championship hand, the cards he'd waited years to throw onto a table.

"I'll provide him," said Thomas.

Whiteside eyed Hunter with amusement and looked at least once into each of the other three pairs of eyes at the table. The noisy excavation continued below them.

"In that case," said Whiteside, the elegant man with a patch of soot on his cheek, "please listen carefully." He smiled. "You'll like this. The story wears well."

Chapter 35

Whiteside cleared his throat. "I've been in double-double games before, even a triple-triple ruse along the line." He shook his head and exchanged a cognizant grin with Hunter. "This one beats them all, however."

He glanced around, seeing that he was center stage. He continued, addressing Hammond, the emissary of U.S. Intelligence, as much as anyone. "Well, sir," he said, "I'll supply you with your bloody missing piece, all right. Your Sandler."

"Our *what?*"

Thomas inclined forward again, instantly baffled. *He* was going to point the finger to Sandler. Not Whiteside.

Patiently, Whiteside repeated, the silence at the table now given an extra dimension of stillness. "Well," Whiteside huffed with studied casualness, "the man's been dead for thirty-one years. What I could never understand is how your Central Intelligence Service, sorry, *Agency*, never managed to learn that for themselves."

The bastards probably did, thought Hammond, and never told anyone.

Hunter sat back in his chair, his hands folded, one thick finger interlocking with another, glancing toward his own chest as if to indicate he'd known it all along also. Hunter *did* look like a bear, Thomas noticed. Whiteside's smugness enraged Thomas.

Whiteside raised his eyebrows slightly, saw the stunned expressions around him, scratched his left cheek elegantly, and mused onward. "Yes," he said reflectively, "I suppose I do owe the present company an explanation. Correct?

"I assure you," he began, "it wouldn't change the current situation the smallest bit."

He turned the calendar back to 1947, a year in which the British Exchecquer was still bedeviled by German pound-sterling notes, printed in Austria during the war. An investigation was in progress, yet doomed to failure. *Someone* was still printing pound notes. No one knew who. Or where.

"It was April of that year, forty-seven, I recall," said Whiteside, "when we were still fairly active in Central Europe. We, meaning M.I.6, of course. We were recruiting Russians. The Iron Curtain had fallen and we wanted people who were behind it. We wanted Russians. But we took what we could get."

What they got, what they managed to recruit, was just about anyone who could exchange a useful tidbit of intelligence for a one-way ticket to the West. "Poles, Hungarians, Czechs," continued Whiteside nostalgically, "we could have set up our own League of Nations in exile, we recruited so many."

"Why didn't you?" asked Daniels sarcastically.

"Afraid your Congress wouldn't want to join," Whiteside shot back. "Touché. May I go on?"

Daniels motioned an open hand to indicate Whiteside could.

"In forty-seven we recruited a Hungarian, man named Walter Szezic. He was a young man then, midtwenties, and had been in the non-Communist resistance in Austria and Hungary during the war. Fine fellow, really."

"They all are," Thomas intoned.

Whiteside ignored the remark and dwelt on Szezic. "Szezic stayed in Hungary for three years, until being uncovered in 1950 and being smuggled out in one battered piece. But when recruited he had told several stories, all of which were later confirmed . . . except one.

"There was no way of confirming that lone story. But since it wasn't important to Szezic that he deceive us on that point, and since all the more important information we received from him was true, we took this as the Lord's truth, also."

The story concerned a spy, a man the Russians had planned to slip into the West since before the war. A man not identified by name, but rather by the identity he took.

"The spy was run by Moscow," said Whiteside. "Years in the making; straight out of the KGB building on Dzerzhinsky Square. But he would have a control in New York, too. He'd be run in the United States and had been trained to assume the identity of a wealthy German-American industrialist."

No one said it, but one name bolted into the listeners' minds.

"Sandler," said Whiteside, though it wasn't necessary. "The spy had memorized every facet of Sandler's life; he'd been given the man's voice, the man's face, practically the man's mind, in that he'd memorized the faces and relationships of everyone Sandler had known before the war. An extraordinary undertaking by our friends the Reds," said Whiteside, not without deep admiration.

Thomas fidgeted nervously, beginning to sense the inevitable implications and consequences of Whiteside's story. Leslie glanced back and forth between Whiteside and Thomas. Hammond spoke.

"Why should we believe *any* of this?" he asked.

"Perhaps you shouldn't. But proof *is* available." Whiteside held up a hand. "Not with me now, unfortunately. No. But I could provide it, if necessary."

Thomas's mind was leaping ahead, to the identity of the spy, to the controlling agent in New York. The pieces were fitting together, gliding uncontrollably like the needle of a ouija board. "Just *tell* us what the proof is," Thomas interrupted.

Whiteside told. Szezic, after his hasty departure from Hungary in 1950, led M.I.6 agents to the confirmation of his story.

The German-American industrialist, Sandler, had been instructed eastward after the war by his control, the "patriotic American." There he was met by Russians and shot summarily. The double took his place.

"Sandler's body was buried in Austria," said Whiteside wryly, "in a manner fitting a man who'd led a double life. The local Reds built a special coffin for him, one with a false bottom. He was sealed within. Then when a local peasant died, the local was given the upper deck. They both went into the ground together. Clever, don't you think? Same principle as the London buses. Who'd think of looking for a missing body in a grave already occupied by another man?"

"Jesus," mumbled Thomas to himself, almost disbelieving the fiendish ingenuity involved.

"Anyway," said Whiteside. "When Austria joined the West in 1955 we went to the cemetery. In the dead of night we brought up the coffin, abducted the half of the population whom we desired, and returned the other occupant to his eternal slumber. We took the body back to London. We obtained Sandler's dental chart from his New York dentist—a man who still practices, if you care to confirm it with him. Or have a tooth fixed. No doubt, it was Sandler. You can even examine the body now, if you wish to come to London."

"Where?" someone asked.

"A churchyard in Earl's Court," grinned Whiteside. He turned to Thomas. "You've been there. The girl thought to be his daughter is buried right next to him. Wrong name on his tombstone, of course. Couldn't have a real name. But we did think it would be fitting to keep all the important bones in the same general area. Don't you agree?"

"The parish minister puts up with a lot," grumbled Thomas, remembering the man in the presbytery who'd watched them so intently.

"The parish minister," gloated Whiteside, "is Szezic." He noted Thomas's surprise and drove home the point. "We wouldn't put celebrities in just *any* churchyard, you know."

Whiteside grew deathly serious again. "But I'm off from the most important point," he said. "Szezic told us *why* the agent was inserted into Sandler's identity. The Russians, he said, had liked the German counterfeiting plans so much that they decided to launch their own scheme with *their* own master engraver. Undermine the currency of the West. Call into question the West's financial foundations, and you've gone a long way toward shaking the earth out from under our side. Don't you all agree?"

No one *dis*agreed.

"And at worst," he added, "they'd have a way to finance their postwar intelligence operations in the West."

The first attack came on the pound, said Whiteside. "We had a pretty fair idea who was doing it. We asked for U.S. cooperation against Sandler, but couldn't get it," he intoned angrily. He looked at Hammond. "Correct or incorrect, Mr. Hammond? Your Treasury Department was never interested in helping."

"Right, right," twanged Hammond tiredly. "Just go on."

"So it continued for years," said Whiteside, turning from Hammond and seeking an audience in Leslie and Daniels. "Until we *had* to take matters into our own hands. Trouble was," he added with an exasperated breath, "the man in New York running the Russian spy during the war was *still* active. Frightful! He managed to warn the man in Sandler's identity. They put a second double in Sandler's place. And that's the man who was taken down."

"Killed, you mean," corrected Thomas.

"He wasn't living when we were finished shooting him, if that sounds better," said Whiteside crankily. He turned to Leslie. "But there remained a further problem. When Sandler had been recruited in New

York, no one had planned on the human side of the man. No one ever imagined that Arthur Sandler would fall in love with a barmaid in Exeter, marry her, and have a child." His longest and most thoughtful pause followed. "After his 'assassination' the Sandler estate started receiving letters from Elizabeth Chatsworth. The escaped spy knew that she was a breach in the carefully secured plans; she could have called into open question the postwar Sandler identity. So he set out to Europe to kill her. He succeeded, but was witnessed by not *his* daughter, but the daughter of the man he was impersonating. Now the daughter became a witness. Years passed. And he kept trying to eradicate her, too."

"But why did he wait?" asked a flustered Hammond. "Why did he wait almost eight years to strike at the woman?"

"Silly," snorted Whiteside. "Sandler's wartime romance was a secret. It was the one facet of the man's life the Russians didn't know about." He cleared his throat slightly, then glared directly at Thomas Daniels. "And," he added, "I think by now everyone in this room knows the *source* of their elaborate background file on Sandler."

Thomas Daniels felt everyone's eyes turn in his direction.

"It was a grand, grand game for the Reds," Whiteside continued. "Masterful. They swapped their best engraver for our best engraver, inserted their man inside of one of ours. But they'd had the *time*, that was the crucial part. As early as 1941 they'd known whom they were going to replace. The only way to know that was to know who'd been recruited. And the only way to know who'd been recruited was to have the recruiter in their own control." Whiteside sighed. *"Their own recruiting sergeant. Masquerading as an American recruiting sergeant."*

Thomas felt Whiteside's glare sizzling upon him. He averted his eyes and an image flashed before him of his father, flag pin on his lapel, campaigning for Eisenhower, Goldwater, and Nixon, and vociferously calling for the bombing of Hanoi. What crap, Thomas caught himself thinking.

"I suppose," said Whiteside with sudden gentleness, "that we needn't dwell on the point."

Whiteside pursed his lips slightly as the truth hung in the air. He seemed thoughtful, while Hunter sized up the audience. Hammond's face was a disgusted, why-wasn't-I-ever-told-before scowl. Leslie was transfixed, wanting to believe that the man who'd sought to kill her for so long was not her actual father. Thomas Daniels seemed off on another thought altogether, thinking more of the control, the man "running" the Sandler impostor, in New York. William Ward Daniels; lawyer, superpatriot, Soviet spy!

Then Whiteside was glancing around, his eyes making contact. "Well, gentlemen? Quite a story, isn't it? And true." He laughed, a short popping snort. "No reason to lie at this point, is there?"

Hammond appeared pensive, not wanting to trust immediately. "The Department will want to see your 'confirmation material,' " he suggested weakly.

"Of course," agreed Whiteside.

"So much for Sandler," Hammond professed lamely.

"But not so much for the man who tried to kill me twice," Leslie shot quickly and bitterly. *"He's* somewhere."

Hammond scoffed. "But after twenty years?" He shrugged. "Could be in Manchuria by now."

"I don't think so," said Thomas Daniels, distinctly and coldly.

"Nor I," said Leslie.

Whiteside's eyebrows were inquisitively upraised again. "Oh?" he asked, as if he were ignorant of the subject.

"Not with all this counterfeit circulating," Leslie reminded Hammond.

"Certainly not," Hammond was quick to agree.

"In any case," Whiteside said in summation, "I think we now understand whom we're all looking for. Not Arthur Sandler. But a spy who inhabited Arthur Sandler's identity for nine years."

Thomas was about to pursue the point. But the chipping of concrete was less in the basement now. One of the agents from below trudged up the cellar stairs and appeared, dusty and fatigued, but concentrating on his task.

"We found a wooden box," the man said. "About nine feet by three feet."

The four men and one woman at the table looked at the man with mixed anxiety and expectancy.

"It'll take another hour to chip it free," he said. "Then we can open it." He glanced from one face to the next, then added sardonically, "I suspect everyone'll want to be present for the unveiling." A beam of sunlight eased through a torn curtain. It was ten A.M.

"Children of the cold war," thought Thomas. "That's what we are. She and I." He was still at the table, looking across at her. "How insolent we've always been to think we controlled our own lives."

He considered the events which had brought them to that table, listening to the sinister chipping below. Not simply the events which had touched them directly, but the larger scheme of things. The Iron Curtain and the purge trials. Korea and McCarthyism. Hungary. Rudolph Abel.

Cuba. U-2 Flights. The Berlin Wall. Vietnam. Czechoslovakia. He could see the Fifties and Sixties flashing before him like a nova. He and Leslie McAdam, the offspring of spies, were brought together not by anything they'd done themselves, but rather by the flow of history, by the -isms of the Twentieth Century, by the galloping paranoia of the postwar years. By the insanities and inanities which afflict governments.

The conference at the table broke. Nervously, sensing the advent of a major development, the five perused the interior of the Sandler mansion, wandering from bookcase to china case, inspecting filth-encrusted sinks and admiring 1890s clocks. Thomas was alone on the fourth floor, examining the walls and hallway panels, wondering what unexpected hollowness might be discovered. When he heard footsteps on the floor above him, heavy footsteps at that, he climbed the stairs and encountered a familiar face and shape.

Hunter stood in the vast hallway and front corridor of the fifth floor. He'd looked all around him, found nothing of overwhelming interest on the other floors, and was now looking upward, toward a long wooden set of stairs which ran to a closed door leading presumably to an attic.

"Top to bottom," he mumbled, to no one first, then to Thomas, who was standing nearby. "That's how we're to search this place. Top to bottom." His conclusion, unsaid, was clear. He'd start at the top and work his way to the bottom. Logic, always. He looked to Thomas. "Coming with me?"

"Is that a return invitation for inviting you here in the first place?" Thomas asked.

"Just being friendly," growled Hunter. "We were just looking after you, you know."

The night at Suzanne's, the chemically induced unconsciousness, and the feel of strong arms on his body, came back to him. "Of course," he said.

"So you got jostled a little. You're alive."

"You can go on to the attic without me," he answered. "I'm going downstairs."

"Have it your way."

Hunter put his foot on the first step as if to test it, then gradually shifted his entire weight onto the step. Then the next. Then the next. He eased his way up the long slatted stairs to the attic, a step at a time, but less cautious with each step.

Thomas watched him halfway, then turned. He'd return to Leslie and Hammond, whom he seemed to trust just that much more, to see where their own progress was leading them.

The first sound he could hear was a slow cracking noise, somewhat like the tearing of wood when a tree is about to fall. But the sound grew in intensity to a quickening clattering burst and Thomas spun around to see the stairs with Hunter collapsing.

They flew apart as a deck of cards might, the underpinnings flying loose and relinquishing their support at the precise moment when Hunter had primed the trap on the tenth step.

The weight of the bulky man intensified his sudden plunge. He collapsed as fast as the staircase, thundering into a pile of falling dust, beams, and steps, as the remainder of the staircase—the sturdy wooden steps he'd never reached—collapsed and crashed down upon him. Part of the attic floor followed.

To Thomas, standing in safety thirty feet away, the moment seemed frozen in time, taking many seconds more to occur than it actually had. Seconds afterward, having seen the burly, bear-shaped Hunter collapsing with the real estate, Thomas had the sensation of having watched it in slow motion.

The collapse had taken only three seconds, yet Hunter too had a similar sensation of slow motion, of seconds which seemed like minutes, though at the first sound of the cracking wood he'd known. The stairs had been a trap, set for any outsider who ventured toward the attic.

The pain was another matter. The pain was instant, recognizable immediately. Hunter lay beneath the crashing steps and beams and felt the unspeakable torment in his two legs, parts of which were crushed beneath him, pinned into impossible positions as the legs of a discarded doll might be. But unlike a doll's legs, Hunter's consisted of breakable bones, flesh, blood, and nerves.

He howled in pain, bellowing like an animal caught in an iron-claw trap. The bellowing didn't stop. It was a torrent of profanities, obscenities, and *help me!*'s even though Thomas sprang immediately to Hunter's aid and began digging him out from under the last steps to fall.

Leslie arrived next, followed quickly by Whiteside and Hammond. They'd heard the crash. They'd heard the yelling. The beams of their lamps illuminated the room with strangely cast shadows and streaks. Thomas shouted, "The steps collapsed!" but it was apparent to anyone with two eyes.

"We'll have to get him out of here," said Hammond, giving word to the obvious. Hunter's face was white, excluding the beard, of course, and the streaks of blood from forehead cuts and gashes.

Thomas helped separate him from the wooden planks which had enshrouded him. Thomas could see the pain and pleading on the man's face, the anguish, and the very human blood that was pouring from his veins. And the two bloodied, horribly contorted legs which might never function properly again for the rugged Hunter.

Thomas winced. For the first time he looked upon Hunter not as a brute, not as an adversary, but as another human being, a man with feelings, blood, and beliefs. Hunter had believed strongly enough in an ideology to work for it as a career; just as Hammond did, just as the real Arthur Sandler had and just as other men—including his own father in a differing manner—had. And this, crushed legs in a crumbling house for a cause that would probably never be considered important, is where it had brought Hunter. Thomas looked at the fallen steps and wondered what he believed in, himself.

Could have been me on them, he thought. Could have been me.

His thoughts were interrupted.

Hunter had been extricated and was wallowing in pain a few feet from where he'd fallen. Hammond and Whiteside were fashioning a makeshift stretcher from sheets and a pair of strong boards. Hammond would arrange to get him out to an unmarked ambulance.

But something was still falling. Leslie noticed, too.

"What's that?" she said.

There was paper drifting down like leaves in the wind. Peacefully and calmly, a draft in the attic was rustling a few papers from the great stacks which were upstairs.

Small papers. The size of dollar bills.

The same shape and texture of dollar bills. Some printed, some unprinted.

All attention, even Hunter's, drifted to the spectacle. Money was floating earthward; not from Heaven, but very definitely from above. From the impromptu atelier in the attic.

Money, drifting through the ripped-away floorboards.

Dollar bills. Dollar bills with only one side printed, the other side magically bleached away. Blank sheets, having once been dollar bills but now with both faces bleached.

And others, finished products, so to speak. Fifties. Hundreds. Crisp, clear, and perfect, the production of masters. Or at least *one* master. A small unspendable fortune drifting down on them, yet only the bottom tip of the large green iceberg.

Hammond stood there awestruck, seeing the same bills that had been presented to him in the Treasury Department. He was onto the source, or at least very near to it, and his heart pounded in his chest. He watched the money drifting down, like snowflakes now, a piece at a time.

"Yes," said Whiteside, kneeling by Hunter to comfort him, but angrily addressing the speechless Hammond. "Not so amusing now, is it? Not when they're your bloody dollars instead of sterling." He paused and bitterly snapped, "Help this man, confound it," he demanded. "Can't you see he's in agony?"

Chapter 36

The opening of the oak box was delayed by hours. The excavators, working with the caution of archeologists, chipped up the floor as carefully as possible, unwilling to destroy anything of potential significance.

Meanwhile, Hunter's tormented body had to be removed. It was carried out through the pantry wall by Thomas, Whiteside, and Hammond. Whiteside telephoned a British doctor in Manhattan, one always on standby to treat emergencies of local agents in the field, emergencies which wouldn't be met with snooping questions.

An ambulance was brought to the corner of Eighty-eighth Street and Park Avenue where, after a painfully circuitous route through dark underground sewer corridors, Hammond guided the injured man up to the street through a manhole.

The massive body of Hunter, now useless, like a big crippled bear who'd been wounded by riflemen, was eased into the back of the ambulance. He had one arm across his face, in the effort of trying not to yield to the torment of his shattered bones. He writhed slightly, moaned though he tried not to, and bordered on a merciful unconsciousness which Thomas, watching him, wished would descend.

Whiteside looked to Hammond and Thomas, then glanced back toward the house.

"I should go with him," Whiteside said. He also knew he should stay, finish the Sandler inquiry as best he could.

"I'll keep you informed," said Thomas. "You can trust me."

"I'd like to come back," he said.

Hammond grimaced slightly.

"We won't be there in another two hours," said Thomas. "I'll contact you."

Whiteside looked at the groaning Hunter. He glanced back to Thomas and offered his hand. "All right," he conceded. "I don't know how much use an old man is in this, anyway."

"I'll never take an old man for granted again," said Thomas. He offered his hand. Whiteside accepted. He then hopped into the back of the ambulance. Thomas's last vision of him was as he was placing his arm on Hunter's shoulder, as if to comfort his fallen associate.

"He's almost sentimental, know that?" said Hammond with distrust as the ambulance pulled away. "There's something about him . . ." He caught himself and changed the thought. "Good thinking, anyway," he said.

"About what?"

"Telling him we'll be gone in two hours," said Hammond.

"I suspect," said Thomas, "that we will be. You'll see when we dig the nails out of that box."

Still, the securing of the buried box was an arduous procedure. A false top had been installed across it, solid beams which pinned it beneath the floor.

The clock dragged. The hours were unyielding.

Hammond remained in the underground mausoleum, watching his workmen slash and chip with their hammers, wedges, and chisels. Thomas and Leslie waited upstairs now, talking in the semidarkness. They held flashlights, carefully pointed away from the windows.

On the top floor the counterfeit had been inspected by Hammond. Yet now it lay ignored, an item of secondary importance.

Thomas and Leslie were in a ground-floor sitting room when they heard Hammond's footsteps on the stairs, walking up from the basement.

"Come on down," Hammond said, though urging was hardly necessary. "I wouldn't want to miss this if I were you."

When they returned through the basement, down the creaking stairs, among the dust-laden furniture and down into the altar room for the Andys, Thomas sensed a strange disquiet in his soul. The sense that something vile or revelatory was on the brink. He'd never opened a buried box before.

Yet he had an instinct. He sensed what to expect.

When they walked into the room, there were great chunks of concrete stacked beside the altar. Great huge blocks which the two excavators had chipped away. Thomas looked at it.

"Don't worry," said Hammond. "We recognize the principle of private property. When this is all over, we'll seal up everything like new." He paused and a sly grin crept across the lines of his face. "Unless we find something we need to keep, of course."

The huge oak box, discolored with age, was broken free from the concrete. From somewhere one of the excavators produced a slim iron bar with a prying device on one end. Using the hammer, hitting the end of the bar for leverage, he broke the wood and pulled the nails from the top of the box.

"Put the lights on it," said Hammond. Leslie and Thomas shone their lamps downward, onto the wooden top of the box. The two excavators reached to different ends of the lid and forced it up. A nauseating, foul stench wafted upward.

At first there was a creak. Then a crack, and the men seemed to fumble for a second, off balance when the lid came free.

They lifted.

Up it came, and they slid it away onto the concrete to the left of them. The lanterns, and every eye in the room, were directed downward into the contents.

Two dead empty eyes, undisturbed for years, stared upward absently.

The five living souls present gazed into the vacant expression of a skeleton, of one whose life had departed years earlier. Fully clad in a man's suit, the suit which he'd worn when death had come to him.

Thomas felt like throwing up. Hammond looked equally sickened. The men with the hammers and chisels looked upon the discovery with horror. Leslie, perhaps steadiest of all, studied the skeleton as if to discern its identity. Then she, too, averted her eyes, looking toward the sealed canine tombs.

But the man in the box would not go away. He would have to be dealt with. No one spoke immediately.

Thomas squelched the nauseated feeling in his stomach. He was transfixed by the sight before him; it was so unreal and so unlike anything he'd ever encountered that, like a crowd jockeying for position around a bloody traffic accident, a morbid streak of curiosity within him was riveted to the coffin. The hollow eyes of the skull transfixed him. The assemblage of teeth, perfectly preserved, seemed to form a ghastly smile.

But the real touch of surrealism was the disintegrating suit on the decaying body, the suit which the owner had worn to his own execution.

Perhaps Thomas sensed an affinity for the man who wore three-piece suits to work. He looked at it carefully, as if he'd seen it before.

Something made him lean down, even though repelled by the odor. Something instinctively drew him to the corpse.

Hammond watched Daniels's reaction, as if perceiving something. "What is it?" Hammond asked.

Thomas said nothing. He reached into the box, gingerly touching the stained shirt at the collar, carefully avoiding touching the neckbone.

Thomas pulled. Gently, as if in respect for the dead. The skull rolled slightly, as if to change its view. The teeth remained frozen in a grin.

"The identity," said Thomas in a voice shaky and not far above a whisper. "The second identity that your missing spy *slipped into.*"

Leslie stared distastefully at the skeleton, a sickened feeling growing in her stomach. Hammond did not yet understand. Not completely.

"The spy inhabited the identity of another man, Arthur Sandler, in the first nine years after the war," said Thomas. "Then that didn't work anymore. A new man was put into Sandler's identity. That man was killed, freeing the spy. But the spy needed somewhere else to go. A little research, a lot of plastic surgery, an ocean of nerve, and he slipped into another man's life. Who'd look inside another man for a missing spy?" Thomas paused. "How fast can you get a small airplane?" he asked.

"Within an hour or two," answered Hammond. "From LaGuardia. Why?" Hammond was frowning, massive bags forming beneath his eyes.

"We'll need it right away. Your spy is planning his escape. He may already be gone."

"I don't follow."

"Don't you?" asked Thomas, standing. "It was all over the front pages of the newspapers this week."

"Oh, my God!" Leslie suddenly gasped. "The fishing fleets!"

Thomas managed a half smile and a nod. "Exactly." He turned back to Hammond. "Shine the light in there," he said, motioning to the oak box and its crumbling inhabitant. "It reads like an engraved invitation."

Hammond leaned over. Leslie, transfixed by the sight as much as she was disgusted by it, peered over Hammond's shoulder. They both crouched for a closer view.

At the collar of the suit was a store label, Dunhill Tailors of New York, dated 1954. It had been a new suit. The man who'd worn the suit had been of the opinion that top-quality clothing would last forever and survive even longer than the wearer. Time had proved him correct.

Beneath the tailor's trademark was another label, the client's name. The letters were faded and stained by blood two decades old. But they were legible.

Hammond and Leslie read at once.

The letters read simply A. ZENGER.

PART EIGHT

"A different man," said Thomas. "As complex and simple as that." There was no smile on his face, not even a hint of one. Only tension and fatigue. It was five A.M.

They stood, the three of them, on the edge of a small windswept landing field at the Marine Air Terminal, a small subport of New York's LaGuardia Airport. Leslie shivered slightly and pulled her coat tighter. Hammond dropped a half-smoked cigarette, muttered something about having to quit sometime soon, and extinguished the butt with a toe. They watched a small plane belonging to the United States Treasury Department, taxiing slowly toward their end of the runway. It had been fueled; a pilot had been hauled out of bed. The craft was ready.

Hammond motioned with his head toward the small plane, the door to which had opened. "We're ready," he said.

They walked toward the airplane. Leslie boarded first. Hammond and Daniels stood before the steps to the plane. Hammond reached into his coat and pulled from it a small thirty-eight-caliber pistol. "Know how to use one of these?" he asked.

"Unfortunately, yes."

"Take it."

"Will I need it?"

"I doubt it."

"Then I don't want it."

Hammond slid it into Thomas's coat pocket. "Keep it as a good-luck charm. I'll catch hell in Washington if you go along and I don't equip you with something."

"What about you? It's *your* profession."

"I'm protected," Hammond said simply. He was. He wore an identical small handgun on his belt. And within the plane, should it be needed, a specially equipped long-range rifle, disassembled and in its case.

Minutes later, the plane was airborne.

Gradually, his entire life made sense. Thomas understood the man his father had wanted him to become.

As the coastline of the northeast unraveled with infrequent yellow lights below the window of the airplane, Thomas was lost in thought. He had the disquieting sense of having never known his father at all. It was as if he'd spent his life standing too close to a mural, never having stepped back to gain the proper perspective. The image of the saint in the iron coffin, the one in the church at North Fenwick in Devonshire, appeared before him. The iron image of the man on the outside, the shell presented for the world to see. But within? The soul of an entirely different inner man. And what eyes could see that, obscured as it was by a lead mask and illusory image?

Illusion, never reality, he thought. Distance, never scrutiny. An interior of betrayal and treason, disguised by an iron mask of patriotism.

Thomas understood that his father had never done anything without a reason, other than perhaps being born and dying. (Thomas examined those events, too; everything was subject to question now.) Equally he understood what sort of a man his father had tried to create in his only son. Tried and failed.

The private schools, the mingling with the very rich, the exposure to the criminal dregs of capitalistic American society, the blood sports, the guise of an extreme right-wing father, the easing into the legal profession, the engendered reaction to white-collar criminals, and the inheriting of a law office with no further criminal clients to represent. It was as if every image of greed, every exposure to oppulence, every suggestion of inequality and unlawfulness, had all been carefully geared to create a reaction in Thomas Daniels. A reaction leftward. Sympathy (overt? covert? Thomas could choose) to the destruction of the American system. Sympathy to the beliefs of the father, whether or not those true beliefs were ever known to the son.

Thomas saw the sky brightening in the east. The sky had an illuminated glow, though not yet light, the grayish-blue brightness before dawn.

He looked around the airplane. The pilot was steady at the controls, smoking a cigarette and appearing in charge. Every once in a while the airplane would buffet slightly.

Hammond was wide awake, on edge, an exhausted man with worn nerves and a winding-down body. Too tired to sleep, too sleepy to converse. He was probably thinking of his wife, of his retirement, of the so-called sunset years that would follow. Would he approach them with enthusiasm or fear? Thomas wondered. He studied Hammond in the darkness. He was a tired man, the sort of man who makes mistakes—unthinking and expensive mistakes.

Could Hammond pull a trigger if he had to? Could he pull one fast enough? Or did he carry a weapon simply to inflate his fading courage?

Thomas's eyes moved a quarter inch. He saw Leslie.

She was reclining in her seat, as motionless as the death that had long been intended for her. Leslie McAdam, he thought, turning over the sound of her name in his mind. Trapped in a world of terror and duplicity, locked into an identity which was hers but wasn't hers. Gifted with the paternal talents of the artist, damned to the vengeance of the bogus father. Unwilling to use her real name of Sandler, unable to advertise the name of McAdam. A life on the run, jumping from shadows, until protection could be purchased from a bunch of sleazy white-collar headhunters in Washington. Sell us your soul, they'd told her. Help us kill. We'll give you your own life in return. Thomas weighed the exchange. He probably would have made the same decision himself. What are ethics when your life is at stake? Crucify your ethics on a cross of expediency. Why not?

He thought of his father, the man living a lifetime of illusion and deception. In retrospect, it seemed so clear. So obvious. Why had no one ever seen it?

A committed Marxist, probably from boyhood. Growing up on the Lower East side of Manhattan, racism and ethnicism and class inequity all around him. The sweatshops. The Depression. Educating himself in the Public Library as a teenager. Scrounging admittance to City College, where the brilliant radical thinking would hone his scalpel of a mind. Somewhere there he'd been recruited. Somewhere then he'd turned into a spy. Was it a Calling he had sought for himself or was he, like a priest, Chosen?

It must have happened early, thought Thomas. Sometime in his father's nineteenth year. As a freshman. Thereafter the guise started. The guise of the self-made right-wing zealot, the criminal lawyer seeking to bilk the legal structure for all it was worth, at the same time undermining it; sending despicable wealthy capitalists off to combat Nazism in Germany, then cashing them in, arranging for their slaughter, and introducing a master spy as a replacement. The master spy who inhabited the identity of Arthur Sandler, then leaped, like a possessing demon, into the identity of Adolph Zenger.

"The ruthless bastard," Thomas caught himself thinking, conjuring up the image of his father, tousle-haired, center stage in the courtroom, cunning, arrogant, shrewd, brilliant as ever. An image that lived in Thomas's mind, an image of the father whose blood flowed in Thomas's veins. Yet could Thomas indict him for his principles, for believing so fervently in a system other than what Thomas believed in? The real failure of the father, Thomas realized, was within a force that no man could control.

The force of nature and human character. The father was an extremist, the son a man of moderation. No lifelong ruses, no connivances, no deceptions or calculations could in the end swerve Thomas Daniels. He was a man of the sane center, or at least liked to think he was. So now he was in an airplane with dawn breaking over Rhode Island, on his way to undo—or end—what his father had spent a lifetime helping to construct.

The pilot threw a switch in the cabin. Soft lights flickered on above the heads of Hammond, Leslie, and Thomas.

The pilot spoke to them. "Better be waking up," he said; "we'll be setting down in another twenty minutes."

Leslie came quickly to consciousness. Hammond had always been awake and jittery. Daniels yawned. Good advice from the pilot, he reasoned. An airplane should always have as many safe landings as takeoffs.

They touched down a few minutes before dawn on the southern coast of Nantucket Island. By prearrangement an empty, unmarked Massachusetts State Police car had been left for them at the airfield. The keys were in the backseat ashtray.

Hammond tossed the rifle and its carrying case into the rear seat. Leslie joined it. Thomas, after a moment's hesitation, sat in the front with Hammond.

"Know the way, huh?" asked Hammond. "Let's hear it."

Thomas began to direct them. Halfway through the ride, he became again aware of the loaded pistol, safety catch in place, which Hammond had given him.

Two images flashed before him.

He thought of Leslie whirling, pistol in hand, in the basement of the Sandler mansion, a finger squeeze away from killing an innocent man by accident. And then that image was replaced by a separate vision, one resurrected from longer ago. In a forest in Pennsylvania, Thomas stood, rifle in hand, watching a struggling deer coughing blood and trying to flee though a shoulder had been shattered by Thomas's bullet. He remembered the terror in the animal's eyes, the blood it had coughed, and his father's hand on the rifle, prohibiting Thomas from firing a merciful second bullet. "Let the blood flow," Daniels, Senior, had said. "That's the way of nature." His father had owned a deer rifle with an American flag carved on its stock.

Leslie leaned forward to Thomas and spoke. "I was meaning to ask you . . ." she said. "How did you have the nerve to bring Whiteside face to face with me."

"There was no nerve at all," he admitted.

She was perplexed. "But he was insisting I was an impostor. Suppose he continued to claim—"

He was already shaking his head. "I went on the assumption that he and Hunter were who they said they were," Thomas explained. "And by that time I knew you probably were, too."

"How?"

"You appeared for all the world to be an elaborate hoax," he said. "There's no way I couldn't have drawn that conclusion."

"And so?"

He motioned to Hammond, bleary-eyed and steering the car. "Then you didn't have me shot, despite the fact that you'd already shot someone that same day."

"What did that prove?"

"Maybe nothing. But I figured an impostor would have had me killed. I knew too much."

She leaned back in her seat, thinking. "Clever," she said.

"Call it a lucky guess," he conceded. "I was still pretty nervous."

Dawn was breaking. "We're almost there," he said to Hammond.

Chapter 38

The borrowed State Police car pulled to a halt before the old house inhabited by the man known as Zenger. Between Hammond, Leslie, and Thomas they continued to refer to him as Zenger. They had no other handle for him.

The radio in the car, in the ten-minute drive from the airport, had been turned to a Cape Cod station. The lead story continued to be the heavy accumulation of Soviet and Polish fishing trawlers in Cape Cod waters, just beyond the territorial limits a hundred miles south of Nantucket. The fishing vessels, equipped with elaborate antennae and radar devices not usually necessary for fishing, had drawn attention not just from the local radio and fishermen. Virtually every spare Coast Guard boat was monitoring their movements. Their presence was *that* unusual. It had to signify something.

As the State Police car pulled to a halt, the three of them stepped out briskly. Their breaths were in small clouds before them on the cold, windy morning.

"Curtains are down," said Hammond, his eyes set back from the bags beneath them and the lines which surrounded them. "He's expecting us."

"A lot of people sleep with the shades down," Leslie suggested.

"Yes," said Hammond in thought, as if reminded of the obvious and embarrassed that he'd slipped and missed it. "Of course."

Hammond looked at the rifle case on the backseat of the car and seemed to make a decision. "We're close in," he said. "No need for this." He closed the car door on the left rear side and left the long black case on the seat. "Doubt that we'll hear a shot fired in anger," he said, forcing a smile. Thomas could see. Hammond, the fading professional, was seeking to reassure himself. "Promise me this," he said, "don't tell anyone how this ended. You know, arresting a wasted old man in his pajamas, pulling him out of bed at this hour of the morning."

"It *hasn't* ended yet," Leslie reminded him.

Damned amateurs, thought Hammond. Always rooting for excitement. "Soon," he offered. "Why don't you two cover the back. I'll knock on the front door."

It seemed logical, a routine procedure to make what was now a routine arrest. Thomas and Leslie walked quietly around the side of the house, noting that each shade was drawn. They then stood to the side of the back door, their backs to the ocean and the waves. Thomas glanced upward. The sky was undecided: It didn't yet know whether to be blue or gray that day.

A minute passed. Then another. Thomas felt like squirming within his clothes. He exchanged a glance with Leslie as if to ask, Hey? What's keeping Hammond? Has he knocked yet?

Thomas felt his hands wet within his gloves. He was conscious of the pistol in his coat pocket and he begged the fates that he'd not have to draw it, much less pull a trigger against a human being.

Both of them fixed their sights on the doorknob, waiting for the slightest movement of it to indicate a hand on the opposite side.

The force of the explosion was so intense that it rocked both Thomas and Leslie off their feet and onto the ground. Glass shattered somewhere in their presence and they could feel the shards and splinters flying to the hard ground around them.

They landed on their backs, stunned and severely jolted. They looked at each other as if in a daze. Then they realized. The explosion had been at the front door.

Where Hammond had been.

They staggered to their feet and ran. Leslie's hand had already wobbled to the pistol she carried. She'd released the safety catch, but it was meaningless now. The target had already fled, leaving only a trap for those who followed.

They rounded the house and saw Hammond, or what was left of him. It was immediately clear what had happened.

The career man, in his fatigue, had tired of knocking at the door and had tried the doorknob. Yes, the door had opened, but the reception had been warmer than Hammond could have ever expected.

The front door had been booby-trapped, the last vicious act by a man of malice and deception. Zenger had fled, knowing that it was now a matter of time before others came for him. He had left his calling card.

The body of Hammond was thrown pathetically fifty feet from the front door. It lay broken and bleeding, the clothes on the front torn away, the skin roasted and seared by the force of the explosion. Mercifully, he lay face down, his arms and legs twisted into impossible contortions and splintered at the limbs.

For the first time, Leslie showed signs of breaking, repeating "No, no, no," over and over and pleading with no one in particular, "It was meant for me, it was meant for me!"

Thomas looked at the appalling sight, Hammond dead without question, Leslie standing, holding the pistol at her side, seeing what the years had brought her to, and the picturesque old house now starting to burn.

A rage built within Thomas, overcoming his fear. He was gripped with a sense of the unfinished, of wanting to add finality to this case.

He gripped the pistol in his pocket. He turned toward the house. He ran through the burning doorway.

The wind, fortunately, was sweeping the smoke outside, though feeding the flames at the same time. He envisioned himself trapped in the burning house, dying of smoke and flames just as his office had died weeks earlier. Every streak of common sense told him to leave the house. His anger pressed him onward.

He wanted the man who'd inhabited Zenger's identity. Face to face, he wanted him. It was, of course, just what the quarry would never have allowed.

He barged through the hallway, feeling the heat of the flames behind him. Into the dining room where the table had been rocked against the walls and where the picture windows had now been blown out, along with the curtains. Every piece of china from the antique cabinet lay in particles on the carpet.

"Come on out!" Thomas roared to the man who'd creased his skull with a cane. "Come on out, God damn you!"

In return, silence. There was no one there.

How brave you are! Thomas thought to himself. You *know* he's long gone. Failure again! You're used to it! You must *like* it!

He pushed through another doorway, the doorway to the den. The door had been half unhinged by the explosion. Thomas stood by the old man's chair. (*How* old? No one knew now!) He recalled the old man's pontifications on the Sandler case.

Don't get involved! You'll get everyone killed! She's an impostor!

He looked around. The curtains in that room had been blown out the shattered window, too. Thomas looked at the sea.

Beneath the waves, the old man had ranted. *A long trip. And I won't be coming back.*

Thomas stared at the gaping hole where a window and curtain had been. He stared at the sea beyond.

He saw the speck in the ocean. He knew what it was.

He ran to the window and glared down to the pier. One of Zenger's two boats remained.

The other was the speck. Zenger was on his way. His way where? Home. After all these years. After decades in America, the master spy was on his way home. To his rendezvous beyond U.S. territorial waters.

The smoke was thicker. Thomas wondered whether he still had a way out. He turned. He ran, stumbling over an overturned rocking chair, coughing as he ran through the smoke of the hallway.

He could hear Leslie calling to him, pleading just as he suddenly emerged from the flaming front doorway. She was on her knees, uselessly, by the side of Hammond's scorched corpse.

"Get the rifle!" he yelled.

"What?"

"He's already escaping. By boat! Get the rifle!"

She turned and ran to the parked car, ripping open the back door, grabbing the black case, turning and running after Thomas.

They ran down the incline behind the house, down the hillside to the shore and the pier. To the remaining boat.

To Thomas it was clear. To Leslie it was becoming clear. What had the old impostor said about the ocean?

Beneath the waves.

Thomas cursed that Russian and Polish fishing fleet. *Of course* it was where it was, a hundred miles to the south, drawing the Coast Guard and naval reserves to the area. It was a diversion, and a damned good one, drawing all attention to that area. The rendezvous vessel for the master spy would slip in and out virtually unnoticed. Brilliant, cursed Thomas.

He and Leslie ran the quarter mile from the flaming house to the dock, their sides aching and their lungs ready to burst. They ran down the dock. Canvas covered the remaining boat.

Thomas tore at it until it began to rip. The canvas peeled away from the Chris-Craft slowly, jerkily tearing from its fastening pins. Once enough was pulled away for the two of them to crawl into the craft, Thomas led the way, pulling Leslie along.

The dashboard of the boat was locked, a wooden panel pulled into place over the ignition and controls. Thomas looked at it with anguish and smashed it with his fist.

Leslie was totally calm. She reached to the fire ax and handed it to him. He knew what to do.

With three or four crashing strokes, he broke through the panel. He then cut through the woodwork that led to the ignition wires. He crossed them and gunned the craft's diesel engine.

The boat roared to life.

"Where'd you learn all about ships?" she asked.

"My father joined a yacht club," he said. "Remember?"

"I never knew."

"You do now," he said.

He threw the throttle into reverse, turning the ship in the small docking area. Zenger's craft was even less of a speck than it had been before. Thomas looked at his compass, estimating the direction Zenger had gone. He looked at the fuel gauge. Zenger's final revenge. Hardly any. No matter. He threw the throttle completely into the forward position, letting the craft speed forward as fast as possible across the choppy, bumpy salt water.

Zenger was on the horizon, distantly, perhaps three miles out now. A mere dot. "Come on, damn it," Thomas cursed at the boat. "Move!"

The boat skipped across the jerky waves, splatting and even banging on the choppy water as it bullied its way through the rough ocean. The pursuit was insane; Thomas knew it. But he also knew that Zenger's escape, or the escape of this man who had inhabited Zenger's identity, had been planned for years. A standby, emergency escape, ready on a few days' notice whenever necessary. Either Thomas stopped him now, or the master spy, his father's associate, would never be seen again in the West.

Minutes passed. The speck remained at a stationary distance on the horizon. Thomas watched the fuel needle sink toward the E. He pushed the boat. They did not appear to be gaining.

He heard clicks and the clink of metal behind him. He glanced over his shoulder. Leslie was assembling the contents of the gun case.

A long-barreled, high-powered rifle, equipped with a special Browning telescopic sight. She had to be dreaming, he thought. The only way would be to get close enough for a decent shot.

Then again, it suddenly flashed into his mind, Zenger had to be armed, also. A further thought hit him: Who was he to play games with professionals like this? Hammond, a professional, already lay dead, the result of one small mistake. Was Thomas that much better than Hammond? He doubted it.

His common sense screamed at him. "Turn it around! Go back! While you still have fuel enough to return!"

Leslie spoke. "It's together," she said, raising the rifle and checking the sight. "I'm loading it!"

She bolted the rifle and slid a long six-bullet magazine into it. She stood up and looked over his shoulder.

"Straight ahead," she said, tense but encouraged. "I think you're gaining."

"Impossible," he muttered.

He squinted at the horizon. No, she was right. For some reason Zenger had cut his engines. They *were* gaining.

Thomas looked at the compass as their craft continued to move in a straight pattern toward Zenger's boat. The speck on the horizon was larger, more elongated. The compass told them that they'd altered their course.

Leslie stood behind Thomas, glancing at the compass, frowning. "What's he doing?" she asked in a half whisper.

Thomas paused for two or three seconds before answering, a signal to her that he wasn't sure. "It looks like he's turning," she said. "But why? There's nothing to turn to."

She looked back to where they'd come from. The island was smaller now. They approached international waters, greater depths, and trickier currents. The fuel needle was on E. The water was tangibly choppier, the bottom of their small boat being battered hard by the four-foot waves.

"He's crazier than we are," he said.

"He doesn't do anything without a reason," she answered.

He nodded. He knew that.

Zenger's ship took a zigzag pattern now. Their pursuing boat traveled a straight line after it, drawing closer. Then Zenger's craft seemed to turn in an arc, going out to deeper waters. Its radar scope was on, spinning quickly amidst the elaborate antennae on the roof of the boat.

Several more minutes passed. They knew they were beyond U.S. territorial limits now. No other boat was in sight. They drew nearer. Zenger seemed to be leading them in an arc now, as if he were looking for something or waiting for something, but were still trying to keep a respectable distance from his pursuers. It was starting to rain. They were within a half mile.

Then Zenger's craft veered sharply leftward, as if he had seen something. He had. Moments later Thomas knew what.

Perhaps a mile away, there was a thin black vertical line breaking through the water, leaving a long silver wake. The line resembled a large iron pipe, traveling upright as if to defy gravity. It broke the surface suddenly and was moving toward Zenger's craft.

Leslie and Thomas saw it at the same time, through the gray rain and water. "What the . . . ?" she began to ask. And then she knew. It was all so painfully obvious. Yet Thomas had realized it, not her.

"It's his escape," said Thomas. "We're not going to catch him. He's made it."

She slammed the loaded carbine against the cushioned seats. The sound made Thomas jump, scared the weapon would discharge.

"Full speed," he said. "Come on," he coaxed the boat. "Move!"

He glanced to the fuel needle. It was below E. No way they'd have the fuel to return, he realized. Only if they could overtake Zenger's boat.

He watched the black line traveling through the water, rising now, cutting a brisker wake.

"Holy Jesus," he said. "Just look at it."

The black line rose and was joined by other black lines. Lines of iron and steel. They were closer and the line was readily identifiable. A periscope. And the rest of the Soviet submarine gradually became visible.

Thomas felt an incredible shudder. As Zenger's ship neared its destination, the contours of the submarine rose like a slumbering giant from the ocean. Its outline was gray and jagged, like the waves, the water, and the sky. It was far larger than he had ever imagined one would be, far larger than a small cruise ship, for example. It rose to the surface, cut its own engines, and seemed to come about, turning its side to the two small pleasure craft that approached it. They resembled minnows charging a whale.

A few yellow deck lights were visible. Thomas drew closer. Zenger's small craft drew near the submarine and turned its side to it. A party of sailors emerged on the deck, lowering a long rope ladder down the sub's side. Zenger drew closer to the submarine.

Thomas looked up. Through the gray mist he could see the markings on the topmost point of the submarine. The red hammer and sickle of the workers' paradise to the East, defiant and strong in the international waters off Massachusetts. They were on a rescue mission of sorts, picking up a spy of three decades' service. The least they could do was whisk him

away in fluorescent, air-purified, underwater safety back to the Mother-
land.

Zenger was alongside the submarine. He abandoned his own small
craft, leaving it to drift to oblivion in the north Atlantic. He was pulling
himself up the ladder, aggressively and gamely, a man of fifty-odd well-
conditioned years rather than a man of seventy-six or eighty-two.

Their own boat lurched and the engines spat and hesitated. Thomas
looked to the fuel needle a final time. Their supply was finished. The last
drop was gone. A red light flashed on the dashboard and the needle
pointed far below E. They were, at half a mile from the submarine, as far
as they could go.

The boat rocked with the waves, starting to turn sideways in the current
which would carry them farther into the Atlantic.

"We're out," he said. "Finished. Failed." He whacked the dashboard
in disgust with his fist.

Zenger was scrambling up the rope ladder.

"Not quite," she snapped bitterly.

She went to the rifle, grabbed it angrily and went to the starboard side
of the boat. It was rocking with the waves but she started to kneel. She
pointed the rifle across the railing of the boat, seeking to steady it.

He looked at her, almost disbelieving what his eyes saw.

"You're not?" he asked.

She looked at him. "After everything *he's* done?" she asked, as if to
imply insanity to his question. "You'd let him go?" She paused, then
added, "We're even, you know. He tried killing *both* of us three times."

"What's the range of the rifle?"

"Five hundred yards with accuracy," she said. "Beyond that? Wind and
luck determine everything."

The rain spattered the boat. They stood in the back, getting wet with
the gray mist. She looked at the safety catch and seemed to fumble with
it.

"Ever fired one of those?" he asked.

"I know how it works," she allowed. She looked at him as if to offer
it. The boat rocked spasmodically. She said nothing, asking with her eyes.

Suddenly his instinct propelled him forward. He thought of his life,
arranged for and conspired against by forces he'd never known. He went
to her side and pulled the rifle away.

He examined it quickly. Zenger was at the top of the ladder, being
helped onto the deck by sailors with sidearms.

Thomas looked through the sight, zeroing the two fine cross hairs in
on the man on the submarine deck.

Zenger was on his knees, stumbling slightly.

The small craft rocked, then eased slightly. The rifle was moving with the boat.

"Put your hand on the barrel," he said, propping it on the railing. "Help me steady it."

She did.

"All I can do is aim high and hope."

"You know your way around rifles," she commented.

He glanced at her, taking his eye off the cross hairs for only an instant.

"My father taught me," he reminded her, realizing the irony. "We used to go deer hunting."

She looked at the deck of the submarine. "An impossible shot," she said. "Damn!"

He aimed high, waited for the peak of the wave, sighted the weapon again. He fired in that one instant the boat stood atop the wave crest.

They watched the deck. No reaction at all. The bullet had sailed into the gray expanses over everything. He lowered slightly and fired again on the next crest. Nothing. A third time. Nothing.

Zenger stood, seeming to brush the dirt and water off himself, secure in the knowledge that the pursuing ship had run out of fuel and was stranded. Perhaps the submarine would wham it on the way home. Why not?

Thomas lowered his sight dramatically, approaching desperation.

He fired the first of the last three bullets in the magazine.

The sailors on the deck and Zenger looked in his direction with suddenness. Perhaps they'd heard the rifle for the first time. The wind had shifted slightly. Instead of blowing from the side it now blew from behind the smaller boat.

They could hear the noise. And they'd looked below them, hearing the sound of a steel bullet hit the seamless iron hull of the submarine.

Thomas fired again. A second or two later a large yellow deck light several yards from Zenger seemed to burst and extinguish itself. Now the sailors began to scramble, back toward the hatch which would lead them down and under the deck to safety.

Zenger stood alone on the deck, looking back as if to inquire indignantly as to who was shooting at him. Never imagining that another shot could come so close.

A siren sounded on the submarine. A dive signal.

"He's got us beat," Leslie cursed.

Thomas fired again. And missed.

He felt a sickened sensation in his stomach.

The siren on the submarine was still audible through the gray mist. Thomas glared through the sight at his tormentor. Almost instinctively, Zenger sensed that his opponents had thrown at him their last offensive weapon.

The master spy stood calmly on the deck, exhilarated at being shot at and missed, and grinned in their direction.

Then, with the quintessence of the American gestures that he'd learned over thirty years, the spy raised two hands toward the small boat. Each hand's extremity was marked with a sole upraised center finger, the universal—but particularly American—gesture of ill will.

"We're beaten," Thomas mumbled bitterly. He slapped the rifle in a fury.

"We *can't* be," she snapped coldly.

He looked at her in frustration and almost anger. What did she want him to—?

"Try another magazine," she said.

And disbelievingly she held out another steel-cased magazine, six long bullets therein.

He looked at her and looked at the weapon. He looked at the deck of the submarine.

Zenger had turned. He walked defiantly and cockily toward the open hatch which would lead him on a fluorescent and air-purified trip to another world, one in which he would be a hero.

"No way," Thomas Daniels said. "He's gone."

She grabbed the rifle from his hands as an inspecting drill sergeant might. Quickly her hands had torn out the empty magazine, sent it overboard and slammed the full magazine into its place.

The wind felt the same. The boat eased from its rocking for a few seconds. She braced herself against a cabin wall and held the rifle's butt against her shoulder, quickly bringing the weapon into a perfect firing position. Her movements were precise, practiced, and comfortable.

Moments later she began firing, aiming not quite so high and not quite as leftward as Thomas had. She pulled the trigger quickly in a rapid succession, firing four, five, and then six shots, trying to spray the area where Zenger was.

There was a delay of several seconds before any bullet sailed the distance between the rifle and the submarine. Thomas squinted and watched.

He had no idea which bullet found its mark, whether it was the first or the final. But the fact remained that as Zenger stepped the last few yards to the hatch, the lower half of his skull exploded with the impact of a viciously tumbling bullet.

The man's body went limp and fell immediately, the red explosion in the back of the head being instantly apparent even at that great distance.

The gray rain continued to fall.

Other sailors emerged from the hatch, gawking, incredulous at first. Thomas and Leslie stared with their naked eyes as three sailors pulled the fallen body toward the hatch.

Leslie set down the rifle. She had no quarrel with the Russian sailors. They had their duty just as she and Thomas had had theirs. The seamen reclaimed a body; Thomas and Leslie had reclaimed a soul, an identity. The body had always belonged to the Soviet Union. The identity? That had been borrowed.

Leslie picked up a floodlight from the small boat's cabin. The light could be flashed on and off. She blinked an internationally understandable cease-fire signal to them.

The sailors stood on the deck, working nervously for a few seconds, hoisting the fallen, semibeheaded body by its red shoulders. They dragged it below.

Minutes later the submarine began to move. Thomas and Leslie wondered if it would ram them or sink them; it easily could have. But, as if in reciprocation for the voluntary cease-fire and the surrender of the spy's body, the submarine turned eastward in the ocean. It began moving on the gray surface, pointing away from them, until it was lower on the horizon.

Then only the periscope was visible, breaking through the waves. Then nothing. The ocean was vacant, except for two small pleasure craft, both adrift and powerless. For a moment it was as if the underwater goliath had never been there. Then they felt its wake, rippling from a mile away.

Leslie sat on a cushioned seat within the cabin, her dark hair soaked and matted, an expression of exhaustion across her face. For her, the long intrigue with her father was over.

For several seconds, neither spoke.

Then, "Lucky shot," she offered.

He looked at her, understanding. "No, it wasn't."

There was a pause and he continued. "No one makes a shot like that on luck. No one guesses how to fire a rifle with accuracy like that."

She nodded and a slight, unwilling smile crossed her face.

"How long have you known?" she asked.

"Known?" he answered. "For about two minutes. Suspected? For a

long time. Ever since I learned you had gulled your own foster father, George McAdam, into thinking you were dead. Where'd you learn it all? From him?"

She nodded. "Learn from the best," she said. "George McAdam was one of the best British agents of his day."

"And now I'll bet you're one of the best. But not British. American."

She shrugged. "I try," she answered. "It's really the only thing I'm trained to do. Not much money in painting, you know."

"Would you honor me with an honest answer or two?"

"Of course."

"Why me?" he asked.

She almost laughed. "It's not obvious?"

"Oh, I understand that part," he said. "My father was a double agent, recruiting for the Americans while all the time he was working for the Russians. And he headed a postwar network—"

"—financed by counterfeit English and American banknotes," she continued. "A network which grew old but continued to compromise British and American Intelligence. When William Ward Daniels died, he was just about to be uncovered. He was lucky he died when he did."

"But then why'd you come to *me*?" he insisted.

"Because the network was still working very well after his death," she explained. "From our perspective it was clear. He'd passed the leadership on to someone else. You."

Thomas Daniels was without words. The final piece fit neatly into place. He knew the reason he'd been sucked into this treacherous vortex of events: He'd been under observation the entire time, by the American government *and* by the British government. He was a suspected spy, suspected of inheriting the position from his father. Just as William Ward Daniels had probably intended.

"Of course," she said cheerfully, "we soon saw that we'd been wrong. You knew nothing. The ranking spy was someone else. We were totally baffled, but you solved it for us. You led us to Zenger."

He considered it. The drizzle persisted.

"What about the money?" he asked.

"The Sandler estate?"

"It's yours, isn't it?"

She shrugged. "A fortune built on treason and counterfeiting? I can hardly ask my employer for that now, can I?"

"No," he mumbled. "Of course not." Thoughtfully, he added, "So there's really just one final question."

She knew what it was. "Montreal," she said. "That part's all true. I teach. I'm an artist. It's a fine cover. From time to time I disappear on an assignment, none ever as special as this, though."

"And there's a man, isn't there?"

She thought for a moment. "I'm sorry," she said. "I live with him. I love him."

He would have said more, though he didn't know exactly what. But then suddenly she was looking past him, over his shoulder. She bolted upright and suddenly screamed, "Thomas! Jesus!"

She pointed, her soft fatigued expression exploding into a look of wide-eyed terror.

He whirled. He saw it, the submarine, rising near them no less than a hundred yards across the water, streaking straight toward them. His mouth flew open, and like most instants of stark, heart-stopping fear, the moment seemed frozen in unreality.

The submarine was going to demolish them. Unmistakably.

They would have jumped, but there was nowhere to jump to. They would have swum, but swimming was suicidal. The water was too cold, the current brutal, the waves enormous.

The sub steamed in at them. Fifty yards. Thirty.

Then it bore sharply leftward, kicking up a gargantuan wake.

Thomas realized, thinking, So that's it! Brilliant to the end! They won't smash us, they'll capsize us instead!

No direct hit on an American ship, merely a deluge of water.

The submarine, slashing through the surface of the ocean, passed within twenty-five yards and then began diving. A massive wave, followed by another and another, burst forth from the sub's wake and—rising thirty feet in the water—rolled violently toward the small Chris-Craft.

The first wave battered the small boat, the second threw it lopsided up upon its crest. The third wave hit it head-on, propelling it sideways through the water.

Thomas and Leslie clung to the boat with all the strength they had. He remembered yelling "Hang on! Hang on!" and they did.

But their boat was on its side now, and the frigid water was still rolling over it, rising steadily.

Beneath the waves, Thomas thought. Zenger's words raced back.

Slowly but inexorably, as the sub dived from sight a final time, their small ship was going down.

PART NINE

All in all, Aram Shassad was pleased, as pleased as he could be under the circumstances. He and Hearn had made an important collar.

The case dated back a while, almost a year in fact. Two holdup men had been working out of town, trying out their show in New Haven, when a ballistics test in a Connecticut liquor store linked them to a holdup slaying in Yorkville a year earlier.

The New Haven police had a lead or two. One gunman's sister, it seemed, lived in New Haven with her three children. She and her kids were scared to death of him and his apparent partner. Some loose talk here and there, and on a warm day in early September 1976 Shassad, Hearn, and six other detectives and uniformed men closed in on an apartment in Brownsville. Months of detective work ended in a mad scramble for pants.

Then there'd been that other case, the one which Shassad and Hearn had been reassigned to in the interim period while the Yorkville liquor store trail had gone cold.

The Ryder-Daniels case, as Shassad termed it generically. Shassad thought of it that first Monday after Labor Day when he by chance was driving alone across Eighty-ninth Street.

He saw a solitary figure on the southeast corner, standing alone, apparently waiting, while a beehive of construction men and equipment surrounded the old Sandler mansion on the opposite corner.

"Son of a bitch," thought Shassad, pulling his car to a halt alongside a fire hydrant. "Daniels."

His curiosity overwhelmed him. He parked and stepped out.

Ryder-Daniels had been one of the most perplexing cases. It was now damned to remain forever in limbo, solved but not really solved, closed but having never reached a satisfactory conclusion.

Oh, there'd been the token explanation. But Shassad had never liked it all that much. Too pat. Too set. Too . . . too . . . Oh, hell. He'd put in a lot of hours. He deserved more than seeing two Federal agents one morning in his office way back during a cold stretch of March.

Rota Films had been a front, they'd explained, as if he couldn't have told *them* that. A counterfeiting operation, using film cans to smuggle money and plates in and out of the United States. Well, he'd conceded, he'd known they were doing something. But he hadn't known what. As for Mark Ryder, the straying young husband who'd stepped out the wrong door at the wrong moment, the Feds had wrapped that one up for Shassad and Hearn, also. A bad case of a mistaken victim, they'd confirmed. And Shassad had already gotten that far, too.

But as for the killers, they'd said, Shassad needn't bother anymore. The two men had been dealt with, one having been sent afloat beneath the Manhattan Bridge, the other having taken a nasty tumble off a Nantucket ferry. All this in confidence, of course, the agents had told the city detectives. The case was all wrapped up and delivered, including that dark-haired young woman. Nothing further for Shassad to do.

"What about that prick Daniels?" Shassad had asked.

The question had been met with shrugs. "Forget him," they'd said. "He's in bad shape, anyway."

And Shassad hadn't seen him again, much less bothered to do anything more than think of him occasionally. Not again, that is, until this warm, open morning in September.

"Hello, Daniels," said Shassad, walking amiably and casually to the man standing alone on the corner. "Nothing quite like an old familiar face, is there?"

Thomas turned toward the voice and saw the detective approaching. For a moment he didn't recognize him. Then he did. "Hello, officer," he answered without acrimony.

Daniels looked back to the house. He watched. Shassad stood next to him and eyed the large crane in place beside the old structure across the street.

"I know it's not important anymore," Shassad tried cautiously, "but I'm a curious sort of guy. . . ."

"What's that mean?"

"It means I never really got more than half a story. You. Some girl. The Sandlers. A boat." He paused, hoping Thomas would expand on it. When Daniels didn't, Shassad tried, "I'd be grateful for whatever you could tell me. Hell. I'd just like to know. To scratch my own itch."

Thomas could feel the sun's warmth. It was going to be a hot day, he could tell already, one of those misplaced summer days which arrive too late each year. One breeze did sweep across Eighty-ninth, rustling a few leaves which had prematurely fallen.

"Well?" Shassad asked. "Come on. Give me a break."

There was so much, really, and it was all shooting through Daniels's mind. Primarily there had been the frigid water, that's what he was thinking of now. There had been the titanic wake from the submarine, the swamping of their small craft and his own mad flailing and floundering through the turbulent, freezing water toward the only thing left afloat— Zenger's boat, the one he'd rode in out to his rendezvous point.

He remembered the panic as he looked through the waves, loosing sight of Leslie.

Then, as his arms and legs started going numb from the cold, he'd reached Zenger's abandoned boat and—shivering and chattering his teeth—had blasted the boat horn to attract her, wherever she was. And just a few seconds later, he remembered, he was buckling to the floorboards, exhausted and overexposed, shivering in what was the advent of a near-fatal bout of pneumonia. Moments later, attracted by the horn, she'd climbed aboard beside him, and had collapsed to the floor with him.

An hour afterward a Coast Guard cutter—attracted by something large and unidentifiable on its radar screen—had come upon them in the drifting boat. He'd been in no condition to explain anything. Not for a while. Leslie was whisked away by a man named Lassiter from Washington. Thomas hadn't seen her again.

Shassad sighed and was almost about to leave. "Okay, Daniels," he said. "Have it your way. Don't tell me."

There was movement on the crane across the street. The yellow sun glistened off its metal.

"It all revolved around the girl," Daniels said. Shassad froze, knowing when to listen. "A girl in the Sandler family. Sort of."

Daniels glanced at the detective as if he hardly cared whether Shassad knew or not. He was speaking out of a therapeutic need to talk. Nothing more. Shassad knew it and listened.

"A remarkable woman," Daniels said. "Bright. Perceptive. Educated.

Could be ruthless, could be sensitive. She could do a lot of things." He thought. "Know what she could do best?"

"What?"

"Teach. She taught me that I should get out of law."

"Oh, yeah?" pondered Shassad. "What're you going to do instead?"

"Who knows?" Thomas Daniels answered. Then he exclaimed, "Look!"

Daniels gazed across the street and so did Shassad. The towering crane was moving now, and suspended from the tallest extremity was the bulbous iron wrecking ball.

The ball crashed into the wall of the mansion, hitting it solidly on the crosstown side and caving in the old walls as a gingerbread cake would crumble to a little girl's hands.

The ball swung away and a gaping wound was evident in the side of the house. Girders and rusting pipes were revealed and seemed like a skeleton beneath the mansion's flesh. Then the ball swung again, hit, and swung countless times more. No one bled much for an old building on a prime corner lot; not when a white-faced luxury high rise could soon be erected in its place.

Shassad watched the destruction, wondering what emotion he should feel and watching Daniels at the same time.

"A wealthy old woman used to live there, didn't she?" Shassad finally asked. "The family had a lot of money?"

"Once they did," replied Thomas.

"Not now?"

Shassad waited for an answer and none was immediately forthcoming. Finally Thomas, watching the Sandler estate crumble, its history with it, merely uttered a question to answer another question.

"Who knows?" he said.

Shassad thought about it for a few seconds. Then, seeking to ingratiate himself, he broke into a broad smile and attempted humor.

"Well, what the hell?" he suggested. "Stay a lawyer, Daniels. Maybe an heiress will turn up and all you smart lawyer boys can get rich."

Daniels turned slowly and looked at Shassad, his face arranged in an expression which Shassad simply could not read. Only one thing was clear. Shassad knew he'd said something wrong.